BLACKFIRE RISING

ELIZABETH DONALD

FALSTAFF
BOOKS
WWW.FALSTAFFBOOKS.COM

BLACKFIRE RISING

Be silent in that solitude
Which is not loneliness – for then
The spirits of the dead who stood
In life before thee are again
In death around thee – and their will
Shall overshadow thee: Be still.

Edgar Allan Poe

THE COLD ONES

THE COLD ONES

The scream from the street was harsh and high-pitched, piercing through the closed door of Sara Harvey's bookstore.

Sara dropped her coffee cup, paying no heed to the splash of brown liquid across the book she'd been reading. She grabbed her Beretta from under the counter as she ran to the door and shoved it open.

Jeff Pagliei lay in the middle of Main Street, his head leaking blood from a nasty gash along his upper brow. His screams were high and hoarse, a man's voice made into something animalistic, pain and fear turning any words he might be trying to utter into shrill, meaningless cries.

Something hunched over him, gnawing on his arm.

Jeff was a thin, cheerful fellow who worked as a community service officer, writing parking tickets so the cops could deal with real crime like spray-painted park benches or skateboarders on Main Street sidewalks. Now Jeff's uniform shirt was splashed with gaudy streaks of blood and tiny chunks of flesh. His free hand pounded ineffectually at the shaved-bald man whose face was bent over his arm.

"Stop!" Sara shouted, leveling her weapon at them.

The attacker raised his head. Blood covered the lower half of his face, and Sara felt something in her chest twist as she saw a shred of Jeff's armflesh in the man's teeth.

"Help me," Jeff cried.

Sara ignored him, training her gun on the attacker's glaring face.

"Oh my God," she whispered. "Parish?"

Parish Roberts growled at her—actually *growled*, Jeff's blood dripping from his mouth. His eyes glowed with malevolent rage, yet somehow emptiness lay behind them.

Behind her, Sara heard the door to Gary Stover's gun shop bang open. She didn't turn around. She knew Gary had at least two guns, both aimed at Parish.

"Everybody drop the guns!" shouted another voice. Sara glanced to her right and saw Chief Russ Matthews, running toward them with gun drawn but aimed downward. The small police station was a block away— the frightened faces peering from the shop windows on Main Street must have called for help.

"Chief—" Sara began.

"Drop it, Miss Harvey!" Matthews snapped.

Sara lowered her gun, but didn't drop it. She knew without looking that Gary was following her lead. She kept her eyes on Matthews, trying to gauge whether he was tense enough to shoot if she raised her gun again.

Parish suddenly dashed for the nearest shop. Gary moved fastest—he raised his gun and fired, even as Matthews shouted "Stop!" again. Gary's bullet slammed harmlessly into the wood frame of the shop door.

Parish vanished through the door, and there were more screams inside.

Gary was already moving into the shop, Sara behind him. Matthews shouted in the street, but the tiny shop door was too small for all three to fit through quickly.

At first, Sara couldn't see anything. Rows of floral-scented candles on elegant wooden shelves blocked her view. Incense and delicate mood music filled the air.

Gary moved down the first aisle on point. Sara followed quickly, covering the corner and shifting her attention to the second aisle.

Pam Spinks' voice shrieked a wordless scream of terror. Somewhere Sara could hear Parish crashing about, and Pam kept screaming. She was a pretty red-haired woman with a taste for herbal tea, Sara remembered, a holistic earth-mother type now climbing up on her counter and fruit- lessly throwing candles at Parish.

"Get down!" Gary shouted – Pam was in his line of sight. Sara moved around the other side of the display shelves. Behind her, she heard Chief Matthews stumble into the shop, for once not shouting at her.

Pam froze and stared at Parish for the second or so before he leaped. Sara's shot slammed into the far wall, a split second too late.

Parish knocked Pam off the counter and into Gary, whose gun clattered across the floor.

"Stop! Get off her!" shouted Matthews, coming up the aisle behind them. He didn't have a clear shot, but neither did Sara.

"Parish!" Sara shouted, and Parish lifted his head from Pam's neck. He hissed at her, blood frothing his mouth, and coiled as if to jump at her.

Sara fired a bullet into his head, just as two bullets struck his chest from Matthews. Parish's head half-exploded into a mass of blood and oatmeal-like matter, his body thrown back off Pam's still form.

"Stover, stay still," Sara ordered. She kicked what was left of Parish over and grabbed Pam's leg. The pretty lady who liked herbal tea stared at the ceiling, her floral dress covered in blood. Her throat looked like raw hamburger with shreds of flesh trailed over her bodice.

Sara knelt beside Gary and checked over his face. "Safe," she said, and he opened his eyes.

"Shit, Harvey, that was a balls-up," Gary said, standing up. Blood covered his left sleeve. Immediately he scooped up his runaway gun.

"Drop it," Matthews said. "That's evidence."

"Stand down, Chief," Sara said, walking past him out of the shop. Gary followed her, but the chief wasn't giving up that easily. He followed them back out into the street, looking back over his shoulder at the two corpses lying twisted in a spreading pool of blood.

Out in the street, people had begun to come out of the shops. The three police officers that comprised Chief Matthews' day shift were stopping traffic and directing it away from the blood-spattered street. An ambulance squealed somewhere as Mayor Kathy Oh bandaged Jeff Pagliei's arm with a couple of dish towels from her restaurant down the street. Jeff's face was the color of curdled milk as he gasped for breath. His arm hung in a mess of tattered flesh.

Sara walked up to Jeff Pagliei and shot him in the head.

The report seemed quieter than it had in the confined shop, but the sickening sound of Jeff's brains exiting his skull and spraying across the sidewalk was very loud.

"Oh my God!" Kathy screamed, falling backward off her knees. Her arm was coated in Jeff's blood.

Matthews had his gun back up instantly, aimed at Sara. "Drop it or I will fucking shoot you, Miss Harvey!"

But Gary was behind him, his own weapon cocked at Matthews' head. "Not today, Chief," he said. The other officers were running up the block, guns drawn, as Gary quickly disarmed the chief.

Sara trained her eyes only on the mayor. "Romero," she said.

Kathy's eyes were still frozen, and Sara wondered for a second if she'd forgotten. If so, they were truly screwed.

But then recognition dawned, and with it, more terror. "Oh no," Kathy muttered, stumbling to her feet. "Chief, let them go."

"The hell?" Matthews snapped. Gary kept his gun pressed against the back of Matthews' head, just to remind him.

"Stand down," Kathy said, staring down at her shaking hands coated with Jeff's blood. "Take your orders from Major Harvey."

"*Major* Harvey?" Matthews said, holding up a hand to stop his officers. "What the fuck?"

"No time," Sara said, keeping her gun down. No sense upsetting the twitchy police officers. "Accept it and you get your gun back."

"Accepted," the chief said, but his glare was aimed at the mayor. Kathy was still shaking, looking at her bloody hands, and at Sara.

Gary handed the gun back to the chief.

"Go downstreet to the dock, see if anyone else got bit," Sara ordered, and Gary moved off without a word. The dock was only a block and a half from Main Street, and if they were lucky…

She heard a shrill scream and a gunshot.

"Motherfuck." Sara walked toward the gun shop. The chief and the mayor followed her. "Matthews, get your men to shut down the town. Send these people back home and tell them to lock their goddamned doors. Mayor, please shut down the school and get those kids home. A building full of defenseless targets is not what we need right now."

"Dear God," Kathy whispered. She was too shaky for Sara's peace of mind. "Is this really—"

"Yes, it's really happening, so do as I say," Sara snapped, unlocking the chest behind Gary's counter.

Sara Harvey sipped annoyingly bland coffee and tried to ignore Gary's obnoxiousness. It wasn't easy, but Sara had a lot of practice. Gary Stover had been coming on to her with more or less comedic approaches for years.

"I don't suppose you're going back to your own shop any time soon?" she asked, staring out the window. The sky was gray and drizzly.

"Don't want me here when Captain America drops by, I guess," Gary said, leaning back in the chair.

"Actually, you're driving off the hordes of customers." Sara flopped down into the comfy chair behind the counter. The bookstore-coffeeshop was not the worst assignment she'd had, not even close. But as a business owner she left a great deal to be desired. The shop was empty save for Gary, who was drinking a black coffee with two sugars—sweet as a showgirl's tit, he liked to say.

Sara glanced out the window again.

"When's Vaughn gonna stick his hand up your skirt, Harvey?" Gary snickered.

Sara was not in the mood for Gary today. She stood up and walked over to him, standing over him so he'd have to look up.

"Stover."

"Yes, ma'am," Gary said automatically.

"Fuck off."

"Yes, ma'am," Gary repeated. He took his coffee, tossed a smartass salute at her and ambled out the door. GARY'S GUNS was across the street, and did marginally better business than SARA'S BOOKS.

Sara heard a Jeep pull up and stepped out onto the stoop on cue to greet Paul Vaughn. He was out of uniform for once, wearing civilian camouflage as though he were an ordinary hunter, but the Jeep gave a hint. He climbed the short steps to her shop doorway and kissed her full on the mouth, sliding his arms around her waist. When he released her, Sara saw Gary peering at them from his shop window.

Paul followed her into the shop, where he dropped all pretense, letting his hands fall away from her.

"Coffee?" Sara asked, already moving to fill a cup. Black, no sugar. Paul was never one to soften anything.

"Report." Paul was stiffer than usual.

Sara set the cup in front of him. "Stover's seen no increase in gun purchases, except one wacko out on Chesterfield Road who thinks the base on the Island is setting up for an alien invasion."

"Sell him a tinfoil hat," Paul said, sitting down at the counter.

"Not that kind of alien," Sara returned. "Mexicans. They're coming in from everywhere, he declares on a regular basis. He's sure the invasion is imminent."

"Oh yes, the great Mexican invasion of Massachusetts," Paul said. "One if by land, two if by sea."

Sara settled on the stool next to him. "They buy you, too. I put a yellow ribbon in the window, and it confirmed their thoughts on you being my soldier fella. The kiss helps a lot, thanks."

"Hell, Harvey, I just figured you wanted to get your saucy paws on me," Paul said. "Gets lonely out here, surprised you and Stover—"

"Oh yeah, that's real fucking funny, Iceman," Sara said, punching him lightly on the arm—but not too lightly. "Don't think I don't know about the bet you two made in Honduras."

Paul held up his hands in innocence. "That was not about you. That was about the lovely lady in the thong, and it was not actually a bet as that would be ungentlemanly."

"Sure," Sara said, rolling her eyes. "I have spies everywhere, Vaughn. Parish Roberts will not subscribe to the male code, he rats you guys out every..."

Paul's eyes sobered, and Sara was immediately nervous. "Shit. Something wrong with Parish?"

Paul stared at his coffee. "He volunteered, Harvey."

"Fuck!" Sara slammed her cup down, not caring about the spill of hot coffee over her hand, a flash of pain, gone in an instant. "How could you, Paul? Goddammit!"

"Volun-teer," Paul repeated, as if she were a child.

"I don't give a fuck! He's one of my men, he didn't have the goddamn right to volunteer!" Sara pushed back from the counter in fury.

Paul got up to face her. "He said he wanted to prove we could take the treatment and stay human, not be like It. He wanted *to do it. They were close to killing the project."*

"Good!" Sara snapped. "It's bullshit and you fucking know it! There's nothing it can do that training and discipline can't, but it sure as hell can fuck up my men!"

"Tell me something I don't know, Harvey!" Paul returned, his tone back to formal command.

"Yes, sir," Sara replied, but it took a moment for her tone to soften. "Sorry, Vaughn. It's just... Parish Roberts, of all people? Is it too late to sneak onto the Island and get him out of it, talk some sense into him, hit him over the head with something heavy?"

"Too late," Paul said.

There was something in his voice Sara didn't like. "What? What is it?"

"It works," Paul said. "It works so fucking well they're terrified. The white

coats, they're all high-fiving each other, but there's this look in their eyes like Jimmy had, remember? The oh-shit look?"

Sara nodded. "And Parish? What's he like...now?"

Paul hesitated a moment. "He's an animal," he said. "He attacks anything he sees. He won't speak, but he'll sit and stare at you, working it out in his head, then he suddenly lunges. He bit some poor guy right before I left."

"BIT him?" Sara asked, incredulous. "Bit him. Parish Roberts bit somebody."

"Tore a big chunk out of some poor tech's hand, who now gets to be a volunteer too," Paul said.

Sara was quiet a moment. "Dammit, Vaughn. I'm losing my team to It."

"I know," Paul replied heavily, and Sara remembered that they were his men, too. "We'll need to recruit replacements, Harvey. But not until we're done here."

"How the fuck do you replace Parish Roberts?" Sara asked.

Paul didn't answer. "The good news is, if the testing wraps up soon, we'll get to move on without It."

"Gee, and I was getting so good at schlepping coffee," Sara said, trying for her usual sarcasm and failing.

Paul stood up, a ghost of his former smile on his face. "Carry on, soldier," he said, ruffling her short-cropped black hair.

"Quit that," she said, ducking his hand. "I'm not a puppy."

"Sure hell you're not," he said, and walked out into the drizzling rain.

"I should've listened to that idiot out on Chesterfield Road," Matthews muttered. The chief's hand kept drifting to the pistol by his side, as if reassuring himself that it was still there. "He made more sense than the two of you."

Sara and Gary finished loading the guns. Gary had taken a brief moment to change his shirt. Sara couldn't blame him. Some of that blood had belonged to Parish. She couldn't think about that yet.

"Chief, you have the authority under martial law to shoot anyone outside their homes after dark," Sara said, walking out of the gun shop. "Aim for the head."

Matthews kept walking beside her. "I am not shooting the good people of this town just for stepping out of their homes, ma'am."

"You'd better," Sara retorted, snapping the last holster closed on her belt as she walked. She reached the dock, where Gary was lighting the bodies on fire. Parish lay on top, his eyes staring at the sky, and Sara averted her gaze. Gary saw, but for once he didn't say anything.

"Stover, the runaround," Sara ordered, then turned back to Matthews. "Martial law. Don't be an idiot. Looks like we got them all, but until we do a head count on the Island there's no way to be sure. If we can't contain it, you're the last line of defense for the mainland."

"That's why I'm coming with you," Matthews insisted.

Sara rolled her eyes. "When did *you* serve in the Marines, Chief?" she asked sarcastically.

"'92 to '04, Second Battalion 24th," he retorted.

Sara paused, taking a real look at the chief. He had none of the middle-aged beer gut that seemed to take over older cops. His eyes were clear and his hands steady, even if he still looked at her as though she were the real threat, an unpredictable equation in his town.

Hell, to him she probably *was* the threat. Sara put a bullet in Jeff Pagliei's head before the chief's eyes, and Pagliei had been one of his men. A community service officer, a glorified clerk. But still one of his men.

She knew what that felt like.

"Combat?" Sara asked, watching his eyes.

Matthews nodded. "One tour in Afghanistan, later Iraq," he said. "I know enough to see you two can't take on a whole island of soldiers by yourselves. My people have the town. I'm not sitting here on the dock with my thumb up my ass waiting to see if you two manage to prevent this…whatever…from spreading to my people."

Sara glanced out over the water. The morning drizzle had given way to rays of sunshine, golden splashes across the waves. In the distance, she could see the Island.

"I sure to God hope we're not fighting them all, Chief," she said quietly. "You come with us, you could catch a bullet or worse. You down with that?'

"It's my town, Major," Matthews replied.

"Then move," Sara ordered, and the chief stepped down into the runaround. Gary revved the engine, and they pulled away from shore. Sara moved to the front, pulling binoculars from the gear box and training them on the Island.

"'Major'?" Gary asked, pitching his voice low so Matthews couldn't hear them over the roar of the engine.

"Paul had to tell them something, in case the fit hit the shan," Sara replied. "Besides. Marine."

"*Semper fi*," Gary snarked, grinning. He had a light to his eyes she hadn't seen in a long time.

"What's with you, Stover?" Sara asked, scanning the beach and the waters near it.

"What." It wasn't a question; it was Gary's idea of response.

"You look like you just got a blow job from a nineteen-year-old beauty queen."

Gary shifted the engine into higher gear. "Just glad to be workin' again, 'Major'."

"Let it go, Stover." Sara lowered the binoculars. "I personally would've been glad if we hadn't been activated."

"Yeah, what's with that?" Gary asked. "Weren't you supposed to get a heads-up from Captain America if the Island went batshit? You forget to mention it to me?"

"Stow that shit," Sara said crisply. "No signal, which means either they don't know Parish escaped or they had no chance to send it."

By now Matthews had moved to the front. "Any of you people consider that whatever the hell you're doing on that goddamn island might be a threat to my town? Or consider telling me about it?"

"Not our call, Chief," Sara replied. "Just following orders."

"Right," Matthews said sarcastically.

Sara scanned the beach again as they drew closer. "Heads up. There's a body."

On the beach, a form clothed in fatigues lay on the sand.

"They fucking left him out there?" Gary said, aghast. Sara spared a glance at him. Gary didn't mind a grotesque attack on two civilians, a team member's head blown off over him, or the prospect of having to fight across the Island. But to leave a fallen comrade out in the sun...that offended him. She would have laughed if her gut wasn't twisting inside her.

"Slow up," she ordered, and Gary coasted the runaround up to the small dock. He slipped the boat's tether over the cleat as Sara and Matthews climbed out. When Gary followed, Sara reached over him and pulled the tether loose, kicking the boat away from the dock.

"What the fuck!" Matthews protested, watching it putter away. "How the hell are we going to get back?"

"We may not," Sara said, pulling her Beretta. "Four runarounds docked on the Island. Now we only have three to worry about. We have to make sure no Cold Ones use them to get off the Island. Top priority is containing the outbreak, Chief. All other priorities are secondary. Am I clear?"

There was rebellion in the chief's eyes. "Cold Ones?"

"That's what we call them," she said, leading them up the dock. The soldier's body lay just beyond the edge of the sand.

Matthews started to speak again, but Sara held up a hand to quiet him. She proceeded on point, gun leveled at the ground with the safety off. Gary fell into flanking posture to the left, and after a moment's hesitation, Matthews took the right, as natural as if he were in fatigues.

About ten feet from the body, Sara held up a hand and they stopped. She edged closer, gun aimed at the head. She could sense Gary tensing as she got closer. She didn't have a read on Matthews yet. She wished suddenly for Parish Roberts at her back, and ignored the underlying thought that Parish was dead, the team broken.

She could smell the soldier now, a gassy putrid stench like hamburger left out on the counter too long. Carefully she used the tip of her boot to kick the body over.

The young soldier's face was half gone, swollen and purple. Something had torn off his nose and lower lip, leaving bloodstained teeth in a ferocious sneer. Flies buzzed around the gaping wound at his throat, where purplish blood had long congealed.

"This was a while ago," Sara said. "He's been here hours, not minutes."

"Trying to stop Roberts?" Gary asked, edging closer.

Sara knelt down. "Maybe."

Matthews came up beside her. "Shouldn't we, y'know, shoot it? Cut off its head or something?"

Sara and Gary leveled identical glares at him.

"He's dead," Sara said, steel in her voice.

"But don't they…come back?" Matthews asked.

"Horror-movie bullshit," Sara said, standing up. "Dead is dead. Body won't move without blood and a heart to pump it. He isn't coming back. We'll burn him later."

Matthews shook his head. "They're not dead? That guy in town, what was he?"

"A Cold One," Gary replied. "No hesitation, no conscience, no feeling. Just a killer."

"Parish Roberts," Sara reminded him stiffly, and Gary subsided.

"Tell me something, boss," Sara said, glancing around the alley. "Why does Chicago always smell like piss?"

"Can't imagine, Harvey." Paul's voice came from the earpiece. It was a weird feeling, as though he were inside her head, but also comforting. "Maybe because you've been wandering the back alleys for twenty hours now."

"Seriously, the whole city smells like excrement," Sara said. "Maybe our people should look into this. A clear sign of a Raptor is the smell of piss in the streets."

"We'll get right on that."

"Ho!" Parish called, and Sara had her Beretta up instantly.

"Confirm, sighting on fire escape to your left," Paul said in her head. "Two civvies on the roof, proceed with caution."

Parish was already climbing the fire escape, Sara right behind him. The shadow above them vanished onto a roof, and screams echoed.

"Fuck," Sara murmured, climbing faster. Parish reached the top before she did, and she heard shouts and gunfire. She vaulted over the landing and onto the roof.

There it was, the fucker they'd been tracking. Shrouded in a stupid black cloak like it was fucking Dracula or something, skulking about in the shadows. Long talon-like nails extended from its bony hands, its pale face hidden in the cowl.

Someone was fighting it. Moving too fast for Sara to get a good look, a stocky man no taller than she was pummeling the Raptor, heedless of its nails ripping through his t-shirt and drawing blood down his shoulder.

Parish stood in firing stance, shouting for the man to move, get the fuck out of the way goddammit, and Sara flanked around the side, angling for her own line of sight.

"Harvey!" Parish shouted, and Sara knew what he was asking.

"Harvey, take the shot," Paul said in her ear.

They were right. The Raptor had ripped up four homeless and two prostitutes while they'd been tracking it through the labyrinthine alleys of Chicago. She should shoot. Fuck the civvie.

But the guy simply would not quit. He beat at the thing with a ferocity Sara had never seen, even in the things she'd hunted.

"Harvey, shoot the fucker!" Paul was getting annoyed.

Sara held up her hand to Parish. Any second now the Raptor would get through the civilian's defenses and gut him with those talons, and they'd get their shot. Let him go down fighting.

The man let out a guttural cry, and he and the Raptor both fell to the roof, *wrestling in and out of the shadows. The thing gave off a shriek of fury—or was it pain? Sara couldn't tell.*

"Goddammit, Harvey, shoot it! You're not doing the guy any fucking favors!" Paul was pissed. She was in for a reaming later.

Sara approached them, unable to tell what was the Raptor and what was the surely-dead civilian. Parish automatically moved around to the other side, covering her. He had Paul in his head too, but he followed Sara's lead. God bless Parish Roberts.

Sara kicked at the cowl, and the Raptor raised its hideous skull-like head, hissing and baring its razorlike teeth at her. She fired a bullet into its head, and it slumped over.

"Finally," Paul griped.

"Bite me, Iceman," Sara muttered. Parish moved in and kicked the Raptor over. They each put another two bullets into it before Sara knelt to check the civvie.

The guy had open, bleeding slashes all over his arms and back, and a nasty one along his brow gushing blood over his face. But his pulse was strong and steady.

His eyes opened and he bucked against her, still full of fight.

"Easy, buddy, you're safe," Sara said.

The sound of sobbing caught her attention. Sara looked over and saw a young blonde cowering against the edge of the roof. Parish went over to try to calm her, but she sobbed in terror, pointing wordlessly at the body of the Raptor.

Sara looked over the rest of the civvie for injuries. His pants were unzipped. Interrupted in the middle of a quickie, she thought, and stifled a grin. He seemed pretty whole for a guy who just wrestled with a Raptor bare-handed.

"What...the fuck was that?" the guy asked, catching his breath and sitting up.

"Buddy, you do not want to know," Sara said, grinning. She held out a hand and helped him to his feet. "Good fight. Wouldn't want to go toe-to-toe with you."

The guy gave her a once-over and leered. "Can't say I would mind it."

Sara ignored that and looked over at Parish. "She okay?"

Parish shrugged, awkwardly patting the sobbing girl on her shoulder. "Not hurt, anyway. I dunno about okay."

Sara turned back to the stocky guy and saw him kneeling beside the Raptor. He pushed back the cowl and exposed its half-destroyed skull, staring at the over-sized fangs.

Sara put her hand on the guy's shoulder. "Think of it as a nightmare, and never say anything about it again."

"Can't do that," the guy replied.

"Harvey, do we have a problem here?" Paul asked.

The civvie suddenly wrenched the Raptor's neck with a hideous wet cracking sound. Despite herself, Sara jumped. There was viciousness in the motion, made worse when he snapped a fang out of the thing's gaping mouth, holding it up to the light.

He looked up at her, a smile spreading across his bloody face. "Name's Gary Stover," he said. "So what do you do, lady?"

Sara advanced on the guardhouse. The door was half-open and swinging in the ocean breeze. As she got closer, she saw a body lying in the door-way, keeping the door from closing.

"Cover," she ordered, and they moved into position as she knelt to check the guard. He was deader than dead, his chest a ripped-open ruin, his eyes staring sightlessly up at the sky.

How the hell did Parish do this? Sara wondered. *Did he tear the guy open with his bare hands?*

"Stover, you keeping count?" she asked. Gary nodded.

"How many?" Matthews asked. He was holding steady, she was glad to see.

"Eighteen," Sara said. "Detachment of six, plus their commander." *Paul.* She wasn't thinking about that yet. "Eight scientists. Plus Parish and the guy he bit before."

She stood up and they kept moving up the pathway to the plain cinderblock building with no windows.

"Major," Matthews began slowly, as if working it out in his head. "You're missing one."

Sara held up her hand, then nosed the door open with a touch of her boot.

The attack came immediately, a screaming banshee launching itself at Sara from the darkness just inside the door. Sara fired, but couldn't tell if she hit it in the split second before it struck her with the force of a speeding car. Sara practically flew backward, her ass hitting the ground hard as the thing above her slashed a hand toward her face. She blocked it with her gun hand instinctively, and the gun flew from her grip.

The screaming, twisted face above her darted its teeth toward her throat. Sara blocked it with both hands, grabbing it by the neck to keep her hands away from its mouth. *Don't get bit don't get bit don't get bit* her mind chanted on repeat, as if that was the worst thing that could happen to her right now.

Come to think of it, that *was* the worst thing that could happen.

The thing was beating at her arms, as Sara held it off by its throat. "Shoot!" she croaked. What the fuck were they waiting for?

Something slammed into the banshee's side, flinging it off Sara. It rolled away into a crouch and coiled to spring. Matthews and Stover shot together, and it fell back, twitching.

Sara hauled herself back up, scooping up her gun. She and Gary advanced on it.

Not a banshee. Not a Raptor. The dying thing on the ground was Capt. Kim Hill, her plain face twisted in hate and gasping, coated in blood.

"What a fucking ballsup," Sara murmured.

Hill hissed at Sara, and Gary shot her in the head.

Then he turned to Sara, suspicion in his eyes. Sara glanced over her arms and ran her hands over her face and neck. "Nothing."

Gary motioned toward her left arm with his gun. There was a rip along her sleeve. Sara shrugged off the jacket and displayed her unmarked arm to him.

Gary lowered his gun. "No offense, Harvey. Just gotta be sure."

Sara nodded and stalked back to where Matthews stood. "You were saying something right as you tipped her off to our approach?"

Matthews' eyes acknowledged his mistake, but he didn't relent. "You said eighteen. Six soldiers, including the guy on the beach, the guard, and her." He pointed to Hill's body. "Their commander makes seven. Eight scientists makes fifteen. The guy in town and the other volunteer makes seventeen, not eighteen."

"Yeah," Sara said. "You can do math."

Matthews waited. Sara did not expound. The silence grew, but if it was a staring game, neither was giving in. Finally Matthews spoke. "Major, who else is on this island?"

Sara turned away and did not speak.

Sara coughed again, fighting the gorge rising in her throat. She knew if she puked now, she would never fucking hear the end of it.

"Watch it, she's gonna hurl!" Gary crowed.

"Fuck you, Stover," Sara managed, and passed the cigar back to Jimmy. Her stomach settled down, still uneasy, but she was no longer in danger of puking her dignity in front of her men.

Jimmy took a long drag without so much as a cough. Sara glared at him. "Sorry, ma'am, I guess it takes a real man to smoke a cigar." Jimmy grinned with that face so damned young he made Sara feel like an ancient crone.

"Keep it up, Bell, and you'll get that cigar inserted in an uncomfortable place. Lit." Sara chanced another sip of her beer. Her stomach accepted it, declaring truce.

"Hey, where's Captain America?" Gary asked. "Ain't he good enough to drink with us?"

"He's outside, getting some air," Parish said. He was drinking a plain Coke tonight, but Sara had covered for him and called it a Jack and Coke. Parish was no teetotaler—God knew they'd put away a few together—but his stomach was no easier than Sara's after the day of work they'd put in. It was amazing even Gary could eat—he'd put away most of the platter of food all by himself. They talked big, but no one else was really eating tonight.

"Air," Gary sneered, flipping the last shred of plantain chip into the air and catching it on the back of his hand. "Air on this fuckin' island stinks worse than Chicago."

"Nothing stinks worse than Chicago, 'cept maybe you." Sara grinned, and others laughed. Gary flipped the chip at her and she deflected it easily.

"Go get Captain America to come in here and down a beer with the slaves," Gary insisted.

"You better quit calling him that or he's going to fuck you up someday," Sara returned.

"I can take him," Gary declared.

Jimmy and Parish both stifled laughter behind their drinks. Sara shook her head. "I'm gonna see that someday, and my money's on Vaughn," she said, standing. "You bad, Stover, but you ain't THAT bad."

Gary flipped her off. "Go get the boss, Harvey, tell him we're buying."

"You're buying," Sara corrected, and walked out of the dingy bar to the moonlit street.

Paul Vaughn stood only a few steps away from the door. He rarely smoked, but tonight the ember of a cigarette glowed from his fingers. He leaned against the post holding up the ramshackle porch roof, staring out at the dirt road instead of the lovely expanse of stars above them.

"Yo, boss," Sara said, chucking him lightly on the arm. "The peons are clamoring for your appearance."

Paul turned to her with a ghost of a smile. "They shaking it loose?"

Sara shrugged. "As best they can. Bell's a little shaky, and nobody's got an appetite except Stover."

Paul shook his head. "Stover fucking scares me sometimes."

Sara grinned. "Nobody scares you, Iceman."

"Iceman, Captain America... You guys ever gonna give me a handle that isn't from some comic book?" Paul was kidding her, but Sara saw something in his eyes that she'd never seen before. She stepped a little closer, and this time she held his gaze.

"Vaughn," she said slowly. "You okay?"

"Fine," Paul said immediately. "We all saw It. We're all a little freaked out. Except Stover."

"Yeah," Sara said absently, still looking at him. "I just never saw you freaked out about anything."

Paul broke eye contact, looking back out at the moonlit street. "That thing. It's just... I'd have felt a lot better if Blackfire's orders were to put It in the fucking ground, you know? Boxing it up for cold storage, that doesn't sit too well with me. Not with what that fucker can do."

Sara nodded. "I'm with you there, Iceman. That thing should never fucking exist, let alone be left alive. Unalive. Whatever you call it."

Paul shook his head. "We're just the grunts, Harvey, we don't get to say."

"You the grunt, I'm an independent contractor," Sara cracked, trying to bring some humor back to his eyes. It wasn't working. Something was heavy on Paul's shoulders tonight, something more than the usual burden of leadership. It was a weird job he had, even weirder than hers, and for the first time she wondered if it was too much for him.

"Hey, Vaughn," she said, laying a hand on his arm awkwardly. "We did the job. It's okay." It felt strange to be comforting him, like he was Jimmy the Kid instead of Paul fucking Vaughn. She'd been following Paul since the day he walked into her desert camp. She'd followed him so long she'd forgotten what it was like not to be fighting at his side, his voice inside her head as though he belonged there.

"Sara," he said, turning to her.

She blinked—he never called her by her first name.

"That thing. If It ever gets loose..."

"Shit, that's what you're worried about?" Sara laughed. "They're never gonna let It see the light of day again, Vaughn! Blackfire may be military, but they're not that fucking stupid."

Paul grasped her shoulders, staring at her with an intensity she'd never seen, almost scaring her. The moonlight shone down with harsh brilliance.

"That thing gets its teeth in me, you shoot me," he said. "Do not let me go that way, Sara. The way It kills, It doesn't kill..."

"Hey," Sara interrupted, grabbing his hands in hers. "I got you. You know that, right? I got your back, Paul. All the way down."

He stared at her in silence, then finally he seemed to relax. "Yeah, I know that." Then he did that thing that drove her nuts, ruffling her short hair with his hand like she was a puppy. As usual, she ducked her head in protest.

"Get your ass inside, drink with the guys," she ordered, as if she had the power to order him anywhere.

"Yes ma'am," Paul snarked, and followed her inside, away from the moonlight.

Matthews dragged another body onto the pile. "That makes four more dead," he declared.

Sara turned to Gary. "Still missing two—no, three, including Doctor Death," Gary said.

Sara frowned. "Four. You forgot Vaughn."

"Fuck, I keep forgetting him," Gary said, ticking off on his fingers. "Yeah, he makes four."

"Quit forgetting him," Sara snapped, stalking around the pile in the middle of the room. She poked at the bodies, checking for any signs of life.

"Sorry, Harvey," Gary said uneasily. Sara glanced up at him, surprised. Gary had never apologized to her for anything in all the time they'd worked together.

He shifted his feet, uncomfortable.

"He's not dead, you stupid fuck," Sara snapped. "Stop acting like he's dead and I'm his fucking widow. He's your commanding officer too, and if there's any human being who could make it through something like this, it's Vaughn."

Gary nodded, and didn't even correct her on the technicality that he wasn't exactly under Paul's command, never having been in the service. When Gary stopped poking her with sticks, she knew the shit was bad.

Sara stood up and walked over to Gary. "Stover, gimme the M4."

Gary handed it over. "What're you doing?"

"What I should've done in Haiti," Sara replied, checking its load. "You and Matthews stay here, batten down the hatches."

"Fuck that," Gary said immediately. "No way you're going down there alone, Harvey."

"What the hell are you two talking about?" Matthews asked. Both ignored him.

"That's an order, Stover," Sara snapped. "Stay here, keep looking for the last four. Somebody's got to be alive on this ball of dirt. If I'm not back in ten minutes, set the incendiaries and proceed to the underground dock."

"Harvey—" Gary began, but Sara shook her head in a way that invited no argument.

Sara moved over to the emergency stairwell and kicked the door open. Fortunately the generator lights were still working, casting their orange glow into the stairwell. She pivoted at the lower landing, keeping her corners covered.

Gary's right, this was fucking stupid, go on and split up your undersized team, Harvey, good plan.

The door at the bottom of the stairs was closed. EMERGENCY EXIT ONLY – ALARM WILL SOUND.

Sara stepped back, the M4 ready. She kicked the door release bar hard, and the door banged open with a report that would have made her jump if she hadn't already been so tense.

No alarms, no guards. For a moment, Sara wished there were six armed guards converging on her, guns raised, wanting to know what the fuck she was doing in the lower level without clearance and an escort. The only other time she'd been down here was with Vaughn. She'd give just about anything for Vaughn to be with her now.

He might be here. He might be waiting.

Fuck that. Sara Harvey did not want to face Paul Vaughn hopped up on the crazy.

The room beyond the lying-ass EMERGENCY EXIT door was empty. There was a comfortable office chair at the control panel before the giant reinforced window. Sara covered the corners of the room, propping the door open with her foot, before she switched on the lights.

A hiss of fury echoed, and Sara frantically covered all four corners again before she realized the hiss was coming over the speaker.

"Turn off the lightsss."

"Fuck you," Sara replied, moving to the control panel. Behind her, the EMERGENCY door swung closed.

The chamber beyond the glass window was dark, though light shining in from the control room provided a dim outline of the thing inside. Containment was secure, Sara saw. It had not escaped.

"Let me out, Sssssara." It spoke in the strange near-French accent of Haiti, but the sibilant S's were all Its own. She had never wanted to hear that voice again.

"Fuck you," Sara repeated. She found if she simply kept repeating that, it helped her not to look at It. Instead she concentrated on the panel. The electrodes were intact, she saw. Why hadn't anyone activated the failsafe?

"A lot of fun out there, yessss. Parissssh ssssssays hello."

"Nice try," Sara returned, looking for the log book. "Parish is dead, you fucker. In a moment you'll be joining him."

"I'm already dead, Sssssara."

"Not dead enough," she muttered. The log book was on the floor under the console. She risked bending over to pick it up after another quick glance back at the door, flipping through the pages.

"They don't all go mad, you know," It whispered. *"I'm not."*

"That's a matter of opinion," Sara replied, finding the log sheet for today. As of 0600, situation normal. All fucked up.

"Ssssome just go cold, Sssssara," It said. *"Jussst what you want."*

Another hiss, closer this time. It had edged closer to the light, enough for Sara to see Its skin, rotten and gray at bloodless wounds that would never heal. Its solid black eyes moved in Its skull, yet somehow It always seemed to be looking at her. Its gray tongue moved over Its jagged teeth.

"Ssssara, here to kill me," It whispered. *"Are you ssssure thisss time?"*

"I always was, you fuck." Sara flipped the emergency switch, and the floor electrodes activated, buzzing loudly over the speaker. It let out a horrible screech, flying forward into the glass.

A crack appeared, even through the steel-wire reinforcement. Sara pulled the M4 up immediately, keeping it trained on the writhing form beyond the glass.

The buzz wavered and the lights switched off. *Fuck, overloaded the generator,* Sara thought. *Did it get enough juice?*

The EMERGENCY door banged open, and Sara dove for the far right corner. The form outlined in the doorway was vaguely man-shaped, and then the door clicked shut.

It was completely black. Sara wanted to shout out for identification—

what if it was Stover or Matthews? If it wasn't, she'd give away her position.

What about the crack in the glass, *oh fuck, the crack in the glass, did it get enough juice?*

A panting breath to her left, and Sara opened fire.

A scream of agony, and the door wrenched open again, letting in a spill of light. Whoever it was crawled out through the door, and it clicked shut again.

Sara braced her back against the wall and moved away from the glass window, passing the control console, keeping the M4 aimed at the pitch-black room. She could swear something was moving beside her.

The cracked glass, oh fuck, the cracked glass.

Outside she could hear another shout, more gunfire. Someone was alive out there.

Fuck this.

Sara moved fast, past the control panel, and wrenched open the door. The light fell across the room.

No one was there. The glass was cracked, but not broken. The shadows beyond it did not move.

Sara stepped out into the stairwell. There on the floor was the twisted corpse of what once had been a lab technician, his face coated in blood, the back of his head exploded in a mess of blood and brains. Above him stood Gary Stover, his gun hand shaking.

"Dammit, Stover, I said stay upstairs," Sara said.

"Yes ma'am," Gary said, but his voice was different, with none of the usual sardonic smartass.

Sara stared at him. "Stover?"

Then she saw it. His hand was bleeding. Bite wound.

Immediately Sara lifted the M4. "Fuck, Stover, goddammit."

"I know," he said, not raising his own gun. He sat down on the steps, seemingly stunned.

"Goddammit, Gary!" Sara shouted, her voice almost breaking. "I told you to fucking stay upstairs!"

Gary met her eyes, his face unreadable. "I thought you'd need backup. I thought… Somebody's gotta have your back, ya know?"

"I got my own back, you motherfucking asshole!" Sara shouted.

She raised the M4 again.

Gary held out his bleeding hand. "Don't do it," he pleaded.

Sara shook her head, fighting the sadness and fury that were trying to take her over. "Gary, I've got to. You know I do. You know what's gonna happen."

"There's still three left, four including Vaughn," Gary insisted. "You can't take them with just you and Andy Griffith up there."

Sara shook her head. "There's no stopping it, no antidote. You know that."

"But not right away," Gary said. "Please, Harvey. I got a little time. Let me go out the right way."

"Shit," she murmured. "You so much as twitch and I will blow you right the fuck away, Stover."

Gary nodded, and stood back up. He put another bullet in the tech's head. The report was very loud in the confined stairwell.

"Fuck you," he spat at it, and climbed the stairs ahead of her.

"The Lord will cause you to be defeated before your enemies," Jimmy said, his hands shaking. The worn black book shifted in his grip. "You shall go out against them one way and flee before them seven ways."

"Don't stop!" Sara shouted, letting go with the flamethrower again.

The redcap howled as another tooth popped out of its mouth. The heat was intense, as Sara and Parish alternated flamethrowers on it. Sweat beaded on her brow, and she tightened her grip on the flamethrower.

"Not yet!" Gary shouted, firing yet again at the redcap cowering against the stone wall alongside the worn, chipped steps leading to the dark recesses of the castle.

"Jesus, Stover, quit wasting ammo!" Sara ordered, and Gary finally put away his gun. Gary just couldn't get his mind around a critter he couldn't shoot.

"You shall become an object of horror to all the kingdoms of the earth," Jimmy said above them on the steps. "Your corpses shall be food for every bird of the air and animal of the earth, and there shall be no one to frighten them away."

"Fuck, what's that happy shit from?" Parish muttered.

"Deuteronomy," Sara replied.

Outside, the wind screamed against the stone walls and thunder rumbled in the distance, competing with the steady drumbeat of rain against the faraway roof.

The redcap hissed at Sara, its gnome-like face twisted and furious beneath its small red hat, its short white beard covered in soot. It hefted the iron pike in its hand, and Parish rewarded it with another blast from the flamethrower. The flames licked over its skin without effect, but its hat was a little less shiny.

"More Scripture!" Paul ordered, running down the steps past Jimmy with a flamethrower in his hands.

"In the desperate straits to which the enemy siege reduces you, you will eat the fruit of your womb, the flesh of your own sons and daughters whom the Lord your God has given you," Jimmy read.

The redcap lost another tooth, spitting it at them in fury. Sara took over the flamethrower, blasting the redcap back against the wall and scorching the stone behind it black.

When the flames stopped, the hat was mostly dull.

"Almost there!" Gary crowed. "Eat that, Santa!"

Jimmy paused, glancing down at the redcap's hat. The redcap took its chance, darting with preternatural speed between Sara and Parish. She almost blasted it, but stopped at the last second, not wanting to chance burning Parish.

"Christ, are we the fucking Keystone Kops today? Get it together, boys!" Sara shouted.

"I got it!" Paul blasted flames from the steps. The redcap skittered away from him, dashing across the silent foyer shrouded in cobwebs and shadows. The castle itself seemed to groan under the weight of the pounding rain above them, and Sara wondered—not for the first time this fine evening—whether the castle had finally seen one too many storms.

Gary had his goddamned gun out again and fired at the fast-moving redcap, chasing it across the foyer toward the darkened ballroom through the archway.

"Stover, for fuck's sake cut it out!" Sara shouted. "Bullets can't hurt it!"

"Motherfucker!" Gary shouted. The bullets whined off the ground—he wasn't even hitting it, Sara saw with consternation.

Parish followed beside Sara, his breath coming heavily. "Goddamn overgrown garden gnome," he muttered, and Sara couldn't help laughing.

They pushed through into the main hall, where some remnants of furniture remained. A few pieces of old plywood were burning in the fireplace—Paul's idea, to bring the redcap out of hiding, posing as errant "tourists" that had sheltered in its castle.

Gary stood in the middle of the ballroom, the firelight casting his strange shadow dancing up the wall.

"Where the fuck is it, Stover?" Parish asked.

Gary looked at Sara instead. She was pissed, and she let it show. Gary was pissed too, but he was pissed at himself, and that was just fine by Sara. The redcap was small and ridiculously fast, but it shouldn't have gotten away from him in this mausoleum.

"Goddammit," Paul groused as Jimmy caught up with Bible in hand. "This is amateur hour, people!"

"Spread out, find the fucker," Sara said. "Jimbo, you're with me."

As soon as Gary moved, she saw it. Crouched behind the splintered remains of a table, the tall iron spike gave it away, lying nearly flat on the ground.

Sara pretended not to see it, drifting closer to the fireplace. "Second thought, kid, you go with Vaughn."

Jimmy drifted over toward Paul, away from her line of fire.

"Parish," Sara ordered. "C'mere."

Parish stepped into the firelight and the redcap immediately launched itself at him, snarling.

"Duck!" Sara shouted, and Parish hit the floor instantly. Sara blasted the redcap in mid-air, and Vaughn turned his flamethrower on it as well. Hit from two sides, the redcap screamed, writhing within the flames. Parish rolled away from it, ending up by Jimmy's feet.

"Save us, O God of our salvation, and gather and rescue us from among the nations," Jimmy said in a shaking voice, and the redcap howled again. Its iron spike wavered in the air as it twisted within the flames.

"We got it!" Paul crowed.

The redcap let out one final yowl, then fell over.

Sara and Paul turned off the flamethrowers together, and they advanced on the redcap. It lay there in its silly green suit, its face slack. Sara wondered how its clothes didn't burn, but then, it dipped its hat in its victims' blood, so why get picky?

"Is the hat dry?" Parish asked.

Sara leaned over. It looked dry to her. She reached out with the end of the flamethrower—was that a shiny patch behind the ear?

Sara jumped backward as the redcap sprang, jamming its iron spike at her. It missed her abdomen and sank into the meat of her left thigh. Sara fell backward, the pain thrumming up through her body. The red-hot pike was buried deep in her leg, and the redcap was trying to dip its hat in her blood.

"Shit!" Parish shouted. The redcap twisted the pike, and Sara couldn't help it —she cried out just a little. She could smell her own flesh burning, like that luau they'd guarded in Maui last year.

She tried to shove herself backward, but her legs weren't cooperating.

"Get her out of the way!" Paul shouted. Gary grabbed Sara's arms and dragged her toward the fireplace. The redcap clung to the pike and growled at Gary, who responded with a hearty kick, sending the damn thing spinning across the floor.

Paul turned his flamethrower on the redcap again, with Parish circling around the other side. The flames met in the center of the stone ballroom, and the redcap howled in fury.

"Played fuckin' dead, smarter than we are," Sara breathed. She felt dizzy, and her leg was a mass of hot, roiling pain.

Gary glared at Jimmy. "Get your ass over here, kid!"

Jimmy fumbled the Bible under his arm as he scrambled next to Sara, reaching into his pack for the medkit.

"We need some goddamn Bible here!" Paul shouted over the roar of the flamethrowers.

Gary grabbed the Bible from Jimmy. "Help her," he said, and started to read. "'May my enemy be like the wicked and may my opponent be like the unrighteous, for what is the hope of the godless when God cuts them off, when God takes away their lives?' Hey, I like this shit better."

"It's Job, you'd like him," Sara breathed.

Jimmy wrapped his fleece jacket around his hands, protecting them from the hot pike, and in one quick motion he yanked it out of Sara's leg. The pain was huge, raving up through her body as if every part of her had been stabbed with the red-hot pike at once. Sara couldn't help making a sound, just loud enough for the others to hear over the flames and the rain and the redcap's guttural cries. She bit hard on her lower lip.

"Will God hear their cry when trouble comes upon them? Will they take delight in the Almighty?" Gary continued. His hands didn't shake.

Jimmy pressed gauze pads against the hole in Sara's leg, and they soaked through immediately. "Bleeding's bad, but at least it wasn't the chest. You were lucky, ma'am."

Sara almost laughed.

"It hurls at them without pity, they flee from its power in the headlong flight," Gary said. "'It claps its hands at them and hisses at them from its place.' You sure this is a real Bible?"

The redcap screamed again and flopped over. Paul stopped the flamethrower, and Parish followed suit.

"I think it's dead," Paul declared.

"Be fuckin' sure this time," Gary snapped.

Paul turned that cool gaze on him, the one that made Sara call him Iceman. "Watch your mouth, Stover," he ordered, with more bite to his voice than usual.

Gary and Paul glared at each other for a moment, then Paul came over to kneel beside Jimmy. "She okay?"

"Ten-four," Sara croaked. "Fuck, it hurts."

"I think it missed the artery," Jimmy said, his hands still shaking as he added more gauze pads to the wound.

The loud report of gunfire brought Paul to his feet again. Gary was shooting the redcap's corpse over and over, the bullets still bouncing harmlessly off its body.

"Goddammit, Stover, cut it the fuck out!" Parish barked. Sara glanced at him in surprise—Parish was the calmest man on her team.

Gary finally quit shooting it, and Parish stalked past him toward their gear, stashed in the corner.

"Fuckin' psycho," Parish muttered.

"The fuck?" Gary shouted, grabbing Parish's arm. "You got somethin' to say?"

Parish threw off Gary's hand with a temper that surprised Sara. "You're whacked, man, you're fuckin' out of it," he snapped. "You let Santa Junior here get away from you, you kept shooting it when you knew it wouldn't do no damn good, and Harvey got hurt! You totally fucked up!"

"That's enough!" Paul ordered, and they shut up. "You want to get pissed at somebody, Roberts, get pissed at me. I'm in command."

They kept glaring at each other, but their tempers seemed cooler.

Paul turned back to Jimmy. "Seriously, how bad is it?'

Jimmy checked the gauze. "Bleeding's slowing. I think she's gonna be okay. We really need to get her sewn up by somebody better than me, though. And those burns need antiseptic treatment."

Paul leaned over and ruffled her hair.

"Quit that," Sara said.

He smiled down at her. "Don't you go doing that again, Harvey."

"Is that an order?" Sara asked quietly.

"Damn straight. I can't manage this motley crew without you," he said, standing up. "Roberts, get the hat. Stover, get the van backed up to the foyer. I don't want Harvey out in the rain any longer than she has to be. We've got a med clinic in Lockerbie, we can get there fast if we hustle."

"Aye," Parish said, and knelt beside the redcap. Gary stalked out into the rain without answering—Sara was going to have to kick his ass for that. He needed to show respect for Vaughn or she was going to boot him off the team, no matter how good he was.

Jimmy placed another bandage over her leg. His hands were still shaking.

The three of them stood on the underground dock. The water lapped quietly at the metal plating beneath them, and the sun shone at the end of the passageway out to the open sea.

"Shit fuck piss motherfucker," Gary murmured. It was almost a mantra to him, stringing together as many curse words as possible without connecting them in any fashion.

Three empty boat slips. One still filled.

The M16 was empty, and Sara laid it on the footlocker by the boat gear. Sure enough, four hand weapons were missing from the locker.

"One was the boat Roberts took to the mainland," Gary said.

"We brought that one back and set it free," Sara replied. "Two for the mainland."

"Maybe they weren't heading for the mainland," Matthews offered.

Sara grabbed the keys remaining on the pegboard. "Not taking that chance, Chief," she said. "You gonna stay here for the firebombing or follow us through?"

Matthews shook his head as though it were a choice. "I'm with you."

Sara stepped over to the console and keyed in her code. The boat began to lower in the water. She tossed the keys to Gary, and the men clambered down into the boat to get it prepped. Sara kept typing.

"Harvey, you coming or what?" Gary called.

"One second." Sara pressed ENTER and vaulted down into the idling boat. As soon as she hit the deck, Gary had it moving backward fast and hard, turning out of the slip and heading to sea.

"Stover," Sara said, and Gary shifted out of the seat. Sara took over for a moment as Gary leaned over his pack, flipping the detonator.

As the boat shot out into the sunlight, Sara heard the first of the explosions begin. She switched positions with Gary again, letting him steer as she trained her binoculars on the Island. Blossoms of flame shot between the trees, as explosion after explosion ripped through the complex.

Good fucking riddance.

"What were you doing up there?" Matthews asked.

"Final detonation sequence and an encoded message," Sara replied. "Letting the powers that be at Blackfire know they got a mess here. I'm sure Vaughn already sent them one, that was protocol, but—"

"But Vaughn didn't exactly send us any warning, so we don't know he had time," Gary finished.

"Stow that shit, Stover," Sara said, with less heat than she intended.

Gary kept the boat steady as Sara switched on the sonar. "Harvey—"

"Shut up, Stover," she said. "Two boats missing. One's got Cold Ones on it. Stands to reason Vaughn would take the other one after them. He's not gonna let them on the mainland. He must not have known about Parish, or maybe Parish got free later. He's chasing Cold Ones across the goddamn ocean, and we're gonna catch up and help him."

Gary turned to her, and for the first time there was honest anger in his face. "Goddammit, Harvey, your balloon ever fuckin' land?"

"Stow it, Stover!" Sara ordered. Matthews grabbed the wheel.

Gary wasn't stopping. "He's dead, Sara, he's fuckin' dead so give up the goddamn fantasyland!"

Instantly Gary was facing the business end of Sara's Beretta.

From behind him, Matthews tried to interject some reason. "Let's all calm down," he tried, but Sara could see the chief's free hand resting on his own weapon.

"Are you done, Stover?" Sara asked, voice cold. Her fury was already passing, replaced with dread at the way Gary's eyes were darting back and forth, unreadable to her.

Gary Stover as a Cold One, not good. Put a bullet to him, Harvey.

"Not yet," Gary said more quietly, as though he could hear her thoughts. He turned back to the wheel, and Matthews gave it up to him without protest.

Sara lowered her gun and glanced back at the radar. "Got a blip north-northwest, heading straight up the coast," she said. "Not straight toward land, sort of paralleling the coast."

"Roger that." Gary turned that way and kept the boat cresting the waves faster. The boat rose and fell with the waves, the sea breeze in the sunlight drying the sweat on Sara's brow. She had always loved the sea, and if it weren't for the situation she'd be enjoying the hell out of the ride.

Matthews retreated to the back of the boat, watching both of them warily. She couldn't blame him.

Up ahead, they saw a runaround identical to their own, floating in the waves. "Harvey, that our mark?" Gary asked.

Sara checked the radar again. "Separate contact. Two marks now, one still going strong. That one's not going anywhere."

"We've got to check it, though," Matthews insisted.

Sara and Gary met each other's eyes. "We've got to catch that last boat before…" Sara's voice trailed off.

"If there's anyone to save," Matthews began.

"There'll be no one to save if a boat with Cold Ones hits the mainland," Sara insisted. "Parish caused the deaths of three people in five minutes in a quiet town. What if that boat reaches Boston?"

"We can spare five minutes," Matthews insisted.

"We don't have time!" Sara snapped, glancing at Gary.

Gary looked at her. "We have time," he said quietly, gripping the wheel.

Matthews glanced from Sara to Gary. Sara ignored the chief, but nodded anyway. "Five minutes, no more."

Gary brought the boat up alongside the runaround. Before it was even at a full stop, Matthews jumped across.

"Wait!" Sara pulled her gun and climbed across to follow him. "Goddammit, Chief, wait for me!" She could hear someone speaking to Matthews.

Matthews had his gun lowered. "Survivor! Get a first-aid kit!" He disappeared behind the large white bulkhead in the center of the boat. Sara turned back for the kit.

Behind her, there was the short report of gunfire and a scream of fury or pain.

"Fuck!" Sara shouted, vaulting back over the railing.

"Harvey, wait!" Gary shouted.

Sara didn't have time to wait. She advanced around the bulkhead and saw a bloodstained man in the tattered remnants of a white coat hunched over a struggling Matthews. She fired and the white coat twitched.

But he just looked up, blood coating his face. Bits of flesh were caught in his formerly white beard, now stained a rusty red. Dr. Victor Milan, or Doctor Death as they called him, the man behind the project.

"*Sssara,*" he hissed.

Sara froze.

"*I told you I was already dead,*" the doctor grinned, blood on his teeth.

Sara pulled the trigger. A round black hole appeared in his forehead, blood and brains spraying across the white bulkhead behind him. She kicked his body off Matthews.

The chief was in bad shape. Bites on his arms, blood spouting from his ear, which hung by a shred of flesh. Sara dragged him back onto the deck, quickly checking the rest of the runaround.

Gary leaped down, kneeling beside the chief with the first-aid kit. Sara met Gary's eyes—there were at least half a dozen bites.

"Not gonna be Cold," Matthews insisted. "Sorry I wasn't more h-help."

"Fuck that," Sara said firmly. "You a good man, Chief. Hell, I'd have picked you for my team."

"Thanks," Matthews whispered, his hand pressed to what remained of his ear.

Sara looked around and found the chief's gun where he'd dropped it, just beyond the pool of blood spreading on the deck. She cocked it and held it to the chief's head.

Matthews nodded.

Sara pulled the trigger.

Then she got up and walked past Gary, climbing back into their boat. "You coming?"

Gary stood there for a moment. Then he followed her back onto their boat. Sara grabbed the spare gas can and splashed it across the other boat's deck. Gary lit a match and tossed it over the railing, letting it go up in a whoosh of flame.

As Gary steered them away from the burning boat, Sara unobtrusively got the spare sidearm from the locker under the control panel and slid it into her belt at the small of her back. Now all the guns in the boat were on her, save Gary's one handgun.

She couldn't have much more time left.

***

"I need four coconuts," Sara said, tapping four fingers on the counter. "Bukos."

The old man behind the counter peered at her with terribly bloodshot eyes, clearly drunk. Sara could smell him across the scratched and scarred wooden counter. "Apat bukos?" he asked.

Sara tried not to be obvious about leaning backward. The smell coming off the old man was strong, some local booze mixed with serious halitosis. "You got 'em or not?"

"I get 'em," the man said, blinking at her. He pulled a beaten cardboard box from under the counter and withdrew four small, sadly dinged coconuts from some godawful storage space. Thank God she didn't intend to eat them, Sara thought.

"Salamat, po," she said with difficulty—her Tagalog was miserably insuffi-

cient, and the "po" honorific always felt weird. She passed the old grocer some cash and fled without her change, the box under her arm.

Sara drove through the small town, the sun setting just as she reached the rural road where concrete turned to ruts and cobblestones. The Jeep rumbled along the road as the rosy washes of sunset bathed the sky over the treetops. Sweat beaded her brow, but she didn't turn on the air. It would just make it that much worse when she arrived at the cemetery.

She stopped the Jeep outside its gates, hauling the box out into the darkening night air, muggy and thick. An insect whined near her ear and Sara wished for another Arctic assignment.

Sara followed the path in between the graves, half-overgrown with weeds. She could hear their voices long before she came around the bend where Paul's truck was parked. She switched into stealth mode, sliding between the graves and approaching from behind the truck. She made it almost all the way up to Paul before he sensed her presence and pivoted fast, pulling his gun.

"Motherfuck!" he shouted, lowering his gun. "Goddammit, Harvey!"

Beyond him, Sara was glad to see Gary and Parish with weapons leveled at her, even though they were waist-deep in a grave. Jimmy was just standing there, looking startled. He needed some refreshers.

"Time was I couldn't have gotten near so close to you, Vaughn," she teased. "You must be getting old."

"Older by the second, you keep sneaking up on me like that," Paul returned. "You get the coconuts?"

She shoved the beaten box at him. "Next time do your own grocery shopping," she groused, kneeling by the grave. "How's it going, boys?"

"Wanna take a turn with the shovel?" Parish asked.

"Nah, you're doing so well, I'd just louse it up," she replied. Gary holstered his weapon and went back to shovel duty.

Sara checked her weapon and began to recon the area, as Paul and Jimmy went back to the cauldron. An honest-to-God cauldron, albeit modern aluminum and resting on a government-issue portable stove instead of a creaky wood fire. No sense burning down the Philippines.

Paul cracked open a coconut, spilling its milk into the cauldron as Jimmy stirred it with one hand and read prayers from a beaten old book he held in the other hand.

"Fucking hocus-pocus," Sara muttered as she passed Paul.

"It's hocus-pocus that works, Major," Paul said. Sometimes he still used her old rank, as though she hadn't left the Marines behind years ago.

A blackbird squawked above her, and Sara resisted the utterly irrational urge *to shoot it. "This whole place makes me crazy," she said. "I'd almost rather be in Texas."*

"Bite your tongue," Parish said.

A thudding sound from the grave, and Gary's dirt-smeared face popped up. "Got it, Harvey!"

Paul dumped the rest of the coconut milk and scrambled over to the side of the grave. "Show me."

Parish grabbed the crowbar lying in the soft pile of dirt beside the uneven hole. He wrenched at the wooden coffin hard, grumbling to himself. "If it ain't what we think, this is gonna be nasty..."

Another wrench, and the wood splintered. Parish and Gary yanked up the coffin lid, hauling it out of the way.

"Fuck me," Gary muttered. Then he reached into the grave and pulled hard at the form within.

"Jesus!" Parish shouted, scrambling backward.

"Get a fuckin' grip," Gary said, shoving the body up out of the hole ahead of him.

At Sara's feet lay the statue of a young girl, her eyes closed in permanent repose. The statue was carved from palm, Sara knew without touching her. A perfect replica, left behind in the coffin when the aswang consumed her corpse.

"Almost done here, sir!" Jimmy called from the cauldron, where he stirred the...goop? Sara could never remember what it was called, only that it was important and required a metric fuckton of coconuts.

"Relax, people, we're good," Paul said, brushing the dirt from his fatigues. "Load up the sting rays."

Parish hauled the box out of Paul's truck, pulling out a handful of sharp sting-ray tails. "I miss the Raptor," he grumbled.

"Fuck, I don't," Sara said, grabbing a couple of tails and attaching them to the leather bands at her wrists. "That thing was a pain in the ass."

"Yeah, but bullets killed it," Parish retorted. "Next time, can we go after something that bullets kill, Vaughn? This shit is for the birds."

"Bitch bitch bitch," Paul said absently.

Sara glanced over to where Gary was examining the statue. "Stover, quit fucking around and get over here for your garlic."

Gary walked over, the statue slung under his arm. "Think they'll let me keep her?"

Sara shook her head. "Gary, you are one twisted fuck."

"Wouldn't you like to know." Gary propped the statue up against the back of the truck. "She's cute. Or she was."

"Closest you're gonna get to a woman, anyway," Parish snarked, and Gary aimed a punch at him. For once it seemed friendly, not the usual assaholic bickering Sara was used to breaking up between them.

"There's always Harvey," Gary leered, waggling his tongue at her. It never ceased to amaze Sara that he somehow thought this was sexually attractive.

"In your fucking dreams, Stover," Sara replied, handing him the basket of garlic. "Suit up and stow it."

Sara moved back over to the cauldron, where Paul was glaring. "Goop not working?"

"It's dark now, the aswang should be scouting for food," Paul said. Jimmy glanced up, his eyes nervous. "Relax, kid, it only eats the dead. Standard-issue ghoul, with Filipino twists."

"Is there really such a thing as a standard-issue ghoul?" Sara asked, peering at the oil in the cauldron. "It's not boiling. Is it supposed to be boiling? Gawd, it stinks."

"Nothing makes it boil but the aswang," Paul said. "If we made it right, that is."

Jimmy poked at the viscous oil with a ladle, which Sara fervently hoped someone remembered to throw away before Gary made it part of their camp kitchen. "We got all the plant stems and coconuts, we chanted the prayers—maybe we need more coconuts, sir?"

Sara sighed. "Then someone else is going back to the grocery, because I do not want to smell that old drunk again."

Paul frowned. "The grocer was drunk?"

Sara shrugged. "Seemed. He stank to hell and his eyes were bloodsh—"

Her eyes met Paul's.

"I'm a fucking idiot," Sara muttered.

Paul was already moving. "It knows we're here, people! Perimeter search, fan out! Keep your radios on and weapons loaded!"

Parish and Gary immediately moved apart, between the rows of graves, but still within sight.

Sara scrambled back to the truck and grabbed a string of garlic heads. "Damn, Vaughn. I'm sorry."

"No worries," Paul replied. "It's easy to miss the human form if you've never seen one. The eyes and the smell are usually the only hint you get. We weren't likely to take it by surprise anyway."

"Sir!" Jimmy pointed at the cauldron. "Sir, it's boiling!"

"Lock and load!" Paul shouted.

Sara heard gunfire and Gary's hoarse shouts. "Dog, Harvey!" he shouted into his radio.

Sara pressed her radio. "Copy that, Stover. On alert, boys, it's in dog form." She tossed a sting-ray tail to Jimmy, who caught it easily and attached it to his leather wristband. "Get you some garlic, Jimbo."

Jimmy trotted past her to the truck as Sara and Paul moved out between the graves, Parish a dozen yards to the left as they surveyed the graves between them and Gary's faraway form.

Sara smelled the aswang a second before it sprang at her. It resembled an Irish wolfhound crossed with a St. Bernard, but bigger than both and covered in matted black fur. How could she have mistaken that smell for the local hooch? It was the smell of corpses, the smell of death, rich and rotten in dank earth and rising up toward her with reddened eyes and snarling fury.

She shot it twice and it twisted away from her, growling. Paul circled around the other side and shot it as well, driving it back away from her.

The aswang swiped a paw at Paul, and Sara shot it again to distract it. She unwound the string of garlic from her neck and swung it in front of the aswang toward Paul, who caught it in his free hand. Together they rushed the aswang on either side, wrapping the string around its neck and switching places in dancelike form.

Surrounded by the smell of garlic, the aswang pitched itself back and forth, snarling and shaking its head in an attempt to free itself from the stench. Amazing, Sara thought—it stank like death itself, yet garlic burned it. It snapped at Sara, and Paul shot it again to distract it from her.

"Stover, this week!" Sara shouted. Behind her, she could hear Gary struggling to catch up to them through the tall grass between the gravestones. Parish ran up beside Paul, and Sara motioned him around to her side.

The aswang growled again, snapping at Parish. He rolled out of the way.

"Keep it busy!" Sara shouted, holstering her gun.

Parish shot the aswang twice while circling it, bumping into a gravestone with a muttered curse. Sara climbed up on a gravestone, balancing on its narrow, flat top edge.

"What the hell are you doing, Harvey?" Paul asked, shooting the aswang again from the other side.

"Something stupid!" Sara leaped onto the aswang's back.

The aswang reared up in fury, snapping its head back around, trying to catch Sara's leg in its mouth. She grabbed the string of garlic and pulled it tight, choking it.

"*Fuck, Harvey, are you out of your mind?*" *Stover shouted, finally catching up.*

"*Hold your fire, don't hit Harvey! Yet!*" *Paul shouted.* "*Sting rays only!*"

The stench of the aswang choked Sara, a horrible mixture of rotten meat and filth and garlic. Switching both ends of the garlic strand to her left hand, she grabbed the sting-ray tail attached to her right wrist and drove the tail into the aswang's back.

It let out a shriek, throwing its head back and screaming to the moon. Paul and Parish took the opportunity to rush it, stabbing it in either side with sting-ray tails. It reared up so high Sara thought it would fall over, and for a moment the moon seemed to fill the sky above them. The aswang's giant canine head was nearly silhouetted against it, and she stabbed it in the back of the neck.

It flung its head forward, and the strand of garlic snapped. Sara flew over its head and crashed into a headstone with a monstrous jolt of pain in her midsection. Above her, the aswang drove its head down toward her, its jaws opening.

It only eats the dead, Sara thought. *Then her mind replied,* Maybe it feels like making an exception, genius.

Its head suddenly jolted back upward, a sting-ray tail jutting out of the side of its neck. Jimmy yanked his sting ray back out and the others continued stabbing it over and over, as it howled again.

Getting to her feet, Sara charged at the aswang and drove her sting-ray tail deep into its chest, piercing the heart, or so she hoped. It let out one more howl, then collapsed to the ground.

They didn't speak at first, as each of them stabbed it a few more times to make sure. Then Jimmy retrieved the cauldron, bubbling away, and held it over the aswang's body. They all watched as the bubbles slowed, and finally stopped completely. The aswang was already decomposing, melting away in front of them. By morning it would be nothing but an odd stain on the grass, washed away by the next rain.

"*All right, children, let's clean up our toys,*" *Paul said.* "*Roberts, you and Jimbo get to filling in that grave—with the statue, let's not traumatize that poor girl's family any more than necessary.*" *He turned his eyes to Gary.* "*Stover, you were slow as molasses in January. I want you running laps when we get back to camp.*"

Gary opened his mouth to argue, but Sara shot him a look and he subsided. Gary might be an asshole, but he knew when he was wrong. Discipline was just not his strength—brutal killing skill, that was his particular talent.

The men filed past them, and Sara reached out and touched Jimmy on the shoulder. "*Nice work, kid.*"

Jimmy looked at her, and broke out in a grin so wide she suddenly remem-

bered how young he was. Then he scrambled off after the others. Sara rubbed her abdomen and watched the aswang rot away in front of her.

Paul walked over to Sara and smacked her upside the head.

"Ow!" she protested. "What?"

"That's for being a dumbass, Rambo," Paul said. "That was not exactly the smoothest fight I've ever seen."

"You have a better idea how we could get close enough to stab the fucker without getting bit?" Sara groused.

"Yeah, follow the plan of attack," Paul retorted. "Which did not involve the Flying Major riding it like a goddamn pony."

Sara kicked at the rotting corpse of the aswang. "I missed it," she said quietly. "I was staring at the fucker in good lighting and could've put a bullet in its head then and there, and if I hadn't been such a fuckin' idiot we wouldn't have had to face the dog. I had to make it right."

Paul looked at her. "You know how many mistakes I've made in this job, Harvey?" he asked. "You don't want my 'would'ves-should'ves.' You've never gotten anybody killed, Harvey. Don't kick yourself about missing one stupid aswang. There'll be plenty of chances for you to fuck up for real."

Sara stared at him for a second. "Thanks, Vaughn, that's a hell of an inspiration."

He ruffled her hair again and she ducked away. Grinning, they walked back to the site. Soon they had the dirt shoveled back into the grave and tamped down, the gear loaded, and the guys in the truck, rumbling back toward the inn. Sara and Paul rode together in comfortable silence in the Jeep, the moonlight shining down on the road.

When they arrived at the inn, the guys were already inside and ordering their beers. Paul begged off, claiming the need for a shower "before Stover stinks it all up to hell." The jeers followed him up the stairs.

Sara sat with the men a while longer, letting their conversation wash over her without really taking part. Her belly felt like one giant bruise, but that was okay. It was a good pain, a reminder that they'd fought yet again and lived. The warm glow of the fireplace suffused her, and she floated, calm.

"Harvey, you sleepin'?" Gary cracked.

Sara jerked herself awake. "Guess I better hit the rack," she said, standing. "You boys have one on me." She tossed a twenty onto the table and walked up the stairs, her stomach aching. She pondered the possibility of a shower—she didn't think she had the energy, but longed to scrub the traces of the aswang from her skin.

Paul was stepping out of the bathroom when she reached the upper hallway, clad in a towel wrapped around his waist. "Turning in, Harvey?"

"Yeah," Sara replied, slipping past him into the bathroom. No shower, she decided, leaning over the sink and running cool water. She splashed it over her face and neck, feeling the aswang smell wash away. Instantly she felt much better, until she straightened up and her stomach sent another wave of pain aching through her.

"I better check you out," Paul said. She hadn't realized he was still there, standing in the hallway watching her. Sara started to protest, but he held up a hand. "If you've got something busted, we'll be doing an emergency lift to Manila, so no bitching."

"What, you gonna use your X-ray eyes?" Sara cracked, but she let him follow her across the hallway into her room. As he shut the door, she pulled her shirt over her head.

He turned around and froze for a second.

Sara couldn't help laughing, even though it hurt her stomach. "Relax, Iceman, you never seen a girl in her bra before?"

"It's been a while," Paul admitted. "Lie down, Major Smartass."

Sara kicked off her shoes and lay down on the bed, and Paul sat beside her. She saw with relief he was wearing BVDs under the towel, then realized she probably shouldn't be looking.

"What, you never saw a man in his skivvies before?" Paul cracked.

"It's been a while," she repeated, grinning.

"Hell, Harvey, I didn't know you could blush." Paul's hands pressed against the four quadrants of her abdomen with practiced ease. She grimaced when he pressed the upper right quadrant, where she had struck the tombstone. He checked her eyes and nail beds.

"It'll be a hell of a bruise, but I think you'll live," Paul declared.

"Told you so," she replied, sitting up.

They sat together in silence for a moment, as the long-threatening rain finally began drumming on the roof. The lamplight flickered a moment before it went out.

"Great," Sara murmured.

"Afraid of the dark?" Paul said, reaching out and ruffling her hair.

Sara ducked her head. "I hate it when you do that."

Instead, Paul touched the side of her face. She took his hand in hers, and they sat that way for a while.

"Sara—" he finally said.

"Shaddup," she replied.

And they lay beside each other in the dark, only their hands entwined. They listened to the rain, to the laughing men stumbling up the stairs to their own dark rooms, listened to the sounds of the world going to sleep. Lulled by the drumming rain, they fell asleep at each other's side, still holding one another's hand.

They were two miles off the coast when they caught up with the last runaround. It coasted along the waves under a sputtering engine.

"Maybe the last ones got tossed overboard," Gary speculated.

Sara peered through the binoculars. "Just what we need, zombie sharks." The deck of the other boat was clear, save for a bloodstain on the starboard side. The bulkhead obstructed a clear view. "Go up to port."

Gary followed orders, hitching it tight. Sara waited for him before stepping over the railings onto the deck.

There was more blood, a lot of it. A finger lay beside the white bulkhead. Just a single finger drained of blood, grayish-pink.

"Shit," Gary murmured.

His hand was twitching hard, the gun shaking. Sara backed away, trying to watch him and the boat at the same time.

Put a bullet to him, Harvey! she could practically hear Paul yelling.

In a weird echo, she heard, "Don't shoot! Friendly!" coming up from behind the bulkhead.

"Fuck," Sara breathed. "Vaughn! Get your ass out here!"

Paul Vaughn stepped out from behind the bulkhead, fatigues bloody but whole. "Harvey, get a grip already. I got that one." He indicated the finger.

Sara edged closer. "You okay, Vaughn?"

"Whole and breathing, you can relax now," Paul said. "Put it down."

There was something about his tone that made Sara keep her gun up. "Take off your shirt."

Paul grinned. "Not really the time, Harvey."

Sara shook her head. "Why are you…" Her voice trailed off. Paul was alive, she should be thrilled. The team wasn't completely broken, they could build a new team and drink a toast to the fallen…

Paul cocked his head. "I knew you'd take care of it. I had faith in you," he said. "You did it."

"Harvey—" Gary said in a warning tone. He was shaking badly, biting his lip so hard a bit of blood trailed down his chin. Sara switched to train her gun on him, backing away from both of them.

Paul remained still, leaning against the bulkhead. "We don't all go insss-sane, Sssara," he said, smiling.

No. Sara felt a tear sting the inside of her eye. *All gone, everyone, they're all gone, the team IS broken, it's been broken since Jimmy, I'm all alone here.*

"Oh fuck, Paul, I'm sorry," she whispered.

Paul smiled. "Don't worry, Gary," he coaxed. "Just let it go. Imagine what the three of usss can do together."

"Fuck that," Sara whispered. She leveled the gun at Paul.

His face was perfectly in her sights. She had only to pull the trigger.

Beside her, Gary dropped his gun and fell to the ground, his body convulsing.

Sara backed up another step.

Do not let me go that way, Sara.

She could still see Paul's face in the long-ago Haitian moonlight, pleading with her, nakedly honest in a way he never was before or since. *Iceman.*

"Oh fuck, Paul," she whispered.

Paul took a step closer, and she could see the coldness in his eyes—how had she missed it before? It was the empty gaze of It, devoid of anything save anticipation. She searched for a hint of the Paul Vaughn she knew, the man inside the monster.

They don't all go mad, there must be something must be left of him.

Sara stepped back to the stern, steeling herself. A gunshot rang out, and Paul jerked away from Sara, hissing in fury.

Gary Stover stood before him, gun held in traditional two-handed stance.

Paul recoiled to attack, and Gary shot him in the head.

An irregularly-shaped hole appeared in the center of Paul's forehead, as reddish-black lumps fell to the deck behind him.

He collapsed backward and his body fell over the railing into the sea.

Sara watched Paul float away, vaguely aware her back was to Gary and not really caring. Slowly the sea washed up over Paul and dragged him down into the dark water.

Finally Sara turned back to Gary. "You didn't change," she said in dull amazement. "It didn't work, didn't take."

Gary shook his head slowly. "It did," he said tonelessly. "It did. *I jusst don't feel any different.*"

Sara stared at him, speechless.

Gary took a step back, then lifted his gun to his head.

"No, wait," Sara protested.

"I had your back, Sssara," Gary said, and grinned. Then he pulled the trigger.

Sara stared at his body for a long time. Then she let the sea claim him, floating him away to join Paul in the depths. She set the boat on fire, returning to her own boat to idle away, watching the flames dance on the surface of the water. She washed her hands over and over, trailing them in the sea water beside the runaround.

The sun was still shining. There were no more screams.

INTERLUDE: YANAGUANA

YANAGUANA

She was losing her breath as she ran, and it was not far behind her.

A cold, harsh pain stabbed the back of her throat from breathing too fast as she raced past a startled group of tourists taking pictures of a passing tour boat, its neon piping-lights flashing under the streetlights illuminating the Riverwalk.

She scrambled up the arched bridge over the San Antonio River, leg muscles burning and trembling from exertion. The stone bridges of the Riverwalk made a good vantage point for an escape route, and she spied a stairwell not far along the other side of the river. Those stairwells led to the upper streets, away from the dark water and the danger it held.

All this passed through her mind in the two or three seconds she was on the bridge—she had no intention of letting up on her speed, not if she wanted to stay ahead of the thing pursuing her. Her foot slipped on the far side of the bridge, and hot pain shot through her ankle. But she caught her balance and kept running, fleeing down the sidewalk along the river-bank, past confused couples strolling in the moonlight and a nearly-deserted cafe where a tired waiter cleaned off the last few tables.

She could hear it behind her, its footsteps much softer than hers. Her heart was pounding too fast for the run, fueled with adrenaline and possibly a bit of panic. The few people around her watched in cautious curiosity as they saw her run for no apparent reason. They would see nothing behind her, nothing at all pursuing the strange woman running in the moonlight.

Too slow.

It touched her shoulder, and a cascade of shivering revulsion rolled down her back and up her neck at the same time. She put on another burst of energy, lurching forward, and she felt its vile touch slip away.

She was getting farther away from the tourists now—this late at night, the remaining patrons were mostly clustered around the margarita joints, and the smaller shops and restaurants were shuttered. Her feet pounded along the sidewalk, the sound echoing against the solid rock wall along her right side above the quiet rush of the river to her left. Brightly colored flags danced in the light breeze above her, below white lights and black sky.

So close. Up ahead was a stone staircase that led up, away from the river to the street above the Riverwalk, where cars and tour buses still bustled along despite the late hour.

Oh, but she was flagging hard. Her legs were on fire, she couldn't breathe fast enough to keep up with her heartbeat, and a stitch dug deep into her right side.

She didn't dare look behind her, but she could hear it, that *pad-pad-pad* of its feet so close behind her.

The river seemed louder, rumbling past as though it had not been sedately tamed to carry tour boats and ferries about San Antonio decades before she was born. Its flowing passage along its stone prison grew in sound if not in sight, until the roar of it drowned out her own panting breath.

She aimed herself at the stairs, her escape up to the real world and safety. She couldn't afford to lose any momentum going up the stairs, trying for one more burst from her flagging energy. Above her, she saw someone walking along the street, up where sanity reigned.

Her hand just brushed the cold stone rail when she felt its claw grip her shoulder again.

So close.

Paul Vaughn had been waiting in the tastefully decorated sitting room for more than twenty minutes, which was about fifteen minutes longer than his patience lasted.

The morgue attendant's name was Robbie, not that it mattered. He had long hair bound tightly back from his face and an earring he had neglected to remove before his shift. When Robbie finally opened the door, he got a full measure of Vaughn's glare, which had been enough to melt three-star generals into apologies.

Robbie recoiled. Perhaps he had expected a tearful man kneeling in prayer or sitting with his face buried in his hands, Vaughn thought. That might have been standard for this room, with its soft lighting and carefully nondenominational decor.

Vaughn was standing in the center of the room, almost at full attention, and he cut off Robbie's apologies before the attendant even had them out of his mouth.

"Give it to me."

Robbie hesitantly held out a photograph, face-down. "Sir, I'm so sorry—"

Vaughn took the photograph and turned it over immediately. He stared at it for a full thirty seconds, saying nothing, and his face was stone.

Then he handed it back to the attendant. "I need to see her."

Robbie shook his head. "I'm sorry, sir, that's not permitted here. Once the body is released to a funeral home, you can arrange a viewing with—"

Vaughn held up a hand, silencing him again. "Son, if I pick up my phone and call my supervisor, he will be on the phone to the chief medical examiner of Bexar County in approximately two minutes, and within five minutes you will be ordered to allow me access to the remains. Now, do I have to go through all of that and risk your job and your boss' job, or can you let me in right now?"

Robbie hesitated, and Vaughn pulled out his phone.

"Okay!" he said, shaking his head. "Come with me."

Vaughn followed him down the hallway toward the morgue. He knew he was making the poor kid step outside standard procedure and he might get in trouble later, but Vaughn really didn't give a damn. He wasn't lying about the phone calls.

Robbie led Vaughn into the refrigerated room where the bodies were kept, fluorescent lighting glaring down, the smell of chemicals omnipresent.

He went to the third drawer. "Are you ready, sir?" he asked, solicitous. Vaughn nodded, and Robbie pulled the drawer open.

The woman's body was nude and pale. Vaughn leaned over, staring, inches away from her face.

Then he reached out and moved her head to the side, studying her profile.

"Sir! I must ask you not to touch—"

Once again Robbie didn't get to finish his sentence. Now Vaughn was pulling at her left arm, turning it toward him.

"Sir!" Robbie reached for him, but Vaughn batted him away. "We have photographs of her tattoo, it's what alerted the database to contact you in the first place. I must insist—"

Vaughn didn't care what he insisted. He rolled the drawer open the rest of the way, baring her cold body to the air. He focused his attention on her left thigh, where an ugly, jagged scar creased the skin.

The sight of the scar hit Vaughn like a hard punch to the gut. He slumped over a second, steadying himself with a hand pressed against the cold tiled wall, and closed his eyes, listening to voices from the past.

Don't you go doing that again, Harvey.

Is that an order?

Damn straight. I can't manage this motley crew without you.

Robbie took the opportunity to discreetly close the drawer and moved over beside him. "Sir, is there anyone I can—"

Vaughn straightened up instantly, his manner once again cold and firm. "Thank you for your assistance. Someone will be in touch about arrangements."

He stalked out of the morgue and down the hallway toward the exit doors, passing the awful sitting room on his way.

His phone was in his hand before he reached the harsh San Antonio sunlight in the parking lot.

"It's her," he said, and waited for the profanity on the other end to finish. Parish Roberts had served with Sara Harvey almost as long as Vaughn had, and he had a right to be pissed.

"No marks, no apparent wound, nothing. Just like the others, and I highly doubt it was a heart attack," Vaughn said. "Which means this critter isn't too particular about its choice of victims, so we need to widen the search. I want you to hit that shop she was going to investigate. See if she was there, and where she might have gone afterward. Send Jimmy to the local library for folklore."

Roberts was long-time military and knew when to shut up and just follow an order. "What about Stover?" he asked.

Vaughn sighed as quietly as he could. "Tell Stover to drink some black coffee and run a razor somewhere in the vicinity of his face, because he and I are going to play FBI. He looked a goddamn mess this morning."

"Stover thinks it's a test, because Blackfire wouldn't send us after a critter badass enough to take out one of our best operatives," Parish said.

Vaughn would have laughed if he wasn't having one of the all-time worst days ever. "Stover is putting a lot more faith in our esteemed employers than I would have expected," he said.

Parish hesitated a second. "Speaking of Blackfire... When do we tell them about Harvey?"

"I'm not." Vaughn got behind the wheel of the van and started up the air conditioning right away.

"What?" He could practically see Parish giving him side-eye. "You're not going to report it?"

Vaughn sighed. "We tell them that a target took out one of our best operatives less than twenty-five hours after we hit town, and they will send a massive squad of idiots to stomp all over our investigation. The thing that killed Harvey will go so far underground it'll hit magma."

He knew Parish wouldn't fight him on it. Both of them had been with Blackfire long enough to know that if there was a way to fuck up, Blackfire would find it and immortalize it in a three-page memo distributed throughout the organization to ensure it was properly fucked up.

"We call them once we've got that thing dead," Vaughn said. "Whatever it is. I want its head on a plate." *Assuming it has a head.*

He hung up and got the van rolling into the San Antonio traffic, heading toward downtown and the Riverwalk district. That's where most of the bodies had been found, though nothing had made the news yet—a random heart attack or stroke generally doesn't garner headlines.

Still, he ought to check in case someone had noticed the pattern. He pressed the radio button.

"Butterfly wings, touched once they fall out of the sky."

Startled, Vaughn's hands jerked on the wheel, and the van skidded into the right lane to a chorus of car horns.

"Help me, I'm so lost..."

It was Harvey's voice, and it came from the radio, and that was fucking impossible. The words were from another time, spoken by another voice, but he knew Sara Harvey's voice as well as he knew his own and that was her, even though those were words she had never said to him.

He hit the button so hard it popped off, and the van skidded again. Vaughn spotted a parking lot and quickly pulled over before he crashed the damn thing.

"Harvey?"

Laughter swelled out of the radio, growing louder and more shrill until it didn't sound like her anymore, it didn't even sound human, a high screeching cackle that drilled into his ears.

"Stop!" he shouted, and it stopped as suddenly as it began. The silence was somehow worse, the glowing green light indicating he should be hearing the radio, some inanity or awful music. "Sara?"

Silence again, then the voice, small and quiet, accusatory. *"How could you, Paul?"*

He covered his face with his hands and couldn't answer.

Parish Roberts got out of the cab at the La Villita district, but as soon as he'd paid and the car moved onward, he walked through the district toward a street on the far end. He was already regretting his leather jacket, as the San Antonio sun was warming up a lot faster than he liked. If he wanted Atlanta-level summers, he'd have stayed in Atlanta.

Parish pulled out a handkerchief and mopped his face as he walked past the curio shops and artisans that filled the historic district. He'd been experimenting with growing a goatee, but it was appearing in an alarming shade of gray. Harvey had teased him that with the jacket, shaved head, goatee and shades, he was trying to play Hawk from the old show *Spenser For Hire.*

He wanted to smile at that, but Harvey was dead and there weren't any smiles.

Harvey's dead. That just does not compute.

Soon Parish had passed most of the shops and cafe patios where people sipped iced tea as though the world was still normal. Just outside the official district was another street of shops, a little less clean and cute, but far more interesting to him.

The shop was in an older house, trim and well-kept, complete with wide porch that displayed wooden shelves full of merchandise along with rocking chairs that cried out for iced tea. The battered wooden sign above the porch was painted with the word *Yanaguana.*

Parish stopped a moment to check his reflection in the window glass and decided to ditch the shades. Harvey was right about the Hawk cosplay.

The little bell above the door jingled as Parish stepped into a blissful rush of air conditioning and the smell of burning incense, something jasmine with a touch of spice. His eyes took a few moments to adjust to the lower light after the bright sunshine outside.

Strangely, a bookshelf had been placed almost directly in front of the door—rather than allowing customers to move in before wandering, it forced Parish to choose whether to go right or left into the twisting aisles. He chose right, letting his gaze drift over the titles along the bookshelf as he did. Harvey had always kidded him about his fondness for bookstores —she said he couldn't be left unsupervised in one or he'd lose his paycheck. *Takes one to know one,* he'd said, and she'd ducked her head like she wasn't forever shipping books back to the quarters in Farson she saw maybe twice a year.

These titles were pretty basic tourist fare: *History of San Antonio. La Llorona: Texas' Weeping Mother. The Missions of San Antonio. Haunted Alamo.*

"Be right with you!" a woman's voice called out.

At the end of the aisle he had to turn left, browsing past displays of sugar skulls and dreamcatchers, turquoise earrings and charming pottery in primary colors.

That wasn't the reputation of this shop.

After a few more turns, Parish was pretty lost. The shelving toward the back stretched up at least twelve feet, with cheerful signs warning that unattended children would be given espresso and a free puppy. He had yet to find the store owner or a checkout stand.

He heard a giggle from the other side of a shelf. Parish stopped and glanced between the books, seeing a small form pass the other way. "Hello there," he said, but the small shadow was gone.

He turned another corner and realized he had been traveling in a slow spiral. The bookshelves were laid out in some kind of a pattern, totally unlike the usual shop layout. It spiraled around from the entrance toward something in the center, and the further he traveled into the shop, the more unusual and esoteric the items on the shelves became.

Parish heard that giggle again, and he stopped again to lean over and look through the space above the tops of the books on the shelf. "Hey there," he said in his best Officer Friendly voice. "What's so funny?"

At first, all he could see was the shadow, and then, so suddenly it nearly made him jump, a small pair of brown eyes. It was a girl's face, no older than six years old, with skin as dark as his and a mass of black hair beyond his immediate field of vision. Her eyes looked familiar, so familiar that he… But that was impossible.

"Hey," he said. "Where is—"

The instant he spoke to her, her eyes changed. At first gleeful and amused, suddenly they narrowed, glaring with a spiteful hate completely out of place in her young face. He recoiled, and he heard her hiss, as though she were a snake in the body of a child.

Parish reconsidered his question quickly and moved on through the aisle. The shop had a reputation for the unusual, but this was taking it a bit far.

In between two dusty shelves of former library books, Parish spied a wooden box carved with an Aztec symbol—or was it Incan? It looked like a stylized, ancient outline of an eagle or falcon head, but it might have been from another Mesoamerican culture, and he would never know because Jimmy Bell was their folklore researcher. All Parish knew about Mesoamerica was that the jaguar was big with the Mayans, and you didn't want to put your hand on an Incan bloodstone unless you felt like dying.

"Lovely, isn't it?"

The woman was on the low side of forty, but with a few miles on her face. She wore jeans and an Alamo T-shirt with a shopkeeper's half-apron tied around her hips, long hair caught in a sensible barrette at the nape of her neck. A hand-painted name tag was pinned to her shoulder, reading *Juliet* beside the omnipresent sugar skull. She smiled with the solicitous air of a shopkeeper sensing an easy target. "I'm sorry, that one is just for display. But we do have some lovely curio boxes by the east wall."

"I wasn't actually shopping," Parish said, putting the box back on the shelf.

"Oh?" Juliet's air remained friendly, but he could sense her mentally stepping away.

Parish pulled out his phone and showed her the image. Harvey was severe and unsmiling, even in a candid shot, her short dark hair close-cropped at her ears.

Juliet peered closely at it. "What about her?"

"Was she here yesterday?" Parish asked.

She stepped back for real this time, her smile fading into caution. "Who's asking?"

Parish pulled out his fake-ass ID provided by Blackfire. Of course, it said nothing at all about Blackfire, but pretending to be FBI or Homeland

Security was a nice sidestep to explaining what the hell they actually did for a living. "We're just trying to trace her steps, ma'am."

She took a close look at the ID, and when she looked up, the neutral shopkeeper expression was entirely gone. Her face was cold and blank, as instantly icy as the little girl's eyes had been angry and hot.

"You're not Homeland Security," she declared, and handed the badge back to him before walking away.

Parish followed her through the weird, twisting aisles of odd trinkets, old books and bizarre amulets. "Yes ma'am, and I need to—"

Juliet stopped in the center of the spiral, at what he now saw was a small wooden checkout counter. *Who puts the checkout in the center of the store?* he wondered.

"You need to get the hell out of my shop, that's what you need to do," she said, stepping behind the counter.

Parish tried one more time, putting away the ID and holding up his hands in what he hoped was a nonthreatening manner. "Ma'am, this is an official investigation and—"

He broke off, staring at the business end of a 9mm Beretta leveled straight at his head.

Instinct took over and in the next instant his own service weapon was aimed back at her.

"I don't talk to Blackfire," Juliet spat at him.

Parish nearly choked, but he didn't lower his gun. "How the hell did—"

"Mom?"

Shit. Right behind her stood a boy of no more than ten years old, dark eyes wide in his face.

"Code Black," Juliet said calmly, and damn if the kid didn't duck and roll like a pro operative out of Parish's line of fire.

"We got off on the wrong foot here," Parish said, as if this wasn't the most ludicrous standoff of his career. "I just need to ask a few questions. No need for all this."

Juliet glared at him. "And I said get out."

Parish nodded. "Okay, I'm going to lower my gun, and you lower yours, and you'll be rid of me." He made good on the first part, slowly lowering his gun and keeping his finger off the trigger. "But as I'm walking out, you could shout after me if you remember seeing the woman in the picture, because she was a good friend, and I want to know what happened to her."

Parish backed off a step, and Juliet lowered her Beretta, still glaring.

Another step, and at the back of his mind Parish realized he was never going to find his way out of the store like this. The bookshelves at weird angles made it impossible to see the front door. *She must have a hell of a time with shoplifters, can't see anything,* he thought randomly.

"Two rights and a left," Juliet said, as if reading his mind. "And she left in one piece."

Parish took another step away, praying that wasn't a mistake. "Yesterday? Maybe toward closing time?"

"Answer me something," Juliet said. "And try not to lie."

"Yes, ma'am," Parish replied.

Juliet lowered her gun a little more. "She spun the same Homeland Security bullshit, but she was after local lore, which isn't exactly DHS material. Blackfire has never been good at subtle. What do you people want with my shop?"

Parish holstered his gun, hearing Harvey's voice screaming at him that he was being an idiot, but somehow he got the sense Juliet wasn't going to cap him in her front aisle.

He held up both hands in the universal gesture of *don't shoot.* "Something's prowling the Riverwalk. Three dead so far, no apparent cause of death, and they sent us to figure out if it's our kind of thing. The woman in the picture was Sara Harvey, and it got her last night."

Juliet put the Beretta back from wherever it was hiding under the counter, and Parish breathed a little easier. "She asked a few questions—La Llorona, the ghosts at the Alamo, basic shit like that. Then I figured out who she was, we exchanged a few more words that I wish my son hadn't heard, and she left."

"Did she happen to say where she was going?" Parish asked.

Juliet cocked an eyebrow at him. "We didn't get that friendly."

Shocking. Parish edged closer, still holding his hands up like an idiot. "If she said anything to you...or you know anything about this thing, please tell me. Three people in three nights, it's not going to just stop."

Juliet leaned forward, eyes angry and cold at the same time. "I have yet to see a critter situation that Blackfire didn't manage to fuck up, Mr. Homeland Security. It does not do well for my peace of mind that you're here at all. I don't suppose I can convince you and your stormtroopers to get the fuck out of my city and let us handle it?"

Who is us? Parish wondered but did not ask. He didn't want to face the Beretta again. "I'm afraid they won't let us do that, ma'am," he replied. "But maybe we could help, if you tell me what you know?"

"I seriously doubt it," Juliet replied.

Parish nodded and slowly—very slowly—retrieved a business card from his pocket. "I know, it's a bullshit card, but the number is real," he said. "Call me if anything comes to mind…or you need anything."

Juliet snorted in derision, but she took the card. "Sorry about your friend. Now, two rights and a left."

Jimmy Bell was tired of the library. His job was always research, and occasionally patching up the crew when they managed to damage themselves more than usual. But often he ended up in a library, digging through microfiche records of long-vanished newspapers, and nothing could give you a killer headache like reading microfiche.

The San Pedro branch had the most folklore of any branch of the hundred-year-old libraries in San Antonio. Be that as it may, Jimmy was getting absolutely nowhere searching for any similar instances to the dead bodies they found. Three people, simply lying on the ground as though their bodies had given up their souls without so much as a struggle, and now Sara was one of them.

That did not make sense. Jimmy had no reason to believe Gary would lie to him, passing along a message that dire in advance of tonight's meetup. But the one thing all the bodies had so far was that there was no sign of a struggle, no wound, no damage whatsoever to indicate how these people died. They simply stopped living.

No. Sara Harvey would not have given up without a fight.

Jimmy glanced up at the wall and saw that he would have to wrap up pretty quickly if he wanted to grab a bite to eat before meeting the others on the plaza in front of the old cathedral. He didn't really have much of an appetite, hadn't since Gary called. But he knew that if he didn't eat, he would get tired and cranky and his reflexes would be slow, and that was the last thing they needed when they were going on a hunt.

Jimmy had been alone in the microfiche reading room for quite some time, probably because nobody in their right mind would ever read microfiche unless they absolutely had to. The silence was starting to get to him. Shadows were growing long, and the cinderblock walls felt like they were closing in.

Jimmy pressed the rewind button, and the microfiche came to life, spooling itself back into its container. The images flew by on the screen, still lit up, making Jimmy dizzy. He rubbed his face for a moment and tried not to think about Sara punching him in the arm the last time he saw her, calling him "kid" as though he were not fully twenty-four years old.

He heard the microfiche machine slow to a stop, and opened his eyes, reaching for the switch to turn it off.

225 DEAD IN SHIP EXPLOSION

The headline glared out from the reader screen in early twentieth-century all-caps. It showed a grainy image of a ship listing seriously to port, half of it under water and a stack of sub-headlines detailing how many people had died when the ship blew up in the harbor.

"That's weird," Jimmy said. He thought he had set it to rewind all the way. He pressed the button, and the microfiche machine begin to whirr again.

The images flew by faster and faster, and then it stopped again, this time on a sepia picture of men with handlebar mustaches paddling a boat down the remnants of a street, with screaming headlines detailing hundreds dead in yet another flood, a constant plague on the city.

"Dammit." Jimmy pressed the button yet again. *Who still uses microfiche at this point?* he wondered. In the age of the internet, keeping newspapers on microfiche was about as useful as trying to shoot a vampire.

The microfiche machine whirred faster and faster, displaying headline after headline that had not been there when he first reviewed it. Here was a busload of children killed when their bus stopped on railroad tracks. Here was a picture of a man being hung on the roof of a jail, a noose around his neck as he dropped two stories down for his final moment.

None of these stories belonged on that microfiche.

Jimmy slowly stood up in his chair, his heart pounding faster. He pressed the button to stop the rewind, but of course it didn't do anything. Years of history flashed by, too quickly to read now, and the whirl of newsprint seemed to form a face.

It was an old face, with black eyes and a smooth head. It was a face without a soul, with bloodless wounds cracking its skin.

"Jimmy..." it whispered. *"Sssssssara."*

That was enough for Jimmy. He switched off the microfiche machine, and in a state of near panic, unplugged it as well. He stumbled backward, suddenly very aware of how alone he was in this quiet reference room in the basement of the oldest library in the city.

Where had he seen that face before? It wasn't in any of his research, but it was familiar nonetheless. It was a face he had seen somewhere… Nothing that they had hunted, not that he could remember, but it filled him with dread. The face seemed to know him, seemed to be waiting for him. Something from a dream, the kind of dream that wakes you up in the dark of the night, unsure of whether you have really awakened at all, knowing that every shadow is a lurking threat, every sound a shuffling footstep, and your skin crawls with too many shivers to even think of sleeping again.

A low, chortling laugh came from the microfiche machine, and Jimmy fled.

Another city, another crappy motel. Vaughn was pretty sure Blackfire could afford to put up its operatives in something at least the level of a Holiday Inn, but they insisted that non-chain hole-in-the-wall places were more likely to accept cash and keep their mouths shut in the long tradition of no-tell motels. Personally, Vaughn was pretty sure they were just cheap.

He pulled in by their room door and waited a moment before he got out. The team was going to be frazzled enough without Harvey; they would need him to be Iceman, as she used to call him.

Bite me, Iceman. That particular snark had come on a filthy rooftop in Chicago, minutes after she put a bullet in the head of a creature that should never exist.

Vaughn got out of the van, but before he could even swipe his card at the door, Stover flung it open, his eyes wild and definitely not ready to pass for an FBI agent. "Fuck, it's you!"

"Yeah, Stover, it's me, and you were supposed to be sober by now," he said dryly, stepping into the dingy motel room.

Then Vaughn saw the phone, an older push-button model with a barbell handset. It had been ripped out of the wall, wires dangling out the back, and was sitting in the middle of one of the beds. "What the fuck, Stover? They're gonna charge us for that."

Stover hesitated by the door. "Fuck that, it keeps ringing," he said, his voice unsteady. "Call after call. I ripped it out of the wall, and it keeps ringing."

Vaughn turned to him. "Shit. You have a warding medallion?"

Stover patted his chest. "Haven't gone without it since Maui."

"It's not just you, I had a fun time with the radio," Vaughn said. "This thing is playing games with us."

Stover kicked the door closed in a fit of temper. "It's not a fucking game, Captain America. It killed Harvey, and I wanna know what you're gonna do about it."

Vaughn glared at him. "Stow your shit, mister." Stover had never been his top choice for the team, with his crudeness and his sloppy personal habits. Unlike Harvey and Roberts, Stover had never served, something Vaughn tried and failed not to hold against him. Harvey had usually been able to keep him in line and relatively sober, and his vicious no-holds-barred fighting style made him a match for many of the critters they encountered. But he always rubbed Vaughn wrong.

Stover glared right back, but he subsided. "Roberts checked in. The woman at the witch shop wouldn't give him shit about Harvey, *and* she knows who we are. Nothing from the kid, I assume he'll fill us in at the rendezvous."

"Back up," Vaughn said. "How does some shopkeeper know who we are?"

Stover shrugged. "I dunno, maybe it's a witch thing."

"We don't know that she's a witch," Vaughn said tiredly. "We just know that her name floats around whenever something supernatural happens around here."

"Yeah well, she made Parish for a Blackfire agent and pulled a gun on him, so I wouldn't count on her for details," Stover said. "Now can we get the fuck out of here?"

Vaughn raised an eyebrow. "Who was on the other end of the phone, Stover?"

Stover didn't get a chance to reply. The phone rang, pealing its shrill tone from the center of the bed.

Vaughn glanced at its cord—still unplugged.

He moved to answer it. Stover put a hand on his arm. "You don't want to do that."

"No, I really don't." But Vaughn picked up the receiver anyway.

The voice on the other end was laughing. Sexless, ageless, identifying it was impossible. No words, just a low chuckle, malevolent and sly.

"Who are you?" Vaughn demanded.

The chuckling voice only laughed harder, louder, speeding up until the laughs were mixed with screams and it was many voices, a cacophony laughing and screaming at once, rising until unearthly and shrill, as though it were a record being played too fast.

Vaughn thrust the handset away from him, and it bounced off the receiver and fell to the side on the motel coverlet. Still it shrieked laughter at him, the sound filling the small room until Vaughn resisted the urge to clap his hands over his ears.

He pointed at the corner. "Grab the kit," he ordered, and Stover picked up their field kit.

"*Grab the kit!*" the voice cackled from the phone. Still no identifiable tones in the voice, even with the words—neither male nor female, not electronic but also not human.

"Fuck you!" Stover yelled, lunging forward as if to attack…what, the phone?

Vaughn stopped him and inclined his head toward the door.

As they moved, the voice shifted, became that of a woman. Worse, a woman he recognized.

"*Please... I don't want to forget.*"

Vaughn froze. "To hell with you," he muttered, but his body shuddered involuntarily as if he'd been punched.

Stover stepped in front of him. "Ain't her, boss. Whoever she is. It ain't her."

"*Gaaaaaaary.*"

It was a thin voice, weak and yet sinister, pleading but also sly. Stover started, pale in a way Vaughn had never seen. Now it was his turn to ground the other man, to step in front of his face and wordlessly remind him to stay focused.

The laughter began again, the laughter that was also screaming.

Stover reached for the door handle, his hand shaking a bit. His other hand rested on his service weapon.

For a heartstopping moment, Vaughn didn't think the door would open, that they'd be trapped together in this miserable motel room listening to the voices of the damned until they went mad. But after a moment of fumbling Stover got the door open, and he gave the phone a middle finger as he fled into the darkening parking lot.

Vaughn chanced a glance back, the phone still lying innocuous on the bed.

"*See you soon,*" it chortled.

The kaleidoscope of brightly colored images cavorted and rotated across the ornate architecture of the old cathedral, and its lights played across Vaughn's troubled face.

The air pressure had subtly shifted as darkness crept across the plaza, foreboding rain. The heat was oppressive, the air thick and stifling as dark clouds roiled above the cathedral. The few remaining tourists on the plaza kept glancing at the sky as faraway thunder grumbled.

Stover hadn't spoken a word in the car. Bell had texted that he had had an encounter at the library, and with Roberts' report that their cover was blown, this whole mission was well and truly fucked.

Of course it's fucked. Sara is dead.

Vaughn had already sat through the light show once—it played two times every night, to the delight of the tourists gathered on the stone plaza before the old cathedral that dated back to before there was a United States. The images on the facade reflected the history and culture of San Antonio, minus the ghosts and goblins. San Antonio's real history was pretty bloody, even in the carefully curated version portrayed to the visitors, and Vaughn knew well that the ground held its memory. The cathedral itself was said to be home to a few wayward spirits, and that wasn't even getting near the Alamo's blood-soaked soil.

The images playing across the cathedral's facade were morphing toward the modern era now, which meant the final light show of the night was coming to an end. As it played, more of the tourists began to drift away, heading back toward the Riverwalk for one last margarita or to the meandering taxis for a ride back to their hotels.

But Vaughn and Stover remained, sitting on the stone benches at the edge of the plaza and waiting for the rest of the team, rain or no rain.

Bell was the first to show, looking pale and shaky even for him. He was the youngest member of the team, and while he'd been with them through a few rough encounters, he was more likely to be agitated than any of the others. His voice was steady as he related the face in the micro-film to Vaughn and Stover, but his eyes betrayed emotion.

By the time he was done, the light show had ended, and the plaza was nearly empty, except for a few last tourists and the figure of Parish Roberts crossing from the far side where a taxi had dropped him off. Reaching them, he perched on the edge of a stone planter and filled them in on the crazy gift shop lady.

Vaughn leaned forward as Parish finished his debrief. "Anything else unusual in the shop?"

"You mean besides a civilian pulling a gun on me for asking a question?" Roberts asked. "I mean, that's a bit much even for a Black man in Texas. And how the fuck does she know about Blackfire?"

"I'm marking that for future action," Vaughn said. "In the meantime, we have a critter that has no pattern, no focus, no lore—but it's sure as hell paying attention to us. It's a voice on a phone for Stover, a face on a screen for Bell, and Parish—did you see anything weird? I mean supernatural weird?"

Roberts opened his mouth to speak, then stopped.

"Don't be shy," Vaughn ordered.

"It couldn't have been," Roberts said.

Vaughn spread his hands in an impatient *we're-waiting* gesture.

Roberts sighed. "Look, I'm ninety percent sure it was my imagination, but…wandering around the shop, I saw a little girl staring at me between the shelves."

Vaughn waited. "And?"

Roberts finally spoke again. "And it looked like Katrina." Silence for a moment, as Vaughn mulled that one.

Bell was confused. "Who's Katrina?"

"My daughter."

Bell gaped in surprise, and Vaughn gestured silently not to ask any more questions. Most Blackfire operatives didn't have families, and Parish Roberts was one of the warning stories of how screwed up it could get when you tried to live the Blackfire life with a wife and kid at home.

"I know, it's fucking impossible," Parish said. "And I couldn't see her whole face, so it could just be my imagination. But in Blackfire—"

"It's never just your imagination," Bell finished. "Sara used to say that all the time."

That silence fell again, and Vaughn was torn between gnawing at the problem of their critter like a dog with a bone, and the need to bring the team together without Harvey. She was the one who really led them. She kicked their asses when they needed kicking, reined in Stover's excesses, and brought Roberts and Bell to focus. He didn't have that rapport with them, and he saw them watching him, needing something from him he felt powerless to give.

"I don't know," he said finally. "I don't know what killed her. I don't know what that thing did to her or the three that died before we got here. I don't have any face on this thing. I wish I had an answer for you, but I don't."

The words felt flat and useless, and no one spoke for a few minutes as they waited for the plaza to clear. This was where the first body had been found, and when they hit town, they'd set this rendezvous to scout the streets after their separate missions.

Vaughn watched the lights rise again, the ordinary white spotlights that illuminated the cathedral facade when the lightshow wasn't running. His mind was running over logistics, how to cover the length of the Riverwalk and the plaza at the cathedral and send someone to the goddamn Alamo, all with a teammate down and the whole fucking team spooked and seeing ghosts. Which might or might not be ghosts.

Who are you? he asked the darkness, musing silently as Stover handed out their gear to each team member. *You've got no face I know, but you sure as hell know who we are.*

The shadows stretched far across the plaza, and Vaughn saw another civilian climbing up from the stairs that led to the Riverwalk. He took a quick glance at the team—no one was packing hardware obvious enough to cause concern in the average civilian, especially in Texas. But they'd best get out of sight before…

The civilian stepped into the glow of the streetlights. A woman with dark, short-cropped hair, wearing a leather jacket.

Thunder crashed across the sky, much louder than before and rolling onward as Vaughn leapt to his feet and pulled his weapon. "Hostile!"

The team fell into position without pause or question, Bell fading toward the back since he was primarily noncombatant, Roberts and Stover flanking him as he advanced on the civilian.

Only then did they see what was coming.

"What the fuck!" Stover shouted.

The woman in the jacket dodged to the side, taking cover behind a wide-branched tree at the edge of the plaza.

"Down, boys! It's me!"

"Identify yourself!" Vaughn yelled, his heart pounding.

"Sara goddamn Harvey!"

Roberts glanced over at Vaughn. "You're sure it was—"

"Fucking sure."

They advanced slowly toward the tree, shifting to the right with each step to get a line of sight on her.

The voice sounded just like her, coming from behind the tree—dammit, she was shifting same as they were, just like Harvey would have. "Jesus, Vaughn, what the fuck are you doing? Stand down!"

"Harvey is dead! Don't fuck around with us!" Vaughn yelled back. Then he pitched his voice low. "Bell, help me out here…"

"Uhh…" Bell was fumbling in his pack for his notebook. *"Bismillah ir Rahman ir Rahim…"*

"I'm not a djinn! Cut it out!"

Vaughn shook his head. "If that's a djinn, we're all fucking dead."

Roberts glanced over his shoulder at Bell. "What about a crocotta? They can mimic—"

The voice came back annoyed. "Do I look like a fucking dog? Here!" A standard-issue 9mm handgun clattered to the patio, thrown from behind the tree. "I'm coming out now! Don't fucking shoot, you assholes!"

She stepped out from behind the tree, hands in the air.

Vaughn could swear it was Harvey, right down to the scuffed jacket she insisted on wearing even in the awful Texas heat and the black hair she kept cut short and simple above her ears. She was ragged, a long scratch on the side of her face, and her pants were out at the knees, but it looked just like her.

But it couldn't be. She was dead. He saw her goddamn body. He'd touched it and seen the scar.

She knelt on the concrete, and Stover circled around to the side while Roberts holstered his weapon and moved behind her to secure her wrists with a zip tie.

Vaughn kept his gun leveled at her head. "Talk."

"You talk! What the fuck are you doing?" she yelled, pissed even kneeling on the patio.

Vaughn shook his head, feeling like the ground was spinning under him. It was her, right down to the—

"Prove it," he said. "Prove who you are."

She gave him a glare so authentically Sara—if she wasn't real, then she believed she was real, and Vaughn didn't know which was worse. "How the fuck do I do that? Jesus, Vaughn, you know me! I've been on my own all day and you would not even believe what I've been seeing, I can't reach any of you assholes for twenty-four hours, and you throw down on me at the rendezvous?" She glanced around the patio, deserted and dark as the storm clouds roiled above them. "Also, nice way to blow our cover. We're one police cruiser away from a shitload of Blackfire paperwork."

"The leg," Bell said. "What happened to your leg?"

"Nothing today, kid," she replied. "If you mean my scar, I got stabbed by a redcap in a storm in merry old England, and you helped us kill it by shouting Scripture from Deuteronomy."

Bell faltered, looking again to Vaughn.

"I recruited you," she continued. "You were working Blackfire's labs in Montana, and you helped us contain that mess with the Incan bloodstone. You helped save Dr. Milan's life, but I don't hold it against you."

Roberts snorted at that. "Sure sounds like her, Vaughn." He stepped a little closer. "How do you kill an aswang?"

She sighed. "You stab it with stingray tails dosed with some enchanted goop that requires a fuckton of coconuts. What is this, remedial Blackfire? Vaughn! It's me!"

Vaughn stood still, feeling even more like the ground was unsteady underneath him. "Harvey is dead. This morning. I identified her fucking body. Tattoo. Leg scar. It was her."

Her eyes widened, but she didn't move. "Paul, it wasn't me. Whatever you saw, it wasn't me. You have to believe me, this thing we're fighting, I've been running against it all day and it damn near killed this civilian—"

"Who was Colette Gibsen?"

Vaughn's question seemed to shock her even more than the pronunciation of her death. "Paul...you made me promise. I swore I would never—"

He lifted the gun closer to her head. "Answer."

She was frozen, silent. He kept his finger close to the trigger. "Goddammit, answer me!"

She swallowed. "Your brother's fiancée. Possession case."

Stover and Bell traded surprised looks.

Vaughn lowered his gun and holstered it. "Cut her loose."

Roberts glanced over at him. "You sure?"

Vaughn shook his head. "That one's not on the Blackfire books. If she isn't Harvey, she thinks she is."

"Gee, thanks," Harvey snapped as Roberts cut her hands free. She got to her feet and scooped up her gun, which she quickly holstered. "Somebody explain what the fuck is going on?"

Bell replied by tossing a handful of salt over her head. She brushed it away. "I'm not a ghost, kid. But nice try. Next time you should throw the salt before freeing the hands—oh wait, you can't slap cuffs on a ghost. What the fuck, people! Amateur hour!"

"Watch her," Vaughn said, stalking away a few steps and pulling out his cell. His heart was pounding too hard—it didn't make any sense, and nothing about this mission made sense to begin with. He dialed up the Bexar County morgue and went through the endless phone tree while half-listening to the thing that looked like Harvey as though it were a real debriefing.

"It was chasing a woman along the Riverwalk, and it was about to get her at one of the bridges when I came along," she told them. "Whatever it is, salt helps, but only for a moment. It's not corporeal, so guns are useless."

"Then where were you all day?" Roberts asked.

She shuddered, and Vaughn didn't think Harvey knew how to shudder. "It's… strange," she said. "I've been running so long, I'm fucking beat. I was somewhere else, and no one was there, but each time I turned around, it's like there were people…sort of there, but not? I kept trying to reach you guys, but the phone was dead, and then it wasn't, but when I called your numbers or the motel, I just got this weird cackling laugh—"

Stover shivered in a sudden, full-body jerk that startled all of them.

Vaughn hung up the phone and walked back to them. He came right up to her and stared into her eyes, silent.

She met his gaze straight and unafraid, as always. "It's me, Paul."

Vaughn stared back at her, watching her even as he spoke to the others. "Bexar County morgue has no record of a missing Jane Doe. In fact, they have no record of a Jane Doe at all in the last forty-eight hours. I thought they might have a missing body, then I'd know if we're dealing with a reanimation, a ghoul, some kind of—"

"None of the above," she replied. "Jesus, you're a scary motherfucker when you want to be. It's. Me."

Vaughn kept staring at her. "It's not just that they had no record of Sara's body," he said. "They had no record of my identification. I was talking to the same guy who showed me the body this morning, and he had never heard of me."

They each exchanged glances, and the thing that looked like Harvey seemed more confused than ever.

Vaughn folded his arms. "Since I'm proceeding on the assumption that I'm not fucking insane, it's clear this critter has been creating impossible illusions around us since we landed."

"Bagala!" Bell said, grabbing his field notebook.

"Bless you," said the sorta-Harvey, and Vaughn would have laughed if it weren't so fucking bizarre.

"No, she's a demon! She presides over deceitful death, she incites people to torture each other!" Bell said, flipping through his pages. "I was reading up on her when we were on our way down, she plays games with people and tries to get them to turn on each other!"

The woman shook her head. "Bagala's a Hindu goddess, not a demon. And what the fuck would she be doing in Texas? That's like finding a chupacabra in New York City."

"What happened to the La Llorona theory?" Roberts asked.

Bell shook his head. "She's aimed at kids, the victims so far have been all adults. I was thinking of *el cucuy*, but that also preys on children."

"What about—" Stover began, but his voice was drowned out by an enormous thunderclap, as the wind picked up hard, whipping through the tree limbs and turning the pages of Bell's notebook.

The speakers at either side of the patio suddenly crackled to life, and the voice it carried was the same sexless cackling laughter from the motel phone. Only now it was so much worse, filling the plaza before the cathedral with that awful voice.

Stover moaned, his hand resting on his gun even though they knew it was useless.

"Positions!" Vaughn yelled, and they moved back-to-back, facing all four corners with Bell in the middle. Instinctively Vaughn let the maybe-Harvey take her usual spot beside him.

The cackling laughter grew louder and louder, and the lightshow started up again on the front of the cathedral. Only now instead of bright-colored kaleidoscope images and cheerful music, it was blood, rivulets of dark red cascading over the cathedral as dark figures writhed in pain or ecstasy.

The voice echoed across the plaza, and Vaughn felt vaguely foolish in fighting mode—what could they fight? A disembodied voice? Lights on the side of a building?

"Civilian," Roberts warned, and indeed Vaughn spied a taxi driver chatting on his cell phone, leaning against his vehicle on the far side of the plaza. But he didn't look up, didn't flinch at the voice's laughter, didn't even seem to notice the light show—which had shifted now to hideous images of murder, of capering figures inflicting horrors on terrified faces, as blood flowed down from the spires of the cathedral.

It's just for us, Vaughn thought. *What does it want from us?*

He turned to ask Bell for a hint on Bagala, but Bell was gone. Startled, Vaughn staggered back and realized he was alone.

They had been literally shoulder to shoulder with him a moment ago, and suddenly he was alone on the plaza.

"Paul..."

The voice whispered from the cathedral, soft, yet clear enough for him to hear it. The light-blood kept flowing, only now it formed a face, an ageless, twisted face that once might have been a woman. It grinned at him, an enormous face twenty feet high, wracked in pain and also cunning; its tongue flicked between broken teeth.

The doors to the cathedral blew open, three arched double doors weighing hundreds of pounds each, yet there was no one near them. Vaughn looked back up at the facade, and the woman's face was gone. In her place, the blood flowed down the front of the cathedral and the bodies writhed in its wake. As he drew closer to the cathedral, he saw the faces of his team on some of the tormented, dying bodies.

Beyond the doors lay absolute darkness.

<hr>

La Villita was silent in the dark, the doors of its shops and cafes shuttered against the outside and sun umbrellas closed over empty tables. Parish Roberts nearly tripped over a curb, disoriented.

"The fuck," he muttered. A moment ago, he was at the cathedral, and now he was back at La Villita, half a mile away.

Is this real, or is this the thing? He had no idea, but something was clearly fucking with them.

Parish had his hand on his weapon but didn't draw it. This might be real, or it might be in his head, but if he was really running around closed shopping centers in Texas at night, he sure as hell didn't need to be waving a gun. The last thing he needed was to get shot by some trigger-happy security guard while he was chasing down a supernatural thingamabob.

At the moment, it didn't seem he was in any danger. He was apparently alone, and La Villita was deserted. He tried to get his bearings, moving down the steps of the little church and crossing the sidewalk toward the open-air theater, now dark and still.

Faintly he heard music, a light, haunting melody like a classical air. In the shadows, he could see someone moving.

"Hello?" he called out.

Behind him, the church bells clanged to life, jolting a burst of adrenaline through his chest. They tolled deep and loud, sending reverberations out from the small steeple.

A spotlight switched on, illuminating a circle in the center of the open stage. Beyond it, Parish could see nothing but darkness.

A slim foot extended into the circle, clad in a white ballet shoe, laced up the dancer's dark leg. The rest of her soon moved into the light, a young girl in a pure white leotard with flowing white silk skirts and her black hair bound up in a screaming-tight bun with a soft white ribbon fluttering from it.

The music rose and she began to dance, her body swaying and twisting to the strains of the melody. He recognized it now: *Swan Lake*, and truly the girl was a graceful swan, moving with delicate precision coupled with powerful intent.

She turned again and again, and Parish was drawn almost involuntarily closer to the stage. The girl began to spin, her head snapping back around with each pirouette faster and faster until she hardly seemed human, her easy smile now a forced rictus.

"Stop!" Parish cried. *Was it really her?* "Katrina, stop!"

At the sound of her name, she fell to the floor of the stage in a crumpled heap.

Parish leaped onto the stage and ran to her, reaching out to take her hand.

She looked up at him, and he recoiled in horror.

Katrina's face was covered in bruises, one eye swollen shut, blood leaking from her mouth and nose. The pin-straight hair was now tattered, and there was an ugly gash along the side of her forehead.

"Look what's become of me!" she spat at him, fury and hatred barely contained in her voice.

She rose to her feet, and the white leotard and skirt were ripped and stained with blood and filth. Her hands gripped into claws, and she shoved him away, out of the circle of light, her slim arms working with an unearthly strength. He stumbled and fell back onto the ground.

Katrina slipped beneath the three arches at the back of the stage, melding with the shadows.

"Katrina!" Parish choked on his words, and the light vanished. He was alone on the stage, only a thin white silk ribbon remaining on the ground. "Little dancer…"

He rose unsteadily to his feet, and jumped back down off the stage, scooping up the ribbon like a tiny scrap of sanity, telling him he was not imagining this.

Parish heard shrill laughter and saw a flash of white silk off to the side. He ran around the edge of the stage, toward the stone bridge on the other side that led across the river.

Bright, multi-colored flags danced in the light breeze over Jimmy's head, and he blinked at the harshness of the sunshine.

Off-balance, he tripped over a curb. Fortunately there was a concrete bench right next to him, and he sat down hard instead of falling on his ass.

How did I get to the market? he thought. *And how did it get to be daytime?*

Jimmy's eyes slowly adjusted to the sunlight. The plaza was crowded with vendors and shoppers, a mix of locals and tourists wandering between the booths in the open-air market, the huge pavilion to his left, and the restaurants lining the right. Somewhere a mariachi band played, but closer to Jimmy, he saw a man dressed as Elvis lip-synching to "Are You Lonesome Tonight?" The impersonator gyrated in front of a ramshackle tavern entrance, a small portable speaker at his feet next to a mostly-empty basket with a few dollar bills in it. The Elvis crooning mixed with the cheerful mariachi was incongruous enough that it added to Jimmy's disorientation, and he clutched his supply bag closer as he fumbled for his cell phone.

No signal. Of course.

Is this real? Jimmy thought. *What if it's some kind of illusion?* Something about it had to be unreal, because it had been dark when he was at the cathedral with the rest of the team. Either he was still there and lost in some strange fantasy, or he had somehow been transported in time as well as space, and that was just a little too science-fiction even for this job.

Jimmy fumbled open his notebook and tried a quick dispelling incantation, but all it got him was a strange look from the man selling Mexican street corn. Another vendor was selling cheap jewelry, and a third belt buckles the size of dessert plates. None of them were paying much attention to Jimmy, but instead were calling out to the people passing by on the plaza, some in English and some in Spanish.

The King crooned his lyrics from the speaker and the lip-syncher, clad in a late-Elvis white vinyl jumpsuit, gyrated and occasionally pointed to the basket beside the speaker. A trio of twentysomething tourist kids posed together in front of him for a selfie, then laughed and trotted on without leaving a tip.

Jimmy tried the cell phone again, but there was still no signal. *There is a reason I'm here, let's find it,* he thought. He wandered past the booths on the plaza toward the large pavilion on the left. At least it would be air-conditioned, and maybe he could figure out what the hell was going on.

He walked over to the large double doors leading into the pavilion, and the conversation around him stopped.

It wasn't completely silent—the weird mix of mariachi and Elvis continued its bizarre duet, but the general hubbub of voices had vanished. Jimmy looked over his shoulder, and all the people were still there, shopping and rolling corn and snapping pictures.

But no one was speaking. Not a single person.

Jimmy shoved the door open and entered the labyrinth of the pavilion. Rows and rows of booths, haphazardly designed and some on the verge of collapsing, constructed of wood or grid wall or even milk crates, and they all seemed to go one way or another without any logical pattern. Some booths had doors propped open, while others had curtains tied to the side. This one was selling bottles of Mexican vanilla for three dollars, while that one was selling sugar skull artwork and hoping no one would notice the "made in China" stamp on the back. Earrings and Mexican Coke and tapestries and scarves, some fluttering from dirty fans clamped to the top of the displays, and soon Jimmy was lost in the maelstrom of commerce. He passed a booth selling small pennants emblazoned with a picture of a former president labeled *el pendejo,* and an equal mixture of American and Mexican and Texas flags.

Just like outside, though, no one was speaking. Somewhere a radio was playing piano music, which saved him from eerie silence, but even though he was surrounded by dozens of shoppers and shopkeepers, no one spoke.

Finally, Jimmy stepped over to the woman selling the Mexican vanilla. "Excuse me," he asked. "Can you tell me what time it is? My phone isn't working."

The woman looked up at him, a Latina woman of at least sixty-five years old, her hair braided with streaks of black and gray, and lines around her face.

She glanced at her own phone, which was sitting on the counter next to a trio of vanilla bottles, as if checking the time.

Then she looked back up at him and opened her mouth. Instead of words, a horrible high shrieking sound came from her throat.

Jimmy stumbled back, startled. She kept bleating that same wordless shriek, over and over, blending one scream into the next as though she didn't need to breathe between them.

The vendors and shoppers all froze in place, and they were staring at Jimmy.

Time to go. Jimmy backed up step-by-step, trying to keep as many people as possible in eyesight and still be prepared for an attack, just like Parish had taught him. He wasn't a fighter by nature, and was still learning how to defend himself, but most of what he knew how to do came from the books.

The books. He grabbed the notebook again, and tried a different incantation, this time an old Catholic one from Latin.

The vanilla woman stopped shrieking. Her eyes closed, and when she opened them, they were solid black.

Their eyes. The Mexican vendors, the tourists with their knapsacks and wide-brimmed hats, even the security guard in full pseudocop regalia with his hand on his gun, all of them staring at him, and now all of their eyes were expressionless, solid black, shark's eyes. None of them speaking.

But they were beginning to take steps, one by one, toward him. *Not good.*

Jimmy moved faster, trying to keep his back to the wall of shops and booths as he fumbled his way back to the door. It seemed to have moved —it certainly wasn't by the booth he had remembered when he first came in, but nothing here made sense anyway.

On the far wall of the pavilion he saw a banner, a rainbow-colored drapery in the same colors as the little flags above the open air market outside. Beside it was a shelf display of small crucifixes, some of which seemed to be bleeding onto the wood and dripping to the floor.

Jimmy took the chance, and pushed his way through the staring, silent black-eyed people toward that banner, and below it was a door.

One of them stepped between him and the door. He was an older man, face lined with many years in the sun. He was dressed as a tourist, with Bermuda shorts and a hat, but his eyes were expressionless, solid black and malevolent.

Acting on instinct, Jimmy grabbed one of the bleeding crucifixes and shoved it at the tourist man, who recoiled backward. His mouth opened as if to hiss at Jimmy, but no sound came out, just his gaping mouth lined with unnaturally white teeth.

Jimmy pushed his way past and through the door, and then he was back on the plaza under the glittering flags.

But the silence continued, not the silence of an empty plaza, but the ominous silence of a hundred blank-eyed strangers staring at him and not speaking. The unseen mariachi band had drifted from the light fast-paced music they had been playing into something slower, something in a minor key, dirge-like and dark. It no longer spoke of grilled corn and spicy nachos under a bright sun and colorful costumes dancing on a stage, but of hardscrabble dirt baked by an unforgiving sun and yielding nothing, of rows of shacks cobbled together from corrugated metal and cardboard and a long-dead gas station on an empty road coated in the dust of ten thousand cars that never stopped.

Jimmy walked quickly, not running. Sara had taught him that running feeds panic, and he was close enough to panic as it was. Whatever this was, it was something he didn't know how to fight, and panic would only make it stronger.

But his pace picked up as he went, trying to get to the edge of the market and possibly get his bearings to find his way back to the cathedral.

Ahead he saw the arched entrance to the open-air market, with words he couldn't read written backwards. His hand gripped the crucifix tightly, his palm slicked with its blood, sickly warm.

"Jimmy."

Startled, he turned, and there was the impersonator, grabbing him by the shoulders and shoving his face up against Jimmy's. But it was no longer the smiling dancer he had seen upon appearing here in this weird festival—this was a different face. The ancient face, with black holes where the eyes used to be and dry flaking skin covering a skull-like visage—gray, rotting, stretched tight over the bones. There were wounds on his lips and hands, bloodless cuts revealing black ichor beneath. It was the face from the microfiche machine, the face he had seen in terrible dreams, only now it was here, and its impossibly strong hands tightened on his shoulders as it breathed fetid stench into his face.

The scream built up inside his throat and he tried to hold it in, because screaming would be letting the panic take over, as bad as if he had run, and maybe he should have run, because panic couldn't be worse than that awful reek from the face with no eyes, still incongruously clad in the white Elvis jumpsuit and the tattered remains of the black wig hanging askew off its skull.

Jimmy's hand was in his bag, grasping for anything, anything at all. The thing opened its mouth and Jimmy shoved the crucifix at it. It recoiled, releasing Jimmy's shoulders and making strange high-pitched noises as it stumbled backward.

That was enough for Jimmy, and he ran toward the archway, whether it led to the river or the cathedral or anywhere but here.

Vaughn's flashlight flickered out the moment he crossed the threshold into the cathedral foyer.

He smacked it a couple of times, standing next to a large white marble sarcophagus just inside the entrance. The flashlight flared once and died again.

"Figures," he muttered, and pocketed it as he entered the cathedral itself, casting a wary eye on the sarcophagus to the left engraved with the names of the Alamo dead. In his business, the dead rarely stayed quiet.

While the outside of the cathedral had been ancient, weathered stone in Gothic engraving, the inside was shining white from the gleaming floor to the arched ceiling high above him. He passed beneath the organ loft and into the main aisle of the empty sanctuary, just beyond what little light shone from the open doors into the shadows of the main aisle.

As he reached the center, light flared from the stained-glass windows lining the walls, as though spotlights were shining through from outside. They cast multicolored shadows of twisted saints and mangled flowers onto the silent pews, moving back and forth over the wood on either side of the aisle.

Vaughn continued slowly up the center, automatically reverencing the altar and making the sign of the cross just as he had been taught as a child. As he did, he heard a low, sinister chuckle from somewhere behind him.

He turned, and the church was full.

Hundreds of shadowy forms filled the wooden rows, all kneeling with heads bowed and gray veils hiding their faces. All the same, indistinguishable as male or female, young or old, and filling the pews across the width of the cathedral in every row.

Vaughn backed up a bit toward the front altar and tried desperately to remember the words of his upbringing. It was odd how easily he adapted to springheels and ghouls and which ghost was repelled by salt and what monster had to be fought with flamethrowers and Scripture readings for the love of God, but try to remember the damn rosary and…

"*In nomine patris, et filii, et spiritus sancti,*" he began, and suddenly his memory flashed, remembering Grandma Marjorie kneeling beside him with Dale on the other side, their fingers moving over the glow-in-the-dark plastic rosaries she had given them on one of their rare visits. "*Ave Maria, gratia plena…*um, *Dominus tecum, benedicta tu in…mulieribus.*"

There was more, but he couldn't remember it. Something *pro nobis,* but it had been too many years. "*Gloria patri, et filio, et spiritu sancto,*" he said again. *You can't go wrong with the Father, Son and Holy Spirit, right?*

It was holy ground, so by basic Christian lore it should be a safe haven, but apparently whatever had infested the entire damn city of San Antonio didn't get the memo. The ghosts remained, veiled heads bathed in the strange dancing colored light streaming in through the stained glass windows. As he looked up at them, the saints in the windows cavorted and danced themselves, sometimes waving at Vaughn, sometimes glaring.

Now would be a good time for a priest, Vaughn thought, and a flare of memory shot up. Not of a priest, but a holy man who was willing to try just about anything to cure Dale's fiancée, the woman whose tormented face had covered the cathedral, the woman whose death ultimately cost him his brother.

"*Exi ergo, transgressor!*" Vaughn called out.

That got their attention. The ghosts all lifted their heads as one, and he immediately regretted it. Their eyes were empty, black holes in gray, desiccated faces.

If they come at me, I'm toast, Vaughn thought. But he had to give it a try.

"*Exi ergo!*" He backed up toward the baptismal font as he chanted. "*Da locum, dirissime, impissime, da locum Christo…*" He always had a bad memory for the Latin. It was Jimmy the Kid who really understood the whole exorcism thing—

The organ thundered to life, a malevolent toccata blasting from the balcony above as Vaughn stumbled backwards. The empty faces of the ghosts swiveled toward him as the music shook the walls.

He bumped into the font, and on impulse, he dipped his fingers into the water and made the sign of the cross on his forehead.

A hissing sound echoed under the roaring organ music, and he saw her in the shadows on the other side of the altar. She wore a long, flowing white robe, and her hair gathered at her shoulders, shrouding her face.

"Vade retro, Satana," Vaughn said, and she recoiled from him, hiding behind the altar in the strange swirling colored light playing across the white marble.

Vaughn searched in his pockets and blissfully came up with a small vial that had held salt. He dipped it in the font and filled it with holy water.

He stepped up around the altar and the organ music responded, crashing from the toccata into a discordant fugue, music with no melody, no sanity, just pealing notes seemingly at random.

The woman in white fled back toward the glorious golden reredos surrounding the statue of the crucified Christ. Vaughn saw with no surprise at all that Christ's head had turned entirely red in the strange lights.

The woman stopped before the reredos, and now she seemed more real to Vaughn than the gray apparitions in the pews, as though she were truly here. *Is she La Llorona? Is that it after all?* he wondered. *No, that's not it, nothing about this damned thing makes any sense at all...*

"Da locum Christo," he said again, hoping that he was actually saying, "Give way to Christ," and not mangling the incantation beyond imagination.

The woman in white turned, and now the reredos shone golden light down around her, banishing the weird reflections and bathing Vaughn in a halo of sunlight. He had to shield his eyes from her brightness, and a quick glance over his shoulder saw that she had banished the specters from the pews, dispelling the shadows. The organ fell silent at last.

Her face.

He looked closer, his hand gripping the holy water vial. If she was Colette's spirit, the ghost he had seen outside, he had to put her to rest. He owed that to Dale. Hell, he owed that to Colette. He'd failed them both.

"Exi ergo, transgressor," he began again, and she merely looked at him, extending her hands—hands, he saw now, that were covered in blood.

He could hear screaming now, echoing behind him from the empty pews, of men and of women, so many wailing voices in wordless agony, swelling louder amid reports of gunfire, screaming grotesquerie and vicious cruelty punctuated by hot explosions and cold fire. It was the cacophony of Afghanistan, the orchestra of combat he had left behind to fight ghouls and beasts with Blackfire, exchanging a hot hell for another, dark and cold.

By reflex Vaughn's hand dropped to his weapon, but he knew it would do no good. Nothing here was going to be stopped by bullets.

Blood dripped from the woman's hands onto the shining steps before the altar.

"Paul." Her voice was soft, gentle—and familiar.

He looked up, and staggered backward, falling to his knees and nearly dropping the holy water onto the floor. "No," he whispered.

The woman smiled, a familiar smile. Her face no longer resembled Colette, living or dead, but a different face, albeit a softer visage framed with long, curling hair she had never worn in his acquaintance.

She was Sara Harvey.

Sara awoke on the ground, mostly upright and leaning against a small stone structure under twisted branches and the night sky.

Struggling to her feet, she saw the structure was a square stone well with a rickety wooden apparatus over its dark opening. Above it stood a wide-limbed, twisted tree whose branches extended far out over Sara's head in the walled garden where she stood.

"Dammit, not again," she muttered.

As a reflex she checked her phone, but it was just as dead as the last time. No signal, and she knew if she tried to call them, she'd just get that weird-ass cackle again.

The garden was shrouded in deep shadows punctuated by thin streams of moonlight, silence coating it like a blanket, but it was not the comforting silence of solitude. Sara knew she was not alone, and whatever walked here was not friendly.

She checked her pockets and found she was down to only a few packets of salt, her service weapon and the flashlight, which still wasn't working. Fortunately, her eyes were adjusting to the darkness as she moved away from the well toward the gated entrance to the garden, and beyond it, the Alamo.

The gate was closed and locked, of course. It was the middle of the night and she was seriously out of bounds. She allowed herself a wry grin at the thought of being caught by the troopers that patrolled the Alamo grounds at night. Surely they'd be just fine with her explanation of having been teleported here by ghosts or demons, right? That would not in any way result in her arrest.

She peered through the iron gate at the white stone fort of the Alamo chapel, illuminated by spotlights, with the Texas flag fluttering over it. Then the air seemed to shimmer, and the rows of switchback lanes for tourists to wait their turn vanished. The walls grew dingy and battered, the pavement transformed to packed-down dirt and rocks, and she could spy a twelve-pound cannon on the far side of what had been the court-yard. The distinctive scrolled top of the Alamo chapel was gone, crumbled or blasted away to jagged stone.

Oh, you have got to be fucking kidding.

Sara looked to her right, where the road was supposed to be, and saw hazy battlements...but also, as if through fog, the shining lights of taverns and shops and passing cars and the relative sanity of the twenty-first century. But when she looked back at the chapel, her view seemed to shift to another time, and the silhouette of a scruffy man braced on the roof with the world's most beat-up long rifle.

Something moved in the garden behind her, something that sounded bigger than a rat or a raccoon. Sara's hand fell to her holster, and she pressed her back against the stone wall, moving away from the gate that turned her into a perfect silhouetted target. Even after all these years, she had to resist the urge to say, "Who's there?"

The form moved between the trees, and in the shadows Sara could not tell if she was in the stately manicured garden with statues and commemorative plaques, or the blasted ground soaked with blood. She edged further away from the gate along the stone wall, feeling into her pocket for salt packets while her other hand slipped her gun out of its holster. All she could find in her pocket was an odd little stone, vaguely heart-shaped by the feel of it, but no salt. The stones beneath her feet clicked and crunched, and she tried to move more quietly into the shadow of another tree.

"Who's there?"

Sara rolled her eyes. "Oh, for fuck's sake, Stover!"

He stepped into the light, his eyes wide, but his gun was holstered. "Harvey?"

Sara motioned for him to join her in the shadows. "Really? 'Who's there?' Are you new at this?"

Stover walked slowly toward the gate, eyes wide. "Uh, Harvey..."

"Yeah." Sara deliberately didn't look back out. "Don't ask me, I just work here."

Stover finally turned and looked at her. "Are we all here? Or just you and me?"

Sara smacked her flashlight again, but it still wasn't working. "I've shown up here three times today. Always night, always next to the well, but this is the first time it's been 1836 out there."

Stover blinked, a confused look on his face.

Sara sighed. "For God's sake, Stover. 1836? The siege of the Alamo? I don't know why we're seeing it, or whether it can hurt us, but I don't care to find out."

"So sorry I didn't bone up on Texas history before this gig," Stover grumbled. "So, if you were hanging out at the Alamo all day, how did Vaughn get word you were dead?"

She shook her head. "On that I've got nothing."

Stover fell in line behind her as she moved along the wall, trying to assess every shadow for a threat. "Well. If it's really you, I'm glad you're not dead."

Sara swallowed a laugh. "Damn, Stover, that's the nicest thing you've said to me all month."

Sara reached the edge of the wall and peered around the corner. She should have been looking at the gift shop. Instead, she saw a darkened horse corral, a few shadowed animals sleepily grazing in the weird moonlight.

"Harvey," Stover asked, his voice somewhat unsteady. "Are we…like, actually here? Like time travel? Because I think I remember how this story ends, and it ain't fucking good."

"Depends on your point of view. Santa Anna thought it turned out all right," Sara said absently, moving around the low fence of the horse corral and toward the side of the chapel. Somewhere she thought she heard a fiddle playing, but that was crazy, right?

Stover followed her around the back, where a low, scraggly field lay in the moonlight instead of the carefully manicured and fenced gardens of the historic site. She turned the corner and damn near ran right into a tall form in the shadow of the chapel.

"Vaughn! Goddammit, you scared the shit out of me!" she hissed.

On first glance, Vaughn was in combat mode, which was not necessarily a good thing. Like her, Vaughn had seen non-supernatural combat and had the metaphorical and not-metaphorical scars. On second glance, however, Vaughn's face betrayed something more than the fight reaction. "Jesus, Vaughn, you okay?"

He looked at her. "Can you see it?"

She glanced across the moonlight field. "Can I see what? That we're kind of in Davy Crockett Land?"

He exhaled. "I wasn't sure if maybe I was cracking up. Because I started today looking at your dead body, Harvey, so…"

"Yeah, we're gonna need to figure that out at some point," she replied, edging toward the far side of the chapel.

As they moved around the corner of the building, the ground shimmered again. One moment she saw a palisade fortified from the chapel wall to the banks of cannons aimed outward at the dark sky, and the next she saw a quiet garden with fountains and statues. Then it would shimmer, and she would see the palisade again.

They dropped low along the chapel wall, and Sara tried to gain a sense of their location. Above them, she heard men's voices and the occasional boom from a not-so-faraway cannon. She leaned back against the chapel wall…and fell onto her rear, suddenly surrounded by light.

"What?" Sara muttered, looking around. All three of them were sprawled on the ground, but inside the chapel, as though they had fallen straight through the wall.

Again, she had that strange double vision, of a clean and solemn room with tasteful interpretive displays here and there…and of a filthy, broken shell of a building, the floor covered with rubble. Shadowy figures moved back and forth, mostly men but also a few women, at least from the shape of their clothing.

"This is beginning to piss me off," Stover muttered, getting to his feet.

Vaughn stood close to Sara in defensive posture, and she noted that at least for now, he was back to treating her like herself, not the wary suspicion that he'd had on the plaza in front of the cathedral. "They don't seem to see us."

Indeed, the shadows seemed to come in and out of focus as though held in a camera lens that was constantly changing. For a moment, Sara could see a woman in a long dress and apron, kneeling beside a man with a bloody strip of cloth tied around his leg. Then a moment later, they were only shadows, and a display case stood in their place.

Sara inclined her head toward the chapel's side entrance, which might or might not lead them out of whatever fever-dream they'd landed in. Vaughn nodded, and together they moved in a defensive posture, though Sara wasn't sure what good fighting would do against shades that were or were not there. You can't shoot a ghost.

As they crossed the center of the chapel, two more shadows stepped out of one of the side rooms.

"Harvey!" one of them whispered.

"Parish! Goddamn," Sara replied.

Parish and Jimmy came out of the darkness, and unlike the shadows around them, they seemed to stay solid. "I'm sure hoping you're real," Jimmy said.

Sara couldn't help grinning. "You and me both," she replied.

Outside, another loud boom echoed, and dust and pieces of stone fell from above all around them. The shadows seemed to be moving faster, and far away Sara could hear more gunfire.

"Oh, Christ, you have to be kidding," Vaughn muttered. "We're supposed to watch the fall of the Alamo?"

"I'd rather watch than participate," Sara replied. "Guys, can you get out the—"

But as she looked at the side entrance, she saw only smooth stone walls. She wasn't sure if the entrance hadn't existed in the 1800s, or if whatever had trapped them here just didn't want them to leave, but her hand on the stone said either way, they weren't getting out through the side of the chapel.

Vaughn was holding something in his free hand. Sara touched his arm and gave him a questioning look. "Holy water," he replied quietly. "From…well. It's been a weird day."

"Tell me about it," Parish said, and Sara saw that he was also holding something: a strip of white fabric. As she looked around, she saw Jimmy was holding a crucifix.

"Where did you guys get that stuff?" she asked, but another explosion drowned out any answer they might have given. The gunfire was closer now, and they could hear the sounds of fighting, of shouting and fury, of men screaming, the clang of metal against metal and the unlovely sound of blades stabbing flesh.

Vaughn gestured to the left, and they formed a defensive posture in a corner behind where the altar had once been and would be again, trying to stay away from the moving shadows. Bell was fumbling with his notebook, trying some kind of incantation, and Stover tried the default salt packets, none of which seemed to dispel the illusion—if it was an illusion, they could have time-slipped to 1836 as far as Sara knew.

Then the chapel door blew open, with a shining burst of light and fire, and now there were no more shadows. Instead, the ghosts solidified into people, fighting men seemingly as real and solid as Sara herself, and the uniformed army rushing in clashed in a cacophony of screams and shouts.

One of them turned toward the team, where Sara and Vaughn stood on point. His face shifted from the normal-appearing soldier's face above the white-crossed uniform to a hideous skull-face, gray and desiccated, and he ran at them with a bayonet affixed to his rifle.

Vaughn and Stover fired together, but the bullets went right through the skull-soldier and whined off the stone ground. Sara grasped for salt, but as it rushed forward, the soldier suddenly vanished.

It wasn't alone, though. The ghosts of the Mexican Army had spied them, and now the ghosts of the Texans joined them, all advancing toward the team.

"Oh fuck!" Sara cried.

Vaughn was shouting something that sounded crazily like Latin to her left, and Parish gripped that strange slip of fabric as he whispered something Sara couldn't hear. She leveled her gun at them—it might not help, but she was pretty much out of ideas. *The fucking Alamo, it figures.*

From behind the ghosts, she heard a high, unearthly cry. It sounded like a scream, but not one from any human throat. It was shrill and strange, and it cut through the din of the battle, silencing all other sounds.

The ghosts froze still, and faded a bit, as though the camera lens had shifted again.

The scream came a second time, and the ghosts turned away from Sara and her team toward the doorway.

Silhouetted in the strange light shining into the chapel was the figure of a woman. She held in her hands a small, strange sculpture that resembled a skull, something ancient and carved from either a white wood or bone. The skull-face on the sculpture was ritualized, with large, round eye sockets and rows of flat teeth.

The woman raised the sculpture to her mouth and blew into it, and that horrible shriek echoed through the chapel again. *It's a whistle, or a trumpet, something like—* Sara cut off her thought. Whatever it was, it was working.

The ghosts faded back, shimmering into the darkness, and the room shifted with that strange veil again, as the battle faded, and the museum came forward.

The woman stepped into the chapel, and Sara moved away from Vaughn and walked toward her.

"It's you," she said.

"Obviously," the woman replied.

Parish strode forward and pointed at her. "This is her, Vaughn—Juliet, the woman from Yanaguana. From the shop."

"You were being chased by…what the fuck was it?" Sara asked.

"Hush now, you're in a church," Juliet replied, glancing around as she gripped her weird skull-whistle-thing.

"Was it Bagala?" Bell asked.

Juliet rolled her eyes. "What would Bagala be doing in Texas?"

The room was definitely more solid, but Sara didn't feel relieved. "She's the one it nearly got on the Riverwalk last night," she said to Vaughn. "Something was chasing her, but I didn't get a good look at it. I fired, and then I blacked out and woke up on the Alamo grounds."

"Sorry about that," Juliet replied. "I meant to thank you for distracting it, but then it knocked you into the half-world and I didn't know how to get you out. You really caught its attention, folks—you've all been knocked in and out of the half-world since you got here."

"What the fuck is the half-world?" Stover asked.

Juliet sighed, and addressed her answer to Parish instead. "I told you. Blackfire never found a situation they couldn't fuck up."

"You're in a church," Sara reminded her.

"You told me Sara was at the shop," Parish accused.

Juliet shrugged. "I didn't know if you could be trusted with the truth. I hoped I could get her out on my own. Then you all kept getting knocked into the half-world, and the portents have been going crazy all day."

"I asked you—" Stover began.

Juliet stared at him. "Get any fun phone calls today?" At Stover's recoil, she smiled, but there was no humor in it. "This thing has lived here a long time, hiding in the waters. It plays on your fears, it knows your guilt. If it can lure you into the half-world, you'll see a mix of what it wants you to see and what you make from yourself. If it keeps you there long enough, your own fears can kill you."

Vaughn spoke hesitantly, which was so totally unlike him that Sara did a double-take. "So…identifying Harvey's body this morning, that was…it was…"

"Your version of the half-world, yes," Juliet said, fiddling again with her creepy death-sculpture. "The thing you fear the most."

Sara raised an eyebrow, and Vaughn suddenly found his service weapon very interesting.

"Come on," Juliet said. "The Aztec death whistle only shakes it off for a little while. We have to move."

"Lady, who the hell are you?" Stover asked, but they followed her anyway out into the courtyard.

The moment they stepped out of the chapel, the bright light vanished, replaced by cold moonlight. The bustling street, plaza adorned with flags and ordinary streetlights were still gone. Instead, Sara saw hardpacked Texas dirt stretching to the rows of adobe huts along a wooden palisade. "Uh, we're still not in Kansas anymore," she muttered.

"Bite your tongue, you're in Texas," Juliet said. "Tommy!"

From the dark recesses of the walled garden to the right, a small form appeared and walked through the moonlit plaza toward the Alamo chapel. The boy was carrying a wooden box, she saw—a box carved with the stylized glyph of an eagle's head.

"The hell?" Parish asked, pointing at the box. "I saw that today—"

"*Cuauhtli*," Juliet said. "We've never been able to determine the true name of the creature that hides here, but we know Aztec artifacts affect it."

"Do any of you have a sunstone?" Tommy asked.

"You're kidding, right?" Parish asked.

Tommy shrugged. "I have a theory that we could capture it in a sunstone if we could combine the death whistle with—"

An explosion cut off Tommy's words, a burst of fire raining dirt on them from only about ten yards away.

"Cover!" Sara cried, and they made a dash for the walled garden, only to be stopped by another explosion.

Sara pivoted, and they followed her along the wall toward the front plaza—where the square stone well was now outside the walled garden, she saw with little surprise. Beyond it was a small platform with two cannons, operated by shadows. Explosions and gunfire echoed around them, and they sheltered at the corner of what seemed to be the hospital, or whatever passed for it back then, Sara thought.

Tommy held open the *Cuauhtli* box. "The icons," he said. "Put them in this."

Sara and Vaughn exchanged puzzled looks.

A bullet impacted the stone above their heads, and Sara dropped by instinct, hunkering down close with the others behind her. "What icons?"

"I think I know," Parish said, and he wound up the white silk ribbon into a roll and placed it in the box.

Bell looked down at the crucifix in his hand as if seeing it for the first time. Then he dropped into the box and wiped his hand on his pants as if it were dirty.

Vaughn added the vial of holy water, and looked at Stover.

"I got nothing," Stover said. "I didn't go into the whatever-world, I just got crank phone calls."

Juliet looked troubled. "It should do," she said. "And you?"

Sara shook her head. "I don't seem to have any... Twice I ended up here today, but it was just...the Alamo. No icons."

But even as she said it, she remembered, and she pulled the tiny heart-shaped stone from her pocket. "Wait...is this—?"

Juliet grabbed it and threw it in the box. Tommy closed and latched it, and then they were chanting in a language Sara didn't recognize.

"Sara...." Parish warned, and she looked up.

The ghosts were circling around them, still fading in and out, some of them Texans, some Mexican soldiers, and all dead. Their faces were skulls, and they looked more solid by the moment.

"Juliet, if you've got an idea..." Sara muttered. She and Vaughn aimed their guns, for whatever good it would do.

Tommy continued the chanting, as Juliet raised the death whistle again. "When I blow, run for the well," she said. The boy nodded.

Parish and Stover circled around, standing on either side of the kid.

The ghost-soldiers stepped into the wash of cold moonlight, solid and fearsome.

Juliet blew into the death whistle. The shriek came from the skull, louder and stronger than before, and Tommy dashed toward the well, Parish and Stover running alongside. The ghosts came at them solid, and they wrestled with them back-to-back, fending them off the boy as he scrambled for the well.

A trio of Texans came at Juliet, bayonets aimed at her chest, but Vaughn and Sara moved in front of her and fired over and over. The bullets passed right through them, but somehow their defiance seemed to dispel the ghosts into shadows, perhaps bolstered by the death whistle.

Tommy leaned over the side of the well and let the box fall.

At the splash, a wave of energy rolled outward from the well across the Alamo plaza. The ghosts shimmered, and Sara felt the ground shift beneath her feet as though something enormous moved beneath the surface, some titanic beast rolling over and shaking the earth.

She lost her balance and fell backward, landing on her rear for a record-breaking third time today. When she looked up, she saw them all on the ground, clustered near the well—which was back inside the walled garden where it belonged.

The gate stood open, and beyond it she could see the chapel, its scrolled top intact with spotlights and flags signaling the twenty-first century.

Sara reclined in the old wooden rocking chair on the porch of Yanaguana, sipping her iced tea. It was crazy sweet to her East-Coast taste, but Vaughn was on his third glass like a good southern man. The guys were all relaxing in some form or another, save Parish, who was tossing the ball back and forth with Tommy in the front yard.

"There's still something I don't understand," Jimmy said.

"There's a metric fuckton I don't understand," Stover muttered.

Jimmy ignored him. "The creature, whatever it is…it's been here forever, but it suddenly started killing just this week. Three people fell into the…what did you call it?"

"The half-world," Juliet said, pouring another cup of iced tea and handing it to Vaughn.

Jimmy nodded. "They never found their way out, and they died. So, what set it off? Why start killing now?"

Juliet looked somber. "I'm not sure. I think it's been killing quietly for a long time—taking the homeless, runaways, people no one will miss. But this jump in activity was strange, and it caught your attention, which is never good for critters."

"You use words like that, and it makes me think you're Blackfire," Vaughn said quietly.

Juliet laughed. "Not a chance, my IQ exceeded their limits."

"Hey now!" Sara protested.

"No offense," Juliet replied. "Y'all are okay, even if you did nearly get plastered all over the floor of the Alamo. But don't expect me to wear the Blackfire t-shirt."

Parish called over from the front lawn. "Do we get t-shirts, Vaughn? I've been in ten years, I think I deserve a t-shirt."

"I think I deserve a vacation," Sara declared.

Vaughn ignored them all. "How long do you think the… I can't pronounce it."

"Cuauhtli box," Juliet said.

"That," Vaughn said. "How long will the thingamabob hold it?"

Juliet shook her head. "No idea. It's bound to water, and no one is likely to disturb the water in the Alamo well for a while. But if it gets free into the Riverwalk again, it could be a problem."

Vaughn raised an eyebrow. "So of course, you would call us for help."

Juliet laughed and said nothing.

Sara looked up at the sign. "Yanaguana… What does that mean, Juliet? Is it some kind of incantation? A sigil protecting your shop?"

Juliet smiled. "Typical Blackfire, seeing zebras for horses. Yanaguana is the original name of San Antonio."

Sara dropped her face in her hands. "I've been doing this job too fucking long."

INTERLUDE: TO PROTECT AND SERVE

TO PROTECT AND SERVE

Adam Horowitz squatted beside the remains of Sam Weller and tried to figure out which part was his head.

The footsteps behind him in the alley were annoying, but not entirely unexpected. "You must be the FBI," he declared without turning around.

"What makes you say that, Detective?" asked an unfamiliar male voice.

Horowitz stood up and turned around. The man standing just outside his crime-scene tape was maybe in his early forties, but his eyes were much older. His sandy-blond hair was cropped too short for his hard-chiseled face. He wore a leather jacket that poorly concealed the camouflage underneath. He could have been in slacks and a tie. It wouldn't help. He was a guy born to wear a uniform.

The woman beside him wore camouflage pants with a tank top and leather jacket almost, but not quite, the same cut as the man's—a little more motorcycle than flight jacket. Shades hid her eyes even in the faint light of early morning, and her black hair was cropped almost as short as the man's. She'd be pretty if she weren't so severe.

"Because I told Hernandez not to let anyone in," Horowitz said, glaring over at his partner. Juan Hernandez looked sheepish. "However, I gotta take it back. You're not the Feebs, so who the hell are you and what are you doing in my crime scene?"

The man fixed Horowitz with ice-cool eyes. "If you're so sure we're not FBI, why don't you tell me who we are?"

The woman was motionless. She gave Horowitz the creeps, in a hot kind of way. He was tempted to tell them to fuck off, but some instinct made him abstain.

"You're in fatigues with no insignia," Horowitz told the not-Feeb. "You're standing practically at attention, and you haven't shaken the haircut yet, so you're ex-military. Pretty recent."

No reaction or acknowledgement. It was like talking to camo mannequins. Hernandez rolled his eyes behind their backs—he thought Horowitz was showing off. Maybe he was—the guy just rubbed him the wrong way.

Horowitz pointed at the woman next. "She's ex-military too, and she's packing under that jacket, which makes me goddamn nervous. I'm not sure how the hell you got past my guys with a sidearm, but I'd appreciate it if you could produce some ID and turn her weapon in to the officer on duty."

The man glanced at the woman, a ghost of a smile on his face. She didn't budge. "I'd like to see you try to disarm her, Detective."

"Then she's outta here, and that's assuming you've got concealed carry permits," Horowitz declared. His patience at an end, he was about to signal to Hernandez to get the fuck over here and get these yahoos out.

That's when the man finally produced some ID and introduced himself. "Captain Paul Vaughn, Blackfire Division. We're who the Feebs sent instead."

Horowitz checked over the ID. Vaughn offered to shake; his grip was firm and strong. "I don't believe I've heard of Blackfire Division," Horowitz said.

"You wouldn't," Vaughn said, handing over an envelope. Horowitz slipped it open—a letter from the police chief, instructing his captain to give Vaughn "all professional courtesy" and accept his assistance with the case.

"And her?" Horowitz asked, glancing at the woman.

Vaughn didn't turn. "Major Sara Harvey. Professional badass."

Harvey folded her arms across her chest. She did not offer to shake hands.

Horowitz glanced down at the sorry remains of Sam Weller. "I was hoping for one of those profilers, you know, someone who could actually help me catch this motherfucker."

"I think you'll be surprised what we can do," Vaughn said, stepping over the crime-scene tape and kneeling beside the remains. "Tell me what you know."

Horowitz surrendered. "Four dead so far. The first two were dealers working the streets near the harbor. The third was a homeless guy, found him in his cardboard box in the park. Last night it was a john trolling for a pro in the alley between the refinery and the dock."

Vaughn peered at Sam Weller's twisted, broken fingers. "All four found outside, pants around ankles?"

Hernandez nodded. "Clearly a sexual bent," he said. "He pulls their pants down before he makes them kneel to do God knows what—there's abrasions on the knees with ground-in dirt. Then he shoves them down on the ground and sodomizes them with something goddamn huge and barbed—it rips the hell out of them. The M.E. says if they'd lived they'd be using colostomy bags."

"But that's not what killed them," Harvey said.

It was the first time she'd spoken. Horowitz glanced at her, impassive behind the sunglasses. "That hasn't been released, ma'am, and it wasn't in the file we provided to the FBI. You mind telling me how the fuck you know that?"

"Let's skip the need-to-know dance and get to work," Vaughn said, standing up. "Your people haven't identified the toxin yet, I presume."

Horowitz glanced down at Sam. "And we don't know if it's what killed Weller here yet, plus he never broke fingers before, so maybe it isn't the same guy."

"Same guy," Harvey said.

Horowitz looked at her. "No sign of injection on any of them except the third, who was a habitual drug user and had arms like Swiss cheese. We're assuming whatever implement is being used for the sodomy also injects the toxin. It kills pretty damn fast, but it sure-hell isn't painless."

Harvey shifted around to get a clear view of Sam Weller. She did not flinch from the blood, or the piece of intestine curled outside the ruin of his buttocks. Horowitz wished he could be so unmoved. She stared at it from behind her sunglasses as though taking a mental picture.

Horowitz turned back to the body. "Vicious, well-planned, consistent and just about the worst goddamn way to die I can imagine."

"Major Harvey will take over your patrols tonight," Vaughn said, coming around the other side.

"Just a goddamn minute!" Hernandez protested.

"I'm staking out this whole district to the docks, so please keep your men out of my way," Harvey said.

Hernandez looked at Horowitz, gaping.

"I cannot just clear out of a six-block radius that's being hunted by a serial killer!" Horowitz snapped. "My squad are good people, and—"

Vaughn laid a hand on Horowitz's arm. "I'm sure they're good, Detective. But our team is experienced in this kind of hunt, and we can work better without any help."

"Just who the hell do you think you are?" Hernandez demanded.

Vaughn ignored the question. "I do believe you were requested to give us every consideration."

Horowitz folded his arms. "I'll be there too, Captain."

"Done," Vaughn said without hesitation. Harvey's head snapped toward Vaughn.

Vaughn handed Horowitz a slip of paper with an address. "Be here by eight p.m. if you plan to join us."

Hernandez threw up his hands.

"One last request," Horowitz said. "Tell her to take off the shades. I'd like to see the eyes of people I'm going to trust with my city."

Vaughn nodded to Harvey, and she pulled off the sunglasses. Had he thought she could be pretty? She could be beautiful, but her gray eyes were cool, almost as icy as Vaughn's. Horowitz couldn't imagine what these two had seen, but whatever it was had frozen them into human statues.

They stalked away, and Hernandez stepped over the pool of Sam Weller's blood to sidle close to Horowitz. "This is a bad fuckin' idea, buddy."

"Tell me about it," Horowitz said.

***

Horowitz hadn't quite known what to expect, but a flea-ridden motel wasn't it.

He pulled into the Elmwood Motel and parked next to a nondescript black van. As he walked toward Room 23, he passed a shaved-bald Black man lounging against the side of the van. The guy wore a long black leather coat and affected a casual air as he smoked his cigarette, but Horowitz could tell the guy was carrying under the coat and watching Horowitz intently out of the corner of his eye.

Horowitz reached the splintered door of Room 23 and knocked. The door opened and a gun barrel was in his face.

Horowitz instinctively dove to the side and pulled his own weapon on the short, stocky man behind the gun in the doorway.

In that same instant, Harvey slammed into the stocky guy, pinning him to the wall and knocking the gun harmlessly out of his hand.

"Goddammit Stover!" Harvey shouted.

Horowitz glanced to his right, where he could see Leather Coat braced against the hood of the van, his own gun aimed at them.

"What the fuck, Harvey!" Horowitz exclaimed.

Harvey released Stover, a thirtysomething white guy with an ugly, jagged scar along his brow, still healing. Vaughn and Harvey had been ice, but this guy was fire, a temper waiting to boil over.

"You must be the cop," Stover said without a shred of remorse.

"Jesus, Stover, you trying to fuck up already?" Leather Coat said incredulously, holstering his own weapon and walking toward them. Horowitz felt stupid still having his gun out, so he reluctantly put it away.

"Parish Roberts, meetcha," Leather Coat said, offering his hand. Horowitz shook, still watching Stover.

"Honest mistake," Stover said.

Vaughn appeared behind Harvey. "Give Stover back his gun, Harvey."

"If I must," Harvey muttered, scooping up the handgun and giving it back to Stover with a glare. "I told you we got stuck babysitting a local, Stover. Try not to get your stupid ass shot until I've had a chance to kill you."

Horowitz decided to ignore the 'babysitting' crack. "Is this your whole team?"

"What, ya want cheerleaders too?" Stover snarked. "Though Harvey would look cute in one of those short skirts."

Harvey leveled a stony glare at Stover. Personally, Horowitz would skip needling Harvey, but Stover didn't look like he was firing on all cylinders.

"What's the plan?" Horowitz asked.

"Plan is you do your best not to get us killed," Harvey said shortly, and disappeared into the room.

"Don't mind Harvey, she's a lot nicer than she seems," Roberts offered.

"Sure." Stover grinned. "She's all heart, warm and cuddly like a pit bull."

"Cut the shit," Vaughn ordered. "Gary and Parish, you'll take the alleys between Beale Street and the docks. I'll be on the roof of the theater at the end of Beale."

A muffled curse came from the room behind Vaughn. Vaughn actually cracked a smile, glancing over his shoulder. "Yes, Harvey, you get the civvie. You'll be in the park along the riverfront."

Horowitz thought of reminding them that he was a veteran police officer, but decided to shut up.

Harvey didn't say a word as she drove the Jeep to the river. The sun finally dropped below the horizon of Arkansas, and she slipped the omnipresent sunglasses into a coat pocket near her sidearm.

The breeze drifted off the river, cooling the sweat on Horowitz's brow. As Harvey pulled into one of the few public parking spaces adjacent to the downtown park overlooking the water, Horowitz looked out his window toward the docks. A small crowd of tourists waited on a rickety gangplank to board one of those steamboat replicas for an over-priced dinner cruise on the water.

Horowitz reached for his door handle and Harvey gripped his arm to stop him.

"What are we waiting for?" he asked.

"Them to leave," she said, indicating the tourists.

Horowitz sat back and waited as the last washes of sunlight faded across the twilight sky. "I'm going on faith here, Harvey, but I don't see how you guys are doing anything more spectacular than my people could manage, and we've got a lot more feet on the street," he said. "Maybe you could let us poor stupid cops in on your big secret government ways?

"Maybe you could shut the fuck up," she said.

Horowitz sighed. "When the yahoos are gone, exactly what are we doing on the riverfront?"

"We're bait."

Horowitz blinked. "We're what?"

Harvey looked at him. "This fucker is attracted to sexual energy. So the plan is for you and me to sit on a bench and fake making out. The boys are moving west on Beale with a supersonic thingamabob—don't ask me, I don't know the tech. It'll drive the fucker away from the crowds along Beale toward the river. It'll come down to the water and find us."

"I think I hate this plan," Horowitz said, trying to be funny. "You know how this guy kills, right? And so far he ain't all that interested in women."

"It never is." Harvey pulled a gun—a nice Beretta. She checked the load and slapped it back into place.

"You don't think the guy will notice the two lovebirds are wearing guns?" Horowitz asked.

"No." Harvey opened her door and got out. Hilariously, she locked her door before slamming it shut. Harvey's Jeep taking a walk was about the last potential crime on Horowitz's mind.

Still, he got out and followed Harvey down the hill, past the old Civil War cannon line toward the riverwalk, a sidewalk that meandered along the canal that divided Mud Island off the Tennessee shore of the Mississippi.

"Wait!" he called, and Harvey slowed enough for him to catch up. "God, you suck at stake-out," he muttered. He slid his hand inside hers, and instinctively she almost pulled free.

"Shit, forgot." Harvey clasped his hand and leaned closer to him. They walked slowly, hand-in-hand, as Harvey muttered something under her breath he was pretty sure he didn't want to hear.

They crossed the street and stepped onto the riverwalk, strolling under the old shade trees. They passed a homeless person's stash of blankets and bottles half-hidden behind a historical marker and made their way to a bench in the shadows by the water.

"Here, sweetheart," Horowitz cracked, unable to help himself. Harvey shot him a glare, and somewhere he heard a tiny thread of laughter. It certainly wasn't coming from Harvey. He glanced around, nervous.

Harvey lightly tapped her left ear, and he spied the smallest earpiece he'd ever seen perched on the curve of her ear.

"And here I thought we were all alone," Horowitz said, sitting on the bench.

She sat beside him, and he slid his arm around her shoulder. He'd never felt anyone so tense, as though she was made up entirely of one taut muscle that never relaxed.

"Lean into me," he whispered, and she did so almost as an afterthought, her body pressed close against his.

Horowitz leaned against her as well, his mouth close to her unencumbered ear. "Well, at least I'm snuggling with you out here. No offense, but Vaughn really isn't my type."

A laugh! A snort, at least, but a sound that definitely resembled honest-to-God laughter escaped her. She also relaxed a little more, and Horowitz became aware of a very pleasant female body beneath the camouflage and leather jacket and God knows how many weapons.

He tried to distract himself for a bit by trying to figure out exactly how *many* weapons she was carrying. There was the Beretta under her left shoulder, and the outline of something very like a knife under the sleeve of her right arm. He stroked down her back and felt the outline of another gun at the small of her back.

Her left leg pressed close against his calf, and he felt the hard press of some metal there. He let his hand wander down her side and—this was not making things easier.

"Only one gun, Detective?" she whispered against his collarbone. That was not helping matters either. Neither was the vague sensation that she was laughing at him.

"Usually that's all I need," he said. "How many are you carrying?"

She pressed her lips against his neck, and he exhaled too quickly. "More than you've found."

"Where do you—never mind," he said quickly.

A light puff of air against his neck told him she was laughing again, that silent can't-let-it-show laughter.

"If this wasn't so damn serious, I'd think this was some giant practical joke by the guys at the precinct," Horowitz muttered. "Is there a hidden camera somewhere?"

"Dear Jesus, I hope not," Harvey murmured.

Slight chatters in Harvey's earpiece. "They sighted it behind a club on Beale," she said.

"Sighted *it?*" Horowitz asked, fighting the haze that seemed to have fallen over his working brain. "You all keep saying that, calling him 'it.' I agree he's pretty damn vicious, but—"

"It's not a him," Harvey said quietly. "Not a him, her, or other. It's an it. A thing."

She paused as the earpiece squawked at her. "Shut up, Vaughn," she argued with thin air. "He's quite literally risking his ass out here, he has a right to know."

The earpiece squawked some more, and Harvey yanked it off her ear in frustration. She pulled back a bit and looked Horowitz straight in the eye.

"It's a Tanzanian creature called a popobawa," she said, her voice direct and without a hint of sarcasm. "It lives for hundreds of years by essentially fucking men to death with a member that is massive and barbed, injecting a natural poison into their bodies that kills them… Not quickly enough. Your FBI request sent up the red flags we saw. It's out of its native territory by two continents, it's all screwed up and breaking its own rules. It's a vicious killer and we're the bait for it, and they should have told you or made you stay home. But we were short one team member after our last sortie and we needed someone on the bench with me. Sorry."

Horowitz didn't know whether to laugh or shove her in the river. "I'm just supposed to believe that? It's an assfucking vampire? Where's the camera?"

"Believe it or don't, but it's the truth," she said.

He stared into her grey eyes, clear and beautiful. "All right," he said. "Why am I here instead of backing up one of your guys on Beale, or with Vaughn on the roof? Why did they put me on the bench?"

Harvey sighed, looking out at the water. The breeze drifted against her face. "Because Paul Vaughn is a fuckhead and I'm gonna rearrange his teeth," she muttered.

Horowitz blinked. "That's not really answering—"

"I said you were hot," Harvey said, and a blush actually stained her cheeks. "After we met at the scene. I was stupid enough to say it in full earshot of the guys, and they're assholes I'm going to *kill* for this, but that's why Vaughn put me on the bench with you, and he just thinks he's so fucking funny…"

Horowitz slid his hands on either side of her face and kissed her full on the lips.

After a moment's surprise, Harvey met him fully and with abandon. She slid her arms around his shoulders for real, and he felt the strength in her arms, an almost scary power in her body as she pressed close against him.

He stroked her back, lightly rubbing his fingers over the exposed skin at the back of her neck. It was stupid, a teenager's fall through the rabbit hole, but he felt like the river itself had changed its course to flow around them, isolating them from the rest of the world. It scooped them up on that little park bench and carried them away, rocking on a magic sailboat out to sea under the crystalline moonlight. It was the power in her arms, the moonlight in her grey eyes, that little breath of air when she almost laughed. His hand smoothed back down her side to the curve of her back…and found the gun.

Sanity reasserted itself. Stakeout. Horrible monstrous killer. Bait.

Horowitz broke the kiss, gasping for a breath.

"Right," Harvey said, sounding a little breathless herself. Good to know he hadn't lost his touch. Horowitz fought the hammering pulse in his blood, trying to remember what he was supposed to be doing, all his training…at this point he'd settle for his name. Started with an H, right?

Harvey grasped the earpiece and stuck it back in her ear. "I'm here, Paul, quit your bitching."

The earpiece squawked louder than ever. Harvey winced and cupped a hand over her ear. "It's coming," she whispered. "Grab me."

Horowitz grinned. "Yes ma'am." He slid his hands around her waist again, and she grinned back at him—grinned! By the stars! Screw the popo-whatever, this was possibly the best stakeout of his life. Not that that was saying much.

She pressed her cheek up against the side of his face, her breath whispering past his ear. He shuddered against her and felt her hand descending down between their bodies. His heart hammered until he realized she was carefully pulling her gun from its holster.

"Don't move," she whispered, flicking the safety off with the gun still hidden between her chest and his.

Her left arm crept around his back, ostensibly as a caress—but it felt more protective to him now.

"Visual acquired," she murmured, and with their ears so close he could hear Vaughn almost as well as she could. "Shadow form, twenty feet away."

Vaughn's tinny voice said something about moving in.

"Not yet," Harvey said. "Still in shadow form. We can't hurt it until it's solid." She paused for more squawking. "Thirty feet. What's your ETA?"

Horowitz tried to turn his head, but her arm around his shoulder tightened, stopping him. "Don't," she said. "Don't…turn around."

Was it possible a moment ago he'd been kissing her? Now he was frozen in terror. He felt horribly exposed, his back to the deepening shadows of the park. Was it all a bunch of crazy bullshit? Were they literally jumping at shadows? Was it really some weird Tanzanian thing? He couldn't believe that. It might be a random crazy guy, it might be nothing but shadows, and he couldn't turn his head to see for himself. His life depended on this woman, this crazy soldier girl in his arms.

Suddenly he found he was okay with that part.

"Twenty feet."

Her left arm tightened against his back. "Move your hands off me," she whispered.

"If I had a nickel…" he whispered back, obeying. That light breath of air said she was laughing again, but her body was back to that tense band of muscle. He slid his own hand to his sidearm, the back of his neck crawling.

A horrible screech split the air, as a burning acrid stench suddenly overwhelmed them. Harvey's arm shoved hard against Horowitz's back, propelling him off the bench and onto the ground. Harvey leaped up onto the bench and fired in two-handed stance.

Horowitz rolled over and stared at hell itself.

Giant and black, its wings stretched at least ten feet across. It rose above the bench, screeching from its twisted beak below a single strange orange eye that seemed to glow in the reflection from the river lights. Covered in sleek black fur, it reached toward Horowitz with clawlike hands.

His horrified gaze went lower. He saw what it had for him.

Horowitz fired his own gun from his prone position. He struck one of the wings, tearing a hole in the thin, fibrous material. The popobawa screeched and banked toward Harvey.

She fired into its trunk, hitting it at least three times. "Now would be a good time!" she shouted. Horowitz realized she was talking to Vaughn and the others. Where the fuck were they?

The popobawa rose higher—the bullets hurt it, but didn't seem to be doing much about killing it.

Horowitz struggled to his feet. "Not real," he whispered. "It can't be real…"

That horrid orange eye focused entirely on Horowitz, malevolent and filled with a strange fury that hadn't been there a moment before. The popobawa dove again, screeching, its claws reaching for him.

Harvey fired, tearing through the wings, but it struck Horowitz hard, knocking him off his feet back onto the ground.

Its nightmarish face screeched above him, its breath the foul stench of dead things, mixed with the dusty rotted smell of its fur-covered body. *Like the world's most hideous bat,* he thought, trying to lift his gun against its body. He pressed the gun barrel against its trunk.

Just as he fired, something knocked the popobawa off him. The bullet tore through fibrous wing instead, and he heard Harvey cry out.

Oh shit. He'd shot her.

Horowitz scrambled to his feet. The popobawa was on the ground, wrestling in and out of shadows with Harvey. He aimed, but couldn't risk a shot. It screeched and its claws flashed; Harvey cried out again.

On the ground, Horowitz saw her earpiece. He grabbed it fast and jammed it in his ear.

"Goddammit, where the fuck are you geniuses?" he shouted.

"Horowitz, that you? We're on our way!" Vaughn said.

"Screw 'on your way,' it's killing Harvey!" Horowitz yelled.

"Then you fucking kill it!" Vaughn ordered.

Horowitz rolled his eyes, tracking the popobawa with his gun. "No shit Sherlock, bullets don't work, what do you suggest?"

"I don't know, hit it with something!" Vaughn retorted.

Horowitz ran forward and kicked the popobawa hard in the side.

It raised its hideous beak, screeching like a deranged owl. It pulled away from Harvey, crouching as if to fly at him.

Horowitz shot it twice more in the trunk. It screamed, rolling away between the trees.

"Report, Horowitz!" Vaughn was practically screaming. Past the circle of trees at the edge of the park, Horowitz could see the three of them running full-speed along the cobblestone wharf, packing enough heavy arms to get them stopped by any cop…if he'd had cops in the area.

Horowitz ran over to Harvey. She struggled to her knees, shaky and slashed with blood. "I'm okay," she whispered, breathless. He helped her to the bench while her shaking hand reached for the gun at the small of her back.

"'Okay,' she says." Horowitz checked her over in the dim glow of the faraway streetlight. "I shot you, I know it."

Vaughn's response in his ear was blue with profanity.

Horowitz saw something move out of the corner of his eye, and instinctively he protected Harvey, trying to aim his gun at every shadow that might seem to move. He heard footsteps—it was the Three Stooges, running up the riverwalk as fast as one can run carrying an M-4.

"About time," Horowitz said as a bizarre shivering fit struck him. He gestured with his gun barrel toward the shadows between the trees. "It vanished over there."

Roberts and Stover fanned out between the trees, Roberts aiming some kind of gizmo that resembled a radar gun.

Vaughn knelt on the ground in front of Harvey, looking for all the world like a man about to propose marriage. He shone a penlight in Harvey's eyes.

"Get that fucking thing outta my face," she said with something like her usual growl.

"That's my girl," Vaughn said, grinning. "How bad are ya, Harvey?"

"Ninety percent," she said. "Scratches to the side, bumps and bruises. Bullet graze on the arm, no big. It compressed me with its weight and I couldn't breathe, no leverage to get free." She pointed at Horowitz. "Saved my ass. Be nice to him, Iceman."

Vaughn stood up and stared at Horowitz, but his gaze was decidedly less friendly than before. "Thank you."

Roberts and Stover trudged back up the hill. "Fucker is gone," Roberts said. "It went to shadow mode. We won't get it again tonight."

Horowitz holstered his gun, mostly because he really needed to sit down and wait for the world to stop spinning. "It was…it was really a monster," he said, still incredulous.

"And it's nicely fixated on you now," Vaughn said.

Harvey muttered an oath. "You even said it, right? You said, 'It can't be real.'"

Horowitz looked at her. "Yeah. I was a little freaked, excuse me."

"No, it's definitely going to hunt you now," Harvey said. "It's infuriated by people saying it doesn't exist. It marks them for its victims. Really pisses it off."

"Fuckin' glory hound," Stover said. "Oughta get it a publicist, maybe it'd stop fucking men up the—"

"Stow it," Vaughn ordered. "Parish is right, we're done for the night. You two wrap up the shit, pick up the shell casings and haul back to the motel. I want you rested for tomorrow night." He turned to Horowitz. "You are staying with us tonight."

Horowitz sighed. "I'm betting I have no choice?"

"Not unless you want to wake up with the popobawa in your bed." Vaughn leveled an icy stare at Horowitz. "It really wants you now."

"Can it, Iceman," Harvey said, standing up. "Horowitz, ride with me. The rest of you do as you're told."

The ride back to the motel was quiet. Horowitz was trying to sort out what he'd seen, and he wasn't doing so well with it. In twelve years on the force, he'd drawn his weapon only twice and never had to fire. For a moment he tried to imagine filling out the forms and reports on this incident, and stifled an inappropriate—and somewhat hysterical—giggle at the thought of "description of suspect."

He glanced over at Harvey. She'd shrugged off the leather jacket, and blood seeped through the makeshift bandage Roberts had wrapped around her arm. A few inches over and she'd be in critical condition or dead. She was dealing with that part better than he was.

At the motel, Roberts and Stover had the guns laid out on one of the beds before they even walked in. For some reason, Vaughn had changed from his camouflage into a suit. It didn't look right on him. "I've got to report to Blackfire," he said.

"Give the pencil-pushers our best," Stover griped. "Tell 'em it's a good thing we don't need more than one sonic array per team."

"Stow it," Harvey said, and Stover subsided, but not without a sullen look at Vaughn.

Vaughn ignored him, taking another look at Harvey's arm. "Parish, you get a good look at this?"

"She should be all right if she takes it easy," Roberts said. "Which means she's probably going to need real meds soon, 'cause Harvey never takes it easy."

"Standing right here, perfectly capable of hearing you," Harvey said.

Roberts ignored her, looking directly at Vaughn. "You tell Blackfire we need a goddamn medic more than we need a second sonic array."

"I'll tell them again," Vaughn began, but Roberts was on his feet.

"No, tell them this," Roberts said, getting in Vaughn's face. "Tell them we needed a fifth tonight, so we let a civilian in on the operation who ended up shooting our second-in-command."

Horowitz winced.

"And if that bullet had hit mid-chest she'd be dead now, because I can't fake it through a gunshot wound," Roberts snapped. "We need a fifth, someone with medical training. Or next time we lose someone. Maybe someone we can't afford to lose."

"Enough," Harvey snapped. "We can't afford to lose anyone, Parish."

Roberts was silent a moment, then grinned at her. "I dunno. I could stand to lose Stover."

"Fuck you too," Stover said from the far bed, where he was cleaning two handguns.

"Concerns are noted and logged," Vaughn said, straightening his tie. "I have a meeting. Enjoy the luxurious accommodations." He stepped out into the cool night air.

"He's kidding, right?" Horowitz asked.

Roberts reclined on one of the narrow beds. "Hell, this is paradise after Venezuela. Remember that dump, Harvey?"

"I remember that Stover snores," Harvey said. "That's why I told Vaughn I don't bunk with you two anymore." She stretched. "I'm outta here. Good night, boys. Get some sleep."

"Where's he sleeping?" Stover asked, pointing a hopefully-unloaded gun in Horowitz's general direction. "He ain't sleeping with me."

"I'm already sleeping," Roberts said from the other bed.

"God, it's like fucking kindergarten in here," Harvey said. "C'mon, Detective, you can sleep in Vaughn's bed, at least until he gets back. I think there's a couch in there anyway."

Horowitz did not miss the look Roberts and Stover shot at each other as they left Room 23 and went next door.

While the first room was covered in equipment and sloppy, this room was pin-straight. Two identical duffels sat at the foot of each neatly-made bed. It looked like nobody had slept in the room yet, save for the duffels. Or perhaps they were simply treating it like a military barracks.

Harvey went to the large mirror over the sink and looked at her arm, peeling back the bandage.

Horowitz hovered behind her. "I am so sorry," he said. "I didn't—"

"Friendly fire, it happens," Harvey said crisply. "I'll pop a few antibiotics so it doesn't infect. Just another scratch."

"Just a scratch," Horowitz said, incredulous. "I shot you."

"And I used you as bait for a rapist demon, I think we're even." She faced him, the wall clearly back up behind those lovely grey eyes. Wolf eyes, cool and detached, yet with live fire burning behind them. "Don't freak out too much, Horowitz. We need you clear tomorrow."

"Adam," he corrected.

She blinked. "Excuse me?"

"My name is Adam," he said. "And you're Sara. At least when we're away from the rank and file, can we use first names?"

After a brief hesitation, she nodded. Then she walked past him to the bed nearest the door and opened her duffel. She started taking off weapons and he pretended not to watch.

"This is what you do, then," Horowitz said. "You fight things like this. All the time."

"That's Blackfire," she said, removing the clip from the Beretta. "Contracted to the U.S. Department of Defense. They call us in when something is a little too extraordinary for standard procedure."

"Military?" he asked.

"Ex," she corrected. "You were right on that. I was a Marine, reassigned to Blackfire after…well. After I caught their attention."

"How was that?" Horowitz sat down on what he presumed was Vaughn's bed.

"Djinn," she said shortly. "You probably know it as a genie."

Horowitz gaped. "Three wishes, lamp and all that."

Harvey looked at him, and something awful clouded those grey wolf's eyes. "It was a draw."

Horowitz stared at the blank television for a moment. "So genies are real, giant rapist bat-things are real… What else is real?"

She didn't answer, laying the Beretta and its magazine on the table next to her bed.

"What's real?" he repeated. "Ghosts? Vampires? The Loch Ness monster?"

"All real, though she really hates being called a monster," Harvey replied.

Horowitz decided to just let that go. "Witches?"

"Very friendly and mostly harmless, unless you threaten to drop a house on their sisters. They don't think it's funny." Harvey pulled a small knife out of a pocket somewhere…he didn't want to think where she'd hidden it.

"Demons. Poltergeists. Leprechauns. Bigfoot. They're all real," he mused.

"Don't be silly," she said. "There's no such thing as leprechauns."

Horowitz stared at her for a long moment, and finally burst out laughing. Harvey cracked a thin smile—two in one night!—and he laughed even harder.

"Shh, don't make me sedate you," Harvey said finally, and his laughter tapered off. She smiled then for real, and the smile lit up her face in a way that made her seem utterly different. Younger—his own age, even. He realized he had no idea how old she actually was.

He kept watching her as she moved around the room, seemingly finding little tasks to keep occupied. But there was another question he had to ask.

"How do you sleep at night, knowing the thing under the bed is real?" he asked.

"Bourbon," she said crisply.

"Seriously," he said, catching her wrist in his hand as she passed by.

Harvey stopped then, sitting down beside him. "I can sleep because my men are on the other side of that wall," she said. "I can sleep because we have each other's backs. They're my team, my family. We've seen some serious shit together. My world has demons and popobawa—yours has skeezy child molesters and drug-crazed idiots shooting a clerk for forty bucks in the till. How do *you* sleep at night, knowing *those* monsters are out there?"

"You've got a point," Horowitz admitted.

But then, he would have said anything just to keep her talking. He hadn't let go of her wrist, he realized, his fingers stroking the skin inside her arm, surprisingly soft. Her eyes held him, grey and cool, like the stillness of a forest after a spring rain leaves mist between the trees.

She turned her own hand, letting it trace his fingers ever so lightly. Her touch erased the memory of the popobawa, dispelling the strangeness and horror of its existence with the energy growing between them.

"Aw hell," she sighed, and leaned forward to kiss him.

It was like before, only even more powerful. Like they were swept up together away from the sordid little motel and crazy awful night into that quiet stream that held them apart from everything else in the world. Now there was no voice in the earpiece, no duty to remember.

Instead there was *her*, the strength and dominance in her body, pressing him onto her bed with a force that excited him even more. He met her hard and full, his clothes shed as fast as he could manage. This time when he pressed against her curves, nothing was between them. Nothing to stop them.

It was intense, a fierce coupling that drove them together, passionate euphoria resonating through him like nothing he had felt before. They rose together, pounding through the waves that coursed through them. He had that sense again of being on a sailboat only they could feel, of the vastness of the ocean separating them from the world. The boat was spinning, the world was spinning out of control and the only thing he could cling to was her, the power and beauty of her.

He cried out softly, unable to hold it in. His hands tightened on the spread beneath him as she shuddered to a stop. For a moment she lay full-length on him, that awful tension ebbing away from her like water flowing out of a cup.

Then she slipped off him and lay pressed against his side, his arm curled around her, and for a moment she seemed at peace. The sail was full, and the world's spinning slowed nearly to a stop.

Horowitz drifted awake in the dark motel room, and it was at least a minute before he realized they weren't alone.

He startled upright at the shadow across the room.

"Very disappointed," Vaughn said quietly from the chair beside the small table. The light from the bathroom backlit him, leaving his face in shadow. "Both of you slept right through when I came in. Sloppy of you. Totally unlike her."

Horowitz glanced down at Harvey. She was still asleep, her face peaceful in a way he hadn't seen for even an instant when she was awake. She had pulled on a tank top and underwear before falling asleep, but the sheet covered her to her neck.

Horowitz felt ridiculous, like a kid caught hiding in the closet by his girlfriend's father. "Uh, Vaughn…"

"Shut up, you idiot," Vaughn said tersely. "You wake her up and you'll have bruises to show for it."

Horowitz was pretty sure he had bruises already, but he wasn't about to tell Vaughn that. What was he supposed to do? Declare his intentions? What the hell were his intentions? There was an unreal cast to the entire night, starting long before he and Sara… He quickly tried to think of something else before he embarrassed himself.

Too late.

"Lie down, Horowitz," Vaughn said in that maddeningly calm voice. Feeling supremely stupid, Horowitz lay down. Somehow that was easier, talking when he couldn't see Vaughn's impassive, shadowed face.

"I don't know if we violated some protocol or something, but if so I was unaware—" he began.

"Do you ever shut up?" Vaughn snapped—but quietly, tempering his tone. "I knew before I left, you moron. You've been gazing at her like a lovestruck private since we arrived. It's why I left."

Horowitz frowned at the ceiling. Then his heart triphammered in his chest.

"Attracted to sex," he whispered.

"Do me a favor and don't tell Harvey," Vaughn said tightly. "I'm not sure if she can kick my ass or not, but I'm in no mood to find out."

Horowitz clenched his fists on the fugly coverlet. "Just bait again. God, you are one cold-blooded motherfucker, you know that?"

"As a matter of fact, I do," Vaughn said.

"She will completely kick your ass," Horowitz declared, but softly. He didn't want Harvey waking up during this conversation any more than Vaughn did.

"Believe me when I say this was not my top choice," Vaughn said with more than a little heat in his tone.

A light breeze drifted over Horowitz's face, and he realized the window was open. "Shit," he whispered.

"Don't move." Vaughn's voice was very low. The bathroom light clicked off, and the only light now was the moonlight, bathing the room in its cold white glow and leaching the color from everything in its path. The shadows fell everywhere, and some of them moved.

Don't move. Sure, don't move. Horowitz spied his gun lying on the bedside table. It was within reach, but he didn't dare twitch.

Shadows danced around the room. A passing car shone its headlights, eldritch patterns moving across the ceiling and walls. Horowitz heard Vaughn's chair creak.

Something touched Horowitz's arm. It was scaly but warm, with long talon-like nails scraping along his skin. It was the most horrible sensation he had ever felt, that talon scraping along his inner arm and digging into the blanket at his waist.

Horowitz tried to remain still, his heart pounding. He wanted to look around, but it seemed all he could see was Sam Weller and what was left of him. The blanket slid lower slowly, tugging past his mid-thigh. That horrible smell was back, acrid and choking.

Mentally Horowitz planned how he could flip over and reach the gun in one fast motion. He'd do it in five seconds. Five heartbeats. What the fuck was Vaughn doing? Waiting for it to kill him?

A talon touched his bare leg.

That was enough for Horowitz. He scrabbled over Harvey to grab at the gun.

But the popobawa was faster, slamming him face-down into the mattress. His hand succeeded only in knocking the gun to the ground as the talons dug deep into his sides. Hot blood coursed under his belly into the sheets.

Now Harvey was awake—how long had she been conscious? She fired a gun she'd had under her pillow—damn, he should have reached for that instead. Some part of Horowitz was still a cop, trying to fight even as the talons ripped into his back, shoving the blankets lower. He struggled, horrid visions of the dead men flashing before his eyes, of

Sam Weller's intestines outside his body. His heart pounded in his chest.

Harvey's gun was joined with another—Vaughn, he presumed, firing from the other side of the room. The popobawa twisted and screamed, a dark horror rising above the bed.

Harvey stopped firing long enough to reach between the bed and the bedside table, pulling something out—what the hell was it? A crowbar? Whatever it was, she slammed it into the popobawa and it flew off Horowitz, screeching.

He tried to move, and found his limbs were heavy and useless. Warm, sticky blood coursed from the slashes in his back and sides and hot pain rode in waves through his gut.

"Harvey, get the fuck out of the way!" he heard Vaughn shout.

Horowitz turned his head to the right and saw Harvey hacking at the popobawa with a long, curved sword at least three feet long. She stabbed it again and again as it tried to fly out the open window, where Stover and Roberts were waiting with what looked like a giant net made of some kind of shiny silver material.

"Harvey, goddammit!" Vaughn shouted.

Harvey wasn't listening. The popobawa slashed at her with its talons and she swung the sword, neatly severing three of its clawed fingers. It recoiled, screaming, and she drove forward, skewering it through the midsection into the wall.

It writhed, pinned on the wall like the world's most grotesque butter-fly. For a second both Harvey and the popobawa were silhouetted in the moonlight, locked in their last second of combat, the deadly dance fading even as its thrashing slowed to a stop.

That's when Horowitz finally grayed out, feeling the coldness steal over his body as the blood soaked deeper into the bed beneath him.

As darkness swept over his vision, he saw Harvey turn toward him, the moon beams falling over her shoulders in a shower of cold silver light. A wolf's moon.

Juan Hernandez was sitting beside his hospital bed when Horowitz woke up.

"I told you this was a bad fucking idea," he said quietly.

Horowitz practiced breathing in and out a couple of times and tested his limbs before replying. "How long?" he whispered.

"About two days, short a few hours," Hernandez said. "I just got here this morning, once those Blackfire fuckers bothered to tell me where the hell you were."

Horowitz moved a little and was rewarded with stabbing pain in his sides and back. "How bad?"

"Moderate blood loss, but no permanent damage. Something like two hundred stitches, I don't know," Hernandez said. "You gotta not scare me like that, buddy. Can't go to all the trouble of breaking in a new partner."

"I'll do my best," Horowitz said. "Are they gone?"

"They're gone," Hernandez confirmed. "Tore out of here. It was that woman came to tell me where you were. She wouldn't say nothing, and the assistant chief himself told me not to ask. So I'm not asking. But any time you want to talk, I am a giant ear."

Horowitz tried to speak again and coughed instead. Hernandez hustled to get him a cup of water—a little too quickly, belying the easy-going tone in his voice. Hernandez held the cup to Horowitz's mouth and helped him sip.

When Hernandez laid the cup on the little rolling table beside his bed, Horowitz saw something shiny and metal lying on it. He grasped it, turning it over in his hand.

It was a small metal disc engraved with a vaguely-Christian symbol he'd never seen before, and a small amber crystal attached by a short chain.

"What's this?" he asked, showing it to Hernandez.

Hernandez frowned at it. "It looks like a St. Christopher's medal, but the symbol is kind of screwed up. Since when are you Catholic?"

"It would be a shock to my rabbi." Horowitz stared at the disc more closely. A slight pressure to the latch snapped it open like a sideways locket, with the hinge on the top.

Inside it read, "The road of life is long and hard. I choose the path that serves. I pray for guidance and protection, wherever I may go, whatever I may do."

Horowitz snapped it closed again, and the amber crystal flashed a tiny bright light for a bare second.

"Guidance and protection," he whispered, clasping it in his fist.

INTERLUDE: DEAR KATRINA

DEAR KATRINA

Dear Katrina...

Parish's hand paused, his pen hovering over the crisp white sheet. He was seized with the overwhelming urge to rip the smooth blank paper into pieces, or crumple it into a ball and aim for the trash can on the far side of the featureless barracks room, where it would join at least four other balled-up sheets with few words scribbled on them.

He fought off the urge, because he was not going to waste yet another sheet of paper, not when he had only written *Dear Katrina* on it. That was just goddamn stupid.

Dear Katrina: From the day you were born, you were the light of my life.

Cliché. Meaningless. The thing everyone says. Worse: She'd never believe it.

Dear Katrina: I'm sorry I was gone so much that you barely recognize me. Now it's likely you'll never see me again. Have a good life. So long, Dad.

It had the benefit of truth. But there had to be more to say than that. Parish took a swig from the beer that Vaughn had nabbed for him from the officers' club. At Parish's rank, it was just Bud Light pisswater. Whatever weird microbrew shit this was, it was definitely a step above that. As last drinks go, it wasn't bad.

Dear Katrina...

God, was he this much of a fucking coward? Never mind the fights he'd survived, the wounds, the lost comrades, the long nights where he couldn't sleep, the bright sharp stabs of terror when he contemplated this next mission. What was all that compared to writing a letter to a teenage girl?

Dear Katrina… If you're receiving this letter, it means I never had the chance to say the things to you I always wanted to say.

Better. Straightforward and truthful, and maybe that's what was needed. A dash of truth. She deserved that much, didn't she?

It means I died. I can't tell you how or why, and whoever delivers this letter won't have any answers for you, either. I beg you not to seek them out, not to try to solve whatever mystery might be shrouded around what happened to me. Maybe you won't even want to, because God knows I was barely there to begin with. But trust me when I say that nothing you find out will make it right, or better, or even sane.

He paused, and then scratched out the last sentence. Forget the mission. Forget what he was about to do. She wouldn't have any reason to care. There were more important things to say. "Don't screw this up," he said aloud to the empty room, and took another swig of the beer. "You only get one shot."

God knows I was barely there to begin with.

I want you to know I'm okay with it. Being dead, that is. It's not quite what I hoped for, but I know what I'm doing is important. That's probably not much comfort for you, but I want you to know why I had to volunteer. You have to know why I was gone so much, why your mother fell out of love with me. Why I abdicated my life as your father for something else.

I owe you that much, and more.

Rambling. Backing and filling, dancing around the real message. Parish reached for the page, ready to ball it up and aim for the trash can, two points.

Then he glanced up at the clock, which told him 1600 was less than half an hour away. Maybe if he kept filling pages with nonsense, he could waste his last chance to speak the truth. They'd come for him, and Katrina would have nothing but useless balls of paper.

"Fuck that," he muttered.

I always loved you, Katrina. Please don't ever think I was gone because I didn't want to see you. I've tried to think of a way to say what I felt, and I never was any damn good at words. I just know that from the day you were born, you changed the way my universe moved. Does that sound weird?

Yes. Fuck it—he was committed now.

Everyone in this world walks about as the center of their own personal universe, and everything else sort of revolves around them. Friends, family, school, work—it's all in orbit. That's not ego; it's just the way the human mind operates.

But you changed the orbits of my planets, little dancer. I was on leave when you came, thank God, because I couldn't have borne knowing that your mother was in labor and I was on some godforsaken base on the other side of the planet. I was there when you were born, and I heard your first cry, and from the moment your big brown eyes first looked at me, you had my heart.

I won't lie and tell you I had no choice. There was always a choice. I could have mustered out, could have taken my little pension, could have even turned down this mission. I could have hung the uniform in the closet and gone to sell insurance in an Atlanta suburb. I would have had you and your mother, a small house with a fence, and a dog. I'd have barbecued on Sunday afternoons, taken you to the ball game, and maybe been able to sleep at night.

I think about that sometimes, usually when the nights are long, in the Philippines when the storms are raging, or in a crappy motel when the sirens blare past the thin walls. I think about the life I could have had, take it out of my mental shoebox like a photograph and look at it. I try not to do it too much, like it'll fade if it's exposed too much. But I can't help it, that little snapshot of that other life, where I didn't have do what I do.

You always had the starring role.

He paused for a quick glance at the clock. 1546.

You can't explain "duty" to a baby. You can't use "honor and service" with a toddler. I tried to explain to your mother, but like I said, I never was any good at words. I needed to show her why I couldn't pass up the opportunity that the mission presented. Not an opportunity for me, of course; the opportunity to make a difference, to protect people in a more direct, meaningful way than any other I know, more than a cop, more than a firefighter or even a soldier.

I don't blame your mom, little dancer.

Parish paused again, and took an extra-heavy swig of the beer. He'd promised himself he would be honest in this letter, his very last chance to be straight with her. Was it really honest to say there was no blame? That was another picture he didn't want to look at, and the stab under his heart when he thought about signing the papers, the coldness in her eyes as she accepted them back from him.

I don't blame your mom, little dancer. I was gone for whole years of your life, things I'll never get back. They are the great regrets of my life. I know you probably don't believe that, and that's fair.

But you should know I wept over the pictures your mom sent me, and even more when the pictures stopped coming. She had a right to a life, and when she asked me to let her go, I agreed.

I never stopped loving your mom. I know she doesn't believe that, either, but I want you to know it, because you're so like her. Voice and eyes and smile, I look at you and I see your mother as she was when I met her. There are days when I wish I had fought for her, for us, wish I hadn't just let her go. But I also knew I was too far gone then, too deep in the things I can't tell you even in this letter. I could never give her the life she deserved. The life I dreamed about at night.

Parish looked back up at the clock. 1551. Nine minutes until they came for him. That pinprick of fear was now an icicle right in the center of his heart, and his stomach roiled with it. He'd been doing this long enough not to pretend he wasn't afraid. Only a fool pretends he isn't afraid. The trick is not to let the fear stop you.

He bent back to the page. There was more to say and not enough time. Never enough time.

I saw you when you were twelve. It was the Nutcracker, when you were the only girl in your ballet class picked for the big stage performance. I was lucky, and we weren't far away. My commander gave me a one-day leave, and I was there, way in the back where you couldn't see me.

Parish couldn't help grinning, remembering how Harvey had pushed through the damn paperwork to give him a twenty-four-hour pass in the middle of an operation. Chicago was one fucked-up mission to begin with, and Vaughn wanted to cancel the pass. Harvey told him if he canceled Parish's pass, she'd staple Vaughn's tongue to the bar table. Parish wasn't absolutely sure if she was kidding, and neither was Vaughn. They'd finally compromised on a twelve-hour pass, which was barely enough time to see the show.

You looked like an angel, twirling about in the fake snow under the spotlight. You were the only Black girl on the stage, a beautiful ebony swan among all the ducklings. I stood there with tears streaming down my face, and when they buzzed me to return to the mission, I didn't want to go. I swear I didn't.

Truth. Truth above all. 1554.

You've grown into an amazing young woman, Katrina. I know your mom did right by you, and I could always rest easy knowing she was taking such good care of you and teaching you all the things you needed to know. I don't have any right to be proud of you, but that never stopped a father from busting his buttons over his little girl, and I'm no exception.

You're going to do great things at school and in life, and someday there'll be a young man who looks at you the way I looked at your mom. He'll move heaven and earth for you.

I wish I could be there to see it. I wish I could have back those years I missed. I wish I could talk to you one time, just to tell you all the things in this letter that you may not ever receive.

A father only has a short window of time to hold his daughter's hand, to be her hero. It's gone much too fast, and only a true fool would waste it on something as nebulous as "duty."

I guess that's really what I wanted to say, little dancer. I was a fool, and I'm sorry. If there's an afterlife at all, I'll watch out for you as much as the Almighty lets me. When you finish school, when you marry that dashing young man, when your own little ones are born, you might get the feeling that someone is watching over you and smiling with all the love in the world.

And you'll be right.

Parish stared at the paper, pen still poised over the empty space at the bottom of the page, as the clock ticked over to 1602. He was still staring at it when Vaughn knocked discreetly on the door and came into his quarters.

Parish didn't look up. "Doctor Death fussing for me?"

Vaughn never used the nicknames. "Dr. Milan is anxious for your appearance, yes. I told him he could wait until Christmas if that's what it took. You take all the time you need, Parish."

Parish's hand hovered over the sheet, but the pen didn't move. "I think I've said all I can say." He looked up directly into Vaughn's eyes. "You'll make sure she gets it?"

Vaughn rested his hand on Parish's shoulder. "Straight to your black box in today's dispatches. You have my word." He paused. "Parish, you do not have to do this. We can find another guinea pig for Milan's science fair project. You can take a little more time, think about it, maybe talk it over with Harvey—"

Parish laughed out loud and swilled the rest of the beer. "The last thing I need to do is talk about it with Harvey. I like my teeth just the way they are."

A ghost of a smile crossed Vaughn's face. "Noted and logged."

Parish bent to the letter again.

Have a wonderful life, little dancer. Please believe that your father loved you.

He signed it, folded and sealed the envelope, then gave it to Vaughn. As Vaughn put it in his jacket pocket, Parish almost grabbed for it back—too much, it was too much.

Fuck that. Truth above all, right?

Parish stood and shrugged on his uniform jacket. "Time to dance?"

BLACKFIRE

1

Sara Harvey thought she was doing pretty well until the corpse started in with the puns.

All she wanted at the end of her day was a quiet drink, something to relax the muscles and the mind. Each day she managed to find something to do, something to fill the endless hours between sunup and sundown. The least she could get as a reward was a simple drink in relative peace.

On a good morning, Sara woke when the encroaching sunlight crept across the cheery light-blue bedspread and reached her eyes. On a bad morning, she lay awake through the predawn hours, listening to the soft murmur of the waves outside her bedroom window, listening for the wordless voices of the sea.

She showered and dressed in her usual black-tank-and-camouflage whether or not she felt like getting out of bed. Discipline compelled her, but like as not she'd be pacing the floors through the dawn anyway, so there was no point in lounging.

The ocean breeze floated through the open windows of the rose-covered cottage, carrying the constant rushing sound of the waves and the smell of the salt water mixed with the fading roses. The cottage was pleasant enough, though as far as Sara was concerned the kitchen was essentially a large room to hold the coffeemaker and the bottle of Jack Daniels. She drank her breakfast on the back porch beneath a bower of roses, watching the early morning rays dance across the ocean below the line of cabins.

Then she wandered.

Sara roamed the island every day, browsing a bookstore on Broad Street or stopping to listen to the street musicians on Main. She took a different path each day just in case anyone was tracking her. Habit.

There was a candle shop on Washington Street. Sara avoided it. It was irrational, but she couldn't help it. The smell of scented candles made her heart pound too hard in her chest.

Lunch was a picnic on the beach, as far away from the tourists as her bicycle would take her. The landlady arranged a daily lunch of albacore tuna or roast beef on ciabatta bread, a wedge of Danish cheese, a crisp tart Granny Smith apple and a microbrewed beer kept cold in a slim foam sleeve. It waited on her porch every morning, no matter how early Sara rose.

Much of the sandwich and at least half the cheese ended up fed to the gulls, who always appreciated her.

The beer did not go to waste, however.

The landlady was a plump, friendly island woman named Martha, who managed a half-dozen cottages sprinkled along the beach. Sara's tiny cottage was within sight of the ocean behind a low picket fence, but the upstairs could be barricaded against assault if necessary. Sara kept the guns in the upstairs closet. Not that she ever went about unarmed, but no one from the bookstore owner to the barkeep at the Brotherhood of Thieves could have found the Beretta on her person.

Martha insisted on cleaning the cottage once a week, even though Sara made no mess at all. It was the longest she had slept anywhere since leaving home at eighteen, unless you counted her quarters in Farson, and she took care of the slightest spill or misplaced pillow. On the mornings Martha cleaned, Sara delayed her departure, sitting on the porch a while longer and watching the ocean as Martha changed the sheets and swept the floors. Sometimes Martha sang to herself as she cleaned, a pleasant on-key alto switching to humming when she couldn't remember the words.

Each week Martha asked whether Sara wouldn't like something a little different in her daily lunch, or perhaps a breakfast or dinner menu. By the third week, she even invited Sara to dinner at home with her husband. Sara politely declined in as few words as possible.

In the afternoons, Sara rode her bicycle out to Steps Beach and latched the bike to the railing before descending to the water. There she sat, staring at the endless blue expanse of the Atlantic, the dance of the waves below.

She watched. She listened. Occasionally she spoke to the ocean, unless she heard footsteps approaching. This time of year the tourists were growing scarce—most of the Americans in their oversize shorts with cameras perpetually hanging around their necks had returned to their homes with their picturesque memories of Nantucket, ready to pick up the threads of their ordinary lives.

That was probably what the islanders thought of her, Sara thought. Another tourist, albeit late in the season. Someone who would stay a while, spend her money and leave without a fuss, going back to her faraway home in some place more prosaic. Sometimes a friendly shopkeeper or waitress would ask where she hailed from, and she told the lie without thinking: Virginia, near Shenandoah. They believed despite her utter lack of accent. What could she tell them, the truth?

Sara waited at the beach until an hour or so before sunset. When the first tinges of pink graced the sky, she climbed the steps as though patrolling the foothills of the Andes—it was a way to stay in shape, at least.

Then she rode out to Brant Point as fast as she could, as though racing the sun. She always reached the lighthouse before the golden rays turned amber and purple, painting the sky in its washes of color.

Sara watched the sunset from the wrong side, staring out at the Atlantic as the sun slipped over the horizon behind her. And when it was almost dark, she would go to the Brotherhood of Thieves.

She picked it because she liked the name, and because no one bothered her there. She sat alone in the large, plush couches beside the roaring fireplace and listened to the conversations at the bar, watched the couples ascending the stairs for dinner. Sometimes an enterprising fellow would offer to buy her a drink, and she politely declined. If he tried a second time, she left.

One of them followed her out into the street once. Drunk beyond all good taste and at least five years too young for her, he trailed her out to the bike rack and slobbered something about how she was too hot to be stuck up. She ignored him as she unlatched her bike.

Then he touched her arm.

Half a second later he was lying flat on the cobblestones, Sara's boot against his throat and facing the business end of her Beretta.

"Fuck off," she said. The slob nodded as fast as he could with her boot under his chin.

After a while the barkeeps spread the word, and the come-ons stopped. Sara was left alone to drink and stare into the dancing flames, watching the random patterns they formed.

She supposed they talked about her, the tourist who had been here so long, still paying a weekly rent in her rosy cabin by the sea. It cost a bleeding fortune, but it hardly mattered.

Once she tried to imagine it from their perspective, and thought they might be worried: a woman who rarely spoke and never smiled, always alone. And yet she could not bring herself to pretend a fiction for them, to assuage their concerns.

I'm not here to kill myself, she would have told them. *I'm just...waiting.*

The ocean never spoke back to her.

After many drinks at the Brotherhood of Thieves, Sara would switch to water for the last hour, just enough to ensure she could cycle back to the cabin without a problem. It would be ironic indeed if she fell off her damn bicycle and dashed her head open on Nantucket's picturesque cobblestones.

She rode through the darkness each night to her cottage by the sea. She spent the days waiting for the night, and when it came, it welcomed her. And yet it held no rest.

It didn't matter how hard she rode the bike.

It didn't matter how many steps she climbed.

It didn't matter how much she drank before the fire.

She could not sleep.

The endless roar of the ocean failed to drown out the screams, even though they were only in her head. None of them had screamed. Hissed, perhaps. The blood frothing Parish's mouth right before she shot him in the head. The dead look in Gary's eyes. Matthews' bloody ear hanging off his head by a ragged shred of flesh. Paul's voice with that horrible lisp.

Haunted. There was a ghost tour on the island, set off each day from the faux-Greek Athenaeum that served as the Nantucket library. Sara had never joined it, even in her endless wandering search for something to fill the daylight hours. What did they know about ghosts?

On the last night, Sara had less to drink than usual. A blessing in disguise. On a whim, she'd picked up a nice bottle of twelve-year-old Glenfiddich, single-malt, with which she intended to toast the ocean under the brilliant starscape. Out of habit, she still went to the Brotherhood of Thieves, but ordered only one bourbon before tossing some cash on the bar.

"Everything all right, Miss Sara?" the barkeep asked. His name was Dennis. She'd never asked, but that's what they called him when they thought she wasn't listening. He had about twenty years on Sara, with shaggy blond hair starting to run to gray and a thick beard.

"Just fine, Dennis," she replied.

"Sure you don't want me to call you a taxi?" Dennis asked.

"I've got my bike," she said, surprised. He'd never offered this before; an old hand like Dennis knew how to judge when someone had had too much, even for a bike.

Dennis gave her a cynical smile. "They got taxis with bike racks," he said. "That's a powerful fog out there tonight. Could get to be a bad ride."

Sara looked out the front window, past the hanging sign of the colonial gentleman balancing money in one hand and a miserable slave in the other. The Brotherhood of Thieves was named after a pamphlet written by a fierce abolitionist. Someone who fought against demons.

The fog was as powerful as Dennis implied. Pea soup would've been a breeze beside this thick, cottony cloudstuff that filled the street outside, barely dispelled by the replication gas lamps. Now she knew why the islanders sometimes called their home the Grey Lady.

"I can handle it," she told Dennis. He raised a skeptical eyebrow, and she gave him the cool look that stilled even Paul Vaughn in his tracks.

Well, sometimes. There was the time that… Oh, but it hurt to think about Paul.

Dennis raised his gnarled hands from the bar. "I ain't your father. You just be careful out there, Miss Sara. Fog ain't just fog here on the island—it's a living thing. Careful it don't bite."

"Noted and logged," Sara said, and tossed an extra dollar on the bar. "Take care of yourself, Dennis."

"You too, Miss Sara." The dollar disappeared like a magic trick and Dennis smiled. Sara almost smiled back—it was the longest conversation she'd had in months.

She stepped out into the fog, and it enveloped her, a curtain of cool moist air surrounding her body and stealing inside through her shallow breaths. It was a thick gray filter over her eyes, dulling the sharp colors and bright lights along the street—like falling into someone else's dream.

Sara's trusty bicycle was right where she left it, the bottle of Glenfiddich discreetly wrapped and hidden under her light jacket in the basket. She unlocked it and pedaled slowly, as though riding underwater.

She was almost past him before she really saw him. An indistinct shadow, and anything shadow-like made her look twice. But quickly she discerned the old-fashioned cloak and tricorn hat. Another costumed reenactor, one of the historically inclined that wandered to entertain the tourists with little first-person discourses about Nantucket in the olden days, loitering in the thin yellow light of the gas lamp diffused by the thick fog.

She had already cycled past him when she realized it was awfully late for reenactors. Even at the height of the season, the tourists were well into their cups by this hour.

Slowing, Sara glanced over her shoulder.

The man in the cloak was following her.

He strolled along the cobblestone street, his heels striking hard on the stones. Sara's bike was much faster than his walk, yet he was not far behind her.

Coincidence. Don't get too paranoid yet, Harvey. Save that for the real nervous breakdown.

Funny how her internal voice still sounded like Paul.

Sara pedaled faster, her bike whizzing along the sidewalk where the concrete was smoother. In daylight she'd have stayed to the street, but no one walked at this hour, and she suddenly wanted to get back to her safe little cottage with the roses fading in the cool fall air and the sound of the sea rolling through the windows. And the guns in the upstairs closet.

Three more blocks and Sara looked over her shoulder again.

He was still only a dozen yards behind her.

That wasn't possible. He'd have to be running, and that right quickly. But he wasn't running. He strolled, he meandered. Surely he wasn't watching her from the shadows under that wide hat brim. Surely she was being paranoid.

Think, Harvey, Paul said in her head. *If he's following you, is it a good strategy to lead him to your cottage? If he already knew where you lived, he could easily wait to spring there when you're coming back tired and drunk.*

The tail meant he didn't know where she lived. Assuming he was following her at all. Therefore, leading him to the cottage was a bad plan.

Suddenly Sara put on a huge burst of speed and banked fast to the right, turning down a side street away from her usual path. She pedaled as fast as she could, cranking up to a speed that really would be unsafe if anyone wandered into her path.

She turned again, doubling back around the block in a circle. She'd come out behind him, but she wouldn't mind waiting in the shadows a few minutes until he passed out of sight, if only to make sure.

Sara pedaled a little more slowly now, coming back up to Washington Street near Main. She drifted over to the side and came to a stop past a discreetly fenced trash bin, breathing a little heavily. She peeked around the corner of the closed and dark shop—the candle shop, she saw with a wrench in her gut.

The street was empty.

Paranoia, she thought, her hand relaxing from the grip of her hidden Beretta. She straddled the bike again.

He sprang over the trash bin, flying at least fifteen feet in the air. His cloak fluttered behind him like insane bat-wings, eyes glowing bright red in the dim fog.

Sara staggered backward, her foot catching on the bike pedal. Off-balance, she was only able to get one arm free to defend herself as the springheel struck her, knocking her flat on the ground.

Its dark face split into a jolly grin, mad fire dancing in its eyes. It tore at her shirt with its taloned fingers and Sara felt hot lines of pain sizzle along her abdomen.

Wake up, Harvey! She struck at it, but couldn't seem to get any purchase. She hoicked a knee hard into what she supposed was its groin. It must have had some kind of impact, because it rolled off her with a grunt.

Sara leapt to her feet and pulled the Beretta. The fucker sprang straight up into the air just as she pulled the trigger, the report very loud in the alley. The bullet struck the cobblestones as the springheel reached the roof of the candle shop.

She tried to track it, Beretta aimed upward, but it sprang again, leaping impossibly high and fast over the rooftops and vanishing into the fog.

"Fuck me," she muttered, scanning the roof line. *A goddamn springheel in Nantucket, you have to be kidding.*

Sara heard raised voices and saw some lights down the road. Someone must have heard the shot. This was not a good place to be. She got back on the bike and debated holstering the Beretta, but she risked the bag in the basket instead so it would be within faster reach if she saw the springheel.

This time she rode directly home. It could follow her if it wanted—she'd rather have it there, where she had a damn arsenal in the closet, away from this quiet street where it could hurt the civilians.

Along the way she passed a police car, flashing lights but no siren. They might or might not find her bullet, Sara reasoned, but they'd never match it to the gun.

She rode quickly past Martha's pretty little house—also covered with roses; obviously she had a talent for them. Sara felt eyes on her and knew she was being followed.

A fucking springheel. So much for vacation.

Sara rode the bike right into the little fenced-in yard and dumped it on the grass, grabbing the bag with the Glenfiddich and the Beretta as she ran up the front steps and into the cottage.

The quiet ocean cabin was too full of shadows tonight. Sara bolted the door fast and sprinted back to the kitchen. *Lock the doors, then get to the M-4 in the closet.*

She ran through the kitchen to the door.

Red eyes stared through the back-door window.

Sara grabbed into the bag and the springheel vanished before she could get the Beretta free. Cursing, she ran out the kitchen door, dropping the bag on the small porch table and racking the slide of the Beretta.

"Come out and play, you fucker," Sara murmured, glancing to the left and right in combat stance. No sign of it. Could it be hiding in the long shadows by the fence, on the other side of the large white rock in the center of the back yard? Maybe it leapt over the fence into another yard. Thank God none of the cabins were occupied right now—all empty save for Martha's house at the end of the row.

Sara's traitor mind shimmered them into life. Parish stalked along the north side of the cottage, methodically kicking the bushes while Gary blasted a hole in anything that moved on the south side and Paul chided them both through their earpieces. She'd had Paul in her head for so many years, he was still there, still talking inside her head from the goddamn grave—

A shifting sound above, and Sara fired twice, straight up through the roses. A howl split the air as the springheel leapt from the rose bower into the back yard, crashing into the low white picket fence.

"Martha painted that fence, asshole," Sara said as she fired again.

But it sprang, impossibly fast—*faster than a speeding bullet, ha ha that's funny*, she had time to think before it slammed into her. Her gun flew out of her hand.

Very sloppy, Harvey.

She wrestled it in and out of the shadows, slamming fists into skin that felt at once hot and cold, hard and leathery, more like reptile skin than human, but oh so hot and somehow greasy. Its eyes flared again like the dancing flames of the Brotherhood of Thieves were contained inside its skull. Mad hate bound up inside its blackened skin, it wanted to burn down the world, she could see it in the grinning gape of its jaw as it inhaled—

Inhaled. *Shit.*

Sara rolled away barely in time, fetching up against the big white rock as a jet of flame issued from its mouth and set the grass on fire. Sara grabbed for her gun, but it leapt between her and the weapon. A sound like laughter came from its jagged teeth, and it coiled to spring again.

Sara scrambled for the cottage and more guns. It sprang after her, leaping faster than anything should be able to walk or fly. It hit her hard, a flare of pain across her back, and she flew forward into the little cherrywood table beside the Adirondack chair where she sat every morning.

Sara landed on the deck, the broken bottle shattered beneath her. The smell of scotch wafted up in a sickly mix with the roses twined on the bower. She felt its talons grip her jacket, dragging her away, toward the shadows where no one would see.

She grasped the remnants of the bottle.

It flipped her over and dove at her.

Sara jammed the broken bottle straight into the springheel's throat. Black blood poured out of its throat and over Sara's hands, but she pushed harder, aided by its weight pressing down on her. It choked on its own blood, flailing above her, the dancing flame in its eyes flickering and fading.

With all her strength, Sara shoved the springheel off her body and into the roses. It scrabbled at the bottleneck jutting from its throat, its black blood spraying on the crimson rose petals above it.

Sara scrambled back down the steps and grabbed her Beretta. Then she got to her feet and walked to the thrashing, dying springheel.

"That was twelve-year-old Glenfiddich, you piece of shit," she said, and blew its head off.

Sara Harvey sat in the dark and watched the ocean.

The M-4 was slung over her shoulder, but she was pretty sure she wouldn't need it. She'd only reloaded the Beretta, grabbed another sidearm for good measure, and sat on the big rock in the center of the garden, waiting.

The springheel lay in the shadows between the shattered remains of the fence and the rock. Sara kept glancing at it, just to make sure it wasn't moving, but unlike other creatures, bullets seemed pretty goddamn final. Even so, she'd followed procedure and beheaded it with her small camp axe before she made the call.

Not exactly the smoothest fight I've ever seen, Harvey.

"Shut up, Paul," Sara muttered. She took a swig from the Jack Daniels. It wasn't Glenfiddich, but it would do.

The blood hadn't completely washed off her hands. Damned resilient stuff. Blood may be thicker than water, but maple syrup and tar both cling harder than blood and this stuff seemed to be a combination of the two. She longed to go down to the ocean and trail her hands in the surf until they were washed clean, but she needed to stay with the body.

Besides, it would take more than the Atlantic to wash her hands clean.

Wow, that was fucking pathetic, Harvey, Gary bitched. Now she had Gary in her head, too. A few more voices and she could officially sign up for the rubber room.

"What do you know, I'm finally ahead," the springheel wheezed.

Sara nearly fell off the rock, scrambling to her feet and pivoting the Beretta at the springheel's head.

It was impossible. The damn thing was somehow drawing air through the tattered, stringy remains of its neck, whistling slightly as it grinned up at her. She could see the shreds of flesh moving as it drew air through the severed windpipe.

"You're dead," Sara said in disbelief. She glanced at the bottle and shook her head. "You're dead, stay dead!"

"Funny how you keep ssssaying that, Ssssara," the head lisped. "That'sss you all over." It lolled about on the grass, the empty sockets seeming to look at the bloody remnants of its body. "Then again, that'sss me all over. What a messs."

Sara shook her head hard. "No, no you're dead, I killed you, fucker, you're dead!" she shouted.

"And at breakneck ssspeed. Or wasss it an idle throat?" It grinned around its blackened teeth.

The eyes were still blackened, empty sockets; no flame danced in them. But they seemed to grin maliciously, below the gaping empty cavern of its half-destroyed skull.

Sara's gun hand shook a bit. "Dead," she insisted.

"Assss a doornail," the springheel said through its mad grin. "And yet I ssssspeak… Ssssara sssells sssseashells by the ssseashore…"

Sara shook her head, heart pounding and head spinning. The ground seemed to tilt under her feet.

The head rolled back and forth, chanting at her through its crazed grin. "You killed me and I came back, you kill me again and I come back again, but *they* never come back, do they, Ssssara by the ssseashore? Never never never never—"

"Fuck you," she whispered, and shot it in the mouth.

The head flew apart into a mess of stringy, red-black chunks and splats. Too many shots, even if Martha did sleep like the dead—oh, bad choice of words.

Sara backed away from the springheel, the horrible lisp finally silent. The part of her that remembered how to be an operative tried to analyze it: springheels were imitative, they copied the voices of people and even animals to blend into their surroundings, one mimicked a London police officer well enough to lure a young girl out of her house—

Jesus Christ, Harvey, your balloon ever fuckin' land? It was dead!

Yeah, it was dead. That didn't always stop shit from causing her trouble, God knew. But it was also decapitated, and that killed just about everything. A springheel that could keep talking after its head was cut off, that was a whole new ballgame.

You really think it was talking to you? Paul asked.

Of course, it wasn't Paul. It was never Paul. Paul wasn't in her head any more than he was speaking to her from the waves endlessly crashing up on the sand. It was never Paul when the phone rang, and it was never Paul's steps on the stairs when she heard phantom creaks in the middle of the night, and she would never hear his voice in her head again.

That meant her imagination—far too vivid for her line of work—had sailed far over the edge of "taking some time off" and into a new world of post-traumatic whatthefuckever that meant only she was desperately screwed.

"Jesus," Sara whispered, and sat down in the middle of the yard. She was still there, Beretta firmly grasped in her hand, when Blackfire arrived.

2

Nathan Thacker was a sonofabitch, and Sara didn't care if he knew exactly what she thought of him.

The cleaners already had the fence almost completely rebuilt and the sun hadn't even come close to rising. It wasn't the team Sara usually worked with; their leader was some grunt named Burns that Sara had never met and therefore did not trust. Three of Burns' minions washed the springheel's black blood off the rosebushes, occasionally swearing when the thorns got them, while Burns smoked and pointed a lot. It would have been funny if Sara had been someone else.

"You'll have to lie about the burned grass," Thacker said, looking over the back yard. "Say you knocked over the barbecue or something."

"She'll be thrilled I was cooking," Sara said.

Thacker gave her a long, appraising look Sara didn't care for at all. His blue eyes were barely lined, his hair still sandy-brown without much gray. He might be a decade older than Sara, but she felt a hell of a lot older than he looked.

Thacker leaned against the porch trellis, still with that appraising gaze. "You look thin, Harvey. You're supposed to be resting out here, not fighting monsters."

Sara rolled her eyes. "It's not like I went hunting for the goddamn thing. It followed me home like a fucking puppy. Second, I'm not resting.

I'm waiting for you to get your goddamn thumb out of your ass. Where's my dismissal?"

"Red tape," Thacker said absently, picking up a shard of the Glenfiddich bottle the cleaners had missed.

Sara slapped the shard out of his hand.

Thacker instinctively turned in a defensive posture. While Burns' hand rested lightly on his sidearm, the rest of the minions just stood there and looked at each other. Sara was mildly disappointed. There were seven of them, faceless and nameless cleaners supposedly well-trained by Blackfire, and if she'd really intended to hurt Thacker, they could have stopped her. Probably.

"Down, Harvey," Thacker said in that maddeningly calm voice. "I can still bring you up on charges."

"Fuck you," Sara said. "I want my goddamn dismissal, Thacker."

Thacker leaned back against the rose trellis, and Sara saw Schaller relax his posture a bit. "What if I said you were the best operative we ever had, and we aren't all that eager to lose you?"

"I'd say you're more full of shit than standard for this outfit," Sara retorted.

Thacker raised an eyebrow. "I'm not kidding, Harvey. You were second-in-command of the most disciplined, efficient team we've ever had."

"Disciplined." Sara laughed humorlessly. "Man, you guys are really out in space. Either that or the other teams must suck donkey balls. Either way, not my problem."

Thacker glanced around and lowered his voice. "If it's a matter of money—"

Sara held up a hand. "I'm going to pretend you didn't go there, and then I don't have to knock your teeth down your fucking throat."

Thacker was silent a moment. "Look at it from my perspective, Harvey. We took a hell of a loss at the Island, both financial and in manpower. I need to recruit a new team, and I'd like you to take it."

Sara shook her head, but Thacker didn't stop. "You'd be in command, and team leaders have a lot of discretion. You'd have your pick of new recruits. We need you, Harvey, you're—"

"The best, right," Sara finished. "Thacker, you're so full of shit it's dribbling out your ears. I didn't do a damn thing that would be any use to you. Paul Vaughn made that team, not me."

"Paul Vaughn is dead."

Sara turned on him, and for a moment Thacker took defensive posture again. Something in her eyes must have told him she was thinking about ripping his throat out with her fingernails.

Sara took a deep breath and stared at the silent black sea instead of Thacker. It made her less homicidal. "I'm no good to you, Thacker. You don't want me in the field. I'm done. Give me my fucking dismissal and you'll never see me again."

"That's what I'm afraid of," Thacker said.

Sara stared at the ocean.

"Look," Thacker said, coming up beside her. "I really have been trying to get your paperwork pushed through, in spite of my own better judgment. Merrifield is against the pension."

Sara groaned. "He's still blaming me."

Thacker ticked them off on his fingers. "Dollar value attached to the installation, the hush money, extreme sanctions, etc. He thinks you should be held accountable."

"Maybe I should," Sara said, still looking at the ocean.

"I disagree," Thacker said. "I read the reports, I read the objections to the whole project you and Vaughn filed before they even got to the Island. When the shit went down, you got the job done and saved us from a very serious situation. I don't blame you."

She looked at him. "Good. Because I blame you."

That got through Thacker's cool demeanor. His face was honestly shocked, almost hurt, if that were possible. "Sara—"

"Stow it," Sara snapped. "Am I getting my dismissal or do I need to introduce my fist to Merrifield's face?"

"How about this?" Thacker asked. "I've got this team to put together—"

"I'm not doing it, goddamn you!" Sara wished heartily for her lost Glenfiddich.

"Just help me screen them, train them, shape them into something resembling a team," Thacker said. "I've got a handful of soldiers, a couple of brainiacs and a potential leader. But they're not a team yet, and that's something you know. Help me get them moving, and I'll get your papers pushed through, Merrifield or no."

"Fuck you." Sara stalked off the porch and back into the kitchen. The bottle of Jack was still open, and she debated pouring herself another shot. It was probably a bad idea with Thacker just outside. *What the fuck,* she thought, and poured another shot anyway.

Thacker came in just as she bolted it down. He stood in the doorway, watching her.

"Spare me the lecture," Sara griped, putting the glass in the spotless sink.

"Wouldn't dream of it," Thacker said. "Wouldn't do any good anyway. It amazes me you were a Marine, Harvey—you were always too headstrong for anyone to give you orders. Except Vaughn, of course."

Sara didn't answer.

"Harvey, do this thing for me," Thacker said. "It could help with the pension."

Sara glanced at him. "Merrifield's an asshole, but is he that big an asshole? He'd pull the pension just to spite me for not dying at the Island?"

"I don't know about spite," Thacker said, opening the refrigerator and staring at the empty shelves. "He's definitely putting all the stoppers he can. Jesus, Harvey, don't you eat?"

She shut the fridge door in his face. Then she leaned against the sink with both hands braced on the edge. She found if she didn't look at Thacker too much, she didn't feel the need to beat the snot out of him. "I'll do it."

Thacker leaned forward. "What? I didn't quite—"

Sara grabbed Thacker by his jacket and shoved him against the fridge. She got right in his face and held him there, almost kissing distance, if she could stand him. "I'll do it. Then you get me my dismissal and no more bullshit about the pension. Is that clear? No. Bullshit."

"No bullshit," Thacker agreed.

Sara pulled him away from the fridge and shoved him none too gently out the kitchen door. She took great pleasure in slamming it in his face. Then she stalked through the darkened cottage toward the stairs. She knew there was another bottle upstairs.

But at the top of the stairs, she paused a moment to look back out at the sea through the half-dome window on the landing. It rolled up on the sand, black and cold, and she listened again for its wordless voices.

She would miss the sea.

3

Sara focused her binos on the quasi-clean diner windows across the empty parking lot.

It was a tiny chain diner, one of thousands littered along major high-ways and open twenty-four hours for your cheap dining pleasure. This one perched near the off-ramp of a disused highway in Nowhere, Indiana. Its overbright windows shone the only light still blazing in the dark hours long after everyone else had shut down for the night.

"Tell me what you see," Thacker said.

"What is this, remedial tracking?" Sara groused. Through the window, she could see Kay Riordan sitting at the counter, stirring what must be very bad coffee with a plastic spoon.

The waitress wandered Riordan's way with a carafe of more sludge. "Want a warm-up?" Sara heard her ask through the earpiece Riordan was wearing.

"Sure," Riordan said, moving her hand out of the way so the waitress could splash about a half-inch more coffee into her cup.

"Waitress is Paige by the nametag, no more than seventeen by the look of her," Sara said, bored. "Apron weighs heavy as she moves, which means a lot of tips, but mostly coin." Sara swept her view over the counter. "Textbooks are probably hers. Advanced-placement biology, and beat-up —not for show. She's college-bound, so she's working for the money.

Light burn on the back of her arm; can't tell at this distance if it's grease or chemical."

"She's too small of stature anyway," Thacker said.

"Whatever. I don't believe half the shit in the briefing papers anyway." Sara switched targets. "Riordan's awful. Slacks and button-down blouse blends in an office building, not here. Jeans would've been a better choice and would've given her more protection. I'd be suspicious."

"You're suspicious of everyone," Thacker muttered.

"I have reasons." Sara watched Riordan add sugar to her coffee and spill a little on the counter. Riordan swept the spill into her hand and dumped it on her saucer. "She was a waitress. Riordan, that is."

Thacker sighed. "No cheating. I said don't look at the file."

"Bite me." Sara adjusted the binos. "She cleaned up spilled sugar. She doesn't want to stick the waitress with extra work and cleans up after herself. She respects Paige without knowing her, which is identification. Either Riordan did time in an apron, or someone she knows and respects —a mother or aunt, maybe a grandmother. Female, definitely. The sort of thing men don't think of."

Thacker let that pass. "Tell me about the men."

Sara listened to Paige deliver Riordan's order to the grill. "Cook is Douglas to Paige, not Doug, and his hands look like construction. Bottom fell out of that industry here a few years ago, so this is likely not his primary choice of occupation. He winces when he straightens up from the grill—bad back, which could be the lack of knees—"

"Or could just be a bad back," Thacker pointed out.

"He smiles too much at Paige, which is creepy but not indicative of monstrosity," Sara recited.

She refocused again, this time on the janitor swabbing the floor not far from Riordan. "Working with bleach, he doesn't seem to mind the smell. He's not terribly careful, which isn't uncommon in a place like this. I can only tell so much from his ass—can I come back to him when he turns around?"

"Lazy. Whaddya want, the jaguar teeth front and center?" Thacker adjusted a dial, and they heard the sizzle of frying bacon more clearly. "Heads up. Here he comes."

A tall young man with a severely short haircut walked in from the parking lot.

"Welcome," Paige said, cheerful and bright. "Steve, would you mind moving your bucket? Thanks… Sit anywhere you like, sir."

The newcomer picked a spot at the counter a few stools away from Riordan. "It's Dan, not 'sir,'" he said with an easy grin. "Dan Jacobs, at your service, pretty miss."

Paige's plain face broke into a glorious smile. "Would you like a menu?"

"Love one," he said, winking at her.

Sara groaned. "Military cut, linebacker build—he's military or Dad was, and probably football in high school. No older than twenty-four, but he hasn't been carded in a long time. His face is older than he is."

"Ow!" Riordan jerked hard, wrapping a paper napkin around her finger. A red stain bloomed on the paper, dark enough to be seen through Sara's binos.

"You okay, miss?" Jacobs asked her, and Riordan nodded. She got up and walked toward the restroom. The napkin fluttered to the floor in front of Steve's bucket, and he picked it up. As Riordan disappeared into the restroom, Steve slipped the bloody napkin into his pocket.

"Bingo," Thacker said.

"He could just be tidy," Sara replied.

Jacobs turned on his stool and slipped his hand into his pocket. Without looking, he withdrew a small vial of liquid. The next time Steve's mop came near him, he spilled it onto Steve's bare hand.

The liquid turned bright purple.

"Fuck!" Sara shouted, grabbing for her sidearm.

"Wait!" Thacker ordered.

Steve shoved Jacobs back against the counter. Jacobs shoved back and Steve stumbled away, his entire body off balance, long stringy gray hair swinging in his face.

"What the hell!" Douglas shouted from behind the counter.

Steve grabbed the mop handle and smashed it against the edge of the counter, breaking it in half. He jabbed the broken end toward Jacobs like a wooden spear.

Jacobs reached down toward the wet floor. Before he could touch the floor, however, Douglas came running around the corner, armed only with a spatula.

"Jesus, Thacker!" Sara shouted.

Paige just stood there, staring at them with her fists jammed against her gaping mouth. Sara's estimation of her went down by the second.

Douglas leaped between Jacobs and Steve even as Jacobs reached to stop him. "Have you gone crazy, old man? Back down!" Douglas shouted.

Steve howled, a guttural sound that seemed to come from far lower than his throat. He bared his teeth like a hissing cat.

Douglas recoiled for a second as Jacobs tried to haul him out of the way. Paige finally broke her paralysis and fumbled a cell phone out of her apron pocket.

"911, what is your emergency?" Thacker said into his headset behind her. Sara shook her head and muttered to herself as Paige screamed into the phone and Douglas grappled with Steve and his mop-spear.

"Is the altercation still going on?" Thacker asked in his best official voice. "Yes, thank you miss, we'll have someone there in a minute. Stay out of the way and stay safe."

Jacobs finally succeeded in wrestling Douglas off Steve. As soon as he did, Steve howled again…and lost his concentration. His face shifted just enough for his eyes to glow a little, his teeth protruding further than should be possible for a human, ears poking free of the tangled hair.

Douglas recoiled in horror, his body getting between Jacobs and Steve again. It was just the opening Steve needed—he slapped the wooden spear upward, driving it into Douglas' side and yanking it out again.

"Aw hell," Thacker said.

Douglas fell to the side and Jacobs charged forward. Half a second later, Riordan burst out of the restroom, braced in a two-handed firing stance.

"Down!" she shouted.

Jacobs hit the floor.

Riordan fired twice, exploding two rivers of blood down Steve's uniform shirt. Steve fell backward, half into an empty booth.

"Dammit, Thacker," Sara began, but he held up a hand to silence her.

Paige screamed in a shrill, girlish voice that made Sara want to slap her. Jacobs scrabbled over to Douglas, grabbing the towel from his apron and pressing it hard against the wound.

Riordan advanced past them toward Steve, who was struggling back to his feet. "Jacobs, I need you."

"Busy here!" Jacobs leaned into Douglas' side as the cook moaned.

Riordan jerked her head at Paige. "Get over there and help."

Paige just stood there, frozen with her mouth open in preparation for yet another scream.

"Now, candy-ass!" Riordan snapped.

Sara liked her.

Riordan kept her weapon trained on Steve as he struggled toward his feet.

Steve growled again, and even through the binos Sara could see he had completely lost control. The teeth were now oversized jaguar fangs, jutting from a lantern jaw malformed by any human standard.

Paige scrambled around the counter and knelt beside Douglas. She fluttered her hands over him a second, and Jacobs unceremoniously grabbed her hands and shoved them against the towel he had pressed into Douglas' gaping wound.

"Don't move," he said.

Pivoting, Jacobs slapped his hand down into Steve's bloody footprint.

Instantly Steve fell back down, twitching on the floor.

"Don't move!" Riordan called, setting her gun down on the counter. She pulled a cigarette from her pocket and lit it.

"Now's hardly the time!" Paige protested, but Jacobs gave her a glare that shut her up, his hand still pressed into the footprint.

Riordan took a drag on the cigarette and blew the smoke at Steve.

The janitor's whole body shuddered and shriveled inside his clothes, the skin crumpling and folding in on itself. His face rippled, the teeth more prominent than ever, eyes bulging and turning orange.

He thrashed on the floor, blood pumping from the wounds in his chest.

Riordan leaned over him, blowing more smoke. Steve's flailing arm caught her in the midsection, and she flew backward, slamming hard into the corner of the counter. Riordan fell to the floor.

Jacobs scrambled toward her, letting his hand slip away from the footprint.

Steve popped up as though lying on a spring.

"Shit!" Jacobs cried as Steve slammed into him, jerking and thrashing.

Jacobs wrestled with him for a moment, finally knocking him flat and pinning his arms. "Now!" he called over his shoulder.

Riordan struggled to a kneeling position. *"Desapareça!"* she cried, scrabbling about on the floor for the lit cigarette. It had fallen beneath one of the stools and by some miracle had not been squashed.

Grabbing it, Riordan wrenched Steve's huge misshapen jaw open and shoved the lit cigarette between the snapping jaguar fangs.

Steve let out another howl, horrible and plaintive at the same time. Behind them, Paige screamed again as Steve's body shriveled smaller and smaller until Jacobs could let him go.

In another moment, he broke into dust, gray powder inside bloody clothes on the floor he had washed.

Sara stood behind Thacker, wearing her sunglasses of doom. She had not said a word.

It was effective. Jacobs and Riordan stood in front of Thacker giving their reports, but kept glancing at Sara as if trying to analyze her as a potential threat. Not the kind of threat that Steve the demonic janitor presented, but a very real threat nonetheless.

Janitor. Sara could never figure out why the shape-changing critters didn't just go sun themselves on a beach or something. With all his powers, he chose to push a mop around a ninth-rate diner in the middle of nowhere? Or lurk in a Chicago alley, or man a grocery counter in the Philippines… Who could figure out the demon mind?

"We could have presented the tobacco more quickly," Riordan said— ah, they had reached the second-guessing and backpedaling portion of the debriefing. At least they weren't turning around to watch the cleanup team as they eliminated every shred of evidence that a kuru-pira had ever existed in the diner.

Thacker glanced over at Sara.

Sara took off the sunglasses.

"Slow as molasses in January." Sara glared at Riordan. "Did you fall in the toilet?"

Riordan didn't flinch. "The cut was deeper than I intended, and took an extra moment to bandage," she said. "I did not realize the situation had…"

Riordan trailed off, carefully not looking at Jacobs.

"Had gotten totally out of hand," Sara finished, shifting her glare to Jacobs.

Jacobs remained impassive, but Riordan actually blushed. *Uh oh. Trouble here.* "Mr. Jacobs, care to explain?"

Jacobs didn't look at Riordan as he replied. "The civilian was in the way. I attempted—"

"Fuck the civvie," Sara snapped. Even Thacker looked askance at her then, but she didn't care. "When you have a supernatural in your sights, you contain it. If there's a civilian in the way, you shoot through it."

"Him," Riordan said. "You mean shoot through *him.*"

"I was not speaking to you," Sara retorted. She began ticking off points on her fingers. "Jacobs was too quick with the identifier solution. Another two minutes of observation would have given Riordan here a chance to slap on a band-aid and get her ass back out here, while you could see if—"

"It *was* in disguise, ma'am," Jacobs interrupted.

Thacker closed his eyes in pain.

Sara tilted her head silently. Then she stalked around Thacker and leaned directly into Jacobs' face.

Something in her eyes must have told him exactly how badly he had fucked up, because he backtracked instantly. "Apologies, ma'am."

Sara glared daggers directly into his eyes. "Go back to the desert, corporal."

"Permission to speak, ma'am?" Riordan asked.

"Denied." Sara fired a stony glare at her as well. "We need one of you. We don't need both. So far I don't see a reason to keep either of you." She turned away, effectively dismissing them. "Colonel Thacker, a word?"

Thacker walked with her to the parking lot outside the diner. The sun cast its early rays over the horizon as the cleanup team loaded its equipment into the plain white panel van hilariously labeled ACME CLEANERS.

"You take care of the girl?" Sara asked.

Thacker nodded, keeping his stone face. "She's got her college paid for and is doing her best to forget any of it ever happened. The cook will get the same offer with a free hospital stay to boot."

"Standard surveillance in case one of them gets chatty," Sara said.

"I'm playing your game, but I'd love to know what the fuck you're doing to the kids," Thacker said.

Sara faced away from the diner. "Tell me what they're doing right now."

Thacker peered over her shoulder. Sara sighed. No subtlety at all. "He's rubbing his face with his hands. She's… I think she's chewing him out."

Sara tried not to smile. "Thought so. I let them think I'm going to get rid of one of them. Next round, I can see what they're made of."

Thacker shook his head. "You make no sense, Harvey."

"They're too close," Sara said. "You pulled them out of combat duty after what, a close encounter?"

"Devalpa," Thacker said. "It got two of their unit before they figured out how to bind it."

Sara nodded. "Nice work. They've got brains. They've also got a bond that's far too close. Jacobs there, he was more concerned with keeping Riordan safe than killing the critter. She's just as bad, trying to leap in and protect him when I was in his face. Are they fucking?"

Thacker stammered a second. "I really couldn't say."

"If they are, they're out," Sara stated. "If not, they may still be unusable. He's all protector, first the cook, then Riordan. She's got the subtlety of a sledgehammer."

"Sounds familiar," Thacker gibed.

Sara ignored him. "Now they have a problem. Do they try to curry favor with me to get the other on the team? Bad. Do they undercut each other for the supposed one spot? Worse."

"They weren't that terrible, considering their inexperience," Thacker insisted. "I might point out that you've been known to take some alternative approaches to—"

"And that's as far as you go down that road," Sara interrupted. She slipped her sunglasses back on and turned so she could watch them, leaning against the side of the van. Thacker motioned them to come out, and they walked out like soldiers. They didn't look at each other, and they didn't look at Sara.

Not bad.

<hr>

Dan Chamberlin was waiting for them outside the bar. Sara hated him instantly.

For one thing, he was in a suit. Oh, he'd taken off the tie and the jacket, but the shoes had a high gloss and unbuttoning the collar didn't make the shirt any less Brooks Brothers. He was the sort of guy who had a suit permanently implanted on his skin.

For another, he looked at Sara with the most annoying mixture of respect and tolerance she'd ever seen.

"Major Harvey, it's an honor," he said, offering his hand in greeting.

Sara ignored his hand. "Leave it as Harvey. I'm retired." Out of the corner of her eye, she saw Jacobs and Riordan exchange glances.

"My mistake," Chamberlin said, retracting his hand. "I've read all about your work. It's a real privilege to be able to consult with a veteran like you on my team."

Sara slipped her sunglasses on, despite the late hour. She didn't want Chamberlin to see her roll her eyes.

Diplomacy is not your strong suit, Harvey.

Sara ignored Paul's voice for the billionth time. "He alone in there?"

Thacker looked at Chamberlin. "We haven't gone inside yet."

Chamberlin actually pulled out a notebook to tick off the plan. "A simple recon pass should proceed first, to identify if there is anyone too close to the subject to be an obstacle. Then we can regroup out here and decide which approach is likely to be the most effective."

Sara fought the mad urge to slap the notebook out of his hands. "Define your 'recon pass,' Mr. Chamberlin."

Chamberlin glanced at the others. "Corporal Jacobs here is the closest to his age. We'll send him in to buy him a beer."

Sara pulled off the sunglasses, no longer caring if Chamberlin saw her annoyance. "Thacker?"

"Your play," Thacker confirmed.

Sara turned to the Bobbsey Twins. "Riordan, lose the ponytail."

After the barest hesitation, Riordan pulled the rubber band from her hair. Sara reached toward her, and the younger woman recoiled by habit.

"Get a grip," Sara muttered, even though she was pleased with the girl's instincts. She caught Riordan's copper hair and mussed it a bit, letting it tumble around the shoulders. She tugged off Riordan's jacket. "Gimme the piece."

"Now hold on a second," Jacobs protested. "She can't go in there unarmed—"

Sara shot him a glare. "Do you usually go armed to have a few beers, corporal?"

Jacobs zipped it. Sara neglected to mention that she herself did go armed to have a beer, but she was hardly the picture of normalcy.

Riordan had already removed the clip from her sidearm. She unbuckled her shoulder holster and slipped it off her arm, handing it to Sara.

Sara placed it inside the van and removed her own boot knife, handing it to Riordan. "Put this on."

"Where?" Chamberlin asked.

Sara tried not to grin. It was close. "A woman's gotta have a secret or two."

Riordan did grin at that, suddenly looking as young as she undoubtedly was. She slipped the knife into her waistband at the small of her back and glanced herself in the black-tinted window of the van. "Good enough?"

"Unbutton the top two," Thacker suggested.

Sara glanced at him. Thacker remained impassive. Sara really tried not to smile. She didn't want to smile. Riordan unbuttoned the top of her shirt.

Suddenly all the men acted a little uncomfortable.

"Go get him," Thacker said.

Riordan walked toward the bar, a little more swing to her hips than usual.

"Is this entirely appropriate? Using a female team member as a sexual enticement?" Chamberlin asked.

Sara snorted. "I'll tell you a story sometime."

Thacker raised an eyebrow. "Really?"

"Yeah, but then I'd have to kill you." Sara climbed into the van and switched on the monitors. "Shit, audio's not working."

Jacobs climbed up beside her and started fiddling with dials and switches. "Do we have to do this a lot, ma'am? I mean, how far does the job go?"

"Relax, Corporal, she's just got to get him out of the bar," Sara said.

"It just feels inappropriate," Jacobs groused.

"You know how many critters out there are attracted to sex, Corporal?" Sara asked. "Sometimes the only way to catch them is to use ourselves as bait, or hang around in places where they're likely to show—effectively using unknowing civilians as bait. How much do you like that?"

"Not much," Jacobs admitted. "But this isn't—"

"This is Riordan, and it bothers you to see her in a sexual or romantic situation," Sara finished, pitching her voice lower so the other two outside wouldn't hear her.

Jacobs stiffened into a military mannequin. "I would feel the same about any fellow—"

"Bullshit," Sara interrupted. "A blind man could see that you and Riordan are a little closer than standard for teammates." She checked her tone. "Maybe it's surviving the attack of the devalpa, maybe she's the little sister you never had, maybe you're fucking like bunnies when we're not looking. Don't know, don't care. I do know it's going to get one or both of you killed and destroy your team before it even gets started, so before I'm done one of you's gonna be gone. Now shut up and fix my audio."

Jacobs was literally speechless, staring at her until she kicked him in the leg and he scrambled to working on the dials.

Sara hauled herself out of the van to confer with the others.

"Audio yet?" Thacker asked.

"Your equipment sucks, Lord and Master," Sara snapped.

Chamberlin blinked. "Shouldn't we have a second pair of eyes inside?"

Thacker looked at Sara, who nodded. Chamberlin turned toward the van and opened his mouth. Sara slapped a hand over it, shutting him up before he could utter a sound. Shocked, Chamberlin stumbled backward.

"Ms. Harvey, your diplomacy skills need work," Thacker observed.

Sara shook off the echo in her head. "Bite me." She slipped off her most obvious gun and doffed her cover. "You can't send Dudley Do-Right in there. He'll be made in about ten seconds. I'm going in."

Chamberlin recovered the power of speech. "With all due respect, Harvey, I thought you were here on a consultant basis only—"

"I'm recruiting," Sara replied.

She stalked off, aware that they were watching her. As she went, she turned on her audio jack—for whatever fucking good it would do them.

As she walked into the dark, smoky bar, she was assaulted with the sound of a yunwhi slowly being boiled in enchanted oil—or perhaps it was an escaped banshee?

No, it was a badly-bleached blonde up on the stage singing some country song with bleary eyes fixed on the small karaoke screen in front of her. She was attempting a soprano refrain with an alto voice and none too aware of the pitch. That didn't stop the enthusiastic applause from a group of equally drunk young women in the corner, or the hooting approval from a trio of young men near them.

Over at the bar, a few older men watched with amusement while a fortysomething woman in a beer-slogan T-shirt sloshed up some booze in glasses of questionable cleanliness.

At the far end of the bar sat Peter Camden, one tumbler glass in front of him. It was deceptively empty, but Sara knew without even looking at his eyes that it had been filled at least twice since his arrival.

Riordan was angling her body just so he could catch a look between the unclasped buttons. A second glance at Camden told Sara two things: he appreciated the view, but he wasn't buying.

Sara climbed onto a stool directly across the U-shaped bar. Riordan saw her, but barely let on. *Good girl.*

"Help you, hon?" the bartender asked.

Sara nodded. "Gimme a Miller Lite."

"Yuck," Thacker said in her ear. *Now they get the audio working.* It wasn't as though a dive like this was going to have Fat Tire, Sara thought—but remembered not to say aloud. The beer arrived and she plunked her cash on the bar, but didn't touch her drink. Not while she was working.

Camden turned to Riordan and said something with finality in his body language. She wilted just a bit—that had to sting the old ego, acting a role or not, Sara thought. Riordan looked over at her and Sara jerked her head almost imperceptibly to the side. Riordan got off the stool and went to an unoccupied table with a mild *his-loss* flounce.

Camden picked up on it as Sara had intended. He was good—he slid off his stool and wandered, ostensibly toward the men's room.

"On the move," Sara muttered, quietly enough to be buried under the caterwauling behind her, but loudly enough for Thacker to hear her.

Sara slipped back toward the dingy short hallway and found the alley exit door slowly swinging closed.

"Rabbit!" she said, running out the back door.

Camden was just beyond her line of sight. Sara dodged his first swing easily and blocked the second, stepping close to elbow him hard in the solar plexus. To her surprise, he twisted away just enough so that she hit a rib instead. Camden grunted and backed away.

A second later Riordan banged the door open, the boot knife out and ready. "On the ground!" she snapped, raising it in offensive posture.

Sara held up a hand to still her. "Wait," she told Camden. "Just here to talk."

Camden glanced up the alley and saw the van, pulling through with Chamberlin behind the wheel. The other end was blocked by a dumpster, which left him pretty well trapped.

"Talk." Camden rubbed his side. "This doesn't feel like 'talk.'"

Sara held up her other hand to keep the dimwits in the van. "How drunk are you, Dr. Camden? We need to have a conversation."

Camden glared at her. "Who are you?"

Sara inclined her head toward the van. Riordan faded back to it, but kept the knife out and ready. Good girl.

Then Sara turned her attention back to Camden. "You're the genius. You tell me who we are."

Camden glanced at Riordan. "She was either a plant or a hooker. Too young, too interested too fast."

Riordan cocked an eyebrow, and Sara resisted the urge to laugh.

Camden looked back at Sara, taking all of her in at a glance. "You're older, military or recently ex."

"It's the haircut, always gives me away." Sara walked a couple steps closer. "Come on. You can do better than that."

Camden glanced down at her boots. "You've been near the ocean lately, at work or at play. And you were injured no more than three years ago, fairly serious, right leg."

Sara didn't flinch. "I do not limp."

"Not anymore," Camden said. "I'd say the leg is perfectly healed except for the scars. But you limped on it for quite a while, and you've never quite trusted the muscle since then. It's not enough to impair you, and now that I've mentioned it, you're putting more weight on it as if to prove me wrong. That tells me you're very conscious of appearing strong, and you are strong, but not as strong as you want others to believe."

Sara rolled her eyes. But Camden wasn't done. He stepped closer, an expression on his face that was half analytical, half smartass, and still somewhat vacant, like he was looking past her to something else.

"You're older than you look, but only in the eyes," he said. "You've seen some serious shit, and it's still with you. It's recent, too—that jacket's been with you through some level of violence, and you never quite get all the stains out no matter who you hire to clean it."

Sara couldn't help herself. She glanced at the right sleeve, but it was impossible to see anything in the stupid orange glow of security lights. She thought the bloodstains were only in her mind.

Camden looked satisfied with himself. "Thought so. You've killed people."

Sara leveled her glare at him in the orange-yellow light. "Not people."

Camden blew out his breath in frustration. "Goddammit. Thacker, get your ass out here!"

Thacker climbed out of the van, followed by Chamberlin and Jacobs.

Camden folded his arms, defiant. "I've told you twice now. The answer is no."

Chamberlin stepped forward, his goddamn notebook in hand. "We were hoping you might reconsider, Mr. Camden."

"It's Doctor Camden," he snapped. "I have three doctorates—"

"Yes, sir, I know," Chamberlin said, unruffled. "Technically it's two doctorates, in biological anthropology and vertebrate paleontology, as well as an M.D., though you've never practiced."

"I said no, I meant no." The slur in Camden's voice was so slight only Sara may have noticed it.

Thacker moved past Chamberlin. "This is the third and final time we'll approach you, sir. I truly hope this time you'll agree."

Camden flipped him the bird. Sara suddenly liked him.

"You're about to lose your tenure, Professor," Chamberlin said, unperturbed. "With your reputation, you aren't likely to get another university appointment. Isn't a position with Blackfire preferable to leaving your profession entirely?"

Camden glared. "Hunting rare species throughout the world and snuffing out organisms that could add to our understanding of the biological diversity of this planet? You can suck it."

Chamberlin snapped his stupid notebook closed and turned back toward Thacker. "Clearly, this isn't—"

Sara stepped between Camden and the van. "Hey, fuckhead."

Camden refocused on her, and his surprise was apparent on his face in a way he likely wouldn't have allowed completely sober.

Sara stared him down. "We only kill the critters that kill us. It isn't for sport. It's important."

Camden snorted. "You gonna give me the 'your country needs you' speech too?"

"Hell no, that's their schtick," Sara said, tilting her head toward Thacker and Chamberlin. "But I can tell you that we keep people safe. We need somebody with brains on the team, someone who can tell us when we're hunting a dangerous critter and when we're aiming a bazooka at a harmless mimi."

Camden almost smiled. "Australian, aren't they?"

"See?" Sara said. "Even half-drunk, you can help us. And help yourself. Where else are you going to get the chance to observe a real chupacabra?"

Camden raised an eyebrow. "No bullshit?"

Sara folded her arms. "I am absolutely no bullshit whatsoever."

"That, I can attest to," Jacobs muttered.

Sara stepped closer. "Take a look at this team, Dr. Camden. Those kids? They're gonna be in the line of fire, and they need someone to keep them safe and patch them up when they get hurt. And they *will* get hurt. With you there, they just might see their twenty-fifth birthdays."

Camden sighed. "The tenure committee meets next week."

"And we know what they're going to decide," Chamberlin said.

Sara let a terse smile across her face. "Come on. It's us or teaching high school biology."

Camden shuddered. "Do I have a choice?"

"There's always a choice," Thacker said. "But are the other options really that attractive?"

Sara clapped Camden on the shoulder, but her hand dug tight into his flesh. Camden looked at her in surprise. She leaned forward and pitched her voice low, so the others couldn't hear. "Just keep the booze off-duty, Doc. That understood?"

Camden looked at her and nodded slowly. Then he followed Sara to the van, while Thacker and Chamberlin looked at each other in surprise.

Riordan had discreetly buttoned her shirt back up. "Sir, do you mind if I ask you a question?" she asked.

Camden nodded. "Only if you promise never to call me 'sir' again."

Riordan nodded with a shy smile. "Why were you going to lose your tenure?"

Camden stared up at the sky for a moment, seemingly lost in thought. Sara was about to poke him when he replied.

"I put in a sabbatical proposal," he said, and climbed into the van.

Riordan looked at Sara in confusion. "I thought that was allowed for professors."

Thacker grinned. "Not when you propose to study dragons in their natural habitat. They think he's a lunatic." He paused a second. "They might be right."

Riordan covered her smile with a hand and climbed into the van with Jacobs. Only then did Sara let herself smile—a smile that quickly faded as soon as Thacker looked at her. "There. You've got a team."

"Not quite," Thacker said. "A few empty spots, and some trial missions to run them through their paces. You know how it goes."

Sara sighed. "I did my job, how long do I have to—"

"Missing the beach?" Chamberlin asked.

Sara leveled a glare that made Chamberlin recoil a moment. As she climbed into the van, she heard Thacker murmur to him, "Don't. Trust me, don't."

Natalia Ivanova saw the business card lying on the floor after he finished on her.

He was an easy one. At first, they sent her the rough ones. They beat her and choked her, and they held her down with brutal hands while they did her. They called her names in their rough language and barked orders she could not comprehend, then struck her if she did not comply.

Later Natalia realized that Anna knew she would fight them, and so they sent her the ones that wanted a woman to fight. The ones who liked it that way.

Once she stopped fighting, they sent her the meek ones, the ones who just wanted an unresisting piece of flesh. The things they made her do weren't nearly as painful.

While they grunted above her, she could lie still and pretend she was walking by the river in St. Petersburg. She loved to walk by the river, watching the starlight play on the waters under the bridges. No matter how awful things had been in St. Petersburg, she could run to the river and bury her sorrows in its gentle susurrations, let its waters flow over her heart and still her soul.

But the river was sour for her now, because of Terry.

The meek ones would try to talk to her sometimes, before or after they did her. She nodded like she understood, because then they wouldn't get mad and hit her. They never seemed to realize she could not answer.

The fists she understood well enough.

At first, Natalia tried to get free. The room was bare of everything, only a mattress in an iron frame with a thin blanket, a sturdy wooden chair with no arms and a pail to use as a toilet. There were no windows in her room, and the door had never been left unlocked a moment since she stepped through it. There were always two of them when they hauled Inez and Sasha and Natalia to the shower, naked and cold. Three against two, but the men always had guns.

And there was Anna, the woman who really ran the house and the men. She was not weak.

It was Anna who brought the food. Anna reminded Natalia in her halting Russian that they were like sisters and had to help each other. Natalia wept and told Anna that she wanted to go home, but Anna slapped her and told her to stop being a baby.

Natalia was only two when her parents died in a car crash. No one remembered them. She could not remember them herself, only images. A soft hand, a smile, the smell of tobacco. She remembered the children's home, and the people who came to look at her, but nobody wanted her. Later she found out someone had—a couple in America—but then they got a divorce.

Natalia did poorly at school, but it didn't seem to bother anyone. As soon as she was big enough, she ran away from the home. Being nearly of age, she thought they did not look for her very long.

Natalia was a waitress when Terry walked into Pietro's diner. Terry was an American, with lots of cash and an easy smile. He came by every day and ordered a hamburger, and Natalia would try to get Pietro to cook it clean.

After her shift, Terry and Natalia walked by the Okhta River and Terry kissed her in the moonlight. There was only the soft susurration of the water and the quickening beat of her heart, until she led him to her tiny room at the top of the stairs. It was the most exciting, intoxicating and beautiful night of her life.

Terry wanted her to come back with him. *America is the land of opportunity,* he said. He told her about schools where she could learn something better than slinging hash on the diner counter. Natalia tried to tell him she had been terrible in school—her eyes wandered over the page and she simply couldn't comprehend the Cyrillic letters. But Terry's Russian was weak, and he didn't get what she said. *You'll learn,* he said, and stroked her hair.

Terry handled everything, papers and plane fare. Natalia left St. Petersburg with a backpack full of clothes, her charcoal pencils, sketchbook and the cheap metal cross they had given her at the children's home. It was all she had.

The airplane was amazing, but the airport was a little frightening—everything was in English, even the signs on the walls. The letters were even more confusing than Cyrillic, and Natalia soon gave up figuring out anything written anywhere. Everyone spoke so quickly, and the few times Natalia tried to speak to someone, they looked at her strangely. Terry spoke to the men at the desks, showed them his papers, and they waved them onward.

Natalia peered out the car windows as Terry drove her through the city with the wide streets. He rolled past some street where the colored lights blazed brightly and amazing music rolled from them in waves of glorious sound. This would be her city, and it felt so alive and vibrant. She was excited and eager to explore it.

Then they came to the house, and Terry led her over the threshold. Anna was in the living room with Keegan and Clayne. They stared at her like a farmer inspects a cow, and Clayne handed Terry some money. Natalia tried to ask Terry what was happening, but he told her to go with Anna and he'd be along.

Anna brought her to the room with no windows.

Natalia had not seen Terry since.

She refused to eat at first. She managed three days, and Anna grew more and more angry. She slapped Natalia, scratching her skin with her fingernails. She rubbed mashed potatoes in Natalia's hair, and oh the smell, it made her stomach hurt.

On the third day she could not help herself. She ate.

The first time they sent her a customer, she fought him off. He stomped away angry, her scratches on his face.

They sent Keegan to her. He had a thin wooden stick, round and about two inches thick. It did not break anything. But he found ways to hurt her with it she never knew.

Then he took her on the floor.

Natalia tried to think of the river, but it seemed far away and murky. He kicked her when he was done.

Sasha said it wouldn't be so bad if Natalia would stop fighting. Sasha was like her—Russian, though she had never been to St. Petersburg. Natalia wondered if Terry had kissed Sasha in the moonlight and told her stories of the land of opportunity, but did not have the heart to ask in the brief time she was in the showers with Sasha and Inez. Sasha spoke Russian, and those few moments in the showers were the only thing keeping Natalia sane, she thought.

Sasha was right. When Natalia stopped fighting and simply lay there, it got better. Instead of the rough, brutish men who laughed while they beat her, they sent her old men who called her Bay-bee and young men with oblong metal tags around their necks who grunted like pigs when they finished.

Sasha had been in the house longer than Natalia or Inez, and she knew how to survive. *You just go away inside,* she whispered.

Just go away. If only it were that easy.

How long had it been? Surely the snows had come and gone at least three times. But somehow Natalia knew it could not be that long. Her hair had not grown that much.

Now she sat on the bed in the room with no windows, the thin blanket pulled up under arms. The man with the tie didn't look at her even once as he finished tying his shoes. He struck the door twice as he'd been told, and someone— was it Clayne?—unlocked the door.

Surely someone smarter than Natalia could have escaped. Broken through the walls, or fought them off during the weekly showers. Taken a customer hostage with a knotted bedsheet. She had been to the movies in St. Petersburg, and she saw what the action girls did.

But they were not Natalia. And somehow she knew there would not be much strength left in her for long.

The door opened, and the man with the tie stepped through.

Natalia slid out of bed and grabbed the business card off the floor in one swift movement. As the door swung closed, she slipped the business card into the doorknob latch.

It jammed. As perfectly as if she had planned it that way.

Natalia's heart beat as if she had run the entire length of the river.

Quickly she wiped herself as clean as she could with the edge of the ragged blanket. Then she pulled on the short plaid skirt and buttonless shirt that were all the clothes she was allowed to wear. She made the two loose front parts into a knot. It gaped to her waist, but she didn't care.

At the door, her hand faltered. Horrible things would happen to her if she tried to escape. They would send Keegan back to her with the wooden stick.

And he had other things. Worse things. Sasha warned her the one time Natalia whispered in the shower about getting out.

"Don't," Sasha breathed, glancing to the open doorway where Clayne watched Inez with idle lust. Clayne could not speak Russian. But he did not like it when they spoke and sometimes hit them when they talked too much.

Inez did not talk. She was small and thin, brown with long straight hair and narrow shoulders. Her dark eyes were empty. When Natalia looked into them, she saw silent screams.

Natalia did not want to die of silent screams.

She listened at the doorway as the customer's footsteps descended the stairs with whomever had let him out of her room. She waited at least a hundred-count later, waiting until she was really sure they were alone. It was very late, so late that they were not likely to have more customers tonight.

It was quiet downstairs, and it was only quiet when Anna was ready for sleep. When customers came, Anna was by the door. The walls were thin, and Natalia could hear the footsteps, the grunting in Inez's room next to hers.

Inez. Sasha had the hard glitter of flint and steel in her eyes, but could Natalia really leave poor Inez? She looked fourteen, but her body was even younger. *That's what the men like*, Sasha said.

Slowly, Natalia turned the doorknob and pulled the door open. She caught the business card—illegible to her, covered in English letters and numbers—before it fell to the floor. She slid it into her waistband on impulse.

As silently as she could, she pulled the door open. An inch, and then another. The shadowed, dingy hallway was empty. To the left lay the other two rooms and the shower room.

To the right, the stairs. Down the stairs, out the door. She remembered.

It was dark downstairs. Could Anna be asleep? Could a simple girl from St. Petersburg have that much luck?

Natalia left her door open rather than try to close it quietly. She slipped away from Inez's door with a silent prayer of apology. She would come back, she vowed. She would find whatever police or action girls existed in this country and come back with guns and knives and other things to get past Keegan and Clayne and Anna and even Terry, if that's what it took.

She heard Terry's voice sometimes; she knew he came to the house once in a while. At first, she screamed when she heard him, begging him to help her. He never came. At least she had never heard his voice grunting in Inez's room.

The stairs were made of wood and had no carpet, descending into the unknown darkness of the small, shabby living room. Natalia remembered when she was a little girl in the home, how she would get past the sleeping matrons to get to the cookies hidden in the kitchen. She was caught at first, but she learned to step on the wooden planks closest to the bearing wall. That's where they creaked the least.

Step.

Natalia was a little girl, and the only consequence of getting caught would be a scolding for sneaking after sweets again. She was a little girl, her hair in a braid down her back, and there were cookies waiting for her downstairs.

Step.

Natalia was a young girl, and there was a book downstairs she had forgotten when the matrons shooed them upstairs to sleep. It was an American book translated into Russian, and in it the teenage boys asked the girls to dance and sometimes they kissed. The matrons would never let her read it if they found it behind the flour canisters. She had to get downstairs and find it. Besides, it was a really good book. That's why her heart was beating so fast.

Step.

Natalia was a grown girl, and she had all her worldly possessions in her green backpack. She was running away and would never have to go back to stupid school again. They would never pull her braid again and tell her she was a loser orphan that no one wanted. She would run into the city, and no one would ever make her do anything she didn't want to ever, ever again.

Step.

Natalia was a young woman, and she needed to get down the steps quietly because old Mr. Petrovich on the second floor got cranky when her footsteps woke him up early in the morning. She didn't mean to make noise, but she was on early shifts at the diner, and she needed to leave before the sun came up. If she didn't have to be up for work, she would never rise until the sun's rays peeked over her windowsill. But those eggs wouldn't poach themselves.

Step.

The living room of the house in the land of opportunity. It was empty and dark. From the half-open door on the far side of the living room, a spill of golden light came from Anna's bedroom. A low, throaty laugh came across the room like a skittering spider—Anna had a visitor. A man. No wonder she left the door untended.

The door.

The front door was locked, of course. But the deadbolt could easily be turned from the inside.

Turned.

Natalia's hand hovered over the doorknob. For so long the world was four dingy walls, a creaky iron bed and men who grunted and spent themselves on her. Beyond the door, that was the real world. The real land of opportunity.

Natalia grasped the doorknob.

It turned in her hand.

She managed not to scream as she stumbled backward. The door swung open in front of her, and Keegan was in her face in an instant, fist slamming into her stomach before the surprise faded from his eyes.

He shouted something in English as Natalia scrabbled for the doorway. Keegan kicked her hard in the side, and Natalia felt something inside her snap like a wet twig. A flood of agony went through her chest and she cried out.

The lights came on and suddenly Anna and Terry were there. Anna was buttoning up her shirt. In her haste she had missed a button, Natalia thought in a crazy disjointed stupor.

Keegan was still shouting, but not at Natalia. He shouted at Anna and pointed at the door. Anna shouted right back at him, and Terry held up his hands as if to make them quiet.

They would send her back to the room with no windows, Natalia realized with mounting horror as she crawled on the floor. They would send her upstairs with Keegan and his stick.

Past Keegan's heavy mud-splattered workboots, Natalia saw a sliver of the night sky. Strangely it was now the fall—or was it fall again?—and crickets chirped in a strange cacophony outside. The stars glimmered, just like they did over the river in St. Petersburg.

Natalia slid herself quietly along the floor as they shouted at each other. Her ribs stabbed her with every movement. But a cool breeze wafted through the open doorway, its light breath caressing her sweat-covered face.

Then Keegan stomped his boot down on her hand, and she heard rather than felt three fingers break like pretzels. Then the pain raved up her arm and Natalia screamed as Keegan grabbed her by the hair, hauling her to her knees.

Keegan said something to Terry, and Terry shook his head. Anna shoved Terry then, and he glared at her.

Then Terry retrieved a length of twine from a drawer table beside the stairs. He grabbed Natalia by the arm and forced her to her feet. Her ribs stabbed her again, and she sagged against him.

Fight. She knew she should fight. The air was so close, the outside air that smelled of life and freedom and running water, not the sour-sweet stench of the room with no windows, the smell of hopelessness and empty sex and hate.

"Please let me go," she begged Terry, the only one who could understand her. Anna knew a little Russian, but an appeal to Anna would fall on the deafest of ears. Anna looked at Natalia as though she were a bag of refuse to be thrown away.

"Quiet," Terry ordered in Russian, and Natalia was quiet. Terry didn't look at her while he tied her hands behind her back. Without her hands she could not hope to stop Keegan from doing anything he wanted. Not that she could stop him anyway. Sasha was right, it was better not to fight. Or be like Inez, and escape inside your mind. Once you had hidden your mind, it didn't matter what they did to your body.

Terry glared at Keegan, and for a moment Natalia wondered if they were both going to take her. She thought something in her might break if they did that.

Then Terry propelled her out the door.

Out the door.

The cool night air was only cool by the definitions of the stuffy, airless rooms upstairs. It was a summer night hotter than any she had ever felt, heat that enveloped her in moist air. But it was fresh air, and she gulped it in despite the stabbing pain in her side.

Terry dragged her by the elbow past two parked trucks and into the scrub brush at the end of the house's driveway. It wasn't exactly deep country—there were bright lights along the sky as if the city weren't far away, but there were no other houses in sight. Perhaps on the other side of the trees.

Natalia could hear the river.

It was the soft susurration of slow-flowing water, and again it made her think of St. Petersburg, of the moonlight on the water after the diner was closed and she had nowhere to go but her little room above Mr. Petrovich's apartment. That room had seemed so dull, like a prison cell.

Natalia was suddenly, desperately homesick for that tiny little room. For her own river.

"I will never tell anyone," she said, quietly so Terry would hear her but the others in the house would not. "Please, I will never tell anyone. I do not even have the English to tell them. Please let me go."

"Quiet," Terry repeated.

She had meant to marry him.

Natalia struggled beside him, her hand and her side screaming in pain as he led her through the woods. She didn't know if she loved him, but he was the first to notice her, the first to touch her, the first to...

Tears stung her eyes. Natalia hadn't let herself cry for centuries. It was too hard to stop. Was he taking her home? Was he finally taking her away? Was this all some terrible test? Was this how American men loved their women, renting them to other men first, breaking them in?

Soon she saw the river through the trees, its silvery curtain rippling in the moonlight. It was enormous, wider than the Okhta by far, an inland sea she could barely see across to a place where dim lights shone. There was power in this river, stronger than any she had ever felt, as though the river soaked up the moonlight and shone its beauty in a shimmering ribbon through the land.

Terry pushed her ahead of him down through the brambles, to a little inlet where a small stream emptied into the great river. He forced her down to her knees in the moonlight. Her side screamed in pain and she coughed, some kind of liquid gathering in her lungs.

"Terry," she whispered, and tried her best for English. "Please."

He stared up at the moon for a long moment.

Then he was on her.

4

It was Chamberlin's brilliant idea to split up.

Jacobs and Riordan went with Chamberlin, while Camden and Thacker went with Sara. She tried to tell him that splitting up the team this early was a rookie move, and if he was going to do it then at least the kids should be separated. But already Chamberlin wasn't listening to her.

The club was loud—too loud for Thacker's crappy earpieces to work properly, and much too dark for Sara's peace of mind. Bodies writhed on the dance floor, twisting and gyrating to music far too young for her taste.

She glanced to her left and wondered if she could stash Thacker behind a pillar or something. If Thacker were any stiffer, they'd just have to hang a sign that said COP on him. The funny thing was, Thacker had never been law enforcement. But his face screamed Authority, and the kids on the dance floor gave him a wide berth as though he carried a plague of locusts under his trenchcoat.

A trenchcoat in a dance club. Thacker was hopeless.

Camden, on the other hand, was already dancing with some far-too-young blonde thing who was two steps away from drooling on the floor. Sara rolled her eyes and told Thacker to keep an eye on him.

"What?" Thacker cupped his hand around his ear.

Sara gave Thacker the "stay" signal with outstretched palms and moved away from him across the dance floor. Awkwardly, she shifted her feet from side to side in a feeble dance movement to camouflage the fact that she was actually searching the crowd.

Dancing was one talent Sara had never acquired. Her feet never knew how to move in concert with her arms and hips. Parish Roberts got her out on a dance floor once in New Orleans, some jazz club full of smoky darkness and old wood, and after two songs he declared her… What was it? Hopeless. She'd laughed and bought him a drink.

Snarling. Blood frothing between the teeth. It hurt to think about Parish.

"Harvey, no sign," she said quietly. There was no response—at least, no response she could hear. Probably they couldn't hear her either, unless she shouted with her hand cupped around the earpiece. Subtle.

Reaching the edge of the dance floor, Sara drifted over toward a spiral metal staircase that went to the upper level. Halfway up, she had a better view over the room. The bodies on the dance floor writhed almost in unison, bound together by some strange telepathy that only young people could hear and utterly escaped Sara.

You aren't exactly ancient, Harvey. Paul never shut up. She certainly felt ancient enough, surrounded by Jacobs and Riordan—even Camden, who was within shouting distance of Sara's age, acted young enough that she barely knew him. On the far side of the dance floor, he cavorted with a redhead—ah, he'd changed affections.

"Harvey to Camden," she said into her comm link. Ever since those phone clips came into popularity, it was a lot easier to disguise the comms. "You know the demon is male, right? You're barking up the wrong underage tree."

No reply. Typical.

"Chamberlin to Harvey."

Great. The boss man calleth. "Harvey here."

"Camden's on the potential victims. Join us on the upper level."

He's on them, all right. At least, it sounded like that was what Chamberlin said. "Roger that." Sara climbed the stairs, stepping past a pair of entwined teenagers who couldn't possibly be old enough to drink—and barely old enough for that boy's hands to be where they were.

Sara smothered a slight grin and moved through the upper passageway. There were a number of smaller rooms, where walls and freaky curtains of beads hanging from a stained ceiling muted the music. Through the curtains, Sara could hear groans that had nothing to do with dancing.

"What are you doing here?" It was Riordan, her normally even voice made hesitant in Sara's earpiece.

"Riordan? I didn't get that," Sara said.

Chamberlin chimed in. "Riordan, location please."

"What are you DOING here? Get away, get away from me!" Riordan's voice was high-pitched, almost screaming.

Shit. Sara pulled her Beretta and rushed into one of the rooms, shoving the beads out of the way. A blond teenager had his face pillowed between a brunette's ample breasts, and they flew apart at Sara's entrance as though magnetically charged.

Sara kept the gun aimed at the watermarked ceiling. "You two alone in here?"

"Yes, officer!" the boy stammered as the girl clasped her shirt closed.

Sara didn't bother to correct him. "Get downstairs right now," she ordered. They scrambled past her, leaving the bead curtain swinging in the darkness.

"Back off, right the fuck now!" It was Jacobs' voice now; he must have found Riordan. And he was no calmer than she was.

"Goddammit, one of you give me your location!" Sara snapped into her earpiece.

At least Jacobs was listening.

Sara was already moving. "Camden, Thacker, on the double!"

She raced across the upper level, past a couple of dorky twentysomething college students leaning over the railing and watching the dancing from above. They recoiled at the sight of her gun, but she barreled past them. "Harvey to Chamberlin, where the fuck are you?"

No answer. Sara rounded the corner and counted down three rooms, but it was empty.

Shouting from the next room. Sara burst through the stupid beaded curtain, gun leveled at the room.

Riordan stood frozen against the far wall, hands held outward as if in defensive posture as though she'd completely forgotten the gun holstered at her waist. Jacobs stood in front of her, gun leveled at the man standing to Sara's right.

He was an ordinary middle-aged man, a trucker type with a sweat-stained John Deere ballcap perched back on his head and a beer gut that hung over a giant belt buckle with an eagle carved into it.

"Get out!" Jacobs shouted.

Sara shifted to the left, automatically aiming her gun at the guy in the ballcap. "What the fuck is going on, Jacobs? Riordan?"

Riordan just shook her head silently.

"Personal business, Major, unrelated!" Jacobs snapped without looking at her.

"Fuck that shit, no such thing!" Sara snapped back. "Explain yourself now, Corporal!"

Riordan tried to speak. "He's…he's…"

"Honey, it's okay," Ballcap said. His voice was odd, flat and without inflection.

"Sure to fuck it isn't," Jacobs snapped. "Get the hell out of here right now, asshole."

Ballcap raised his hands and backed slowly out of the room, copping Sara a quick wink as he passed through the bead curtain.

Sara slowly lowered her weapon. "Explain yourselves in words of one syllable, right the fuck now."

Jacobs actually ignored her, moving over to Riordan. "It's okay, Kay. He's gone."

Riordan shook her head. "He's never gone," she whispered.

Sara had had enough. She stalked across the room and grabbed Jacobs by the arm.

To her shock, Jacobs actually swung at her. Good for her he was young and stupid. Sara ducked easily, catching his overlong jab and twisting his arm up behind his back with expert skill. In half a second, she had him pinned against the wall, his face pressed into someone's crudely-drawn genitalia above about nine phone numbers.

Riordan slammed into Sara, apparently recovering from her paralysis. It was almost enough to loosen Sara's grip on Jacobs. Almost, but not quite.

Sara lashed out a side kick that sent Riordan reeling. Jacobs tried to push her off, but she just pressed him harder against the wall.

"You've got about ten seconds to explain before the others get in here and you're charged with assaulting a senior officer," Sara barked.

"He was protecting me!" Riordan cried.

Sara shot her a glare over her shoulder. "You need protection from a civvie with a beer gut?"

Riordan opened her mouth, but no sound came out.

"You know shit," Jacobs snarled.

Sara let him go, at least enough to turn him around and glare up into his face. If he thought she would be intimidated by the fact that he was six inches taller, he was dumber than she thought.

"You two have personal baggage that's going to get you killed," Sara said. "This isn't Tennessee, fuckhead. You're screwing around in here when we have a goddamn demon on the prowl. You ever see what a demon leaves behind when it gets a soul?" She held up a hand. "Of course, how could I know, I don't know shit."

"You know shit about people," Jacobs snapped.

The beads rattled and Thacker came bursting in with Camden about four seconds behind him. Thacker had his gun out. So far Camden refused to carry one. Pretty dumb for a fucking genius.

Thacker stopped still and blinked at them. "What the hell is going on here?"

"It'll be in my goddamn report," Sara said. "These two go sit in the van. We've got a demon to catch."

"I'm good," Riordan said thinly.

Sara shot her a glare. "All evidence to the contrary."

Jacobs got in Sara's face again. "It's not her fault!"

Sara glared at him as the beads rustled again. "You two get the fuck out of here so we can—"

Her voice faded as she glanced over at the beads. Thacker and Camden stood together by the doorway.

Stepping through the beads was Peter Camden.

Two Peter Camdens.

Sara had her gun out in an instant. "Thacker!"

Thacker practically launched himself away from them, dropping to a kneeling position beside Sara with his sidearm out and aimed at the two Camdens. Jacobs was a second slower to react; Riordan took another four seconds to remember she had a gun.

"What the hell!" Camden on the right exclaimed, startling away from the other.

"Who the hell is that?" Camden on the left shouted at himself.

Thacker pivoted his gun toward Left-Camden; Sara shifted to aim hers at Right-Camden.

"Camden!" she shouted.

"Yes!" they both replied.

Sara fought a burst of inappropriate laughter. *It's a fucking Neil Simon comedy in here.* "Where am I most likely to find a blackheart dragon?"

"Saskatchewan!" Right-Camden shouted.

"Ontario, you idiot!" Left-Camden insisted.

Thacker glanced up at Sara. "Which is right?"

"Like I know," Sara muttered. "We could shoot them both, see which one shifts."

Right-Camden groaned. "I knew it was a mistake to join this—"

Left-Camden laughed, a shrill sound that drilled into Sara's ears. She reeled for a second as Left-Camden's eyes seemed to pivot in his face, rotating upwards until the corners of his eye sockets pointed toward his forehead instead of his ears.

Thacker's hand trembled, and his gun lowered. "Oh fuck," he whispered, still kneeling.

Sara holstered her gun fast. "Weapons down! Now!"

Jacobs glanced over at her. "But—"

"Right the fuck now!" Sara stepped in front of Thacker's half-trembling form, as Camden—the real one—faded back into a corner behind them. "It's a djinn."

The djinn's face seemed to ripple, its mouth widening beyond Peter Camden's perfectly ordinary face to stretch almost all the way around its head. Those bizarre vertical eyes lit with an inner fire, not unlike the springheel's unearthly dancing glow.

"Impossible," Thacker breathed.

Ordinarily Sara would be inclined to agree. A djinn in Kansas City was about as likely as a mermaid in Nevada, but she was not about to argue with the evidence of her own two eyes. She mentally recounted the ways she was going to slaughter Chamberlin, sending a bunch of greenhorn newbies after a fucking djinn. They had no chance.

"*Bismillah,*" she said. "Goddamn, I don't remember… Thacker?"

She glanced down at Thacker. The veteran was utterly motionless, his eyes somewhere else, somewhere awful. His mouth had fallen open as the djinn fixed its flaming eyes on him.

Sara reached into her pocket and pulled out a small packet. She ripped it open and flung the tiny puff of salt at the djinn.

"*Bismillah…*uh, *rahmani…*" she recited.

The djinn recoiled with a shriek that should have burst their ears. But the salt landing on its skin did nothing.

"Run!" Sara shouted, shoving Thacker. He lost his balance and staggered, bracing one hand on the floor. Jacobs and Riordan started to move, but the djinn rose in front of the bead curtain. Instead they recoiled back toward the corner where Camden stood frozen.

Fuck, we're dead, we're worse than dead, Sara's mind whispered to her as she grabbed another salt packet. She always kept at least a dozen on hand, but would it be enough to get them out of here? Just tiny bits of salt?

She tried desperately to remember something of the *bismallah,* anything, as she threw more salt in its face.

"Bismillah ir Rahman ir Rahim," she recited, trying to remember any more of the appropriate sura.

The djinn merely laughed, flames dancing in its upside-down eyes.

Sara stepped back. Thacker was with her now, pulling a long dagger from his boot. She pulled her own knife from her small-of-back sheath. It wasn't enough—not against a djinn, which would laugh at bullets and swallow knives—but it was solid iron, and it might buy the others time.

The djinn advanced, and Sara sacrificed another salt packet at it. It passed through the salt as though it wasn't there. Why wasn't it working?

Its jagged teeth were bared, the remnants of its Camden flesh lying in tattered rags on its limbs as a second pair of arms reached out for Thacker. A black, jagged mark on the side of its face stretched from its gaping maw to the coarse, ragged remains of its Camden-hair.

Thacker slashed weakly at it with his knife, and Sara fell into defensive posture beside him. Her mind worked over the salt and tried desperately to remember the *bismallah,* it had been so fucking long, no excuse…

That mark. That jagged black mark across its face. That was new. It wasn't—

"Ssssara," it whispered.

Its face began to change again. Fiery eyes turned black and cold, its face splitting with bloodless wounds.

"Fucker," Sara whispered. She dropped her knife.

Thacker glanced at her. "What? Harvey—"

Sara pulled her handgun and fired six times, right into the center of its chest.

It stumbled backward and fell, arms flailing and thrashing.

Thacker leaped forward and drove his dagger straight into its heart.

It flailed against him, black blood pouring from its chest. It shifted again while writhing on the floor, this time to a creature with bald head and pale face, black jagged patterns seemingly tattooed across its mouth in a hideous sneer. Its eyes sank into its skull in pools of jet black.

Sara advanced on it, her pistol aimed at its thrashing body. "That's not a djinn."

Thacker glanced up at her, still holding the dagger in its heart. "You're sure?"

"A djinn laughs at bullets, but a demon doesn't give a damn about salt," Sara said, kneeling beside it.

The vrees looked up at her and grinned, black blood dribbling from its mouth. *"You let it out, Ssssara."*

"Go to hell," Sara replied.

Its body twitched again, and slowly it faded into smoke before them.

The music downstairs chose that moment to pause for a moment. *Good thing it wasn't when I shot the fucking demon,* Sara thought as she stood up.

Then she aimed her glare at the three in the corner.

"A little tougher than we thought," she said. "Vrees demon. Dutch." She aimed her glare at Riordan. "Mr. Ballcap wasn't who you thought he was. Just a little present from the vrees."

"Ma'am—" Riordan began, shaky.

Sara held up a hand. "I don't give a fuck. Don't share. Just know this, kiddos—everything you've ever seen, everything you've ever done, it'll come back to bite you in the ass. The shitheads we fight, they can take advantage of every chink in your armor. So you get your shit together before you even think about coming up against one of these things. You've got to learn about everything and remember it all."

Like the goddamn bismallah, she thought with chagrin. She had some Qur'an to read before bed tonight.

Chamberlin chose that moment to burst through the bead curtain, his weapon out and ready.

"Where the royal fuck have you been?" Sara snapped. Chamberlin started to reply, but she interrupted him. "Fuck it, I don't care. Take the Bobbsey Twins over there and get the hell out of my face."

Sara knelt beside the fading smoke on the floor, feeling around in the darkness that seemed to be held in a vaguely man-shaped shadow. Out of the corner of her eye she saw Thacker nod to Chamberlin, and the others left.

Thacker knelt beside her. "It was turning into—"

"Yeah, once was enough for that fucker," Sara said.

They both watched the black, smoky shadow dissipate into the stained carpet.

Sara didn't look up. "Didn't know you were afraid of djinn, Thacker."

Thacker picked up his dagger and wiped the black blood off on the leg of his camo pants. "There's a lot you don't know about me, Harvey."

Now she glanced up at him, looking at him as though she'd never seen him before. "Heard you fought one once."

"You could say that." Thacker slid his knife into its sheath and didn't meet her eyes. "Only one Blackfire operative ever beat one."

Sara stood up. "I'd call it a draw."

***

Sara Harvey sat at the bar and thought about the ocean.

Behind her the team—if you could call them that—downed what she thought was likely the third round. If Thacker was buying, it'd be the last round. Camden, on the other hand, was just warming up.

"A vrees demon can read the things you're most afraid of and take that shape, but clearly it isn't bound by the rules of that shape," Camden said with the air of a lecture, as though speaking to a classroom instead of his teammates. "It wasn't affected by the salt, which apparently Major Harvey thought would work."

"Usually it would," Thacker said tightly.

Riordan ticked off her fingers. "So you can shoot most demons, iron and salt work on the Zulu impundulu and your average ghost. You use fire on water creatures and water on fire creatures—"

"Except when you don't," Thacker warned. "Try to memorize some kind of basic rulebook and you'll go crazy. For every ghoul repelled by fire, you'll find one who loves it. The more exotic the critter, the weirder the method used to quell it."

Sara heard a chair scrape.

"Major," Chamberlin said behind her. "Why don't you tell them about the redcap?"

"Thanks, I'll have another," Camden cracked, raising a hand to the barman.

Sara turned around. They stared at her. So young, so eager, gathered around the round wooden table with Thacker leaning back in his chair like a Scoutmaster. Okay, Camden wasn't much younger than Sara, but he acted the same age as the others, genius or not. Even Chamberlin had the fresh-scrubbed look of someone who still had the shine on his skin.

"Nobody's interested in old war stories, Chamberlin." Sara tried to turn back to her drink.

"I think I speak for everyone here when I say bullshit," Camden snarked.

"Please," Riordan said, smiling. She'd let her hair down, and Sara could tell both Jacobs and Camden appreciated it. They had all shaken off the creeps and adrenaline of the early part of the evening, and now were practically glowing with excitement. It was fun again for them, that combination of adventure and intellectual fascination that Sara could barely remember in the dim corners of the past when she had been a new recruit, after Paul Vaughn found her in the desert.

Sara surrendered and moved to the chair at the round table. In the other half of the bar, the jukebox switched into yet another country song. She'd hoped in Kansas City they could have found a real jazz club, but instead Thacker led them right to the most boring suds mill within walking distance of their motel.

"Redcap!" Riordan grinned. "Sounds like a soccer team."

"British critter," Sara said. "Looks like a slightly overgrown garden gnome, complete with pointy red hat."

"Oooh, scary," Jacobs said.

Sara winced involuntarily. "You'd be surprised."

Chamberlin actually pulled out his stupid notebook. "I read that they dip their hats in the blood of their victims, and that's why the hat is red."

Sara nodded. "Fucker is fast, too. Bullets bounce off him and he moves like a goddamn cheetah. Weapon of choice is an iron pike. He's affected by flame because he can only be killed when the hat is dry. That's why he kills, to keep the hat wet."

"Charming," Camden said. "Where did he get you?"

Sara glanced at Camden. "That super-observant thing you do? Fucking annoying."

"I'm betting the left leg," Camden said. "That's why you limp. You were injured there and—"

Sara glared. "I do not limp."

"Peter, shut up," Riordan said, smiling.

"We fought him with flamethrowers to dry out the hat," Sara said. "He moved fast, but we had three on the flamethrowers and—"

"From your old team?" Chamberlin asked.

Sara drank the rest of her bourbon in one gulp.

Thacker stepped in. "Textbook case, one for the records. They dispensed of it in one night."

"Textbook," Sara said with a wry near-smile. "Sure it was. Jimmy read

Scripture because every few verses it lost a tooth. That kept it distracted and slowed it down. Parish and I were on the flamethrowers with P-Paul, and Gary—"

She reached for her drink and remembered it was empty. "Gary kept shooting it, which was a waste of ammo. It played dead, and like a moron I got too close, and it got me in the leg. So we went back to the Scripture and flamethrowers until it was done."

Another bourbon arrived and Sara glanced up. Thacker passed a fiver to the barman, and she nodded thanks.

"That is the craziest shit I ever heard," Jacobs said. "Scripture and flamethrowers?"

"Beats the hell out of coconut goop," Sara muttered.

"The woodcutters of Japan appease the tengu by leaving rice cakes by the tree trunk," Chamberlin offered.

"Tengu are just pranksters," Camden said. "Most of the so-called threats we hunt are unique organisms that are no more dangerous than any other animal that—"

"Beg to differ," Jacobs said tightly.

"Seconded," Sara said.

Riordan shuddered. "That thing in the desert—"

"An ordinary devalpa," Chamberlin blundered in, clueless. Sara wanted to hit him with something heavy. "I read the whole file. They're shapeshifters and can be pretty dangerous when cornered, but they're susceptible to alcohol and can be easily avoided when tricked into imbibing."

"Oh yeah?" Jacobs snapped. "It got two of our unit before we figured that out, *sir.*"

"My apologies," Chamberlin said quickly.

"A shapeshifter is worse than any other snarling beast," Riordan said. "That thing today... I mean, how can you trust anyone or anything with things like that walking around. When anyone you talk to could be a monster in disguise?"

"It's just a matter of finding the right counteragent," Chamberlin said.

Jacobs looked at Chamberlin with something approaching Sara's own disdain. "Have you ever faced any critter, sir?" he asked, putting far too much emphasis on the honorific.

"Stow that shit," Sara ordered, though she noticed he had adopted her own preferred word for their quarries.

Jacobs subsided. "Just seemed as though there was a lot of book knowledge there, ma'am."

"Nothing wrong with book knowledge, Corporal," Chamberlin said, putting his own emphasis on rank. "There is as much study and reading in this job as wrestling and shooting."

Riordan tried desperately to get the topic away from the dick-measuring contest. "What is repelled by coconut goop, Major?"

Sara sighed. "Riordan, I'm begging you. Call me Harvey. Call me ma'am if you absolutely must. Don't call me Major."

"Yes, ma'am," Riordan replied, smiling.

"It's an aswang," Camden said. "A ghoul that lives in the Philippines, supposedly another shape-changer but—"

"Stop right there," Sara said, a little more sharply than she intended. They looked around at each other, a little uncomfortable.

Sara tilted her head toward the bar. "There are ears in the room, folks, and eyes are looking over here too often."

"So what?" Camden asked. "Never understood this whole secrecy thing. Why shouldn't we tell everyone what we know, let them protect themselves?" He stood up, the barest waver in his stance. "I could publish the definitive zoological study on the nesting habits of the blackwater dragon!"

The rest of the bar just stared at him. Thacker yanked Camden back down into his seat. "You're cut off."

Sara downed the rest of her bourbon. "I'm looking at my watch."

Chamberlin nodded and the others rose, tossing dollar bills on the table.

"I'd like to stay and buy Major Harvey another drink," Camden slurred.

"Sorry, I've had too much," Sara said.

Thacker helped Camden to his feet as they filed through the bar toward the door. Thacker's cell buzzed and he answered it, following the others out the door.

The music switched again, and Sara paused. There were couples dancing in the half-light of the bar and the soft glow of the jukebox in the corner as jazz music filled the air.

In the dim light, Sara saw a shaved-bald Black man twirling his partner across the floor on nimble feet as the woman laughed. It seemed like Sara could smell the gumbo cooling in bowls on the table by the dance floor, feel Parish's hand on her waist. They were partners and friends, and he was trying to help her learn to dance. He tried to lead, and she stepped on his foot.

"You just can't let anyone else drive, can you?" Parish laughed.

"You're supposed to be teaching me how to dance," Sara retorted.

"Then let me be in charge for once!" Parish insisted. "Didn't you ever go to prom?"

Sara cocked an eyebrow. "Do I look like a fuckin' prom queen?"

"Harvey, you got no rhythm!" Gary Stover crowed from the table, where Paul Vaughn and Jimmy watched with smiles.

"Be nice or the next lesson's yours, Stover," Sara shot back.

Parish swept her away across the floor. "Don't make me dance with Gary," he said. "I'll sleep with him if I must, but don't make me dance with him."

Sara burst out laughing so hard she lost her balance and stepped on Parish's foot for about the ninth time.

"I give up," Parish said. "You are hopelessly white."

Sara couldn't stop laughing. It felt so good to laugh, so open and free, a release of everything tied up inside her into that dark, smoky bar. Parish just stood there laughing with her, and there was blood frothing in his mouth, and she wrenched away from him in horror. When she looked at the table, they were all covered with blood, Gary and Jimmy and Paul... *Oh God, Paul.*

Paul Vaughn rose from his chair and walked toward her with that glittering coldness in his eyes, still laughing even as he came forward with the black eyes of It, his face splitting with bloodless wounds that would never heal, fatigues spattered with someone else's blood, his hands reaching out for her, bloody mouth open in a hideous grin, his hand on her shoulder, drawing her close—

"Sara!"

Whack—

Sara blocked the second slap automatically, shoving Thacker's hand away from her, free hand dropping to her small-of-the-back holster by reflex.

Thacker's free hand still rested on her shoulder, and she twisted away from it as though it was made of flame.

Thacker held up his hands, stepping back. "Harvey. You with me?"

Sara looked back at the dance floor. Everyone stared at her. The man on the dance floor wasn't Parish. The table in the corner was empty. The team wasn't there. They were dead, and they were gone.

The two don't always go together, Ssssara.

"The team is broken," she whispered.

The barman leaned over. "Miss, you need help?"

Sara stared at the barman for a second before she realized the cause of his concern. He was glaring at Thacker with white-hot spite. Thacker had slapped her. The barman thought Thacker was her husband or boyfriend and he was smacking her around in a public place. It was almost funny. But she never thought she'd laugh again.

"I'm fine," she said.

"Let's go," Thacker said quickly. The barman drilled him with another glare, and they hustled out the door fast.

The cool air out in the parking lot felt good on Sara's face.

"Sara—"

Sara held up a hand between them. "'Harvey' will do just fine."

Thacker walked beside her, following the distant forms of the rest of the team, nearly at their motel doors across the street. "If you ever need—"

"Oh for fuck's sake, shut up," Sara snapped. "I didn't want to be here, you made me be here. I'm doing my job, don't play shrink or I'll rip off your dick and shove it down your throat, got it?"

"You always had a way with words, Harvey," Thacker said dryly. "Look, I've got an assignment for you."

Sara sighed. "That was your phone call? What are we going after next?"

"Probably nothing," Thacker said. "They got a serial killer in Memphis, and we're just ruling out supernatural crankiness."

"Crankiness? This is the technical term now?" Sara said. "I once dealt with a cranky critter in Memphis. I wouldn't want to do it again."

"Good, because you're doing something else," Thacker said.

Sara stopped walking. "Dammit, Thacker, I'm doing my job. Don't you fucking send me away."

"Harvey, this is not a demotion," Thacker said. "I need you for a recruitment. It won't take all of us."

"I am fine," Sara insisted. "I was fine before you dragged me off my island, I'm fine now, don't you dare pull any bullshit with me because I want that fucking pension put through, you hear me?"

Thacker faced her in the awful orange glow of the security lights. "Nobody said anything about the pension, Harvey. Just calm down."

"Don't fucking tell me to calm down, I will not have anyone complain that I didn't fulfill my orders!" Sara snapped.

"I'm not saying that! Goddammit, you are the most obstinate woman I ever—" Thacker rubbed his face. "I need you to recruit a tech geek in St. Louis and catch up with us in Memphis. I have the utmost confidence in you, which is why I'm sending you on to St. Louis alone, and I am equally confident that Memphis has a garden-variety killer and not anything supernaturally cranky, so will you fucking chill already?"

Sara folded her arms across her chest. "Maybe."

Thacker made an exaggerated bow made more ridiculous by the orange security lights. "Thank you, milady. Now, if I have your dismissal, can I go snag a few hours of sleep before I have to listen to Camden puke his guts out?"

Sara glanced at the motel rooms beyond the pair of oh-so-inconspicuous black Jeeps. "He's trouble, Thacker. Unstable, too smart for his own good, insubordinate as hell—"

"Sounds familiar," Thacker muttered.

Sara shot him a glare.

Thacker ignored her. "He's a walking encyclopedia of theoretical knowledge and his observancy skills are goddamn supernatural when he's not smashed."

"I'm pretty sure observancy isn't a word," Sara said.

"Screw you." Thacker trudged toward the rooms. "Don't let the bedbugs bite."

"You wouldn't like to meet a real bedbug," Sara said. "Big as a tennis ball."

Thacker stared at her a second. "That's a thought that's gonna linger."

"My work here is done."

Thacker keyed his door open and went into the room he and Camden shared with Chamberlin. Sara wasn't sure what cosmic genius put her as the cold shower for the Bobbsey Twins, but she was going to fix that situation at their next port of call.

But first, she leaned against the back of the Jeep in yet another anonymous motel parking lot, and tried to find a star beyond the orange glare of the lights.

5

Sara leaned against the van under glowering dark-grey skies. At any moment it would rain cats, dogs, and small barnyard animals, and she wanted to be out of the parking lot by the time the skies fell.

It was nearly fall, and in a sane climate it would be cool in the late afternoon. But St. Louis appeared to be designed by a puckish God, wrapping the city in stifling humidity that seemed more appropriate to deep summer.

Thunder rumbled in the distance as Sara glanced at her watch. They were taking their sweet fucking time. The hulking glass building before her looked more like a corporate headquarters than a city jail, all green and shiny and new-looking in its dilapidated surroundings.

A raindrop fell against her cheek, a touch of blessed coolness. "Goddammit," she muttered, glancing up at the skies.

As if on cue, a pissed-off twerp in a suit pushed open the door, hustling a handcuffed man in an orange jumpsuit before him. The man in the cuffs was no more than twenty-six, with shockingly red hair and a full beard. He had a wiseass grin left over from whatever he'd been saying to the twerp in the suit, which Sara bet hadn't been "happy birthday."

She pushed off the van and stalked toward them, her bullshit identification-of-the-week in hand. "Sara Harvey. Taking custody of the prisoner."

The twerp glared daggers as he shoved a clipboard at her. She signed on the bottom line in her usual indistinguishable scrawl. "I hardly think we need the handcuffs," she said.

"Oh, I like you," the prisoner said.

"Shut up, Mr. Kaiser," Sara replied, handing the clipboard back.

The twerp took the clipboard and handed her a handcuff key. "Unlock him yourself. He's your problem now." He stalked back toward the green-glass jail as dime-sized raindrops marked their dalmatian pattern on the sidewalk.

Sara opened the side of the van. "Haul it," she said, shoving Kaiser ahead of her.

"I'm hauling, I'm hauling!" Kaiser stumbled up into the van and sat on the observation stool. Then he froze at the sight of the surveillance equipment as Sara clambered up after him and slid the door shut.

Just in time. Another thunderclap, and the skies burst open with massive hammering rain, all that pent-up fury roiling in the clouds driving down on the van.

Well, it needed a good wash anyway, Sara thought.

"Name's Mark, by the way," Kaiser said. "And you are?"

"I know your name, Mr. Kaiser," Sara said. "I'm going to unlock your restraints. When I do, you might be tempted to do something fucking stupid. Considering the amount of trouble you're in, I suggest you restrain your natural impulses until you hear what I have to say."

Kaiser shrugged. "No problem, I ain't going nowhere."

Sara reached over and unlocked the handcuffs. Kaiser slid his hands free and rubbed his wrists. "Much better, thank you."

"Don't thank me. You're not my first choice. Not my second or my fifth." Sara flipped open a manila folder.

"Choice for what?" Kaiser asked.

Without raising her eyes, Sara began to read. "Kaiser, Mark Aaron. Born and raised in Fresno, California, where you graduated third in your class. Would have been first except for a few disciplinary issues that led to two short suspensions from school. Attended MIT on a full scholarship, expelled for hacking the grading system."

"I was framed," Kaiser said.

Sara leveled her eyes at him over the folder. "I am completely unimpressed with your sense of humor, Mr. Kaiser."

"I'm getting that." Kaiser looked around the van. "Exactly who are you again?"

Sara returned to the folder. "You've got quite the reputation as a hacker, Mr. Kaiser. Your netname is Wilhelm, appropriate enough since it took the FBI almost the length of World War I to catch up to you. Shouldn't have gone for a bank. They're cranky."

"Also a frame job," Kaiser said.

Sara didn't look up this time. "What did I say about your sense of humor?"

"And you must really think I'm an idiot if you think I'm going to talk to you about my case," Kaiser retorted. "You're not my lawyer, my mother, or my priest. Frame job. That's my story and I'm stickin' to it."

Sara turned a page. "You were four years old the first time you were visited by a ghost."

That caught Kaiser's attention. His mouth gaped open, and he grabbed at the file. Unperturbed, Sara moved it out of his reach.

"You can't have my shrink's files," Kaiser insisted. "That's… You'd have to subpoena them or something, doctor-patient whatever… Goddammit, how did you get that?"

Sara flipped another page.

"There's no such thing as ghosts," Kaiser said, his voice almost desperate. "I know that now. I was a kid. My imagination—"

"Your imagination did not run away with you," Sara said. "You were not hallucinating. You are not schizophrenic. You do not have a brain tumor. You are a sensitive." She flipped the file closed and climbed into the front seat, sliding it into the space beside her seat.

Kaiser sat still in the back, stunned.

Sara looked over her shoulder. "Feel free to come up front. We have more to talk about."

"No shit, lady." Kaiser climbed into the passenger seat.

Sara started the van, the windshield wipers splashing the rain out of the way. Overhead, thunder rumbled hard across the sky. "At least it'll break this godawful humidity. I don't know how people live here."

Kaiser sat beside her, seemingly numb.

Sara rolled the van away from the jail and onto the St. Louis city streets. She intentionally took the long way to the river; they had plenty to discuss.

"About fifteen percent of the population is capable of sensing the dead," Sara said. "Possibly more than that, but they're misdiagnosed as having a mental illness, particularly in the college years. In children it's more likely to be dismissed as an overactive imagination, and many of them learn to keep quiet about it. They rationalize it away, even managing to convince themselves that they're not seeing or hearing it."

"I didn't." The smartass tone was entirely gone from Kaiser's voice.

"Nope. You took meds." Sara pointed to the file. "It doesn't take much to knock it down. I'm guessing you haven't seen anything in six years or more."

Kaiser turned to stare at her. "Who *are* you?"

Sara ignored the question.

"There is no such thing as ghosts," Kaiser insisted.

Sara snorted. "Ghosts. Werewolves. Vampires. Demons. The Loch Ness monster. All real."

"Please, lady. Pull the other one." Kaiser had regained some composure. "What is this, some new interrogation technique? I'm sure it violates—"

"Oh, spare me the TV-lawyer routine. I have less than zero interest in your hacking beef," Sara snapped. "I'm here to make you a once-in-a-life-time offer."

Kaiser glanced around. "Unless my lawyer is in your glove compartment, I'm pretty sure I'm not saying yes or no to anything today."

Sara sighed. "God, I was really hoping this wouldn't be necessary. It's fucking raining." She signaled to get into the interstate and flipped him her badge—her real badge, not the one she'd flashed at the jail.

Kaiser opened it and peered closely. "Blackfire. Wait, I heard of you. Government contractor, right? Security or something?"

"Or something," Sara said. "Specifically, we deal with supernatural threats to American interests here and abroad. Assessment, intervention and protection. My team needs a tech. You sign on with us for five years and your record is cleared. You'll be free to go forth and annoy the hell out of other people. The work is classified, so don't start thinking about writing a memoir unless you want to find yourself down a very deep hole."

Kaiser glanced out the window. "What is the work?"

"Tech, in your case," Sara said. "Surveillance. Recordings. Plus your ability might come in handy, so no more meds."

"Ability," Kaiser snorted. "How crazy are you, lady?"

"Go ahead, say no," Sara said. "I'll have you back at the jail before they serve dinner. You'll never see me again."

Kaiser didn't say anything for a while, as the van rolled over the bridge, rain pounding against the windshield as the wipers squeaked back and forth.

"There's no such thing as ghosts," Kaiser reiterated after a long time.

"This is the part I really hate," Sara said.

She took the first exit, weaving off the ramp onto an older highway that trailed the Illinois side of the river. Then she took a quick right, driving back west toward the river they had just crossed.

Kaiser looked out his window. "Where the hell are we going?"

"Clearly, you need some convincing," Sara said.

Kaiser grinned. "Is this the part where you pull my fingernails out? Let me guess—there's a nest of vampires on this puny little island, right?"

"Like I'd take you to vampires on your first trip out," Sara groused. "Just shut the fuck up."

"Wow, such a pleasant conversationalist. I can see why they made you the official recruiter," Kaiser cracked. "Tell me, how do you kill a vampire? Wooden stake through the heart?"

"Cut off its head," Sara replied without pause as the van rumbled across another bridge, older and narrower than the one they'd just crossed. It carried them over a canal to a man-made island stretched along the eastern shore of the Mississippi. It was a favorite with fishermen, hikers, and Blackfire. "You'd be surprised how many things don't take well to decapitation. It's pretty goddamn final."

"Well, sure, that makes sense," Kaiser said. "I mean, if you're going to suck blood and all that, you need a head. What about ghouls?"

"Salt and iron. Except in the Philippines."

Kaiser shook his head. "I think you're even crazier than I am."

The van rumbled and bounced down a dirt road that became little more than a levee path, tall grass brushing against its doors. The rain still drummed against the van roof, but not nearly as hard as it had a few moments ago.

They rolled up to a gate with razor wire rolled across the top. A weatherbeaten tin sign read ACME DISPOSAL CORP.

"Great," Kaiser said. "Well, even a landfill's better than jail."

"You never shut up, do you?" Sara asked.

Kaiser grinned. "Sick of me already?"

"I was sick of you before I met you." Sara rolled down her window and reached out to the small keypad on a metal post to her left. She keyed in a ten-digit combination, and the gate slowly swung open, allowing them through to the too-symmetrical hills of the closed landfill.

The van didn't want to climb those hills, but Sara pushed it, and it rumbled onward. Kaiser finally put on his seat belt, as the shocks groaned under the weight of the van slamming into the ruts in the road. "I'd make a joke about women drivers, but—"

"I'm armed."

Kaiser shut up.

The van finally crested the steep hill, revealing the vast crater in the center of the island. A trailer rested to the left with three or four men visible just outside it, hauling large plastic-wrapped cargo out of the bed of a nearby pickup truck toward the center of the crater.

The men saw her. Immediately two of them had sidearms out and leveled at the van. Kaiser instantly put his hands up. "Great! Now what?"

Sara rolled to a stop beside the truck. "I'd like my ID now."

Kaiser shook his head, hands still up in the air. "Get it yourself!"

Sara sighed and reached over him to grab it off his leg. "Forgive me for invading your personal space."

"Any time you want, under different circumstances."

The nearest worker came toward her, gun leveled at her head. Sara rolled down the window and held out her ID. "Blackfire, code clearance 2479371."

The worker checked her ID and immediately holstered his sidearm. "Sorry, ma'am."

Sara took her ID back. "Out of the van, Kaiser."

Kaiser climbed out with her, standing in the now-light drizzle beside the van. "What exactly are we waiting for?"

"Proof." Sara pulled binos from the thigh pocket of her camo pants and pretended not to notice Kaiser gaping at her. She was used to carrying a million pounds of crap in the pockets of her pants—it was easier than carrying a pack and she'd be in her coffin before she carried a purse. It was just easier to stuff her pockets like a chipmunk. For some reason, men never got that.

Sara aimed the binos up, but couldn't see anything past the ridge. "Damn." She pocketed them again. "Just stay right there, Kaiser."

"You going for coffee?" Kaiser asked.

"Not going anywhere," she said. "I'm just telling you to keep your ass still. No matter what you see, do not run away. It'll complicate things."

"Well, we wouldn't want that," Kaiser said.

The workers carried all three large plastic-wrapped packages to the center of the crater. One of them produced a boxcutter and slashed the plastic open.

"Shit, that's a body!" Kaiser exclaimed.

"Relax, it's just a skinned goat," Sara corrected. "Though we could always feed you to it if you piss me off too much."

"Feed me to what?" Kaiser asked.

Sara pointed up.

The shadow crested the hill before it descended, shimmering into life as though from thin air. Its camouflage ended as it entered the crater, rippling out of the dark sky in an explosion of golden and rust-red feathers. It was huge, easily twice the size of the van and covered with shimmering golden scales—almost like Camden's dragons, Sara thought.

But it had the majestic head of a lion, with an enormous jaw and golden horns jutting from its head. Its wings were nearly as wide as the crater itself, covered with gold and red feathers as they folded into its body. Its long whiplike tail likewise curled under it as it dipped its jaw down to the first goat.

"I've...seen it before," Kaiser breathed.

Sara nodded. "The ancient Native Americans painted it on the side of a bluff just a bit north from here. Used to be quite the pain in the ass—it ate an injured hiker or two, was hell covering it up. It's been trained for decades. We feed it, it doesn't eat us."

"It's fantastic." Kaiser had lost his smartass again, staring at the creature in wonder.

"Officially the Piasa is protected, as the only one of its kind," Sara said. "We do try not to wipe out whole species, not if we can help it. But if it starts eating people again..."

Kaiser shook his head. "Someone must see it."

"Camouflage," Sara explained. "It sort of bends the light waves around itself. It's there, we just don't realize we're seeing it. It's a shadow, a movement in the corner of your eye."

The workers watched Kaiser, poking each other and grinning. Sara wondered how many times they'd seen someone meet the Piasa for the first time, how something that amazing became commonplace.

Then again, how long did it take before she said things like "garden-variety ghoul" and developed a checklist for curing werewolves?

On impulse, Sara walked down the side of the hill toward the Piasa. Behind her, she could practically sense the workers snap to attention, covering her with their guns. It was not standard procedure to approach the Piasa, but Paul had brought her here once and…

Oh, but it hurt to think about Paul. Paul loved the Piasa. He was one of the few human beings who could approach it.

Sara walked now as he did then, slowly and with eyes downcast to avoid showing a challenge. She spread her arms outward as though they were wings, hunching her body over like a bird of prey.

"That seems like a really bad idea," she heard Kaiser call to the workers.

"It really is," one of them replied—the one who had come to the car. "Major, please come back up the hill now."

Sara ignored him. There was a snort from the Piasa, and she glanced up toward it.

The Piasa stopped eating. It tilted that magnificent head toward her, its giant eyes focused on the small human with arms outspread.

Sara bowed lower. "He can't come anymore," she told the Piasa. "I'm sorry."

The Piasa moved toward her, its giant legs crunching on the bones beneath it hard enough for Sara to feel the vibrations beneath her boots. It lowered its head even with Sara, eyes large and limpid behind the rustling feathers.

Sara met the Piasa's eyes, and a wave of sadness rolled over her like nothing she'd felt in all those weeks by the ocean. To her shock, something like tears welled behind her eyes, though she would not let them out.

She reached toward the Piasa slowly, aware of the increasing tension among the men up on the ridge. Her hand moved toward the Piasa's giant snout, and it would take nothing more than a twitch for the creature to eat her whole.

But instead it turned its massive head to the side, and allowed Sara to stroke the soft, down-like feathers alongside its eyes. She moved her hand with the feathers, brushing it over and over. The Piasa nudged her gently with its snout, and she nudged it back hard, as she had seen Paul do that one time.

The Piasa made a low keening sound in its throat, something that almost sounded like mourning. Did it know? Could it sense that Paul was dead, because Sara was here without him? Could a creature like the Piasa…grieve?

Suddenly Sara hoped that it could. It should grieve a human being who had understood it as an eternal creature beyond their understanding, not a monster to be contained and controlled.

Someone should grieve for Paul Vaughn. If you die and no one mourns you, were you ever really alive? Did you leave any mark on the world?

"Please, Major, come up now," the worker called.

Sara patted the Piasa one more time and bowed her head. "I'm sorry," she said again.

Then she backed away as Paul had, slowly and with arms outspread. When she reached the edge of the crater, she turned and climbed up the side, where the men were twitching. Kaiser's eyes were very wide.

She stepped in front of Kaiser, heedless of the rain, which was coming down heavier now. "I'd give you the 'your country needs you' bullshit, but that ain't my thing," she said. "I need a tech. The powers that be think you'd be a good fit. I don't know if that's true or not—I used to run without a tech and did just fine. But the world is getting more technical by the day and now it's a requirement. You run my surveillance and communications, do our field research and try not to piss me off. In five years, you're a free man."

"See the world, meet exciting creatures and kill them?" Kaiser was trying to be a wiseass and failing, as the Piasa gnawed a limb off one of the goats.

"Make up your mind, Kaiser," Sara said. "The men have other things to do."

In fact, the three workers were eyeing them again. Truth be told, Sara didn't know what would happen to Kaiser if he said no and thus became a giant security risk. No one had ever declined at this point.

Kaiser nodded slowly, eyes on the Piasa. "I'm in."

"Good." Sara nodded to the workers as she climbed back into the van. "Move it."

"Yes ma'am." Kaiser climbed in as well. "Can I ask just one question that you'll actually answer, ma'am?"

Sara sighed. "Goddamn. What?"

"What's your name?"

She blinked. "Oh. Sara Harvey. *Not* Major, no matter what those yahoos said."

Kaiser extended a hand. "Nice to meet you, Sara Harvey. I assume you are the morale officer."

Sara managed not to smile as her phone buzzed on the dashboard. "Not exactly. Your team leader is Dan Chamberlin, you'll meet him in

Memphis. Military liaison is Colonel Nathan Thacker. They're the two you take orders from. I'm a temporary attaché." She reached for the phone.

"Does that mean I shouldn't get 'attached' to you?" Kaiser cracked.

Sara didn't respond, staring at the text on her phone.

"C'mon, surely I get a sympathy laugh," Kaiser coaxed.

Sara looked at him. "We're out of here. Dan Chamberlin is dead."

INTERLUDE

Sara Harvey woke when Paul Vaughn rolled down the window to show his credentials.

"Damn. We there already?" she muttered, straightening up in the shotgun seat of the van and rubbing her eyes.

The sentry shaded his eyes against the sun to examine Paul's identification, his hand resting on his sidearm. Especially as remote as they were, it was a bit overzealous. Either the sentry was very nervous about something, or he was very stupid. Sara was tempted to pull her sidearm on him just to fuck with him, but she was bone-tired. Also, she was likely to get Paul shot in the crossfire, and that was a little extreme just to prove a point.

"Looks fine, sir. Do you know where you're going?" the sentry asked.

"Been there a lot," Paul replied, taking his ID back. "Next time you want to keep your hand off your weapon while the ID's confirmed, soldier."

The sentry straightened up with a nervous salute. "Yes sir."

Sara grinned as Paul rolled through the gate. "I coulda taken him."

"A teddy bear with small arms could have taken him," Paul groused. "Hey, you in the back. Wake up."

There was no response from the rear of the van. Sara unbuckled her seat belt—a clear violation of Wyoming state law—and crawled back over piles of miscellaneous crap littering the back of their allegedly high-tech van.

She kicked Gary Stover none too gently in the side. "Hey, sleeping beauty, wake the hell up."

Gary startled up. "Shit. We're at Farson already? How long since Cheyenne?"

"About five hours," Paul replied.

Parish woke a little more easily, yawning and stretching. "I'm too old for this shit."

"Spare me," Sara said, checking the cargo. All secure. "Any dreams?"

"None," Parish replied. "It's fake then?"

Gary snorted. "Duh."

"Not our call," Sara said. "C'mon, guys, make yourselves at least quasi-presentable. We've got to meet real people in here. It'd be nice if you didn't look like the remnants of a middle-aged bachelor party."

Gary and Parish looked at each other, blinking in unison. There wasn't a single unwrinkled item of clothing between them, and a razor had not approached either jaw in at least forty-eight hours. Gary had a stain she fervently hoped was ketchup on his shirt, and Parish's belt was unbuckled, hanging around his waist like a dead snake.

Sara probably didn't look much better. She ran her fingers through her short-cropped black hair and wondered why they never thought to put a mirror in the van that served as their dormitory more often than not.

Paul rolled the van to a stop by the main building of the Farson complex. Somehow Paul always looked pin-straight, even though he'd been driving wide-awake while the rest of them catnapped their way across Wyoming. His fatigues were perfectly neat, his eyes clear, and somehow he was still clean-shaven. How did he manage that? Did he pull over by the side of the road and run a quick razor over his face? Or did he carry a magic amulet that stopped hair from growing? Either seemed equally possible, which probably meant that Sara needed more rack time.

"Lock and load," Paul said, and Sara yanked the van door open. They erupted out the side while Paul came around the back to open the doors. Parish went to help Paul with the box, which wasn't really heavy enough to need two men, but it was long enough to be awkward.

Gina Wotosi came striding out the door toward them, impeccable as always. She wore a trim pencil skirt, blouse, and high heels every day.

Sara had never seen her in anything as prosaic as pants or, heaven forfend, sandals. Gina's gait was steady and perfect despite heels that were just barely this side of the height commonly known as fuck-me pumps. If Sara ever tried to wear shoes like that, she'd teeter over and fall on her ass, probably with a busted ankle to boot.

"Paul! How marvelous to see you and your team!" Gina gushed. That was the other thing Sara couldn't stand about Gina—she was so goddamn cheerful. Upbeat and friendly, prone to hugs and friendly pats on the arm.

Except with Sara, of course. She'd told Gina two visits ago that the next time she patted Sara she was going to lose a finger. Gina said Sara had problems with authority. Sara was about to reply when Paul stepped in, probably saving her from an insubordination rap. Or jail.

The guys set the box on the ground and Paul stood at attention. Gina flapped a careless hand at him. "None of that, silly. How ARE you? You look fabulous." She hugged him and did that fake-kiss thing where she kissed the air next to his cheek. She also moved with a little more sway to her hips when Paul was around. Sara had enough estrogen in her to notice.

Gary stared at Gina with his openly lecherous gaze, which Sara was used to ignoring. Gina's eye skimmed over him, turning away with vague discomfort. Parish might as well have been invisible.

"And Sara!" Gina said, obviously restraining herself from actually reaching out to her. "My goodness, we have got to get them to lighten up on the regs. You'd look so pretty with longer hair."

"It isn't regulation," Sara said.

"Oh." Gina was barely flustered. "Well, silly me! It frames your jaw so nicely."

"We're not here to talk about my hair," Sara said. "We've got an artifact for you."

Gina looked over at Paul. "What's your thought on it?"

"I like Harvey's hair just fine." Paul's face was absolutely deadpan.

The guys broke up, snickering as quietly as they could.

Gina's smile faltered, then she chucked Paul on the arm. "Silly man! You know I meant the artifact!"

Paul pointed to the box. "It's in too good condition to be real, and none of us have had any dreams or noted unusual symptoms while we've been carting it around. You'll get a full report before we leave, but my gut reaction is it goes in the warehouse of fakes."

"You're probably right, but let's take it to isolation anyway," Gina said. "Come with me, Paul!" She laid a perfectly manicured hand on his arm and led him up the short sidewalk to the windowless cinderblock building.

Sara minced along behind them, mimicking Gina's hip-swaying walk and gesturing with her free arm like the other woman did. Gary and Parish chortled as they followed with the box, which made Gina glance over her shoulder.

Sara desisted immediately, shrugging like *I don't know what gets into these two.* Gina turned away again, keying her code into the front door, but Paul shot them a quick look that said, *Behave yourselves, children.*

They passed the door guards and walked down the cinderblock hallway. Sara waved the boys down the left side, as if they'd forget where the artifact examination rooms were. Sara followed Gina and Paul through yet another keycard door, stifling a yawn. She was much too tired to pay any attention to Gina's nattering.

"We have a number of messages for your team, Paul." Gina ticked them off on her fingers. "Parish Roberts has another court appearance pending—"

Paul held up a hand. "We're taking care of it, yes?"

"Naturally," Gina said. "The last thing we want is one of our team members under oath for any reason." She ticked off another finger. "You've also had three calls from your brother, and he's starting to sound awfully curious."

Paul's jaw tightened and Sara fervently wished she was allowed to hit Gina.

"Don't worry about my brother," Paul said tightly. "I'll handle it."

"But—" Gina began.

"He'll handle it." Sara glowered. Gina glanced back at her, uneasy.

They entered the observation room, where a trio of lab assistants worked at the upper console while Gina led them to the lower level by the windows. In the lab below them, a collection of white coats clustered around a lab table with bright lights centered on an oblong brown stone about the size of a cantaloupe, with a few suspicious red streaks.

"I thought you'd like this one." Gina pointed down at the stone.

Paul leaned toward the observation window. "Mayan blood stone?"

"Christ, Paul, you know everything," Sara muttered.

"Not quite," chirped a young voice. Sara glared upward as a babyfaced kid who looked barely old enough to shave scampered down to their level, his white coat flapping behind him. "Incan, not Mayan."

"Whatever," Sara groused.

"It's a big difference," the kid yammered, oblivious. "The Inca had the far superior civilization, though the Mayans are the ones that get all the attention, what with the calendar and all. The Inca worshipped stone, and despite having a lesser technology and no concept of the arch, the Tawantinsuyu constructed vast cities in less than a hundred years. It's possible they were able to tap into deeper energies than the Mayans and harness them inside—"

"A rock." Sara glared at him.

The kid almost literally gulped, finally figuring out that Sara was not someone to annoy. He switched his attentions to Gina and Paul. "You're just in time. They're about to start the experiment."

True enough, the white coats were filing out of the room—all except one, an older gentleman with creases on his lab coat that belied his impeccable white beard.

Then two assistants came in, one skinny and one heavyset. They were leading a scruffy young man in an orange prison jumpsuit.

"Shit," Sara said. "I thought we weren't doing this anymore? Goddammit, Paul—"

"Major." Paul still occasionally used Sara's Marine rank, especially when he needed to remind her of her professionalism. Sara subsided, glowering.

"Our volunteers are carefully selected and quite well compensated," Gina chirped. "This particular gentleman is serving a five-year sentence for possession with intent to sell marijuana. That gets reduced to ten months in return for his assistance today, so naturally that's a heck of an incentive."

"'Carefully selected,' making sure they have no next of kin to raise noisy questions when something goes wrong," Sara retorted.

"If something goes wrong, we always take care of our people," Gina replied, looking like she wished she could send Sara in for experimentation.

"Something always goes wrong," Sara grumbled.

"A little faith, Major," Paul said quietly. Behind him, the kid was studying his shoes.

Gina pressed the intercom button beside the window. "We're watching, Dr. Milan."

The white beard looked up and nodded. The prisoner looked around nervously. "Who's watching?"

"Don't worry," Milan said, pointing to the chair. "One little prick and that's all it takes."

"I heard that one before," Sara muttered.

The kid beside her snorted, and Sara upgraded her opinion of him half a step.

"The problem is, I got a thing about needles," the prisoner said, shifting his feet from side to side.

"You promised cooperation," Milan said, a warning note in his voice.

"What's his name?" Paul asked. Gina looked at Paul blankly.

The kid spoke up instead. "Donald McAllister. He's about twenty-two, I think."

Paul leaned over to the intercom. "It's all right, Donald. Just sit in the chair and don't look while he draws the blood."

"Don't look?" Donald asked, looking up at the window. His eyes were very blue, Sara realized, a brilliant cerulean blue that didn't seem possible without special contacts.

"That's right," Paul said as Donald sat uneasily in the chair. "I want you to look away from Dr. Milan and fix your eyes on a point on the wall."

Donald laid his arm out for sacrifice and did as Paul said. Milan approached with the needle and palpated the veins.

"You've got to relax your arm," Milan said, still testy.

Sara wanted to smack him. Instead, she leaned over to the intercom herself. "Donald, were you a Boy Scout?"

Donald blinked, and the others looked at her like she had sprouted a third leg out of her neck. "I dropped out in the ninth grade."

"Tell me the Scout Law," Sara said.

Donald shook his head. "Uh. A Scout is trustworthy, loyal, friendly, thrifty— Ow!"

"Keep going!" Sara insisted.

"Trustworthy! Loyal! Friendly! Thrifty! Truthful! Brave! Clean! Uh, reverent!" Donald blurted them out as Milan drew the blood and quickly slapped a cotton ball and strip of gauze tape on the tiny wound in his arm.

"Good job, Donald," Sara said, switching off the intercom.

"He missed a few." Paul had a slight grin on his face.

Sara snorted. "I should've known. You've got Eagle Scout printed on your goddamn forehead, Iceman."

"How did you know it would work?" the kid asked.

Sara's jaw tightened. "Worked on my brother."

Paul glanced at her sideways, but Sara stared ahead, stonefaced.

Milan led Donald to a gurney and put him in restraints. If anything, Donald was more frightened now that the needle part was over. How someone so easily freaked could have been a dealer, Sara had no idea. On the other hand, he might have been a really bad dealer. After all, he did get caught.

Milan took the three tubes of blood he'd drawn and set one aside on the side counter. Then he withdrew a few drops from the second tube in a syringe and brought it over to the table.

Milan glanced up then, a chilling smile creasing his beard that only those in the observation gallery could see. It was the anticipatory smile of a child on Christmas morning, a child who has no fear of breaking his new toys. Sara had always found Victor Milan to be the creepiest person at Blackfire, and that was saying something.

Milan let a large drop of Donald McAllister's blood well up on the needle and dropped it on the Incan bloodstone. The blood rolled across the stone's surface and dripped onto the table as though the rock were impervious as plastic.

The two assistants gathered at the foot of Donald's gurney. Donald craned his neck, trying to see what Milan was doing. The skinny one started asking him questions, meaningless coherency questions like name, age, what year it was, who was president and so on. Donald answered correctly and seemed perfectly fine to Sara.

"Darnit," Gina said. "We thought we'd found a real one this time."

"You can put it next to the Grails," Sara said.

Suddenly Milan shoved the skinny assistant aside and grabbed at Donald's arm. He ripped off the bandage, making Donald yelp more out of surprise than pain.

"Doctor, what are you doing?" Gina asked into the intercom.

Milan didn't answer. He took the cotton ball with its tiny stain of dark-red blood over to the bloodstone and pressed it against the stone with his thumb, as his assistants looked at him in shock.

Donald began to laugh, a low, chuckling laugh that seemed much lower than his regular speaking voice.

Both assistants scurried away from the gurney as though Donald had suddenly sprouted flames.

"Of course!" the kid beside Sara exclaimed, clapping his hands together in excitement. "Anticoagulant is standard in the withdrawal tubes. It must have screwed with the sample—"

Milan stepped over to Donald's gurney. The young man grinned up at him, a smile full of horrid cheer and the glee of dead things feasting on each other. It was strangely a mirror of Milan's own smile, enough that Sara shuddered from the safety of her glass-enclosed gallery.

"What is your name?" Milan asked.

"You know my name," Donald whispered, his eyes alight. The deep cerulean blue had vanished, the irises bleeding completely black as though the pupil had expanded to cover them.

Milan stepped around the gurney and repeated himself. "Tell me who you are."

"*Kay pacha*," Donald hissed. "It is good to be back, old man."

The kid beside Sara tapped madly on some handheld computer thing, muttering *kay pacha* under his breath. Sara wanted to look over his shoulder, but was afraid to stop watching the goddamn fuckarow happening down below them.

Donald's face turned away from Milan, staring up at the observation window. That terrible smile split his face again, and Sara's hand fell to the gun at her hip without thinking about it.

"*Ukhu pacha*," Donald chanted.

"Uh," the kid stammered. "Snake…no, the symbol was the snake…"

Donald wrenched his arms forward, and the restraints popped as though they were made of a child's ball of string.

"Shit!" Sara exclaimed.

Paul hit the intercom. "Doctor, get out of there now!"

It was too late.

Donald's hand was around the throat of the skinny assistant even as the heavyset one scrambled for the door. Milan slammed a hand down on the console and the door locked tight, keeping all three inside.

"*Ukhu pacha*," Donald said and squeezed. The assistant's eyes bugged, and his hands scrabbled helplessly at Donald's arm and shoulder, trying to wrench free.

There was a terrible *pop.*

Sara pivoted toward the door. Paul's hand fell on her arm as if to stop her, and she glared at him.

"*Ukhu pacha*, that's the underworld!" the kid yelped behind Sara. "*Kay pacha* is earth, and *ukhu pacha* is the underworld, which makes him—"

Donald laughed, throwing the body of the skinny assistant to the side.

He advanced slowly toward Milan, ignoring the heavyset one, who pounded on the door and screamed.

"*Sapay*," Donald chanted.

Milan backed up, but he didn't flinch. That much Sara had to give him. Up on the observation level, Gina was frozen into uselessness, her hands jammed against her open mouth. Paul shouted at the workers on the upper level, who were calling other no-name useless people on their stupid phones or fruitlessly throwing switches.

Paul climbed up and grabbed a phone. "Merrifield! Lock down the facility now!"

Below, that awful laughter rose again. "*Capacocha*," Donald chanted.

"Oh shit," the kid whispered.

Sara turned to him. "What? What the fuck does that mean?"

The kid met Sara's eyes, and while he was clearly afraid, there was still a conscious mind working out the problem. "If he's *Sapay*, he's the Incan god of the underworld, ruler of a race of demons—"

"The point!" Sara snapped.

The kid swallowed hard but kept steady. She upticked his rating another notch. "The *capacocha* was the Inca ceremony of human sacrifice."

Sara had had enough. She grabbed the kid by the sleeve of his white lab coat and dragged him out the door.

"Harvey!" she heard Paul shout behind her, but Sara kicked the door shut and scrambled down the stairs to the lab level. Klaxons blared and doors slammed everywhere, and as Sara entered the lab corridor she pulled her gun.

Parish and Gary popped out of the examination room on the left, minus the stupid spear they'd delivered.

"What the fuck, Harvey?" Gary already had his gun out.

Sara nodded to them. "We're working, boys."

"Good," Gary said.

Parish drew his own gun with a sigh. "Remind me never to go on vacation with you, Harvey."

Sara advanced toward the exam room door. "Kid, open that door."

The kid opened his mouth to protest, but Sara's glance stilled him. He snapped his jaw shut without a word and yanked the cover off the electronic keypad. His too-young face frowned at its workings, and he brushed sandy-brown hair out of his face.

"Gimme a bullet," he said.

Sara nodded, and Parish popped a round out of his magazine. The kid shoved the bullet into the circuitry, ducking to the side. An instant later there was a tiny *pop* and a puff of smoke.

Sara and Parish stood side by side, guns aimed at the floor, and together they kicked the door hard. It splintered free of its housing at the first kick and Gary went through on point, weapon aimed at anything that moved. Sara and Parish followed through in flanking posture.

The lights flickered over them, barely registering. The light from the hallway cast vague shadows over the lab equipment. Sara's foot struck an unyielding shape, and she glanced down to the body of the heavyset assistant, lying in a pool of blood, mercifully face-down.

She jerked her head to the side and the guys spread out, with Sara moving over toward the console. She searched for some sign of Milan or Donald, but there was too much in the way, too many things casting shadows in the weird half-light from the hall.

A shot from above them and glass showered down into the room and onto Sara. She ducked and rolled for cover by instinct as Gary and Parish immediately knelt to lower their profile and aimed upward. Sara came back up into a kneeling posture, searching for a target.

Paul lay on the floor of the observation gallery in perfect sniper pose above them. "Harvey, two o'clock!"

Sara pivoted and fired. Her shot just missed Donald, who scrambled out of the way barely in time, ducking behind a shelf of medical supplies.

"*Sapay!*" Sara shouted. "You're trapped. Give it up! Let the host go!"

From her kneeling stance, Sara could see Milan crouched under the console, apparently unhurt. She resisted the urge to shoot him.

The light from the hallway darkened, a tall shadow falling across the room. It was the kid, hesitating in the doorway.

"Get the fuck outta here, hayseed!" Sara shouted.

But the kid ignored her, running across the room even as Donald leapt for him. Parish shouted something lost in the furor—the kid was directly in his line of sight. Gary scrambled around the other side, bumping into a table as he tried to get a visual.

Sara jumped up onto the console, knowing she was blocking Paul's line of sight, but she had to see what the hell was going on.

The kid reached the examination table, his hands stretched out for the bloodstone. The cotton ball had already fallen off, lying innocently beside it.

Donald howled in fury, his ordinary face twisted with frustrated hate.

The kid laid his hands on the bloodstone.

Donald stopped still.

"Hold your fire!" Sara shouted. Parish and Gary straightened up, guns leveled directly at Donald. Behind her, Sara knew Paul had Donald's head in his sights.

The kid's hands trembled, but he kept his hands on the bloodstone. "*Ukhu pacha,*" he said.

"They will eat you alive, boy," Donald whispered.

The kid's hands trembled even more. "*Sapay! Ukhu pacha!*"

Donald let out a horrid gurgling scream, and his body collapsed to the ground.

After a moment, the kid let his hands fall away from the stone. He looked over at Sara. "I could feel it...feel it go," he said. "I guess you can only control it if you're holding the stone."

"Nice to know," Sara said, hopping down to the floor and glaring at Milan, who was still crouched under the console.

Donald groaned. Sara grabbed the shackles from the floor and snapped them on his hands and ankles, just in case.

Then she glared upward. "Gina. Better get your crews in here. This one isn't for the fake storeroom."

Gina's wide-eyed face appeared, silently gaping over Paul's head.

Sara met Paul's gaze over his gun and saw her own aversion mirrored in his eyes, before his cool detachment swept back over and he stood up.

Gary and Parish holstered their guns, and Sara brushed the broken glass off her clothes and out of her hair.

"*Now* do we get the day off?" Parish asked.

"No guarantees," Sara muttered.

Milan climbed out from under the console at last, dusting off his white coat.

Sara gave him her most withering glare. "Hey, Doctor Death. Chalk this one up as a success, huh?"

Milan stalked out without acknowledging her, but Parish gave him a look of such contempt as Sara had never seen from him.

Sara turned to the kid. "How did you know?"

The kid pointed at the bloodstone. "It's activated by touch, it's about control, I took a shot."

"It could've killed you, or taken you over as well," Parish said.

The kid shrugged. "And if it got out of the room, what happens to the rest of the world? It was worth a try."

Sara holstered her gun. "You got a name, kid?"

He wiped the sweat off his face. "James Bell. Jimmy."

Sara leveled her stare at him. "Crazy, stupid, or brilliant?"

Jimmy smiled in a way that made her realize he couldn't be any older than twenty. "Can't I be all three, Major?"

Sara extended a hand to him. "Never call me Major, kid. You want a new job?"

                                  6

                          ____

Thacker was waiting in the lobby at the Memphis precinct when Sara and
Kaiser walked in.

"What the fuck, Thacker?" Sara glared at him.

Thacker didn't smile. "Trust you not to waste any energy on 'hello,'
Harvey." He extended a hand to Kaiser. "I'm Colonel Nathan Thacker,
military liaison."

Kaiser shook his hand. "Mark Kaiser, newbie."

"Waiting," Sara snapped.

"And obviously you know Mary Sunshine," Kaiser said.

Thacker inclined his head toward a bench a bit further from the desk,
where an administrative aide was paying them absolutely no attention as
he stamped things and stapled other things. They moved away anyway,
and Thacker pitched his voice lower.

"Standard recon along the shore last night with a few Bolivian glow
wands, just to see if we could pick up any supernatural energy," Thacker
said.

Sara groaned. "Those things are bullshit."

"They're better than nothing when you've got a crew that doesn't
know how to recognize a supernatural, Harvey," Thacker insisted. "I was
pretty sure this wasn't supernatural, and I'm still—"

"What happened to Chamberlin?" Sara interrupted.

Thacker's jaw tightened. "Riordan found his body on the riverfront just after midnight. Drowned on dry land, just like the others. She was also seen by dockworkers, so she had to play up the screaming witness or end up a suspect. She's in there now, giving her bullshit statement."

Sara glanced around the precinct lobby. Other than one guy frantically arguing into a cell phone and the disinterested aide at his desk, no one was paying them any attention. "And exactly what do they think of you?"

"Uncle," Thacker said.

The keypad-locked door on the far side of the lobby opened, and Riordan came out with a pair of detectives. "Thank you, gentlemen. I hope you find whoever killed that poor man." She offered a shaky-yet-sweet smile that almost could have fooled Sara.

"Thank you for your help, ma'am," said the first detective, whose nameplate read HERNANDEZ.

The other detective stepped around his partner and offered Riordan his hand.

Sara felt her stomach sink. She looked around for anywhere to hide without drawing attention to herself. She slipped her sunglasses on and tried to fade behind Kaiser.

Too late.

The detective froze midway through shaking Riordan's hand as his eye fell on Sara.

"Mother-fuck," he whispered.

Thacker shot a glance at Sara, then turned back to the detective. "Something wrong, Detective Horowitz?"

Horowitz pointed at Sara. "Lose the shades."

"Giving me orders now?" Sara couldn't help saying. But she pulled them off anyway. There was never a secret trap-door to Hell when you really wanted one.

She met Horowitz's eyes, absolutely unchanged after all this time. She tried to keep her own gaze cool, her best Iceman impression. "Heard you were transferred to Atlanta."

"Came back two years ago," Horowitz said. "So, this is what we've got now? It's back?"

Hernandez snapped his fingers. "I remember you. Aw shit. Is this that same fuckhead who—"

"Gimme a second, wouldja, Juan?" Horowitz said, his voice tight. "And...the rest of you?"

They stepped away, Riordan and Kaiser staying mute as they pretended to know each other.

Thacker remained at Sara's side and Horowitz glared at him. "Uncle Nathan, huh." Horowitz turned back to Sara. "Tell me it isn't the same thing that—"

"Don't know," Sara replied truthfully. "You haven't given us shit to work with."

"I didn't know it was one of yours," Horowitz said.

"Then give us access to your files," Thacker said.

Horowitz glared at Thacker again. "I have not invited Blackfire into my case, sir. Technically I could charge you all with obstruction of justice, including the girl."

Sara folded her arms. "Try it. See what happens."

Horowitz turned his attention back to her. "New team?"

Sara glanced away at that. "I'm retired."

"Yeah. You look real retired. How many weapons do you have on you this time?" Horowitz had effectively dismissed Thacker from the conversation.

"None that you're going to find," Sara retorted. "Are you really going to make this personal?"

"Naw, why would I do that?" Horowitz said sarcastically. "Tell me everything and maybe I'll invite you in on the case."

"I don't have anything to tell," Sara said. "Just got to town."

Horowitz sighed. "Still stubborn."

"You have no idea," Thacker muttered.

Horowitz studied Sara intently, as if trying to read her mind. She wished fervently for her sunglasses, but it would have felt like hiding. Instead she looked at his ear, his throat, anywhere but his eyes.

She spied the silver chain disappearing beneath his shirt and averted her eyes.

"Sorry," Horowitz said. "Unless they order me to invite you in, this remains my case and you're out. I don't intend to have a repeat of last time."

"It worked," Sara said, keeping her voice cool.

"You trust Blackfire now? You trust *him?*" Horowitz pointed at Thacker. "They lie. They manipulate and they don't give a rat's ass who gets hurt in the meantime. And I'm not entirely convinced you're any better, Sara."

Sara was surprised to find that actually stung. She slipped the sunglasses on before Thacker or Horowitz could see her eyes.

"That's enough," Thacker growled. If the situation weren't so serious, she'd almost smile at Thacker getting all protective. He signaled to the others, and they followed him toward the door.

Sara started to follow, then stopped and turned back to Horowitz. "Chamberlin was fairly useless, but he was one of mine," she said. "You know what that's like, right? To lose one of your own?"

"I don't want to find out," Horowitz said. "Tell me this. Only men have died so far. Is it the popobawa?"

Sara shook her head. "Believe me when I say, I don't know. I don't think so."

"Well, that's a big screaming comfort," Horowitz said, handing her a card. "Call me when you know something."

She held the card up in mock salute, then followed her people out into the sunlight.

Sara paced the motel room like a caged panther, chafing at the confining walls. She was never very fond of the Elmwood Motel anyway. "Can't you go faster?"

"Can *you* hack the Memphis Police Department's computer system?" Kaiser's eyes rose from behind his laptop, a smartass eyebrow cocked. Sara glared at him. "Then I suggest you let the maestro work."

"Maestro," Camden sneered, tossing a worn tennis ball into the air and catching it. Riordan sat beside him on one of the double beds, reading a beaten-up copy of *Tales from the French Quarter*.

"Aren't you the genius? Shouldn't you be able to fly a computer?" Jacobs asked.

"Bread and circuses for the masses," Camden declared.

"Respectfully disagree," Kaiser said from behind his laptop.

Sara paced faster.

Camden sidled closer and tried to look over Riordan's shoulder. "What *are* you reading?"

"Supernatural fables from New Orleans," Riordan said. "I expect some of them might have a basis in fact and thought it would be good background reading."

Camden peered at the book and probably at Riordan's thin T-shirt as well. "Perhaps you and I could sneak off to the pub and chat a bit about folklore."

Riordan leveled a cool stare at Camden. "Perhaps not."

"I am the maestro!" Kaiser declared.

Sara pivoted mid-pace and went directly to his desk, peering over his shoulder. "Tell me you're in."

"I am in, baby," Kaiser said. "I am slidin' my hand up her skirt and—"

Sara smacked his shoulder.

"Five men in total," Kaiser said without missing a beat. "A homeless man was the first victim, found on the parking lot by Mud Island last Tuesday. Who names an island 'Mud'? Isn't that just asking for floods?"

"Focus, Kaiser." Sara beckoned to the others, and they crowded around Kaiser's laptop.

"A park worker was next, found on Friday by a rock wall in Confederate Park," Kaiser said. "Again, near the river but not by it. A pair of dockworkers earlier this week, both found on the wharf on the same night. Not far from—"

"Where I found Chamberlin," Riordan finished. "Those Bolivian glow sticks didn't—"

Sara held up a hand. "Stop right there. Those glow sticks are total bullshit and if I hadn't been babysitting Red here, I'd never have allowed you out with them."

"I think I prefer Wilhelm to Red," Kaiser protested.

Sara ignored him. "You have to learn to hone your own senses when you're out in the field. You can't depend on gadgets and machinery; half the supernaturals can fuck them up by looking at them cross-eyed. Trinkets and artifacts can help you some, but you never know when there's going to be another goddamn exception. The only rule is that there are no rules. Better to learn to find the things yourself, trusting your gut and instincts, then be lulled into a false sense of security because of some goddamn glowstick—"

She stopped then, because they were all watching her with an identical expression on their faces. It wasn't sarcastic or challenging, it wasn't boredom or even the guarded caution she saw in Thacker's face before he left.

It was interest. Curiosity. Learning. God help them, they were beginning to see her as a teacher, a leader. Dan Chamberlin was supposed to be their leader, and he'd gotten his ass killed the first week. None of them were reeling about it—they'd barely known him, survived exactly one-point-five encounters with him, and he hadn't exactly inspired confidence in the few days he'd been with them. It wasn't like they served with him for years and then watched him blow his own head off before their eyes.

Sara felt it then, that slick clench in her stomach, roiling inside her chest, as she fought off the image of blood and brains spattered across a boat deck. She wanted to run away from their eyes, so young and distant, clearly turning to her despite her best efforts to keep them away. Keep them safe.

She dropped her eyes to the laptop instead, trying to think of the ocean, huge and cold and swelling over her heart to still its beating.

Her eyes focused on the screen, and she pointed. "What's that one?"

Kaiser tapped. "She's not part of the pattern, just another case assigned to your best friend Horowitz. A Jane Doe they found the day before the homeless guy."

The pictures popped into resolution, and Sara winced. The victim was a very young woman, probably no older than Riordan. Her face was frozen in terror, her hands bound cruelly tight behind her back. Her clothes had been slashed off her nude body, and her skin was horribly blue-pale.

Kaiser read the file. "Jane Doe, early twenties, no dental records on file, doesn't match any missing person reports. Extensive signs of physical and sexual abuse, some healed and some very fresh. Your Detective Horowitz posits that she was a prostitute killed by a john."

Sara smacked him again, harder this time. "He is not *my* detective."

"Yes, ma'am," Kaiser said, as neutral as the smartass could manage. His smartass vanished as he scrolled the screen down. "Broken ribs, broken fingers, extensive beating. She was raped by at least two men and strangled while she drowned. Yuck."

"That ain't the word I'd think of," Riordan said quietly.

Camden peered closer at the screen. "All of the victims drowned, but the woman was the only one sexually assaulted and restrained. None of the men had a scratch on them, and none of them were tied up."

"And that in itself is weird," Sara said.

Camden straightened up. "Yes."

Sara pointed. "Riordan, try to drown Jacobs."

Riordan barely hesitated before she expertly grabbed Jacobs by the arm.

"Hey!" Jacobs protested.

"Shaddup, you big baby," Riordan said. She grabbed him in a headlock under her left arm and hauled him over to the table, shoving aside

Camden's health bars as she grabbed the large ice bucket. A can of cashews burst open and flooded the chair and floor.

Jacobs struggled against her with his fists, but Riordan easily shoved his face into the empty bucket.

Camden clapped. "Now with water in it!"

"Oh please," Sara said. "Jacobs, quit being a fuckhead and fight back."

"I don't wanna hurt her," Jacobs said, his voice tinny and silly-sounding inside the bucket.

"Fuck you," Riordan said good-naturedly, shoving his head harder. Jacobs flung her off then, and they grappled on the floor for a minute as she tried to shove his head back in the bucket.

"All right, cut it out," Sara said.

Riordan stood up, straightening her T-shirt. "To be fair, Major, he has always been better at hand combat than I."

"I keep telling you not to call me that," Sara griped. "The dockworkers were big guys like Jacobs here. Camden, you try to drown him."

"My pleasure." Camden approached Jacobs, then stopped short. "Um."

Jacobs glowered down at him. Kaiser snickered.

Camden circled around Jacobs. "Let's say our bad guy got him by surprise."

"He'd have to," Jacobs growled.

Camden grabbed Jacobs around the neck like Riordan had. Jacobs flung him off easily and Camden flew backward into the nearer double bed.

"Oh man," Riordan said, her arms crossed.

Sara held up a hand. "Camden gets remedial hand combat later. Clearly our guy would have to be trained in order to drown these guys." She surveyed the room. "Jacobs, drown Kaiser."

"Hey, I'm a noncombatant!" Kaiser stepped out from behind the desk anyway, turning to face Sara. "He kills me, I'm suing."

"Relax, candyass." Jacobs grabbed Kaiser from behind. Kaiser twisted under his hands and almost slipped free, but Jacobs countered and knocked him down, shoving his head in the bucket as the other man struggled. "Mission accomplished."

"Not quite," Camden said. "It takes a minimum of three minutes to drown."

"I could get out of here in three minutes," Kaiser said, his voice also tinny inside the bucket.

"Don't bet on it," Jacobs growled.

Sara tried very hard not to smile. "Let him go."

Kaiser sat up and shook his head. "You are one weird outfit, you know that?"

Riordan chucked him on the arm. *"We're* one weird outfit. You're stuck with us now, Red."

"Wilhelm," he corrected her.

Sara pointed again. "Camden. Put Riordan's head in the bucket."

Camden looked at her. "C'mon, don't make me the asshole."

Riordan gave him a cool stare. "Do your worst."

"That's what you'll get." Camden grabbed Riordan and tried to force her down to her knees. She twisted away and flipped him onto the bed again.

Jacobs laughed as Camden roused himself again. "I think I hate you all," Camden groused.

Sara stepped up behind Riordan and quickly caught her wrists together behind her back. She grabbed a power cord lying on Kaiser's desk and swiftly bound Riordan's hands together as she struggled.

"Hey!" Riordan said. Sara dodged her backward head-butt easily and kicked her gently in the backs of the knees. Riordan pitched forward and Sara shoved her head toward the bucket. Riordan's torso heaved under her, to no avail.

"See?" Sara told the men. "Even a trained soldier like Riordan has a hard time fending off an attacker of the same size with her hands bound." She released Riordan then, and Jacobs instantly untied her hands.

Kaiser raised a hand. "The bondage is fun and all, boss, but I'm missing the point."

"We've efficiently proven that the woman was killed by a different assailant than the men, the same conclusion the police reached without the assault and battery," Camden said.

"More than that," Sara said, pointing to the pictures on the screen again. "The woman was bound as she drowned. Because you practically have to tie someone up to drown them. It's a terrifying way to die, and the victim struggles with practically superhuman strength. The violence of the restraint causes at least as much damage to the body as the drowning itself."

"Wait," Camden said, scrambling over to the laptop.

"Hold it, skinny," Kaiser said, stepping between Camden and the computer.

"I just want to look at something!" Camden insisted.

Kaiser shook his head. "Look all you want. Touch my baby and you die. Slowly."

Camden grinned. "You can't take me, man."

Kaiser pointed at Sara. "I'll sic her on you."

Camden chose to remain silent. Kaiser brought up the original crime-scene photos again. Camden leaned over the laptop, peering closely. "Here. And here."

"Dead men, drowned on dry land," Riordan said.

Camden looked up. "Nothing. No sign of restraint at all." He pointed at his own throat. "Tomorrow I'm gonna have a slight bruise from Bluto here choking me—"

"Watch it," Jacobs warned.

"And about nineteen others from being repeatedly flipped across the bed, thanks very much," Camden continued. "And you all didn't even kill me."

Jacobs glared. "Yet."

Kaiser rubbed his nose. "He's right. Just an empty bucket, and my nose hurts. If a human being held those guys underwater, they'd have injuries. Fingermarks. Scratches. Something."

Sara nodded. "Top marks, gang. Whatever it was, it drowned them without touching them. And since that's pretty much impossible by modern physics, we have ourselves a likely supernatural."

Kaiser raised his hand. "I say Major Harvey is the next in the bucket."

Sara folded her arms, impassive.

Camden glanced at Kaiser. "You first."

The door opened and Thacker came in, stopping still at the sight of the mess. "My God, Harvey! What have you been doing to them?"

"Waterboarding," Camden volunteered.

Thacker raised an eyebrow. "Harvey, I have a serious problem with this."

Sara signed. "Empty bucket, *el jefe*. I'm not gonna kill any of your children quite yet."

"Hell with that." Thacker pointed at the small table. "What did you do to my cashews?"

Sara Harvey leaned against the brick wall outside the Elmwood Motel. Inside the others were laughing, ribbing Thacker about his cashews, playing "hide the laptop" on Kaiser. It was good to hear laughter among a crew again. It meant they were becoming a team.

It was too bad Chamberlin wasn't around to see it. He wasn't a bad sort, for being completely naïve and unprepared for whatever he had encountered on the wharf. Like most Blackfire operatives, he had no family or close ties. It was depressing that no one would mourn him, beyond the team's dedication to finding whatever had killed him. They were steadfast and determined, but as a matter of pride, not some kind of out-of-control vengeance for a man they had known for less than a week.

Sara stared up at the sky and thought about Paul.

It wasn't very often she allowed herself to think about him, as though bringing him to the surface might make his memory fade, wear it out. It hurt her somewhere she didn't allow herself to acknowledge. She had spent the better part of her adult life walking around with Paul Vaughn inside her head, speaking through the earpiece as if he were part of her.

In a way, he was. Sara Harvey had a life before Paul Vaughn, had been a person before he walked into her desert camp and made her an offer she didn't want to refuse.

But she didn't remember who Major Sara Harvey was. What did she care about, except going where Paul Vaughn pointed? The guys had sometimes asked her if she would step into the military liaison role—de facto commander of the team, as the liaison outranked the team leader— if Paul stepped down. She always replied that it would take the apocalypse for Paul Vaughn to quit.

How easy to joke about the end of the world. Less funny when you're staring it in its twisted, malevolent face.

So many deaths. So many faces disappeared from Blackfire, from other teams, from training sessions. Sara couldn't find it in herself to mourn for Doctor Death, that's for sure. But so many others.

How do you replace Parish Roberts? she asked Paul once upon a blue moon. He had no answer for her. *How do you replace Paul Vaughn?* That was the question she couldn't answer for herself.

Sara rubbed her leg half-consciously. The scar was still there, but she knew Camden was right—the pain was only in her mind. It was her imagination and not a flaw in the muscle that made her limp. It wasn't the worst injury she'd ever had, but she still remembered lying helpless on the stone floor of that long-ago castle. Gary and Parish were sniping at each other and Paul hovered over her and ordered her not to die. As if she would die from a stab wound to the leg. As if she were that fragile, that weak.

No, that wasn't fair. Paul had never thought her weak. But he seemed to worry more about her physical well-being than that of the men. It used to piss her off something furious—she was no more breakable than Parish or Gary, and she didn't need to be swaddled in cotton.

Eventually Sara realized it had nothing to do with her gender. It had to do with Paul's deep and abiding caring for the people under his command. The team was his as much as hers, and he had a talent for connecting with them that she lacked. Her method of discipline was to kick them when they needed inspiration and throw them into a wall when they needed correction. But Paul used his soft voice and that cold stare of his, the one that made her call him Iceman. And they obeyed.

Yet the cool stare had wavered. That time in Haiti, and the night in the Philippines. And that moment in the castle, when his face hovered over hers and he ordered her not to die. She wasn't going to die. She was the one who lived. Always outliving everyone else around her. The last survivor.

Almost.

For the fifth time, Sara dialed the number on her cell phone. She stared at it for a long time, and finally had the intestinal fortitude to press SEND.

A ring, then two. An eternity later, someone answered with an officious-sounding voice. Inside the motel room, the laughter finally quieted down.

Sara asked after the patient, pretending to be a friend of the family looking to send a care package. She pitched her voice higher than her normal scowly tone, the light voice of a careless young woman who can't find her address book.

Then she listened to several sentences of gobbledygook before she got her answer. No, she could not send him a care package, it was not permitted under the current rules of his incarceration. But that meant he was still there.

She hung up the cell phone and listened to the chatter of crickets and nightbugs in the brush beyond the Elmwood parking lot. He was still there. But the team was broken. It had been broken since Haiti, and nothing was ever going to bring it back. Not the voices from the sea, and not the bourbon, and not even the voices inside the room, the ones that had fallen still.

The door opened and Thacker stuck his head out. "Harvey, you all right?"

"You keep asking me that and I'm gonna stick your cashews where the sun don't shine," Sara grumbled.

Thacker didn't smile. "We've got a problem."

"No shit," Sara retorted.

"A new one," Thacker said. "There's been another death."

Sara shoved past him without pause, heading straight for her duffel and yanking out the weapons. "Tell me."

"The body was found less than an hour ago on the wharf, drowned," Thacker recited. Behind him the team gathered its equipment, all business again.

They're starting to look like Blackfire, Sara thought with a strange mixture of satisfaction and dread. "Male victim?"

Thacker nodded. "Sara, it's… It's that cop."

Sara stopped still.

"I'm sorry," Thacker said lamely. "He must have been scouting out the wharf when he—"

"Stop," Sara said. She looked at them all staring at her. There was something horribly familiar in their eyes, the way everyone looked at her when she came back for debriefing at Farson after the Island, that mix of pity and fear. Feeling sorry for her like she was some goddamn civilian victim, and also afraid, because she had touched the demon and lost everything. Would they suffer the same fate if they touched her?

Everything you touch dies, Paul taunted in her head. But Paul would never say that. Paul was an officer and a gentleman. He might cuff her upside the head when she took too many chances, but he would never mock her for the people she'd lost. Not her team and not her family.

"Quit gaping at me like a bunch of fucking zoo animals," Sara snapped. "Lock and load. I want you all in the Jeeps in sixty seconds or I'm putting my boot up your asses."

"Yes, ma'am," Riordan said, and the others followed suit. Camden stared at Sara the longest, for which she heartily wanted to smack him. They filed out as Thacker hefted a duffel with some godawful-stupid equipment in it—Thacker did love his toys.

"Harvey, I read the reports on the popobawa case," Thacker said. "I'll understand if you want to stay behind."

Sara leveled a glare at Thacker that might have stopped even Paul

Vaughn in his tracks. Of course, Thacker was goddamn impervious. She resorted to words. "Fuck. That."

Thacker glanced around. "No one will think the less of you if—"

"Shut the fuck up, Thacker," Sara snapped. "I am not staying here. If it killed him, I'm going to find out what it is and tear its goddamn head off before it hurts any more of my team. I am done losing my people to the fucking critters."

"Your people?" Thacker prodded. He never did know when to quit.

"Until I get back to my ocean, they're my people," Sara said, zipping her duffel closed. "Now get the fuck out of my way."

She stalked past him, out into the cool night.

7

The Blackfire team probably looked like a bunch of assholes striding down the wharf in their black tactical gear with the logo on the upper left chest, Sara thought. If nothing else, the huge cobblestones along the wharf made walking in boots more than a little challenging, and it was hard to walk strong when you're about to trip on your own goddamn feet. The Memphis riverbank had a very steep angle, and the century-old cobblestones were rounded and smooth from many years of rising river water. You could turn an ankle easy.

Thacker led the way so he could schmooze past the crime-scene tape and the very cranky cops milling around—far more than usual. A dead cop is always a bigger deal than a dead homeless or dockworker or even a tourist. Cops take dead cops very seriously, and there was a deeply personal fury on the scowling faces around them.

Sara hung back a bit, telling herself it was time for her crew to figure out how to handle a crime scene, not that she had any reservations about seeing Adam Horowitz dead on the wharf. It was a long time ago, and it wasn't like he was—

"Oh shit," she heard Thacker say. The team parted as if to make a path for her, straight down the cobblestones to the sodden body lying at least ten feet away from the water—and the cop kneeling beside him.

The cop looked up and Sara stopped still.

Horowitz glared at her like she'd spat on his badge, but he was alive, kneeling beside the body.

"Shit," Sara said. "I guess we were misinformed." She arrowed a glare at Thacker, silently promising him pain.

"I really don't care what that means," Horowitz said.

Sara took a real look at the corpse then, and saw with a start that it was Juan Hernandez, Horowitz's partner. His skin was an unnatural bluish-pasty color, his eyes open and full of river water that leaked down his cheeks like tears.

Sara knelt beside him. "Goddamn. I'm sorry."

"Save it," Horowitz said, glaring at her over his partner. "Tell me what the fuck you know, Sara."

Sara glanced up at Thacker. "A moment alone, please."

Thacker looked like he was going to protest, but Sara gave him her best Paul Vaughn Ice Glare and he backed off, motioning the team off to the side.

Sara looked at Horowitz. "I don't know what's doing this, Adam. God's honest truth."

"Bullshit!" Horowitz snapped. "You fucking Blackfire people, you keep your goddamn secrets and move everyone around on a chessboard. Was Juan bait for this fucker?"

Sara met his eyes. "No. On my life and my honor. There was no trap and Juan was not bait. Hell, we don't know enough about this thing to set a trap, Adam."

That barely seemed to mollify the fury in Horowitz's eyes. "Tell me what you know."

Sara kept eye contact—she sensed Horowitz was close to some emotional blowout that would damage not only him, but the investigation. She saw a dangerous glint in his eyes that seemed awfully familiar.

"It's a supernatural, type unknown," she said. "It kills by drowning without touching them. We don't know if it's a critter or a human using some kind of artifact. We don't know why it's only men and only on the riverfront, unless it has to be close to the river to drown them. And I think your Jane Doe was the first."

That was a bit of a stretch, but Sara had an instinctive feeling that Jane Doe was part of it, even if she wasn't killed by the critter. Still, she needed to warm Horowitz up to her next request, because he still looked like he was half a step from throwing her in the river.

"The pro? She doesn't fit the pattern," Horowitz said, some measure of police detachment coming back into his voice. "Female, bound, sexually assaulted. The others don't have a mark on them except they drowned on dry land."

"That's why I need to see her body," Sara said.

Horowitz shook his head. "She doesn't fit the pattern," he repeated. "Hell, if it wasn't for you and your kiddie field trip here in town, I'd still think we were dealing with a serial. He could drown them in the river and then drag the bodies up onto dry land."

"Then you'd see signs of the movement, trails to the water's edge, scuffing on clothes and shoes," Sara said. "You have to trust me."

It was the wrong thing to say. Horowitz's eyes narrowed. "The last time I trusted you, I ended up in a hospital bed. And I don't see any of your team at your back, do I, Sara?"

Sara's breath caught in her chest, and she looked down. Juan's eyes stared up at her, empty and still somehow accusing, river water rolling tears.

"Sorry," Horowitz said. "I guess even Blackfire has transfers and red tape and—"

"Shut up," Sara said quietly. She looked at him, the ocean roiling in her chest. "I know what it's like to lose a partner, Adam. Let me in, and we will find this fucker together. We'll rip out its goddamn heart."

Horowitz looked back down at Juan Hernandez, rubbing his face with his hands. "Juan was my partner from back when we were uniforms," he said. "He was the one beside my bed when I woke up in the hospital after the popobawa. I left him when I went to Atlanta, and when I came back he was exactly the same. He said, 'Ya bring us any peaches?' and it was like I'd been on vacation instead of abandoning my post."

"You didn't abandon him," Sara said.

"He called me Peaches for two months," Horowitz said.

Sara smothered a grin. "Good man."

"The best." Horowitz glanced up and gestured to the police photographer, standing a respectful distance away. "You done, Bierman?" The photographer nodded, and Horowitz reached out with a gloved hand toward his partner's face.

"Horowitz, you can't—" Bierman protested, but Horowitz didn't listen.

He closed Hernandez's eyes, and the river water flooded over his face, dripping onto the cobblestones.

The Memphis morgue looked like an office building. Sara expected something like the crumbling-concrete morgue attached to the old army hospital, the place where they brought the yellow fever victims in the 1880s. That dank hole was so infested with ghosts that Blackfire teams had been sent out three times. Hysterical tourists visiting the nearby museum kept seeing floating lights and heard voices rising from the dark basement. There was always some yahoo posting photos of orbs in doorways—as far as Sara knew, the orbs were just blobs on the lens. But the ghosts were sure real, and she had no wish to mess with them this trip. She had enough problems.

The current morgue was a quiet and serene building that couldn't be more than ten years old. Sara tried not to tap her foot impatiently as Horowitz argued in hushed tones with the white coat who didn't want to let them in. Horowitz tapped his badge for emphasis at least twice—that didn't look good.

Camden was twitching hard beside Sara. He probably hadn't had a drink in twelve hours. Okay, that was unfair, but Camden was far from Sara's top choice for a backup man. Horowitz had absolutely refused to allow the entire team, and Thacker insisted Camden's eye for detail was vitally important.

The white coat was on the phone now, as Horowitz glared around with thunderclouds on his brow. The white coat was everyone's stereotype of a coroner—tall, skeletally skinny, almost no hair and eyes recessed in deep hollows. He looked like he'd stepped out of a bad movie.

"Where's the camera?" That was the uneasy wisecrack Horowitz had made that long-ago night in the park. If only it had been a joke. If only that night so long ago hadn't ended in blood. It turned out all right in the long run, but it felt like Horowitz hated her, and that bothered Sara for some god-unknown reason. Maybe because the last time she saw him, she was with her real team, with the crew that had her back for so many years.

"I can sleep because my men are on the other side of that wall," she'd told him.

They weren't there anymore.

Sara shook off the reverie. God, the way her mind kept wandering, she was going to be practically useless in a fight. She fought down the surge of anger that accompanied this thought: she told Thacker she couldn't be here, that she was used up, no good.

She told Thacker she blamed him for the Island.

But Sara Harvey wasn't much of a liar. She tried to be angry at Thacker because she was really furious with herself, with her inability to move past what happened at the Island and be what she was. If it was a critter, she'd have wrestled it to the ground and cut off its fucking head by now, but it was her mind, her heart, and she'd never been all that good at wrestling herself.

"You coming?" Horowitz asked, with more snippiness in his voice. Well, he'd just seen his partner dead on the waterfront, so he was entitled.

They walked down the hallway to a discreet examination room. "They brought her out here, don't want us back in the freezer," Horowitz said.

As they entered the exam room, Sara saw Hernandez's body laid out on a table, finally starting to dry out. Horowitz averted his eyes as they walked to the other table.

There was no sheet, no modest covering, no respect for the dead. Just a young woman who was very dead.

Deep, ugly purple bruises all around the slim column of her throat, and bloodless cuts on her face. Bloodless because the water had washed away the blood, the water in which she drowned. *She drowned in a mixture of the river and her own blood,* Sara thought.

Looking further down, she saw half-healed cuts and extensive bruises.

"These are the worst," Camden said, pointing to a blooming dark rose on Jane's ribcage.

Horowitz glanced at the file the lab rat had given him. "Three broken ribs, inflicted within an hour of her death. Plus two more preexisting, mostly healed."

"Regular beatings, scars," Camden said, circling Jane's body. "Poorly fed—you can tell she didn't have much body fat to begin with, and whatever she was eating before her death couldn't have been much unless she was fighting illness."

"No contagion we could find," Horowitz said in a monotone. "Two kinds of semen indicate two assailants."

Sara glanced at him. "We boring you?"

Horowitz tossed the file onto the counter. "She doesn't fit the pattern, Sara. She's female, she was bound, she was raped, and clearly the fuckheads who did it were holding her down in the water, so if it's a goddamn supernatural it changed its method and you told me that doesn't happen."

"There are no rules," Sara began, but Horowitz's eye was on Hernandez again. Like Jane, Hernandez had no covering, no modesty, nothing to protect him from their eyes or the cold fluorescent lights.

Horowitz stalked away, shoving the door open and banging into the hallway.

"Shit," Sara muttered. "They'll kick us out in half a second without him."

"On my way," Camden said, hastening out into the hallway.

The door swung shut and Sara turned her attention back to Jane Doe. If she only had five minutes with the body, she'd better make them count.

She noted the deep purple marks on Jane's thin wrists—whatever they used to bind her sure hadn't been padded cuffs. She skipped past the Y-incision and horrible bruising along the sides. She forced herself to look at the bruising between Jane's legs. It was about the most horrible way to die Sara could imagine, and brutally non-supernatural by every measure. Just your garden-variety human butchery. But her gut said there was something here that would make a difference to their investigation.

Moving down to the far end of the table, Sara noted mud and small marks to the bottoms of Jane's feet. Bramble scratches and stepping on rocks, she thought—the sort of impact you'd see from walking through the woods without shoes.

"What kind of pro goes into the woods by the river, alone with a john, and doesn't wear shoes?" Sara wondered, speaking without really thinking.

The kind who isn't a pro. Either Jane Doe was very new at her job— hard to believe with the older injuries—or she wasn't a prostitute. Sara was no expert, but she'd been around the block a few times. Prostitutes very quickly develop a keen sense of survival that told them which johns were trouble, which would be an easy trick, and which were the street equivalent of a great white shark, a mercurial creature that could devour them at a moment's impulse.

"Jane, Jane, who are you?" Sara mused aloud.

"Not Jane," a voice replied.

Sara backed up fast, her heart thudding in her chest as she reached for her gun by reflex. Her hip holster was empty—Horowitz had insisted. *Not again. Oh no, not again.*

Jane's head turned toward Sara at an impossible angle—impossible for life, that is. Sara heard the thin crunch and snap of brittle, dead tendons in the corpse's neck. Her eyes were glittering cold, water trailing from their corners across Jane's face. They had been dull and dry a moment before— Sara would swear to it.

The mouth opened and the burble of river water came from her throat. "Sssssara. You are a hard woman to find."

Sara recoiled, her hip bumping against a table. "Jesus," she whispered. "No, you're dead, goddammit. Dead."

Jane giggled with a deep ragged sound that Sara thought might drive her insane. "That never sssstopped me, Sssara. Ssssweet little Ssssara, far from her ssseassshore…jusssst like little Natalia Ivanova, little girl lossst…"

"Shut the fuck up!" Sara shouted, feeling under her jacket for the small-of-back holster Horowitz had missed. She pulled the Beretta and aimed it at Jane. "Stay dead! Stay dead, you motherfucker!"

Jane lifted her head from the table, more tendons creaking in her neck. "Can't kill me again, Ssssara."

"We'll see about that," Sara said desperately, and thumbed off the safety.

The door banged open. Sara pivoted fast on reflex, aiming at the door as Horowitz came charging in.

"Shit!" Horowitz shouted, one hand reaching out in a defensive motion as the other hand pulled his gun. He pivoted sideways to decrease his profile even as Camden stumbled in after him. "Sara, drop the fucking gun!"

Sara shifted her attention back to Jane, who lay impassive and still. "Not dead yet, not dead yet, sweet Jesus—" She was aware she was speaking aloud, but seemed unable to stop.

Horowitz stepped forward, gun still aimed at Sara. But now he reached toward her with the other hand, a calming motion she found darkly hilarious. "Sara, put it away. It's just a body."

Sara shook her head hard. "Not a body. Not dead."

"Check it out," Horowitz said to Camden, clearly not leaving anything to chance.

Camden scuttled over to the body, trying to keep out of Sara's line of sight. He leaned over Jane's face, checking her pulse, peering into her eyes. Sara resisted the wild urge to warn him, pull him away before Jane lunged upward and bit him.

But of course she just lay there, staring at the ceiling with her dead eyes.

Camden looked up, staring at Sara with uneasy suspicion in his eyes. The way Thacker looked at her, as if she were the shark circling him.

"Dead, Harvey," Camden said. "Stone dead. Deadest woman I ever saw."

Sara's gun hand trembled. She saw it, though she thought—hoped—it was imperceptible to the other two.

"Sara, the gun," Horowitz said. "I'm not gonna say it again."

Sara slowly lowered the Beretta, returning it to her small-of-back holster. Horowitz made a motion as if to take it, but she stopped him with a look.

"Sara, are you all right?" Horowitz asked. At least the anger was gone, replaced by caution and awkwardness, which was entirely worse.

Sara didn't have an answer for his question, so she settled for doing her job. "Natalia Ivanova," she said.

"Who?" Horowitz finally put away his gun.

"Just look it up," Sara said, staring at Jane's—Natalia's—very dead body. "It's her name."

A tiny drop of river water slipped from Natalia's eye.

8

───────

If there was someone in Blackfire who pissed Sara off more than Thacker, it was Gina. If there was someone worse than Gina, it was Merrifield.

The bastard's face was on Thacker's laptop screen when Sara emerged from the shower. Thank God she'd brought fresh clothes into the bathroom with her, because she didn't relish changing in front of Thacker, much less that fuckhead Merrifield. The youngsters—she seemed unable to think of them any other way—were in the other motel room, and she and Thacker were alone. Such joy.

Alone, that is, save for the balding, pasty-round face on Thacker's screen.

"Ah, Major," Merrifield said from his screen. "We were just talking about you."

"My ears are burning," Sara said.

Merrifield was unfazed by the tone of her voice. "I've been reviewing your application for retirement, and given the field reports, I'd say it's appropriate."

"Thanks," Sara said, though it didn't sound like a compliment. "Excuse me—field reports?"

"No need to go into that now," Merrifield said. "Your other request, however—"

"Don't. Don't even," Sara snapped, grabbing the laptop away from Thacker. She held the damn thing up to her face so the webcam could

220

convey her expression. Merrifield's pasty face recoiled a titch, as if she were about to leap through the screen and throttle him. Physics aside, it was a definite possibility.

"I want that pension put through, every dime of it," Sara ordered. "I don't care what kind of subterfuge and layers of government lies you need to develop to get it done, but you get it done."

Merrifield had regained his composure, glancing down at unseen papers. "Major Harvey, I hardly need to remind you that you do not make policy at Blackfire."

"Naturally, because if I did, the policy would make some fucking sense," Sara retorted. "The pension is the very least you owe the people who do the dying for your fucking memos—"

"That will be all, Major Harvey," Merrifield interrupted. "I would like to speak to Colonel Thacker now."

Sara almost threw the laptop, but Thacker grabbed it before she did any expensive damage. "Sir, before we go any further—"

Merrifield harrumphed. "I think it's clear Camden's assessment was—"

"What?" Sara snapped.

Thacker held up a hand, silencing her. "First of all, sir, I do not agree with Camden's assessment at all. In the short time this team has operated, Major Harvey's contributions have been extensive. She personally recruited two team members, including Camden himself. She led the neutralization of a shape-changer and has taught my people more in a week than they could have learned in months from another agent. Plus, with the loss of Dan Chamberlin, we don't have a second and none of them are—"

"That is being handled," Merrifield said. "For now, you remain on task. Any more unorthodox procedures, however, and Major Harvey gets her retirement posthaste, is that clear?"

"Crystal, sir," Thacker said, and clapped the laptop shut before Sara could speak. "Also," he added without looking at her, "that idiot Camden went over my head to Merrifield, and I do not let that shit stand."

"I'm gonna feed him his own testicles," Sara swore.

"Disciplining Camden is my job," Thacker said. "He and I are going out to the shooting range for basic firearms qualifications tonight, and we're gonna have ourselves a little chat about chain of command."

Sara folded her arms over her chest. "He said I flipped out, right?"

Thacker stood up. "He said you aimed your weapon at a police detective and a dead body, ranting about the dead speaking. Oh, and he says you also aimed it at him."

"Shoulda shot him," Sara grumbled.

Thacker reached out as though intending to touch her in comfort, but she looked up and he stopped. "Sara, I want to believe you," he began.

"I want to believe me," Sara said. "God, Thacker, I told you. I said I shouldn't be here. And if it turns out Natalia Ivanova is some random collection of syllables from my fucked-up head, you should box me up before I kill someone."

She took a deep breath before continuing. "I almost did it myself."

Thacker didn't speak.

"Should've," Sara said. She didn't see the walls of the motel room anymore. Just the ocean. "They were all gone. I mean, what the fuck am I supposed to do now? Wander around listening to the dead talking and wait for the one that finally drives me into the rubber room?"

Thacker spoke carefully. "What stopped you, Sara?"

"The pension," Sara said. "Thacker, you're a military man with a military mind and that's pretty goddamn useless. But unlike those assholes up the totem pole at Blackfire, you know what it's like to serve. So don't you let them fuck over the pension."

"Sara, it's not in my control—" he began.

"Fuck that," she interrupted. "You owe me. You owe her. Make it happen. Whatever happens to me, you fix it."

That wary look was back in Thacker's eyes, as though Sara was a volatile substance that needed to be carefully handled or it might explode. "Sara, you aren't planning on doing something stupid, are you?"

"Who, me?" Sara paused. "Relax, Thacker. I want to find this fucker, box it up, and get back to my ocean." She checked her clip and put her gun back in its holster. "And it's Harvey, if you don't mind."

The moonlight fell across the cobblestones in a silver wash along the Memphis riverfront. Sara walked with Riordan, watching the younger woman as much as she watched the shadows.

Riordan was in good military form, keeping her hands free to reach for weapons if needed and orienting her body toward Sara as she scanned for threats. It spoke both of readiness and an implicit trust in Sara, which she appreciated.

"Here's what I don't understand," Riordan said. "You're sure Natalia Ivanova was killed by a human being, so how is she connected to the men on the wharf?"

Riordan, at least, had accepted Sara's theory without question. "Not sure yet," Sara said. "Just a gut instinct."

Riordan frowned. "You don't have some folk tale or Southern gothic legend that might explain it?"

Sara snorted. "I keep telling you, the books are only going to get you so far. Folk tales and legends are important as a basic introduction, but they've gone through so many translations, interpretations and outright bullshit that they'll inevitably miss something or distort the actual facts. You have to trust your gut—something they'll never tell you at Blackfire. Your instincts and experience are the best tools they have to find, control, and neutralize supernaturals." Sara paused. "Don't believe everything they told you when you signed up."

Riordan looked at her. "Is that why you want to retire? Because you don't trust Blackfire?"

"I'm too fuckin' old for this bullshit," Sara grumbled.

"With all due respect, ma'am, that's crap." Riordan didn't look at her as Sara double-taked. "I looked up your record, and you're only—"

"Hush, infant."

Riordan grinned. "Anyway. You've got decades of useful service left in you. And I don't care what Camden says, you're not crazy."

"Thanks, kid. Damned with faint praise." Sara aimed her flashlight under a park bench that was exceedingly familiar to her. Once upon a time she sat on that bench with a man, and ended up with a bullet. Sort of. Nothing there now.

"Your team had a higher success rate than any other in Blackfire," Riordan continued. "You must have been very good, and I just can't understand why you wouldn't want to do what it is you're meant to do."

Sara looked across the darkened park overlooking the waterfront. Empty. Not even the panhandlers loitering for the tourists—the word had gotten out. "Being good at something isn't the same as destiny, kid," she said. "You should remember that before you get too deep in bed with Blackfire. For one thing, they won't let you and Jacobs be together."

Riordan's head snapped around. "What do you mean?"

Sara laughed out loud. She couldn't help it, but she smothered it as fast as she could. "Girl, you and Jacobs might as well have it emblazoned on your packs. You walk in a room and his eye follows you. And you touch him on the arm about six times more than necessary." Sara paused. "It won't end anywhere good, Riordan. Never fall in love with someone on your team. It always ends badly."

Riordan was silent for a moment. "Nobody said love."

Sara rolled her eyes.

"Is that what happened?" Riordan asked. "You loved someone on your team, and—"

"Oh Jesus, quit the pop psychology," Sara interrupted. "You've got to work together without letting emotions interfere. That's what makes a good team. Won't work if you've got personal drama getting in the way. Take a cold shower, bang a cowboy on your days off, just don't let it get any further with Jacobs, or one of you has to transfer out."

They walked the part for a while longer in silence.

"So if you're all burned out and retired, what are you going to do with the rest of your life?" Riordan asked.

Sara glanced at her. "You always this mouthy?"

Riordan grinned. "Yes, Major. Haven't you noticed?"

"For the love of all that's holy, Riordan, if you don't stop calling me…" Sara's voice trailed off. "What the fuck is that?"

Down the hill on the wharf, a man walked along the cobblestones. He moved with a strange gait, half-stumbling and clumsy. Granted, no one looked graceful walking on those huge, uneven cobblestones, but the guy looked drunk.

He came near the water and stopped, swaying back and forth in the moonlight.

"Shit," Sara said.

Riordan was already moving. Younger and faster on her feet, she scrambled down the side of the hill from the park toward the expanse of cobblestones that lined the wharf.

The man stood at water's edge, his body trembling.

Sara approached him from the side as Riordan flanked around him. "Mister, step back from the water."

He stumbled back a step, and Sara gaped. "Fuck! Horowitz, what the hell are you—"

"Help me," Horowitz pleaded, eyes huge in his pale face. His whole body twitched forward, and Sara saw with no small surprise that he was hugely aroused. "Please, help me."

"How do I help you?" Sara asked, one hand on her holstered weapon.

Horowitz's eyes were running with tears—or was it river water? "Don't you hear it?" he whispered.

Sara strained to hear, but there was nothing. Just the wash-whisper of the river, a few cars passing on the bridge, the rumble of the trolley a few blocks away.

She met Riordan's eyes, and the younger woman shook her head. Nothing.

"What do you hear?" Sara asked.

"I'm not crazy," Horowitz insisted, his body trembling. The tears flowed down his cheeks. "Not crazy."

"I believe you," Sara said.

Horowitz took a shaking step forward. Riordan moved to stop him, but Sara shook her head. Instead, she moved in front of Horowitz, blocking his path to the river.

His face was drawn with misery and terror, as if all the sadness in the city was contained in his eyes, streaming with river tears, weeping for them all. "Oh God, Sara, it's so terrible, and so beautiful."

"Fight it," Sara said, rising panic in her chest. "You're not crazy. Please, fight it."

Horowitz jerked another step forward, but Sara pushed him gently back, her palms flat against his chest. As she did, it felt as though something pushed back against her, as though some invisible force propelled him toward her even as she blocked his path. She braced her hands against the firm plates of his vest and anchored her feet as best she could against the cobblestones.

That force tried again, pushing him close to her, and she braced herself as best she could. Horowitz cried out, in pain or terror she could not tell.

"Harvey, what do I do?" Riordan pleaded.

Sara muttered under her breath. "Goddammit, if only I knew what it was…do you have the iron knife I gave you? Try that!"

"Against what?" Riordan asked, kneeling to pull her boot knife.

"Whatever it is, it's behind him!" Sara said.

It shoved again, and Horowitz's body jerked forward. Sara's foot slipped off a cobblestone and she stumbled backward into the water, ankle-deep.

Riordan slashed at the air behind Horowitz. Nothing happened.

"Shit!" Sara slipped another step. Now she and Horowitz were struggling in waist-deep water, that terrible force still propelling him forward.

"Harvey!" Riordan splashed after them. "Harvey, let go! He's going to drag you in too!"

"Fuck that," Sara growled, bracing herself on the slippery stones.

Horowitz struggled harder, his whole body wrenched by something they could not see. "God, Sara, don't let me kill you!"

Sara felt her foot slipping again, deeper into the water. "Riordan! Upper right pocket of my jacket!"

Riordan splashed closer, apparently unaffected by the force pushing Horowitz into the water. Sara's arms ached, pressing harder than ever against the plates of Horowitz's vest. If it wasn't for the vest, she'd be leaving a hell of a bruise on his chest, she thought.

Riordan reached into Sara's breast pocket and pulled out a few handfuls of salt packets. "Oh God, of course," she muttered, and ripped packets open.

Sara slipped again, cold river water rising up under her arms. She felt Horowitz slipping further. "Grab me, Adam!"

Horowitz shook his head hard. "Not…gonna kill you…"

Sara groaned, grabbing his vest and straining to keep his head above water. "Goddammit, would you cut your stupid southern chivalry shit and *help* me—"

"Here, fucker!" Riordan shouted, throwing tiny puffs of salt into the air behind Horowitz.

Nothing happened.

"Shit!" Sara's foot pressed against something round and heavy—one of those giant iron rings that they used to tie boats up, perhaps. She hooked her foot into it and pulled him to her, clasping her fists together behind his back, inside the vest. They were pressed chest to chest, face to face.

"Let me go," Horowitz whispered, terror in his face. "Please, I can't take you with me."

"Not happening," Sara insisted.

Riordan splashed closer to them. She had three salt packets left. "Aw fuck," she said, and threw them onto Horowitz's head.

He jerked hard as though she had thrown acid on him, and that horrible pressure eased significantly.

"Now!" Sara shouted.

Riordan slung her shoulder under Horowitz's left arm as Sara went for the right one. Together they dragged him up the shore, step by step, as that invisible force dragged at his legs like great chains tied to his ankles.

When they were knee-deep and moving faster, something jerked

Horowitz toward the water hard. Sara almost lost her balance, and if not for Riordan on the other side, they might have lost him.

"Haul!" Sara shouted, and they fought their way out of the water.

Horowitz's body jerked hard, convulsing between them as they hauled him up onto dry cobblestones, well away from the river. Carefully they laid him on the ground, and Sara stripped off her jacket to place it behind his head, protecting it from the hard stones as his body jerked back and forth beneath her.

He fell still, eyes closed. Riordan pulled out her cell and tried to dial 911, but it was dead, river water leaking out the sides. "Shit!"

Sara grabbed his vest and shook him. "Adam!" She slapped him hard, once and twice.

Horowitz's eyes opened, and he blinked river water out of his vision. "Sara? What the hell you hitting me for?"

Sara sat back on her heels, out of breath. "Goddammit, you idiot cop, don't you do that to me."

Horowitz coughed a little. "Yes, ma'am."

Sara met Riordan's eyes and saw her own relief and fear mirrored there.

INTERLUDE

They were already well into the exorcism by the time Sara arrived with the salt.

Paul Vaughn opened the door and Sara blinked. Twice. Paul actually had shadows under his eyes, though his camo was pin-straight as always.

"Goddamn, Vaughn, you look like shit," she said, holding up the box of salt.

He took it without a word and vanished back into the dingy Baltimore rowhouse.

"You're welcome," Sara grumbled, shutting the door behind her and following him down the hallway into the tiny kitchen.

She glanced around and resisted checking the corners for roaches. A box with a mostly-uneaten, long-congealed pizza rested on the rickety wooden table next to stacks of musty books. Long streaks of something she fervently hoped was juice decorated the faded yellow linoleum. Through an archway, she could see a couple of thrift-store plaid couches, an Army-issue puke-green blanket wadded up at the end of each.

Sara somehow expected that a Blackfire safehouse would be super-clean and military-straight, but this place looked like college students lived there. Messy ones.

Paul laid the salt on the table and walked through the archway into the living room. Sara followed him and stopped still.

Another Paul sat on the couch.

He had his face in his hands, but he lifted his gaze as Sara and Paul entered and it was Paul again, the same square jaw, the same—

What the hell was she doing? Sara pulled her gun and thumbed off the safety, aiming it at the second Paul. "What the fuck! Vaughn, I'm seeing—"

"Harvey, meet Dale," Paul said, wearily indicating the man on the couch. "Holster your weapon, please."

Dale stood up, exactly Paul's height, but now she could see slight differences. Dale had a five-o'clock shadow, and Paul never did, even in the Arctic. Dale's hair was a little longer, and his clothes were definitely those of a civilian. Sara couldn't imagine ever seeing Paul in ripped jeans, much less a rock band T-shirt. Her brain rebelled at the very thought.

"Meetcha," Dale mumbled, holding out a hand.

Sara felt silly holding her gun on him, so she flicked the safety on and put it back in her holster—leaving it unsnapped, however. She sidled over to Paul. "Is it a glamour? Maybe a trinket of some kind, but I'm seeing—"

"My brother," Paul said tightly.

Sara couldn't help herself. She burst out laughing so hard her stomach hurt. Then she stepped forward and shook hands with Dale. "God, I've been doing this job too fucking long. Didn't even occur to me. What are you, twins?"

A ghost of a smile flitted across Dale's face. "As a matter of fact," he said quietly, moving past her into the kitchen. He picked up the box of salt and went down the basement stairs, leaving the door open a crack.

Sara flopped next to Paul on the couch. "Jesus, Vaughn, you have family? I thought you were hatched in the Blackfire labs."

"You're nine kinds of hilarious today, Harvey," Paul said tiredly.

A man came up the back stairs, an older man with longish salt-and-pepper hair and a beard beginning to tip over the balance to out-and-out gray. Add a red hat and little glasses at the edge of his nose and he'd easily have passed for Santa Claus, but Sara knew him too well to suggest such a travesty.

"Wolf! Goddamn, it's good to see you!" Sara sprang to her feet. "What brings you way the hell to Baltimore?"

"Your man here," Wolf said, nodding at Paul. "He flatters my ego, and I obey."

Paul stood. "I needed the best magic man I knew, Mr. Stewart. That's not flattery. Simply the facts."

"I do believe I've spoken to you about calling me a magic man," Wolf said in a severe tone.

"Namasté," Paul replied.

Sara smacked Paul on the arm. "That's Hindu, you big lug. Wolf, what the hell is going on here?"

Wolf glanced at Paul, who nodded. "Bad news, I'm afraid. Colette is not responding thus far."

Paul swore under his breath and turned away. Sara finally clued in that there was more going on than a simple side job—Paul was far too tense, and Paul was never tense. "Somebody tell me," she insisted.

Wolf indicated the stairs. "Colette Gibsen. She attempted an invoking ceremony alone some months ago, and apparently invited something other than she intended. Now it won't leave her."

"Which one?" Sara asked.

"We don't know," Dale said, coming out of the basement stairwell. On second viewing, Sara decided he looked worse than either of the other two men, drained and miserable. "They keep giving us different names. Pwcca, Kali, Melchom—"

Sara frowned. "Those are all from different belief systems. That doesn't make any sense."

"It's screwing with us," Paul said.

Wolf nodded. "I would be more inclined to say that it is a deceptive spirit, intent on hiding any clues to an appropriate expulsion, but 'screwing with us' will do."

Sara frowned at them. "You tried to start an exorcism ritual without salt? Sloppy."

"We ran out," Paul said.

Dale ignored them. "I'm ready to try again."

Wolf looked at him. "Son, you're fading fast. This is a marathon, not a sprint. You need to get some sleep before we—"

"You think I can *sleep?*" Dale shouted.

By instinct, Sara moved into a subtle defensive posture beside Paul in case Dale went wiggy.

"I can't *sleep,*" Dale insisted in a more normal tone. "She's tormented by the most horrible dreams, many of them too terrible for her to describe to me. The least horrific of them involved a demon slowly slicing her breasts into pieces and forcing her to watch as the blood and liquified flesh leaked out of the cuts."

"Yeesh," Sara muttered.

"By day she sees things that aren't there," Dale said. "She sees faces twisted into something repulsive, shadows behind her in the mirror, and she goes into a terrified screaming fit. Then suddenly she turns to me and it's not *her*, there's something else behind her eyes, it won't let her rest, and I *can't* rest until she's safe."

Sara couldn't help rolling her eyes.

Dale picked up on it right away and he focused his frustration on her. "You got a problem, lady?"

"Yeah. You." Sara folded her arms.

"Harvey." Paul's voice was foreboding.

Sara ignored him and addressed Dale. "Very chivalrous, pal. But you won't do her a damn bit of good if you keel over and we have to ship you off for a nice relaxing date with intravenous fluids and sedatives. Fun for you, useless for her. These guys know what they're doing, so lie down and chill already while we figure out what we know."

Dale glared at her, but Sara gave him her best Paul Vaughn look. It was weird to give it right back to Paul's face. Kind of.

Dale stalked off, and a minute later, they heard his feet going up the stairs.

"Handled with your usual tact and delicacy, Harvey," Paul grumbled.

"Sara was never one for diplomacy," Wolf said. "You've even gotten taller, I think."

"You say that every time," Sara said. "I think you still believe I'm twelve."

"You are twelve, aren't you? Thirteen at the most." Wolf pulled a bottle of water from the avocado-green fridge and sat down to drink it. "I still remember you as the child who insisted on diving off the end of the dock even after her mother told her repeatedly—"

"That sounds like Harvey," Paul said, opening one of the books and flipping through it.

"Yay, fun stories about my childhood," Sara said, flopping into a chair. "Why don't you break out the baby pictures, Wolf?"

Wolf cocked an eyebrow. "I would if you hadn't burned them all when you were fifteen."

Sara reached out to touch Wolf's hand. "There's no way you can possibly exorcise any demon with this much conflict, can you?"

"No, and I believe I've been clear on this point," Wolf said, arrowing a look at Paul. "We all must lend our energies to the common purpose and be unified in our resolve. There is too much tension between the Vaughns to—"

"That is our business," Paul said tightly.

Sara groaned. "Paul, you need to listen. I know just enough ritual to be dangerous, but even I know any ritual that starts with the participants glaring at each other is not going to work. If you and your mirror image can't get along, you need to—"

A loud thump came from below them, and the three of them were on their feet. Sara followed the men down the stairs toward a dim, dirt-floor basement.

Before they reached the bottom, Paul stopped and held up a hand. "Do you have a talisman?"

Sara opened the top button of her jacket and showed him her usual pendant. It resembled a St. Christopher medallion, but was inlaid with a charged crystal and had been altered and blessed by Wolf years ago for all-purpose protection. Paul nodded and went down into the basement.

It was well-lit from a series of bare bulbs screwed into the ceiling. A circle delineated by the stumps of melted-down white candles covered half the floor. Sara could feel its waning energy, like prickling heat on her skin.

In the center, Colette Gibsen lay on the dirt floor, her arms and feet bound in padded cuffs cinched to iron spikes driven deep into the ground. A blanket was crumpled beside her, useless. A bundle of sage lay in a bowl outside the circle, burning slowly with thin tendrils of rich smoke rising from it. Paul picked up the sage and waved it in the air, moving around the circle.

Colette's body was thin beyond belief, and she had sweated her tank top and shorts into transparency in a few places. It wasn't all that warm in the basement, but her drawn face shone with sweat and her blonde hair was matted to her scalp.

Her eyes shone with glee as Sara entered the room. "More friends," she whispered, a high tittering laugh escaping her.

Sara shook her head. "Vaughn, you show me all the vacation spots."

"Why should the Catholics get all the pea soup?" Wolf re-lit the candles and continued speaking words Sara couldn't quite hear. He stepped into the circle and completed the energizing ritual from within, the energy rising around him.

Paul completed his circuit with the sage, waving the smoke toward Colette. She threw a big coughing fit, but even Sara could tell it was fake.

Wolf took out a small flask and poured pure water into Colette's gasping mouth. She spat it out at him, straining against the cuffs. Wolf moved to her feet and repaired a pile of soil that had been kicked about the ground. "Sara, would you do her finger?"

Sara grabbed one of the candles and brought it to the edge of the circle. Wolf cut a doorway in the energy and allowed her in, then re-energized the circle with both of them inside. It was nothing anyone could have seen, especially Sara with her low esper rating, but the energy of the circle felt like a band of heat rising and falling around them.

Sara knelt beside Colette. "Sorry," she said awkwardly as she pulled one of Colette's hands toward her.

"Hello little Sara," Colette whispered, grinning.

"Don't listen," Paul said.

"Don't listen," Colette parroted. "Even if your daddy says hello, don't listen, don't listen to the screaaaams…"

"Nobody's listening," Sara said, and used the tip of her silver knife to prick Colette's finger. Colette screamed as though Sara had stabbed her in the chest, and a drop of blood fell to the floor.

"Dammit," Sara muttered, moving the candle so the next drop of blood sizzled into the flame.

Wolf intoned another invocation, but Sara wasn't listening. Neither was Colette, grinning and drooling at her from the ground.

"Daddy is calling you, Sara," she whispered. "He wants you to find your brother."

"Sara." Paul was reminding Sara to stay grounded, not to listen. He didn't have to worry. Sara knew this fucker inside the girl couldn't possibly have any answers for her.

"Don't I?" Colette giggled.

Sara blinked. *Mindreader, that's new.* "Crafty little fucker, aren't you?"

"Goddess, please help this spirit to find its way," Wolf began, and Sara felt the energy start to shift within the circle.

At that moment Dale burst in. "What the fuck! I thought we were waiting!"

"The spirit had other plans," Paul said. "Stay back, Dale."

"Hellooooo, Dale," Colette singsonged. "Want a drink? Want a fuck?" Her narrow hips thumped up and down in a grotesque parody of sex, rising as far off the ground as her thin frame could manage against the restraints. "Oooh, Dale, God, that's soooo good, don't stop…"

"Shut up," Dale whispered.

Colette laughed. "She faked it every time, Dale. Every. Fucking. Time."

"Dale, wait upstairs," Paul said.

"Fuck that," Dale snapped.

Colette twisted her head back and forth, giggling that horrible high-pitched tittering laugh. "He grunts when he comes, just like a fucking pig."

Sara stood up and arrowed a look at Dale. "You need to go if this is going to work."

Colette's head whipped toward her impossibly fast. "Little girl so far from home. Don't you want to hear your daddy's voice again?" Her voice dropped to a conspiratorial whisper. "Do you know what they made him do to your mother?"

Sara forced herself to remain impassive, determined not to give the creature any satisfaction. Inside, her heart was pounding.

Wolf glanced at Paul, and Sara read some hellish indecision in Paul's eyes for the first time she could remember.

Dale obviously knew what was unsaid. "No!" he shouted. "No, we are not—"

"It's the only way, Dale," Paul said. "It's just getting stronger."

Colette's laughter rose higher and higher until it became screams, shrill and awful. Sara resisted the urge to cover her ears. In mid-scream the tone changed, from a crow of triumph to one of utter terror. Tears leaked from her crystal-blue eyes.

"Dale!" she shrieked. "Dale, help me, please, I'm so lost…"

"I'm here," Dale said, kneeling outside the circle. He started to reach toward her, but Paul put a hand on his shoulder, and he remembered the circle. "I'm here, Cole."

"Don't leave me," she begged him, terror in her eyes. "Please, I'm so sorry, it's lying I swear it's lying—"

"I know, Cole," Dale insisted, tears welling in his eyes. His fists tightened impotently on the ground. "I know, and I'm going to get you free of this, I swear."

"Ask her," Wolf told Paul. Paul shook his head.

"Goddammit!" Dale swore over his shoulder. "It's the first time she's been lucid in days, can't you—"

"That's why we have to ask now, because we may not get another chance," Wolf insisted.

"Somebody start talking," Sara ordered.

Wolf spoke to Sara, but was looking at Dale. "The grounding rituals aren't working, obviously. We need to do a divination ceremony to determine which pantheon we're dealing with, and if it's the one I think it is, there's a way to get the entity to depart."

Paul stood over his brother's shoulder. "Colette, we think we know how to get you free. If we invoke a second spirit, we can ask it to force this one to leave you."

"Not a fan," Sara said quietly.

Dale looked at her. "Suddenly I like you."

"The feeling is not mutual." Sara looked at Wolf. "If we've got one squatter spirit, inviting another seems like a good way to make things worse. Two possessions, no waiting."

"A second entity from the same pantheon could compel the spirit to leave Colette in peace," Wolf said. "The problem is the price."

Dale shook his head. "The price would be your memory, Cole. Your memory since the invocation at least, maybe before."

Colette's eyes widened. "But…that's six months. That's…"

Dale nodded. "Everything."

Colette shook her head so fast Sara thought she was being possessed again. "No, love, I can't. I won't remember any of it. I won't remember *us.*"

Dale lowered his head. "I know."

Colette wept, and Sara wished she could run far away from this place. "The day in the park under the tree. The trip to Chincoteague. Christmas Eve in the apartment. The first…the first time we…"

She dissolved into gut-wrenching sobs, straining against the cuffs. "No, please don't."

Dale looked up at Wolf. Silently the older man cut a doorway, allowing Dale into the circle. He leaned over Colette and brushed the sweat-streaked hair out of her face. "Cole, it's killing you. We can't get you free, we can't… I can't watch you die, love."

Colette shook her head again. "No, Dale, please. Please. Don't do it. Don't make me forget you. Please, I love you, I don't want you to be a stranger. Please, Dale, it was the happiest time of my life, please don't take it away from me, I don't *want* to forget—"

Dale kissed her again, his shoulders shaking.

"We're running out of options, Colette," Paul said. "Your metabolism is way too high, the fever is getting worse."

Sara turned to Wolf. "Hospital?"

Wolf shook his head. "No good. Nothing they can do will touch it, and they wouldn't let us help her."

"Seems like we're doing a bang-up job at that," Sara muttered.

Colette looked past Dale up at Paul. "Have you ever loved someone, Paul? Wouldn't you rather die than forget ever knowing her?"

Paul stood silent, the iceman Sara often accused him of being.

"Please…" Colette's voice grew small. "Please…please don't…"

Her whole body shook, and her back arched like a drawn bow, lifting her off the ground.

Sara grabbed Dale by the shoulder and pulled him away just as Colette's teeth snapped forward, trying to bite at him.

"Pleeeeease doooon't," Colette giggled, that twisted grin back on her face. "Oh, Dale…"

Sara turned to Wolf. "Get us out of here."

Wolf cut another doorway, and Sara hauled Dale out of the circle toward his brother. Dale stood shaking between them as Wolf once again re-energized the circle.

Sara looked from the brothers to Wolf. "Was it fucking with us again? Was that her or not?"

"It was her," Paul said.

"You don't know that," Dale replied. "I don't know that, and I love her."

"I'd rather diiiiie," Colette cackled.

Dale turned to Paul, grabbing his brother by the arms. "Find another way."

Paul shook his head. "I don't know any other way, Dale. Don't you think I'd have tried it by now?"

"Would you?" Dale shouted, shoving Paul away hard enough to make him stumble.

"You all need to get out now," Wolf said severely. Sara tried to grab Dale, but there was no stopping him now.

"You and your stupid Secret Service or whatever the hell you are!" Dale shouted at his brother. "What the fuck good are you if you can't save one dying woman?"

"Stow it, buster," Sara said, trying her damndest to yank him toward the stairs.

Dale pulled away again, pointing an accusatory finger at Paul. "This is your supposed specialty, Paul. You and your spook squad. That's why I called you. You and your people, you fix this!"

Paul shook his head. "They don't know I'm here."

Sara shot a look at Paul.

"What?" Dale whispered.

Paul dropped his gaze. "Just me and Harvey here. This is off the books. If Blackfire knew—"

"*What* if Blackfire knew?" Sara asked. "What did you get me into, Paul?"

"You know damned well, Harvey," Paul said, but he was looking at Dale. "I tell Blackfire what's going on and Colette goes into lockdown. They'll try to catch the spirit, imprison it somehow. They…"

"They'll let her die," Wolf said through gritted teeth.

Dale stared at Paul. "Helluva job you've got, brother. Helluva job."

Sara had had enough. She stepped between Dale and Paul, breaking that horrible tension between them. "I'm telling you now, pal. Up the stairs. Out of the way."

"What, he's from the government, he's here to help? What a fucking relief!" Dale shouted.

"Dale, please," Colette said, and now Sara could not tell at all whether it was the mocking voice of the spirit or the real Colette. If the real Colette had been there at all.

Wolf reached over and took Colette's pulse. "Gentlemen. Her heart rate is extremely high. I am telling you for the last time. Get out and let me work alone, or she is going to die. I doubt she can keep—"

"Please, Dale, let me die," Colette pleaded.

Dale stepped up to the edge of the circle, and Sara moved beside him in case he tried something as disastrous as just stepping through and disrupting it.

"We can try again," Dale promised her. "We can… We can do it again. We loved each other once, we can love each other again."

Colette shook her head. "I won't remember. It won't be the same. Butterfly wings, remember? Touched once, they fall out of the sky."

"I'll remember for both of us," Dale said, his voice shaking almost as much as his hands. "I'll remember, and I'll tell you everything. We can go back to Chincoteague, we can build new memories…"

Colette screamed again, her whole body shuddering.

Dale buried his head in his hands. "Do it."

"No," Paul said.

Dale's head snapped up. "What?"

"She said no," Paul said, and probably Sara was the only one who could hear the roughness in his voice. "She declined. We can't take her memory without her permission."

Dale turned on Paul, nose to nose with him. "It might not be her! We don't know it's really her!"

"You know it is!" Paul shouted, the first time Sara could remember him ever raising his voice outside a fight. Which this might become at any moment. "You know it's her! She made her choice, and you can't accept it!"

"She's dying, you fuck! Help her!" Dale whipped around and pointed at Wolf. "You, start the ritual!"

Wolf looked at Sara. She grabbed Dale's hand and applied the *san-kyo* wrist lock that, ironically, his brother had taught her. The slightest motion brought him extreme pain, and Dale didn't have his brother's training to break it. Sara got him to the stairs and forced him upward, wishing she had a rolling pin to whack him one. It would probably be kinder.

Behind them, Colette screamed. "Dale! Don't leave me!"

Paul followed them up into the kitchen, the echoes of Colette's screams rising from the basement as Sara released Dale. "It's not what she wants, Dale," he repeated.

Dale shoved away from Sara and launched himself at Paul, throwing him up against the wall. Sara was there in an instant, wrestling Dale into a chokehold and pulling him off his brother. She kept him held tight.

Dale looked up at Paul. "Please," he whispered. "I love her. Don't let her die. I'd rather she lived without loving me than... *Please.* I'm begging you, Paul."

Paul stared at his brother, that hellish uncertainty in his eyes. Then he went down the stairs as Colette screamed for Dale to come back, don't leave her, she loved him...

Sara restrained Dale on the kitchen floor, his body writhing and fighting the sobs that wracked his body as the chanting began downstairs. None of them could see the look in her own eyes.

9

The knock at the car window startled Sara more than it should have. She jumped, vaguely embarrassed that she hadn't heard or sensed him coming up to the passenger side of the Jeep.

She pressed the button to lower the window. "Goddamn, give me a heart attack next time."

Wolf Stewart slid into the passenger seat and closed the door. "You couldn't have chosen a respectable place where I could buy you an adult beverage, now that you're old enough to drink them?"

"Good God, Wolf, I've been old enough to drink since God was a little girl," Sara said.

Wolf cocked an eyebrow. "Exactly how old does that make me, my dear girl?"

"Two days older than dirt." Sara chucked him on the arm. "Thanks for seeing me."

"And how may I be of service?" Wolf asked.

Sara looked ahead at the gates. "This is an off-the-books consultation, Wolf. I can't bring you in on this one officially. I don't have the authority."

"Not that I'm complaining about the loss of my fee, but since when?" Wolf asked.

"I'm retiring."

Wolf stared at her. "Really."

Sara sighed. "Don't. Just…don't, okay?"

Wolf followed her gaze and watched Brookside with her, its corporate-smooth white-stone walls belying its true purpose behind the steel gates and wide useless lawn with no trees. "Quid pro quo, Clarice. I'll answer your questions for free. You answer mine."

"God save me from old friends," Sara muttered. The gates to Brookside rumbled open and she tensed, watching a blue sedan roll out into the street. Wolf watched her and said nothing. "Fine. Me first."

She handed him a thin sheaf of photo printouts and the file. Wolf frowned at the photos of Natalia, and flipped through the dead men. "You're sure it's supernatural?"

"Very sure," Sara said. "I barely kept an invisible force from dragging a cop into the river right in front of me last night. It moves like nothing I've fought—draws them into the water against their will, drowns them, and somehow leaves them high and dry on the land without a single drag mark. I don't know how to direct my people—flying totally blind."

Wolf read the file for several minutes before speaking. "It's hard to say without being present and feeling its energy, but it's definitely a water force."

"Thanks, Wolf, I could figure that out for myself," Sara grumbled. "Tell me something I don't know."

"You first," Wolf said, looking at her in that maddening way: concerned and analytical at the same time. He could read her as easily as he could read the file, and she knew better than to lie to him. But the scientist he truly was constantly searched for the cause and effect, the logical result of the energies he manipulated so well. His intellectual calm was comforting and annoying at the same time.

Sara rolled her eyes. "Ask already."

Wolf hesitated a moment, which alone was enough to worry her. "Months go by after the Island and I hear nothing from you. You debriefed and you vanished. Where did you go?"

Sara stared straight ahead. "Nantucket. It's lovely this time of year."

Wolf shot her a look. "And the reason you didn't tell me was…"

"You only get one question at a time," Sara said. "Give me something I can use, Wolf. People are dying."

He closed the file. "Water spirits are tricky beasts. Fire's the obvious enemy, but a strong spirit will just quench it and keep going. Water is often a form of cleansing; your particular creature could be corrupting that into a need to cleanse the victims. Were they up to anything naughty when they were killed?"

Sara frowned. "Not sure. The dockworkers were on their lunch break, dunno about the homeless guy. The cop was patrolling, hoping to get a glimpse of the killer."

"Bad cop?" Wolf asked.

"Good cop," Sara insisted. "At least, he was. Horowitz's partner."

Wolf raised an eyebrow. "THE Horowitz? Detective Adam Horowitz, formerly of the Memphis Police Department?"

"Once again of the Memphis Police Department, and you just wasted a question, and shaddup." Sara fumbled out a notebook. "Tell me some water critters."

"I dislike the term 'critter,' but I obey, madam," Wolf said wryly. "The vilya like to drown people. Vilya are Slavic wood fairies, which puts them more than a little out of their territory."

"Possible." Sara scribbled. "Aren't the vilya the ones with the crappy personal lives?"

"Yes," Wolf said, looking at her in that analytical mode again. "Vilya are cursed never to find their one true love. Once they do, that love dies a horrible death."

Sara groaned. "Lovelorn sprites. Great. Who else likes to drown people?"

"First," Wolf said, ignoring Sara's eyeroll. "Why didn't you ask me to come to you at Nantucket?"

"Gee, Wolf, I figured you could get your own seafood," Sara snarked. "You've kind of got a life and all, didn't figure you wanted to join in on my vacation. Next time we'll do Disneyland, okay?"

Wolf remained silent until she glanced at him. "Use the sarcasm all you like on the monster fodder at Blackfire, Sara Madeleine Harvey. It will not work on me."

The gates opened again, and Sara leaned forward to watch as another car rolled out into traffic.

"It goes without saying that I'm worried about you," Wolf said.

"Join the fucking club. Who else drowns?" Sara flipped a page in her notebook.

"Sirens of all kinds lure sailors to their deaths," Wolf said. "A rusalka, for example—a Russian spirit of a murdered woman, but then it'd also be out of its territory by half the globe. There's also kraken, which I figure aren't likely in the Mississippi River. Your garden-variety ghost isn't generally strong enough to drown, but don't forget that the Mississippi has centuries of sunken riverboats and deadly disasters, especially in the Memphis stretch. That's a lot of energy."

"I thought ghosts couldn't cross running water?" Sara scribbled in her notebook.

Wolf smiled. "What did I tell you when you were a teenager? For every rule—"

"There's a critter that breaks it," Sara finished. "Yeah, yeah, heard that one. I don't think we're talking ghosts here, Wolf. We tried salt and iron both, to no effect."

"Then perhaps a transplanted rusalka," Wolf said.

Sara flipped another notebook page. "Which does…"

Wolf hesitated.

Sara raised an eyebrow at him. "You're kidding."

"It's hell getting old. Give me a little time to look it up, all right? I know there's a spell, but it's in Russian. I'll call you." Wolf placed the file back on the armrest between them. "One more question."

"Wolf, I cannot tell you what happened on the Island," Sara said firmly. "I told you last year and I'm telling you now. National security, and your clearance isn't high enough. Suffice to say it was an utter clusterfuck."

"As only Blackfire can do," Wolf said dryly.

Sara rubbed her face with her hands. "Please, for the love of God, don't bug me about Blackfire. I'm retiring, okay? Gone. Finished. You were right, I was wrong, that's what you wanted to hear, right? It was a bad fit from start to finish and I should have stayed in intelligence where I belonged and thanks to me my whole fucking team—"

She stopped then, becoming aware that her voice had risen to a hectoring rant that sounded more than a little hysterical.

Wolf reached over and touched her hand. She did not pull away, because it was Wolf, her unofficial godfather, the man who stood by her parents the day she was born, the one applauding her the day she graduated at Parris Island. Wolf was the one who would get the somber knock at the door and the folded flag when she was finally too slow on the draw. She could stand for him to touch her.

"I don't have to know the details to know that you fought like hell for your team, and it's not your fault they're dead," Wolf said quietly. "They did their jobs, and they knew the risks, just as you do. I've never seen any leader in Blackfire care about their people like you and Paul Vaughn did."

Sara couldn't help it—her hand jerked away from him when he said

Paul's name. Glittering cold eyes, the spatter of dark-red blood and thicker things across the white boat deck.

We don't all go insane, Sara.

Wolf caught her hand again and squeezed it. Unaccustomed tears caught in Sara's throat, and she swallowed them back down. She hadn't cried in years, and she wasn't about to start now. Her hands shook, but Wolf caught them both in his own hands, turning her toward him. She looked down to avoid his eyes, her unfocused gaze on the simple manila folder holding its slate of death.

"I told you to leave Blackfire because I saw what it was doing to you, Sara," Wolf said quietly. "You're colder than you were. More hard edges. I didn't want to see the girl I knew become a woman who didn't know how to feel anymore. It had nothing to do with your ability. You'd know that, if you weren't in your own little private hell right now." He paused. "You're seeing things that aren't there and sometimes you have to fight to keep control, to tell the difference between reality and your nightmares… What are you using for grounding?"

"Seawater," she whispered, and willed the image of the cool waves to wash over her twisted heart and make it still.

Wolf pressed her hands tightly. "You survived the djinn. You survived the business with the Vaughn brothers. You've survived more disasters than I could possibly begin to list, and probably many more I'll never know, including your parents. But Sara, you are not made of stone. Not yet. Leave Blackfire if it's what you want, but you can't leave yourself behind."

"Is that your question?" Sara asked, steeling herself to look at him.

Wolf shook his head. "I want to know why we're parked in front of the mental institution, Sara. Is he still there?"

Sara nodded. "But I can't, Wolf. I'm not ready to see him."

"Then don't," Wolf said with finality. "You shouldn't, not until you're ready." He smiled a little. "Frankly, if you could face him without any emotion, I'd be afraid you were already gone."

"Not quite yet," Sara said. "You're a good man, Mr. Stewart."

"I'll do in a pinch," he replied.

Her phone rang then, and Wolf waited quietly as she answered it. "Horowitz, slow down. You've got a file from immigration?" She wrote a bit on her pad. "Yes, well, it's nice to know that I'm not completely crazy."

"Not completely," Wolf muttered, and Sara elbowed him.

"I'll meet you at the motel," Sara said. "Yes, the same one." She sighed as the voice squawked a little, then interrupted him. "I am *so* not discussing this right now. See you in fifteen, Detective." She snapped the cell closed.

"Detective Horowitz and a motel room, this is promising," Wolf said.

Sara leveled her best Paul Vaughn ice-glare at him. "Get outta my car."

"Aye, ma'am," Wolf said, kissing her gently on the cheek. He clambered out of the Jeep, but paused with the door held open. "Think about what I said, Sara. Stay grounded. And get out while there's still something left to save."

She sketched him a quick salute.

Sara pulled into the parking lot of the Elmwood not long after Horowitz. He leaned against the side of his car as her Jeep came to a stop.

"Bingo, Harvey," he said, waving a file at her as she got out. "Natalia Ivanova, Russian immigrant, showed up on a fiancée visa and disappeared. No one's seen or heard from her since."

"Not even the fiancé?" Sara flipped through the file. Typical bureaucracy, nothing of interest and a lot that wasn't interesting at all.

"Talking to him tomorrow," Horowitz said. "Gotta handle this carefully if it turns out he's my man."

Sara rolled her eyes as she closed the file. "Your man? What are you, a Mountie?"

Horowitz trailed after her toward the rooms at the far end of the motel, where Sara preferred to stay. The motel butted up against a drainage ditch and thick brush, with a sloping hill that fell away from the building and the street toward a stand of trees. It was quieter and more secluded at that end, which came in handy when Blackfire was in town.

Sara walked faster, knowing that Horowitz wanted to talk in private and she absolutely didn't. He walked faster as well, trying to catch up, but she just wasn't ready for another heartfelt conversation after nearly losing it with Wolf earlier.

"Harvey!" Horowitz called, finally catching up to her. Unfortunately, he also put a hand on her shoulder, and she spun around in defensive posture without realizing it.

Reflexively he put up his hands to block an attack. "Jesus, Sara! What the hell!"

"Sorry." Sara relaxed her posture. "I've got work to do, Horowitz."

He stepped closer. "Sara, I'm—"

"Worried about me," Sara finished. "Goddammit, I'm overdosing on misplaced male chivalry these days. Would everyone stop fucking worrying about whether I'm having bad dreams and just focus on the job?"

"I *am* focusing on the job," Horowitz insisted. "You were right. The name you gave us is the name of Jane Doe. I don't know who or what was speaking to you in the morgue, but I do know it was telling the truth that far. I thought you were wigging out and actually you were doing your job. I wanted to say that I'm sorry."

Sara blinked.

"I'm apologizing," he repeated.

"I get that. Thanks." Sara turned away again, and he scrambled to keep up with her.

"God, you walk faster than—" Horowitz's voice trailed off as his gaze went past her. "Hold up, Harvey." He moved in front of her, his hand on his holster.

Sara followed Horowitz's line of sight and instantly her hand fell to her own sidearm.

Someone staggered out of the brush by the drainage ditch, down the hill past the side of the motel. Someone covered in leaves and sticks, someone pale with clothing in tatters. He moved with poor grace, stumbling a bit.

"Help me," he called, his voice ragged.

Horowitz broke into a run, moving fast down the hill. Sara followed, slamming a fist into the motel room door as she passed it. A second after she ran by, she heard the door open and the team's voices as they poured out of the room.

"Horowitz! Wait up!" Sara shouted, but he was going full-tilt. "Goddamn Boy Scout," she muttered, skidding a little as they ran down the hill.

They were a few steps short of the man when Horowitz drew up, gasping. Sara took one look and pushed Horowitz out of the way.

She was just in time, as the corpse of Dan Chamberlin leapt at them, snarling. It slammed into Horowitz, who in turn knocked Sara to the ground. It came at them again, but Sara's boot caught it in the stomach and sent it spinning away from Horowitz.

At the top of the hill, Jacobs and Riordan appeared. Sara staggered to her feet as Chamberlin switched targets, clambering up the hill toward them. Camden stood by the parking lot, seemingly frozen, with Thacker behind him.

"Romero!" Sara shouted, scrabbling for her gun. "Romero! *ROMERO!*"

"Jesus Christ!" Thacker shouted, bolting back toward the weapons cache inside the room. At least, that's what Sara assumed. Thacker was a lot of things she despised, but he was unlikely to run from a fight.

Riordan skidded to a stop, her hand falling to an empty holster.

Crap. Sara leveled her Beretta at Chamberlin. "Hit the deck!"

Riordan threw herself flat, bless her. But a second later Jacobs slammed into Chamberlin, knocking it away from Riordan. They rolled onto the ground, thrashing in the tall grass.

Sara scrambled up the hill, Horowitz struggling to his feet behind her. The steep slope of the hill made movement difficult. "Jacobs, get the fuck out of the way!"

Jacobs hoisted Chamberlin away from him and rolled aside as Camden ran down the hill, a stupid .22 pistol in his hand.

Chamberlin's head snapped to the side, focusing on Camden like a tiger spying its prey. The shambling bit had been an act, Sara realized—Chamberlin was faster and stronger than it looked. Especially for being dead.

Chamberlin sprang at Camden, who fired wild just as Sara's shot slammed into the side of the motel beside them.

Fucking Keystone Kops, Paul mocked inside her head. *Is this your crack new team, Harvey?*

Chamberlin knocked Camden down, but Riordan was there, her combat boot slamming into the corpse's side. Sara heard the crunch of ribs—they'd already been cut apart with a spreader in the morgue. How was it fucking moving?

Riordan grabbed Camden's dropped .22 and fired at Chamberlin, hitting it full in the chest. Once, twice, he kept coming. Camden rolled his useless ass out of the way as Riordan backed up, emptying the gun into Chamberlin's chest.

Sara skidded to a stop and leveled her Beretta at Chamberlin. She fired, catching the corpse in the leg. Chamberlin staggered, dragging the wounded leg as it kept moving toward Riordan.

Camden crab-walked backward, slipping around in the tall grass as he tried to get to his feet.

Horowitz braced himself beside Sara and they fired together, catching Chamberlin twice in the left arm and once in the side. Some liquid bubbled out of the wounds, a preservative maybe, but it certainly wasn't blood.

Riordan stepped between the corpse and Camden, protecting him with her own body like a good soldier. Sara was suddenly, unreasonably proud of Riordan, even though it was a useless gesture—they weren't going to get it down before Chamberlin reached her. Even though she didn't really care if the thing ate Camden.

But then Jacobs launched himself at Chamberlin, pulling it away from Riordan again even as Sara shouted at him to stay away. They fell into the grass yet again, wrestling among the brush.

Sara struggled up the hill toward them. "Goddammit, Jacobs, get away! Get away! Fucking Romero!"

Jacobs kicked out and Chamberlin's body practically flew backward, leaking from a dozen horrific wounds. There was a hole in its gut the size of a lemon, and Sara could see dark organs glistening.

"Hit the deck!" Thacker shouted from the top of the hill. He stood there braced with the AR-15.

Sara and Horowitz dove to the left, falling into the grass yet again. Jacobs rolled away fast to the right, as Riordan threw herself over Camden.

Thacker fired the AR-15, ribboning bullets through the grass and catching Chamberlin in the lower midsection.

The force of the bullets blasted Chamberlin's lower half apart, separating one leg entirely and pitching it backward into the grass. Once Chamberlin was down, Thacker ceased fire.

"Hold!" Sara shouted, just to make sure.

Thacker advanced down the hill, the AR-15 leveled at Chamberlin's prone body. Sara and Horowitz moved in from the side, guns at the ready.

Chamberlin was barely more than a mutilated torso squirming in the grass, waving one useless arm in the air.

There was no way it could speak. But no one had bothered to tell it that.

It grinned with Dan Chamberlin's mouth, leaking noisome fluid onto its gray lips.

"*Ssso much ssstronger, Ssssara,*" it whispered.

Sara put her boot on the flailing arm, pinning it to the ground. Her Beretta was aimed squarely at its forehead, with Horowitz covering her and Thacker's finger on the Atchisson's trigger.

"What are you?" Sara asked.

A cackling giggle burbled from its mouth. *"Sssara of the ssseasshore,"* it chanted.

Sara stood up and stared at Thacker. He met her eyes and nodded.

Sara aimed her Beretta carefully and put a bullet between Chamberlin's eyes. The head half-exploded across the ground, and Horowitz looked away. She couldn't quite blame him.

But there was no time.

Sara turned and stalked up the hill. "Everybody in the room for debrief! Horowitz, you too. Thacker, get a cleanup crew out here fast. Let's move, people! Our lives just got way more complicated."

Riordan scrambled across the hill to a limping Jacobs, helping him up toward the rooms. Sara shot a special glare at Camden, who avoided her gaze.

As Sara reached the top of the hill, she nearly bumped into Kaiser. He leaned against the motel wall outside the room, a second drum for the Atchisson in his shaking hands.

"Relax, kid," Sara said.

Kaiser looked at her. "He was…dead. Like undead."

"Welcome to Blackfire," Sara said, but she made an effort to temper her tone. *See, Paul, I'm learning.* "You gonna be okay?"

Kaiser looked down at the Atchisson drum for a minute, then looked at her. "I was useless."

Sara grinned. "That's the spirit!"

Kaiser blinked. "I'm supposed to be useless?"

Sara shook her head. "You're supposed to *care* about being useless, which is more than I can say for some people," she said. "You're a noncombatant. You stayed out of the line of sight and kept your ass alive to help us. You got the Atchisson out of the case for Thacker to use, right?" Kaiser nodded. "Then you weren't useless. You did your job and left the fighting to those who were trained for it. There might be hope for you yet, Kaiser."

A ghost of a grin emerged. "You're hell on the motivational speaking, Harvey."

"That's our Harvey, director of public relations," Thacker snarked from behind them. He hefted the Atchisson toward Kaiser, who staggered under its weight. "Box it up, kid. Thanks."

Sara clapped Kaiser on the shoulder and walked into the motel room, Thacker and Horowitz behind her.

She stopped still.

Jacobs sat on the far bed, looking a little pale. Camden ripped up Jacobs' bloody right sleeve as Riordan scrounged the supplies table for the first-aid kit.

"Oh shit," Sara breathed.

Jacobs looked up at her. "It's not bad."

Camden peered at the wound in Jacobs' forearm, for once acting like the professional he allegedly was. "Should be fairly simple to stitch up, the bleeding's already slowing," he said. "Riordan, you found the Betadine yet?"

"I think it's—" Riordan's voice trailed off. "Harvey, what the hell?"

Sara had her Beretta out as the others filed in. "Camden. Move away from him."

Camden gaped at her. "What the hell are you doing?"

"Move away," Sara repeated, her Beretta held in both hands. "It's a bite wound." She fought to keep her voice calm.

Jacobs looked from Sara to Camden, shock and a touch of fear in his face that reminded Sara how goddamn young he was. "What? It can be disinfected, right? What's the deal?"

"Romero," Sara said. "You were supposed to read the file. You were all supposed to read the file."

"It was…classified," Thacker said in a choked voice.

Sara gritted her teeth and willed the calm seawater over her heart to keep her from shooting Thacker first, preferably in the goddamn kneecaps.

"Camden. I'm not saying it again. Move away."

Camden stood up and stepped to the end of the bed.

But Riordan shoved past him, her own gun back in her hand and aimed at the floor. She stood between Sara and Jacobs.

"What the hell do you think you're going to do, Major?" Riordan asked, her voice tense.

"He was bitten," Sara said. "He's going to turn. I don't know how long we have before—"

"Jesus, are you kidding me?" Jacobs shouted. "I'm – what, infected with something? What Chamberlin had?"

Camden scrambled to the first-aid kit. "There has to be something I can give him. Wash the wound, a massive antibiotic, intravenous—"

"Nothing works." Sara's voice was flat and dead.

Thacker moved up beside Sara, his own sidearm in his hand. "Riordan. Move."

Riordan stood straight and tall in the dim light of the motel room. "No."

Sara and Thacker lifted their guns as one, and Riordan raised her own.

"Oh Jesus," Kaiser said, backing away from both sides.

Horowitz had his gun out now, moving to Sara's right and keeping them all in sight. "Everybody stay calm. Let's talk this out."

"You're not killing him." Riordan's voice was as flat as Sara's, and as absolute.

Sara shook her head. "Listen to me, Riordan. Please believe that I'm telling the truth."

"I believe you believe it," Riordan said. "It doesn't matter. You're not killing him."

"There's no saving him," Sara said.

"I don't care!" Riordan shouted. "If it was your man, the one who died, you'd do the same, Harvey. I know it."

Sara closed her eyes a half-second, long enough to will the image away. Paul's body, drifting away into the ocean. "I'd save him if I could, Riordan. I swear to you I would. But there is no way."

Jacobs stood up, his hand clamped over the wound. Automatically Riordan shifted to protect his body with her own. "Kay, they may be right."

"You're not dying," Riordan insisted, keeping her eyes on Sara and Thacker. "It's just a scratch. Just a scratch! I won't let them kill you for it."

"What if they're right?" Jacobs said. In his eyes and his voice, Sara could see a very young man trying to be brave, trying to be right.

Riordan shook her head hard, some of her auburn hair falling loose onto her neck. "Shut up, Dan. You got bit protecting me. You've always protected me, since we were kids. You think I'm just gonna stand aside and let her shoot you like a rabid dog? Fuck that."

Camden stepped beside Riordan, and now he had Jacobs' Smith & Wesson aimed at Sara and Thacker. "Put it down, boss."

"Harvey's right, he's going to die and take us with him," Thacker warned Camden.

"You don't know that!" Camden insisted. "I read Romero, and the Cold Ones weren't dead. They weren't dead, and you know that, Harvey! Chamberlin was dead as a doornail! Whatever was just out there, it wasn't a Cold One, not like before, so we don't know the rules!"

Sara shook her head. "Chamberlin was a skinny drink of water. Jacobs as a Cold One would be practically unstoppable, he could take us all out before we even had the chance to fight back so you fucking idiots *get the hell out of my way!"*

Riordan shook her head. "Not happening, Harvey."

Sara glared at her. "I will shoot you, Riordan. If it means stopping an outbreak, I will shoot you dead."

"Kay," Jacobs protested, touching Riordan's shoulder gently.

Riordan smiled at Harvey, but there was no humor in it. "I know you'd kill us all in our sleep for this job, Harvey. But you'll have to start with me."

Thacker lowered his gun.

"Thacker." Sara chanced a quick glance at him. "Goddammit!"

Thacker shook his head. "They're right, Sara. We don't know for sure."

"I do know!" Sara shouted. "I'm the only one here who knows what they can do! Goddamn you all, trust me. Trust me! Please!"

Her eyes moved from person to person, and she saw the truth—they didn't trust her. The team was broken. The team had always been broken.

"Guns down, everybody," Thacker said.

"Her first," Riordan said.

Horowitz spoke from the corner, where he stood with his gun out and aimed at the floor. "Can I make a suggestion that doesn't involved anyone getting shot?"

"I think we're open to ideas," Kaiser said.

Horowitz pointed to the far bed. "Tie him up. Secure him to the bed, treat him as best you can. If he goes all creepified, we can shoot him then."

Riordan glared at Horowitz.

"Good plan," Thacker said. "Harvey. Lower your weapon."

Sara didn't move. "You motherfucking idiots," she repeated, quietly this time. "He's going to kill you all." Then she lowered her Beretta.

Slowly, Riordan lowered her gun, and Camden did the same.

"Okay," Horowitz said. "Jacobs, get comfortable."

Sara stood perfectly still while Kaiser and Camden secured Jacobs to the bed with restraints. She remained still, leaning against the wall, as Camden got to work with the disinfectant and setting up an IV in Jacobs' good arm.

Horowitz moved over to stand next to Sara, but she refused to relax, eyes focused on Jacobs, hand on her holster.

Riordan sat on the edge of the bed, touching Jacobs' face lightly with her hand as they tightened the restraints.

"Hey, you," she murmured.

"Very badass, Kay," Jacobs said.

"I learned it from you," Riordan replied.

Jacobs grinned. "The hell you say."

Riordan leaned forward and kissed him full on the lips, her hands moving through his hair. She whispered something to him, and his whole body shuddered. "I mean it," she whispered.

Kaiser sidled over to Camden. "Pay up," he muttered, and Camden fumbled out his wallet.

Sara turned to Thacker. "A moment alone, please."

Thacker opened the motel door and gestured to the darkening parking lot. Sara stalked out and walked toward the top of the hill, staring down at the blood and chunks of flesh scattered through the tall grass. Chamberlin's remains had not moved. He was still dead. Deader.

"Cleanup team will be here in a few minutes," Thacker said, coming up behind her.

Sara grabbed Thacker by the jacket and flung him up against the brick wall.

"You fucking shit bastard!" she shouted, not caring who heard or saw. *"You knew!* It's alive and you didn't fucking tell me? It's sending me goddamn zombie-grams and I thought I was losing my fucking mind and you didn't...fucking...*tell...me!"*

Sara punctuated each word by slamming Thacker against the brick wall again.

"I didn't know!" Thacker shouted, tensing his body to keep from being injured, but not striking out at her.

Sara let go of Thacker's jacket and swung a roundhouse punch, which he blocked. "You fuck! Of course you knew! You knew everything about the Island! You and your fucking pals at Blackfire, keeping your goddamn secrets from me and my team, and they died, they all died and it's your fucking fault! How did It escape? *Tell me!"*

"I don't know!" Thacker insisted. "I swear—"

This time Sara caught him full in the jaw with an uppercut, blunting it only at the last second. Thacker went sprawling beside the wall just as Horowitz came out of the motel room.

"Sara, stop!" Horowitz grabbed at her arm.

Sara flung Horowitz off, and he struck the brick wall hard. She stepped forward and swung a ridge hand strike at Thacker's head, but he ducked out of the way in time.

"I don't want to do this with you, Harvey!" Thacker backed away.

Sara feinted and jabbed at him again, but he was ready for her and blocked it.

"Tell me!" she shouted. "How did It get away from us? I electrocuted the fucker and blew up the goddamn Island!"

"I know," Thacker said. "I know, Sara, you killed It, It's dead, you can stop now!"

"No! I can't!" Sara insisted.

Horowitz moved to restrain her again, his hands on her arms. She struggled, but it was a token protest now, not enough to break free.

"I can't stop!" Sara cried. "It's alive, goddammit Thacker It's alive and we're dead, we're all fucking dead, and it was all for nothing! They died for nothing!"

"Sara," Horowitz murmured behind her.

Sara's whole body shuddered, and she felt Horowitz's arms shift from restraint to a clumsy attempt at comfort. She turned to him, unable to meet his eyes, but grasping his forearms with her fists. "It's alive, Adam. I killed It and It's back and God alone knows how many It has now."

Thacker approached her with caution from the side. "We don't know anything yet, Harvey."

Sara lifted her eyes to glare daggers at him. "We know that Dan Chamberlin had to cross half of Memphis to get here from the morgue, Thacker. We know that. So you tell me: how many are there now? And how long do the rest of us have?"

Thacker stood silent, as the Blackfire truck rolled up into the parking lot.

10

It was a long, hot shower before Sara felt human enough to emerge. It was a good thing the Elmwood had a seemingly inexhaustible supply of hot water. She needed to get the blood and other detritus off her skin. But no matter how much water pounded against her skin, that crawling sensation of dread covered Sara's entire body and turned her stomach into a twisting, roiling knot.

She walked out into the room and caught Horowitz and Camden by surprise. They sat at a small table with papers spread across it, heads together and conferring in low voices as Thacker reloaded the guns on his own bed.

"Anything I need to know?" Sara asked.

The men turned and stared at her, silent.

"What?" Sara asked, more than a little snappish.

Thacker put down his Beretta. "I think they're a tad surprised at your attire, Harvey."

Sara glanced down at the scant motel towel wrapped around her torso. "Oh for fuck's sake, I'm wearing underwear," she muttered, stalking past them. "Avert your goddamn eyes if you're so dainty."

"That ain't exactly the word that comes to mind," Horowitz muttered.

Sara clawed fresh clothes from her duffel in the corner as the men theatrically looked at floor and ceiling. "What are you two conspiring about?" she asked, pulling her camo pants up. She turned toward the corner and let the towel drop, ignoring Horowitz clearing his throat.

"Um. We, uh, have an idea that—" Camden's voice trailed off.

Sara finished hooking her bra. "Quit staring at my scars and finish a sentence, Doc."

Thacker sighed. "Camden here has practically got us narrowed down to the likely spot where Natalia Ivanova was murdered."

Sara pulled a fresh tank top over her head. "Explain."

"Oh God, please don't," Horowitz pleaded. "I lived through it once."

"It's not that convoluted if you examine it in the proper context," Camden said, pointing to the photo array.

"Bottom-line it for me," Sara insisted.

Camden scrambled over to her with a photo of Natalia's abused body. "If you examine the juxtaposition of the scratches and abrasions along—"

Sara glared at him. "Bottom. Line."

Horowitz stood up and pointed at the map taped to the wall. "Here. At the curve of the river south of the old bridge, a wooded area that's relatively remote, but a short walk from a pretty seedy district. A couple of taverns, a few houses."

"I was going to get there," Camden groused.

"What's the theory?" Sara asked. "Fiancé changed his mind and went for the cheap method of bride disposal?"

"Not with that much bodily damage," Camden said. "The extensive physical and sexual abuse indicates—"

"We've had a lot of this trafficking shit," Horowitz interrupted. "Girls brought in on fiancée visas and sold into prostitution. They get used up real quick. If they're lucky enough to escape they'll never testify or even report it because any contact with law enforcement could lead to deportation. Mostly they end up working off their sale price on the streets."

Camden blinked. "Sold? Like slavery? Didn't we make that illegal?"

"Right, like that's gonna stop the scumbags," Horowitz griped. "I worked a raid on a warehouse once in south city and found six girls chained to beds. Not one of them was old enough to drive. Sick shit."

Sara strapped on her utility belt. "I've said it before, Horowitz. Your world has more monsters than mine."

"I think we live in the same world," Horowitz said quietly.

Thacker clicked a magazine into place. "If you two are done with the debate, maybe we could go check out the possible murder site."

Sara cocked her head toward the wall. "What's going on next door?"

Camden shrugged. "So far Jacobs seems fine. He's tied down tight, and Riordan and Kaiser are watching him."

"I want another gun in there," Sara ordered. "When he goes, I want someone there who can put a bullet in his head."

Thacker stood up. "You really think Riordan won't shoot him if he turns?"

Sara shook her head against the rising sound of the waves. Paul's head, squarely in her sights. "No, she won't. I don't care if he's frothing blood and trying to eat her brains, she won't put a bullet in his head. She'll sit there and hope for leprechauns."

"Horowitz can babysit then," Thacker said, holstering his pistol. "I need to be with you when you go to the riverfront."

Horowitz raised his hand. "Can I point out that as a police officer, I'm actually the only one legally permitted to investigate and interrogate—"

"Shut up," Sara told Horowitz without looking at him. "It can't be Horowitz."

"And why the hell not?" Thacker asked.

"He's a civilian." Sara holstered another gun.

"Excuse me?" Horowitz said. "Detective. Remember?"

"And still protecting and serving," Sara said, still not looking at him. "You've never had to shoot someone in the head, Horowitz. You could freeze. This job requires someone a little more cold-blooded."

"Gee, thanks," Thacker said.

Sara stared at him. "I know you're ready to shoot him, Thacker. I know you could shoot me, Camden, and the entire team without losing any sleep."

Thacker looked honestly angry, facing her across the narrow bed. "That's a hell of a thing to say, Harvey."

She stood before him, hands on hips. "The only concern I have is whether you would actually do it."

"Well, thanks for giving me that much," Thacker snapped.

"Not because of weakness," Sara corrected. "Whether you've got Blackfire orders I don't know about. Keeping it for—"

"Are you fucking kidding me?" Thacker asked, incredulous. "They're in panic mode, Harvey. Merrifield himself is flying out from Farson as we speak. When he gets here, poor Jacobs is gonna get a bullet in the brain whether he's turned or not."

Camden gaped. "What the fuck?"

Sara glared. "I don't believe you."

"Believe me or not, that's the way it is," Thacker said. "Before the day is out, somebody gets to kill Jacobs. Killing a living human being who may or may not be a threat. That's a whole different level of bad shit, Harvey. I don't know if even you could do it."

Sara folded her arms. "Done it. Read the file. And did you notice where I tried to do exactly that, right next door, and you fucking wussed? You're the reason Jacobs is still breathing, so don't you shove this off on me!"

"Yes, and I'm glad!" Thacker snapped. "I'm not talking about putting some poor slob out of his misery before he turns. I'm talking about killing a young man on my team, and I wasn't ready to do it without checking every option, and you weren't either. You can act all badass, Harvey, but there's a big difference between putting down a supernatural that's a legitimate and present threat to your team and killing an ordinary human being in cold blood. You know that better than anybody!"

He softened his tone. "You couldn't kill Gary Stover either, Sara. That's not weakness. That's being human."

Sara dropped her eyes for a moment. Gary's face as he stared at her in the stairwell, the certainty of death cutting through his usual bluster. She willed the seawater over her heart yet again, but it wasn't working. Even in her mind's eye, there were streaks of blood in the water.

Then she glared at Thacker. "You don't know me as well as you think."

Horowitz stepped up. "All right. I am going to check out a potential crime scene. I need Camden's eyes with me. Sara, I assume, is going to insist on joining us. So I guess that leaves you out, Colonel."

"Fine," Thacker said. "I expect regular updates, Harvey."

"Aye sir," Sara said, and tried to keep the sarcasm out of her tone as she added extra clips to her belt. "But I've got a call to make first."

Horowitz insisted on going in first, even though Sara told him his face screamed *cop* and everyone would go running. The tavern at the end of the road redefined the word "seedy," making the dive where they'd found Camden look like a swanky New York club. The hand-painted sign above the door was practically illegible, and the only real light came from the neon beer sign flickering in the dirt-smeared window.

The youngish guy behind the wooden bar barely looked up when they entered, but once he caught a glimpse of Horowitz, he straightened up.

Three young men toward the rear of the room quietly got up and wandered down the back hallway as soon as they came in.

"Help you folks?" the barkeep asked. He had a scraggly ponytail and about six earrings in one ear. He chewed on a toothpick while he dunked a beer stein in a sinkful of greasy-looking water.

Horowitz flipped the badge. "I'm looking for Terry Keegan," he said. "He works here?"

The barkeep shrugged. "Sometimes he does, sometimes not so much. What you want him for?"

"How about you point him out?" Sara asked, already bored.

The barkeep rested his gaze on Sara. It was a decidedly unfriendly look that swept her from face to breasts to hips and back up, but there was little to be found in his stare of the kind of attention Sara occasionally got from men. It was an appraisal, as though she was a car he was considering buying, or more accurately, a hunk of meat to be cut up and consumed. It said less about evaluating her as a woman or as a threat, and more about what he would do to her if given the chance. There would be little in it that she would enjoy, from the cold glint in his eyes.

Sara was used to men looking at her. She'd served with Gary Stover for years, and if she could have counted the times he stared at her breasts or waggled his tongue at her… But Gary's casual lust was different than this guy. He wasn't about getting his rocks off. He was about hurt. Maybe that was how he got his rocks off.

Horowitz picked up on it as well—she could practically feel him tense beside her. "What's your name?"

The barkeep sighed, switching his gaze to Horowitz. "Victor Keegan, and I ain't served nobody underage so don't go harassing my customers."

"Except for the three kids I just saw scamper out the back," Camden said.

Keegan barely looked at Camden. "Terry's my brother. I can get him here if you want him."

"Why don't you do that?" Horowitz said, his manner decidedly less protect-and-serve than it had been a moment ago.

Keegan waved his hand toward a table and picked up his phone. They sat down, as the few patrons in the dingy bar stared openly at them.

Sara looked at Camden. He was twitching a bit, staring with more longing than she cared to see at the drink sitting before an old tosspot at the next table.

"Soda only," Sara murmured.

Camden glared at her. "I don't need a nanny, Major."

Sara let that one pass as she considered whether Thacker would fire her for feeding Camden to his precious dragons.

They waited silently as Camden's eyes swept the room. Horowitz glanced at him, and Camden nodded. Sara didn't need a psychic link to Camden's super-special observations or Horowitz's cop instincts to know that the tension in the bar was sky-high, not enough to scare those three college students off earlier, but enough that everyone was on edge just because of their presence. Sara stood.

"Where are you going?" Horowitz asked.

Sara rolled her eyes. "Ladies' room, sire."

As soon as she was past their line of sight in the back hallway, Sara turned away from the putrid-smelling restrooms and toward the back entrance where the college students had vanished. Naturally, there was no alarm on the back door to this dive. She pushed through and found a well-worn track from this door curving back around the bar to the dim parking lot.

The door behind her opened. "Subtle, Harvey," Camden said.

"How'd you know?" Sara asked.

Camden cocked an eyebrow at her. "It is unlikely that I would inform you of your tell, Major, as you would then make a conscious effort to change it and obfuscate my analysis in future instances where determining your truthfulness might decide whether I am eaten by a large carnivorous beastie."

"Go back inside," Sara ordered.

Camden shook his head. "Your instincts are right. But that's not the way." He pointed toward the tall grass, shadows and trees beyond the orange glare of the parking lot.

Sara sighed. "Come on, before Horowitz comes looking."

Her hand rested near her holster as Sara walked through the tall grass. Camden stumbled along with her, pointing her this way or that from broken grass or the wave of the land or some such bullshit. They were well beyond the glare of the lights when they reached the trees and the ground became rougher.

"Cars have passed this way," Camden murmured. "That brush is artfully placed, but it didn't fall there."

Sara frowned at the dead tree branches lying in their way. "Looks natural to me."

"That's why you've got me," Camden said. "There's a house on the other side of those trees."

Sara craned her neck, but could see nothing. Camden was an ass, and she didn't trust him, but she had to admit that he could see shit she just couldn't. But she didn't have to say it out loud.

Headlights pierced between the trees, and quickly Sara scrambled into the shadows with Camden beside her. She shoved him down to the ground, pulling her Beretta.

A truck pulled up on the other side of the brush, the headlights painting weird patterns through the dead branches. A young man climbed out, maybe a few years younger than that creep Keegan. He grabbed the branches and pulled the brush out of the way, making space for his truck.

Shit. It must be Terry Keegan. Sara glanced around, trying to think of a way to deter him without giving away her position. Catch Terry or investigate the house?

The house.

She let Terry get back into the truck and roll on through the grass. Now that she was looking, she could see how the ruts were carefully covered up. That didn't make the house their murder scene—it could be a meth house or something.

Sara started to stand up, and Camden put a hand on her arm. "We're not alone," he whispered.

Sara crouched and listened. A moment later she heard footsteps at seven o'clock. Shoving Camden back down in the grass, she pivoted and aimed.

"Chill, Harvey." Horowitz stepped out of the brush.

Sara exhaled. "Sneak up on me too often and one day you're gonna catch a bullet, Horowitz."

"Just returning the favor." Horowitz knelt beside her. "That was Terry rolling away, I bet."

"Dollars to doughnuts," Sara said. "Carnac the Magnificent here says the house we're looking for is behind those trees."

"I said there was a house," Camden said from the ground. "But if Major Pain in the Ass here will let me up, I can show you that what we're really looking for is several hundred yards to the right."

Sara decided to let that one pass. She took her hand off his jacket and Camden stood up, brushing nettles and dead grass off his jacket. He cocked his head to the side, and they followed him further away from the grassy field and deeper between the trees.

Camden made lefts and rights seemingly at random, muttering to himself about brambles and scratches and the Latin names of plants that made Sara want to shoot him. But before long, they could hear the gentle rushing sound of water.

"Here," Camden said, stepping over a fallen log and pointing south.

They stood together by the side of the Mississippi in the moonlight.

"Here, what?" Sara asked. "It's a river."

"Riverbank," Camden corrected. "This is where Natalia Ivanova died."

Sara looked at the water for a moment in silence. The river had its own power, she realized—a different power than that of the ocean, more focused and intense, more turbulent and reactive than the giant rolling mass of the sea. The cool water flowed past this little outcropping and past the flat rock just below them. For a moment, Sara felt calm, as though the river could flow over her like the ocean and still the beating of her heart.

Horowitz was the first to speak. "None of this is admissible. I could get a forensic team down here, but it's been days, and it's rained twice. They'll find nothing, Camden's prognostications notwithstanding."

"Put me on the stand," Camden said.

"Oh, hell no," Sara muttered. "You better read the Blackfire manual."

"To testify to what? The girl had scratches from brambles along the river? No help." Horowitz knelt beside the rock, shining his flashlight around. "If there was blood, scratches, if she left something… We don't even know if—"

"I know," Sara said.

Horowitz looked up at her.

Camden shook his head, suddenly looking disoriented. "Are either of you… Can you hear…?"

Sara looked at Camden. "You sober?"

Camden glared. "I think…there's music playing. Can't you…?"

"I hear it," Horowitz said, standing up.

Sara strained her ears, but could hear nothing past the flow of the water. "I think you both are a little on the tired side," she began, but her voice trailed off when she looked at Camden.

Camden swayed from side to side, his eyes fixed on the river. He took a step toward the water.

"Fuck," Sara whispered.

"Can't you hear it, Sara?" Horowitz said dreamily. "It's…beautiful."

Sara swore under her breath. "We gotta get out of here. Right now."

She grabbed them each by their arms and tried to drag them up the hill, but they were immovable, as if their feet were planted in concrete. "Goddammit!"

"Oh shit," Horowitz whispered, his foot taking a step toward the water.

Sara pulled the paper from her pocket. "This better work, Wolf," she muttered, and began to read the Russian words he'd given her on the phone. She hadn't thought she'd need them quite this soon, but if her last encounter was any indication, she had no other chance of keeping the rusalka from taking at least one of them.

Sara chanted the Russian spell, hoping her pronunciation wasn't too terrible. Hoping it was actually a rusalka and not some critter she'd never seen before.

The sound of the river grew louder, as though the water flowed faster though it looked as placid as ever. The sound swelled until Sara could have sworn the Red Sea was parting in front of them, though nothing could be seen.

Then the voice cut through it.

"Idi ko mne."

It was a woman's voice, choked with water and darker things. It seemed to come from inside Sara's head, as though she spoke through Paul's earpiece.

"Natalia?" Sara asked the river, feeling halfway like an idiot and halfway afraid. She had the Beretta in her hand, and after a moment's thought she holstered it. What was she going to do, shoot the river?

"Idi ko mne."

Sara stepped between the frozen men and the river. "Let them go and I'll try to help you."

Camden took another step, and now they were too far apart for Sara to stand between both of them and the water. She gritted her teeth and stepped in front of Horowitz. No offense to Camden.

Sara repeated the Russian phrases again, and the water roiled before them, swirling into a whirlpool. Horowitz tried to take a step forward and Sara braced herself on the rocks in front of her, arms stretched out as Camden's foot touched the water.

"I'll help you!" Sara shouted, wishing she could speak Russian. "I swear! I will help you! I will help you *now let them go!*"

The water grew even louder, until Sara wanted to clap her hands over her ears. And then it broke, as though something had snapped it in half.

Camden staggered backward and fell into the mud beside the water, an ungainly stumble that would have been funny in other circumstances.

Horowitz fell forward and Sara caught him in her arms, preventing him from falling into the water now rolling placidly by, quiet as ever.

"Sara," Horowitz whispered. "My God, Sara, what is it?"

"I think I know," she said, touching his face gently. "Are you all right?"

"No," Horowitz said truthfully, bracing himself on her shoulders. "She scares me, Sara. But she also…"

"I know," Sara interrupted. She glanced over at Camden. "You alive?"

Camden got to his feet slowly, mud and filth coating his pants. "For the moment. What the fuck was that?"

Sara looked over her shoulder at the river. "It's a rusalka. And we are in very deep shit."

11

The dread Sara felt getting out of the Jeep was half-dispelled when she saw who was directing traffic in the parking lot beside the ubiquitous vans from Blackfire—oops, Acme Cleaners.

"Michel, you son of a bitch." Sara grinned. "You still doing the mop-up work after all this time?"

"As long as y'all make a mess," Roy Michel drawled, pushing off the van and walking toward her. Ridiculously tall at six-five, Roy's shoulder-length gray-blond hair and goatee made him seem more like a rock-band roadie than a trained Blackfire operative, and the koi tattoo on his forearm wasn't exactly protocol. As always he moved to hug Sara, and as always she caught his arm halfway and shook it, her other hand grasping his arm. It was a little dance they did, because Roy couldn't help but be warm and affectionate. It was the Cajun in him, he said—everyone was family and deserved a hug and some righteous food. Sara found it amazing that he could stay so friendly and cheerful given the horrific job he had, a job that regularly drove lesser men screaming into the night.

Behind him, Joy Keeling popped her head around the brick wall of the motel. "That you, Harvey?"

"My God." Sara walked with Roy back toward the hill where Blackfire minions scurried about, picking up grotesque pieces. "Keeling, what the hell you still doing following this big loser around?"

"Just waiting for my big break so I can go Hollywood," Joy said dryly, stomping her boots a bit on the concrete before stepping out of the containment zone. She was approximately half Roy's height and slim of frame, with large blue eyes and fluffy blonde hair that always seemed perfectly coiffed even when she was knee-deep in monster shit. Sara had no idea how she managed it. "How the hell are you, Harvey?"

"Alive," Sara replied. "How are we down there?"

Joy shrugged. "Isn't nothin' to us. Bagged and tagged, we'll be clearing the grass shortly and by morning no one will know you dismembered a zombie here."

"I didn't say zombie," Sara chided.

"Zombie, Cold One, whatever, it's all the same to me," Joy said.

"Make sure them idiots wear their gloves," Roy said.

Joy rolled her eyes so hard Sara's head hurt just watching. "Like I've never done this before. Bite me, you big lug."

"Disrespect for a fellow officer, disregard a direct order in the presence of a superior…" Roy cited.

"I'm on Keeling's side," Sara said, grinning.

Roy cocked an eyebrow at her. "Imagine my surprise. Y'all always ganging up on me."

"Be nice, and I'll gang up on ya later," Joy said, waggling her eyebrows.

Sara held up her hands in defeat. "I do not need to know these details of your marital life."

Horowitz harrumphed behind her, and Sara remembered her manners. "Oh yeah. Roy Michel and Joy Keeling, this is Adam Horowitz, pet detective."

"Real funny, Harvey." Horowitz shook their hands. "Roy and Joy?"

"We've heard every single possible joke, many of them from Harvey," Joy declared, slipping her slim hand into Roy's giant paw.

Roy leaned over and kissed the top of Joy's head. "It coulda been worse. Coulda been Jack and Jill."

"I'm going to skip the next joke, because I've gotta get inside and check on the FUBAR," Sara said. "If we're all alive in a day or two, the first beer is on me."

Roy sobered. "Keep ya head in there, Harvey. I don't know what's going on, because I'm just steerin' the jonboat. But it sound to me like the fit all over the shan in there."

Sara glanced down the hill, where the last of Dan Chamberlin had been bagged in opaque red hazmat sacks. "Better not go far, guys. I think you're gonna be needed."

"We ain't going nowhere," Roy confirmed.

Sara walked into the room, Horowitz and Camden behind her.

As soon as she did, she wished she'd stayed with the rusalka.

Riordan stood by the foot of Jacobs' bed. Her sidearm was in her right hand, but her arms were crossed, the barrel loosely pressed against her own side. Kaiser and Thacker were by the window near Kaiser's cataclysmic pile of technological crap. Kaiser was buried in his computer, barely looking at anyone, while Thacker looked ill.

Jacobs turned to stare at Sara when she came in, and immediately her stomach turned.

He didn't look any different. His skin was the same color, his body just as hale and strong as it had been when she left.

But his eyes… His eyes were empty, dead except for a dancing, malicious glee. Anticipation.

She knew that look.

Sara unholstered her Beretta. "Riordan, how long has it been?"

"He's just not well," Riordan said dully, as though she'd repeated it a hundred times. "A fever. Damn thing bit him, it's to be expected."

Sara looked at Thacker. He shook his head slowly.

"Come on, Major," Jacobs said. "I'm fine. Let me go."

Even his voice was off. Too easy, too simple. The cadence of Jacobs' normal voice was similar to Riordan's, a touch of the Tennessee drawl common to the tiny town where they had both grown up. Sara had only known him for a few weeks, but she could tell the difference, so Riordan must be picking it up. He was too calm. Jacobs was rarely calm. He was a fighter, a big guy who used his strength regularly and trusted nothing else. He was passionate about the job, about service, and about Riordan. But he was not calm.

Now there was no Tennessee in his voice. If Sara had to choose, she'd say he sounded half-French with a touch of the Caribbean, a smooth tone that sounded a bit Creole.

And he was avoiding the letter S.

Sara edged away from the men and toward Riordan. The younger woman was restless, rapping the back of her head against the wall behind her, the gun loose in her right hand—but her finger on the trigger.

"Riordan," Sara said.

Riordan shook her head, auburn hair loose from its customary braid and falling over her shoulders. "He's just not well," she repeated.

"Sara, we're waiting on Merrifield," Thacker began.

Sara kept her gun aimed at the floor and ignored Thacker. "Riordan. It's time to walk out of here. Let us take over the watch."

Riordan's eyes raised to Sara's face, and it felt like falling into a deep, dark well. Riordan looked for all the world like Gary Stover, standing in an industrial gray-cold stairwell with eyes that were already dead, a heart waiting to be buried.

Behind her, Sara heard Camden take a few steps. "You've done all you can, Kay," he said, a desperate tone in his voice that made Sara turn around and stare at him. "It's time to let go."

Riordan shook her head again. She gestured around the room, not exactly aiming the gun at anyone, but Sara didn't like the careless way she was holding it or her sudden abdication of trigger discipline. "He needs some rest, that's all. Just some rest. He'll be fine after some rest."

"Exactly," Jacobs said. "Don't give up on me, Kay. I'm here for you, like alwaysss."

He slipped at the end, that sibilant S giving him away. Sara pivoted her head toward him, and he met her gaze with delight.

It was the gaze of It, the cold and soulless look that lit dead eyes with icy fire. Muted, perhaps, in the dead bodies that had spoken to her in the last few weeks, but now fed by Jacobs' vitality, she was face to face with It at last.

"How did you survive?" Sara asked, still not encroaching past Riordan's comfort zone between the beds. "I killed you, you fuck. How is this possible?"

Jacobs tilted his head toward Riordan. "You aren't going to let her talk to me like thisss, are you, Kay?"

Riordan said nothing, staring at the carpet. Camden tried to take another step, and she snapped to attention, forcing him back at gunpoint.

"Tell me," Sara insisted, holding up a hand toward Riordan, her heart pounding in her chest. "Tell me how you survived."

Jacobs smiled, the horrid smile of things squirming in cellar corners, of sickening smells and living things exploded at the edge of a dark highway at night.

"Oh Sssara," he whispered. "You don't expect me to tell you all my sssecretsss, do you? Little lossst Sssara by the ssseassshore—"

Riordan let out a dry, harsh sob, and her pistol turned toward Jacobs now. "Let him go, you fucker," she ordered. "You let him go and we'll let you live."

Jacobs hoisted himself up as close to a sitting position as his restraints would allow. Sara's eye roved over them fast—they looked secure. They had to be secure. "I don't think Sssara by the ssseassshore would agree," he lisped.

"Then fuck her," Riordan snapped, turning her gun on Sara with her eyes still on Jacobs.

Instantly Thacker was at Sara's side and Horowitz was on the other, guns level with Sara's, aimed at Riordan.

"Stop!" Sara ordered, keeping her eyes on Riordan. "It's fucking with you, Riordan. It can't let him go. We've never seen it happen. Once It has you, It keeps you. It wants you to kill me because It's scared that It can't."

Jacobs laughed, an awful sound that made Sara want to cover her ears.

Riordan shook her head, tears starting down her cheeks. "He's in there, Sara. I know it. He's still inside there somewhere and I can bring him out."

"I wish that were true," Sara said, her voice almost breaking.

"It is true!" Riordan insisted, her voice rising as she shouted at Sara. "It's true and you know it! You killed all those people back on the Island, all those people infected, and they were still alive! They were still alive and you killed them, you bitch! You killed soldiers and citizens and your team, you killed your own man Sara and he was *still alive!*"

Sara shut her eyes, her gut clenching like a slick fist as it happened again, over and over again, Paul's dead eyes and the report as Gary put that final bullet in his head.

"He was gone," Sara whispered, her eyes still shut. Which meant Riordan could shoot her at any second and at that point Sara simply didn't fucking care. Then sanity reasserted, and she opened her eyes.

Riordan looked back at Jacobs. "Where were you born?"

"Union City, Tennessssee," Jacobs said. "It wasss ssso goddamn hot in the sssummertime, but we kept cool, didn't we, Kay? We know all the good ssswimming ssspotsss…"

"Stop it," Camden pleaded. "Kay, please. Let us take over. Don't let him—"

Riordan ignored him. "Tell me something only Danny would know. Tell me…tell me about the prom."

Jacobs smiled again, and Sara willed herself to stop looking. "You called me from the party, after he roughed you up for ssssaying no to hisss tiny dick. You were ssstanding by the sssside of the road in the rain, ruining your yellow dresss. I picked you up and took you home, and we watched the ssssun come up from the lawn chairssss in front of your daddy's trailer."

Riordan turned to Sara. "See? No one would know that except Dan. Don't you think I'd know my best friend? Don't you think I can tell the difference?"

"Yes, I do," Sara said softly. "And you know that's not him."

Riordan moved closer to the bed, and Sara started toward her. Riordan aimed the gun at her, and Sara stopped. "Please, Kay. Don't do this to yourself. Let us handle it."

Riordan sat on the edge of the bed, barely beyond where Jacobs could reach. "Tell me, Dan. Tell me what you told me in the moonlight that night, the night of the devalpa. What did you say?"

Jacobs looked at Riordan, and for the life of her Sara wavered. He looked almost human.

"I told you I loved you," Jacobs said. "Had sssince ninth grade. I sssaid we'd alwaysss be together. And we will, Kay. We will. *Forever.*"

Riordan wept silently, tears flowing down her face. She leaned over him.

Sara started forward again. "Stop, Kay, you're too close!"

Riordan looked over at her. "It's all right."

Then she slid the gun against Jacobs' head and pulled the trigger. The report was very loud in the confined room, and the spray of blood and brains covered the bed and the wall beside it.

"Jesus!" Kaiser shouted, stumbling backward. Outside, there were shouts and the sound of running feet.

"Shit," Camden whispered. "God, Kay, I'm so fucking sorry."

"Me too," Riordan said, gently closing what was left of Jacobs' eyes with her free hand.

Then Riordan lifted the gun to her own head.

"No! Wait!" Sara shouted as they rushed toward her.

Too late.

12

It had been a long damn time since Sara Harvey smoked, but she wanted a cigarette now more than she'd ever wanted anything.

She leaned against the Jeep in the parking lot as Michel and Keeling ordered their team in and out of the blood-soaked motel room.

God, she hated the Elmwood. Blackfire bought it after the thing with the popobawa and kept it as a safehouse, but she'd gladly pay her own way and clean up whatever mess came along if it meant never looking at this motel again.

Horowitz emerged from the black van on the far side of the parking lot, where Thacker was ensconced with the videoconference. Sara had no intention of going near the van, or Thacker, or men. Or, for that matter, humans.

Horowitz walked across the lot and leaned against the Jeep beside her. Sara idly wondered if he was due for a freak-out. Horowitz was a cop, but he was also a civvie, and he'd just seen two people die before his eyes not that long after he was nearly made into zombie chow and rusalka bait.

But a stealthy glance at him made her think twice. Horowitz had a spine of steel. She'd known that since the night on the bench, when the popobawa was doing its damnedest to crush her to death on the sidewalk and he kicked it off her, knowing it would come after him next. No training, no awareness of the supernaturals, but he waded in anyway and did what he could. Serve and protect.

God, she wanted a cigarette. And bourbon. More than anything, she wanted to be back on her island, watching the sea roll in every day and night. She wanted seawater to wash all the blood out of her heart and leave her cold.

"You okay over there?" Horowitz asked.

Sara watched Michel carry a bucket out of the room. A bit of sickeningly pink water sloshed out of it onto the ground.

"No," she said frankly. "You?"

"I want a cigarette," Horowitz said.

Sara almost laughed. "I was thinking the same thing."

Horowitz smiled a little, then sobered. "What happens next, Sara?"

"How should I know? I'm not in charge." Sara leaned back against the Jeep and stared at the sky. There was some horrible wet vacuuming sound coming from the room, and she was pretty sure she didn't want to see whatever would come out next, because now Gary was back to haunt her with a vengeance.

I had your back, Harvey.

"Cut the shit," Horowitz said. "You're the least retired person I've ever seen. Thacker's not bad, but he's not you and he knows it."

"Yeah, I'm doing a bang-up job," Sara muttered. "Another team broken."

Horowitz pushed off the Jeep and stared at her. "What the hell happened, Sara? And don't give me the classified bullshit—we're way beyond that now. What happened to the team? Vaughn, Stover, Roberts? Why are you training this bunch of kids?"

"A few less than there were before." Sara ducked his gaze as if that would also make his questions disappear.

"Stop it," Horowitz ordered, his voice sharp enough that Sara glared at him. "The guilt trip doesn't suit you. You didn't kill Jacobs. You didn't kill Riordan. I don't fully get everything that's going on around here, but I know you are not responsible for their deaths."

Sara shook her head. "I shouldn't have let Thacker stop me. I should've killed Jacobs right away. Bullet in the head, nice and painless."

"You couldn't have done it," Horowitz said.

"Fuck you," Sara said without heat. "All of you, telling me what I am and am not capable of doing. It needed to be done, and Thacker stopped me. Now it's worse."

"You're not that far gone, Sara, it would've been too cold when we didn't know for sure," Horowitz insisted. "Riordan—"

"Riordan could hate me all she wanted, but she'd be alive." Sara glared at the Elmwood as if it was responsible for all the blood on its walls.

"You don't know that," Horowitz said, a softening in his tone that she couldn't read. "To lose someone you love… How do you live with that? To find the other half of yourself in another person and have it ripped away? Could she have lived with that?"

I did. Sara choked back the words, because they were rude. And crazy.

"Maybe, maybe not," Horowitz said, answering his own question. "But it's her responsibility, Sara."

"They're all my responsibility!" Sara shouted, loudly enough that Thacker poked his head out of the van across the parking lot. Without really looking at him, she flapped her hand in a go-away gesture.

More quietly, she continued. "They were my *team.* They were green as the proverbial grass and hopelessly disorganized, but they were becoming a team. And now they're ripped apart."

Horowitz didn't argue with her on that last point, for which she was devoutly grateful.

But then he had to go open his damn mouth again. "Then you build a new team, Sara. Isn't that the job?"

"Sure, just keep marching my people into the meat grinder," Sara said. "The Island and now this. They're gonna bury me so deep I'll never see sunlight again."

"Not likely," Horowitz said.

Something in his voice tripped her wires, but before Sara could ask the question forming in her mind, she saw a Jeep rolling into the parking lot with the very last person she wanted to see at this moment.

Sara muttered a long string of curses under her breath as Harold Merrifield stepped out of the Jeep with Gina Wotosi literally carrying his briefcase. Merrifield wore a gray suit that cost much more than Sara's Beretta, and brushed imaginary dirt from his jacket before walking toward her.

"Hello, Miss Harvey." Merrifield managed to sound punctilious and assaholic just saying hello. For once, Gina was subdued, hovering behind Merrifield like a goddamn stenographer and glancing uneasily at Michel's team still moving in and out of the Elmwood.

Sara folded her arms across her chest and glared. Following her cue, Horowitz walked over to her and stood at her side.

Thacker climbed out of the van, scurrying over to stand between Sara and Merrifield. Kaiser followed him, pale and quiet for once.

"Hello sir, I hope your flight was—" Thacker began.

"Status update please, Colonel," Merrifield said calmly. "I've been informed we're down two more trainees."

Thacker winced. Kaiser stood there looking ill, while Sara just wanted to slug Merrifield.

"Yes sir," Thacker said. "It seems that Jacobs was infected when he was bitten by the potential necroambulator. He was dispatched by operative Riordan, who then took her own life."

"Very sloppy," Merrifield said, examining his fingernail. "Too much personal attachment between team members leads to poor judgment. Miss Harvey knows something about that, doesn't she?"

Sara willed herself not to strangle him with her bare hands. "I've got a question for you, Harold."

"Mr. Merrifield," Gina corrected.

Sara ignored her. "I want to know who classified the Romero file so half my people were wholly uninformed of the proper procedure in dealing with Cold Ones."

Thacker attempted to intervene. "Harvey, no one knew there could possibly *be* any Cold Ones—"

"Necroambulators," Merrifield said placidly.

"I don't believe any of that for a fucking instant, so shut the hell up, Thacker," Sara snapped. "I'm talking to Harold here."

Merrifield's eyes swept over the Elmwood with reptilian composure, taking in the cleaner team still carrying sealed bags out of the room. "I don't believe you are owed any explanations, Miss Harvey. I don't believe, at this point, you are owed anything else from our organization."

Sara glared. "Don't. You are not ducking the pension."

"Let's review your record, shall we?" Merrifield said dryly. "Despite some early successes, you have a long history of ignoring protocol—"

"Usually successfully," Thacker interjected.

Merrifield switched his laser gaze toward Thacker. "Not in the case of Dale Vaughn's fiancée, which as I recall was an unauthorized operation and created the Vaughn situation, which is still troublesome for our organization."

"It isn't about me, fuckhead," Sara snapped. "It's about—"

"Of course, there was the situation in Haiti," Merrifield continued. "A high rate of team casualties under your command, Miss Harvey, culminating in the destruction of the Island, a substantial loss that required significant expenditures in containment. With this confluence of events, I hardly think anything else needs be said." Merrifield turned to Gina, effectively dismissing Sara.

Sara leapt forward, grabbed Merrifield by his high-priced suit coat and threw him up against the side of the Jeep, startling Kaiser into backing away a step and stumbling into Gina.

"She's his daughter, you stupid pencil-pushing fuck!" Sara shouted. "She lost her father to your precious experiment and the very least you owe her is his fucking pension!"

Thacker tried to pull her off, but Sara flung him away easily by throwing an elbow—and he wasn't trying very hard, she noted with a tiny bubble of amusement in the flood of white-hot fury that enveloped her. Horowitz had apparently decided this was an internal matter and was simply observing, silent.

Merrifield wasn't flustered at all. He barely blinked.

"*You* did it, didn't you?" Sara snapped. "What, did you keep an extra vial of zombie juice or something? You started the goddamn experiments again and somehow It survived!"

"I assure you, we did nothing of the kind," Merrifield said, perfectly calm despite Sara's fists holding him against the Jeep.

Sara backed down a second, hot fury boiling in her chest, warring with her instinct that he was at least partly telling the truth.

"Fine," she said slowly. "But you know. You know how It survived."

Merrifield straightened his tie. "As far as I am aware, the original necroambulator captured in Haiti was completely destroyed in the explosion you set off on the Island, which was a significant loss in terms of revenue and infrastructure, as I said."

"Oh for fuck's sake," Sara snapped. "How is It back, Harold?"

"That, in part, is what we are here to discover," Merrifield said. "It is obviously still active in some form, and now capable of possessing the dead, which was not within its apparent capabilities before the incident at the Island. Obviously something has happened to change that, and as the sole survivor of that operation, Miss Harvey, it appears you would be the only one to have that answer."

Sara stared at Merrifield for a long moment as his reptilian gaze swept over her, and she could think of nothing to say.

Horowitz intervened. "Look, I know there's the necro-whateverthe-hell to deal with, but can I remind you that we still have a rusalka to handle? That is one scary bitch, I can personally attest, and I don't think she's going to sit back and wait for us to get back to her."

Thacker nodded. "Wolf Stewart contacted me—he's got more on that and is going to meet us at the river. We're preparing a major operation against the rusalka, and we're going to need everyone on deck. Lock and load in thirty minutes."

Sara nodded, but kept her gaze on Merrifield. Losing interest, Merrifield stalked toward the van, Gina tagging along like a puppy.

Sara waited until they were gone before she turned her glare on Thacker. Kaiser hovered behind him, pale and silent.

But Thacker interrupted her before she could even speak. "I think he's lying too, Harvey."

Sara stared at Thacker for a long moment before she spoke, and a tug of shame at her suspicions. "Not quite lying. But he knows more than he's saying. He's got some idea how It's alive, or unalive, or whatever the fuck we're calling it."

"By the way—necroambulator?" Horowitz asked.

Sara rolled her eyes. "Don't even start. I have less patience than ever with Merrifield's bullshit. Tell me we're working on the potential outbreak?"

Thacker glanced at the van before answering. "Another team is already on the ground and seeking out any possible contagion. So far it seems… Chamberlin came straight here. No stops, no attacks, nothing in the emergency rooms to raise suspicions."

Sara sighed. "A fucking zombie-gram."

"Maybe there's a tie between the rusalka and…whatever It is," Horowitz suggested. "So far it's only rusalka victims It has been able to animate, right?"

Sara stared at the ground. "No."

Thacker blinked. "What?"

She took a deep breath before answering. "The springheel. On Nantucket. It spoke to me after I beheaded it. In the voice of It."

Thacker swore. "Why the fuck didn't you tell me, Harvey?"

"I thought I was going batshit!" Sara snapped. "I told you I wanted out, okay? There were reasons! Post-traumatic whatever, I don't know, I thought I was seeing It everywhere and now I have no idea what's in my fucking head and what's real."

"Let's table the discussion of crazy for a bit," Horowitz interjected. "Especially since poor Mark here has been trying to get a word in edgewise."

Sara took a real look at Kaiser for the first time. The young man looked sick, so damn young and yet years older than he looked when he stood with her on the hill and watched the piasa land. "You steady, Kaiser?"

"I'm beginning to think jail wasn't so bad," Kaiser said, but his usual smartass tone wasn't quite there. "This is probably nothing, but I didn't want to talk about it in front of the suits."

"I like you better every day. What is it?" Internally, Sara pleaded with whatever deity might be listening that it wouldn't be too complicated.

Kaiser studied his shoes. "I haven't seen Dr. Camden since the cleaners kicked us out of the motel room," he said. "I got worried, and I used the trace."

"Trace?" Horowitz asked.

Thacker groaned. "GPS tracker planted on each of you. Camden's is in his belt. Where the fuck is he?"

Kaiser hesitated.

"Fuck." Sara glanced around. "How far is the nearest bar?"

"Walking distance," Kaiser replied.

Sara took a deep breath. "The last thing we need is Merrifield getting into this. You're on Camden duty, Kaiser. Find him, get him out of the bar and keep him the hell away from the Elmwood. You'll still have time to catch up with us at the house."

"Shit." Kaiser looked even sicker than he had a moment ago.

Sara stepped in front of Kaiser, ignoring the other two for the moment. She put a hand on his shoulder. "I know, man. It sucks the wet farts out of dead pigeons. But it's gotta be done, and you're the only one I can spare."

Kaiser looked at her. "You got a hell of a way with words, boss."

"He's an asshole and a drunk, but he's on the team, so we look after him until he's not," Sara said.

Kaiser nodded and climbed into the Jeep. As soon as he rumbled away, Sara turned to Thacker. "Camden's out. He's fucking out. I don't care how brilliant he is, he's got to go."

"Let's see what the situation is before making decisions like that," Thacker said. "Look, I've got to go mobilize the troops. Michel needs to know he's going to have another mess to clean up."

"Tell him we'll be neater this time." Sara watched Thacker walk toward the Elmwood, as she tried to breathe deep and stay calm.

Horowitz stood beside her, still steady even though he couldn't have understood half the shit flying around. Thank God for people who didn't collapse or run for a bottle at trouble, Sara thought.

"I never thought you were about the money, Sara," Horowitz said.

She blinked. "What is that supposed to mean?"

He chucked a thumb at the van. "You threw the boss's boss around the parking lot over a pension."

"It's not my pension," Sara said softly. "It's for Katrina Roberts."

"Who?"

Sara sighed. "Never mind."

Horowitz was quiet for a moment. "This is probably a stupid question, but why aren't we calling in the real police on the raid on the house?"

Sara rolled her eyes. "That is a stupid question. We cut out the civvies whenever we can."

"The murder of Natalia Ivanova is a legitimate non-supernatural crime," Horowitz said. "We should give the civilian courts a chance to—"

Sara interrupted. "You don't get it, do you? We're not raiding the house to arrest the bad guys, Horowitz. We're going to do whatever we can to put the rusalka to rest. If along the way you manage to slap some cuffs on those fuckers, feel free, but we ain't hanging around to testify, you get it?"

"So this is what we do?" Horowitz asked. "Just sweep in, make a mess, let criminals run free and kill supernaturals?"

Sara stared at him. "That's twice you've said 'we' when talking about Blackfire."

He didn't respond.

Sara stood facing him. "No. You're not that stupid. Tell me you're not that fucking stupid."

Horowitz slipped his police badge out of his jacket pocket and stared at it. "I guess I am."

"Goddammit!" Sara shouted and this time she didn't care who heard her. "No. Absolutely not. What the fuck, Adam?"

Horowitz put his badge back in his pocket. "I asked you once how you could sleep, knowing that the monsters are real. I can't sleep, Sara. Not when I'm doing nothing at all to stop it. In Blackfire, I can do some kind of good."

"To serve and protect from things that go chomp in the night? You haven't seen enough yet to know it doesn't work that way!" Sara demanded.

"Yes, I have, and I have to help," Horowitz reiterated.

Sara shook her head vehemently. "Denied. I refuse."

"Well, good thing it's not up to you," Horowitz snapped. "Thacker made the offer, and I took it."

Sara ignored that. Her heart was pounding too hard to stop. "This job… God, Adam, this job tears you to pieces until you're nothing, there's nothing left of you. For God's sake, stay here, be a cop, help real people and go home at night to some sweet little wife and two-point-five kids. Have a life."

Horowitz stared up at the stars. "A life. I woke up slashed to ribbons by a Tanzanian hell-beast and realized there was no life left, and the shadows all moved. I ran to Atlanta and there was nothing there either. Part of me thinks I came back here just to wait for you. For the monsters to come back. I can't have a life. Not anymore. I'm not a civvie, Sara, and I haven't been one since that night by the river. I know the dangers, and I'm ready for the life."

Sara closed her eyes and saw the same tired rerun, Paul's eyes and the bullet in his head, his body floating out to sea. She stepped in front of Horowitz and placed her hands on his arms.

"Adam," she said softly. "I'm begging you. Don't do it. You still have a soul. Please, if…if you ever felt anything for me, do this one thing I ask of you. Tell Thacker no. Tell him you're out. Please."

Horowitz met her eyes, those gray-green eyes of his that first caught her attention looking at her over the mangled body of yet another innocent victim. They were cop's eyes that had seen too much, but still filled with compassion and humanity and the soul she knew was absent in her own cold gaze. He looked at her as though she were the only woman in the world, and for the life of her, she wavered.

"Felt anything for you?" Horowitz said softly. "God, Sara, don't you know that—"

Sara interrupted him, her heart pounding faster. "Say you're out. Please. Say you're out."

Slowly, he shook his head.

Sara took a deep breath, gripping his forearms with her hands.

"They're dead, Adam," she said tonelessly.

"I figured that from what they said," Horowitz began, but she waved a hand to shut him up.

"Parish was the first," she said. "He volunteered for the experiment, and it changed him into one of them. A Cold One. He got loose and started an outbreak. I… I had to kill him."

"Oh Sara, I'm sorry," Horowitz began, but Sara kept talking. If she stopped, she might go mad.

"Gary and I went to the Island, and we burned it all down." She stared at Horowitz but she no longer saw him. "We burned it down, but they got him. They got him and he had my back anyway. We chased them across the ocean, we caught the last few, and they'd gotten Paul. He was Cold. He…"

Her body shuddered, and Horowitz drew her into his arms. For once she didn't fight him. She let him comfort her, but she still could not unbend.

Horowitz spoke above her, but she could hear him inside his chest. "Did you have to kill Vaughn, too?"

Sara shook her head. "I would have. I was ready to do it. Gary did it for me. He spared me that."

"Like you wanted to spare Riordan," Horowitz said.

Sara wrenched away from him then, the horror crawling on her skin like ants. "Then Gary blew his own head off. Just like Riordan. This is what Blackfire does to us, Adam—it burns us up, makes us Cold, just like It. I won't let it happen to you."

Horowitz shook his head.

"Listen to me, dammit!" Sara snapped. "There was a cop with us. Russ Matthews. A decent guy, just an ordinary cop who happened to be there when the shit went down. They tore him to pieces, Adam, and I had to put a bullet in his head. I can't do that to you! Don't make me watch you die too!"

Horowitz tried to draw her back into his arms, but she shoved him away.

"Fuck you then!" Sara shouted. "Fuck you! Go off and play soldier boy and die like the rest! You won't make me watch, and I won't cry when they tell me you're gone!"

The look in his eyes drilled through her heart.

Sara turned away from him then, heartsick and furious. But there were no more words.

13

Sara slammed the stocky woman up against the side of the van, and she wasn't too gentle about it. Anna glared defiantly at her, and Sara had to give her props for that. Anna was unarmed and facing multiple operatives in the dark woods, but she had steel in her spine.

Kaiser stuck his head out the open van door. "We're trying to stay on the down-low here, do you think you can quit smacking my van?"

Sara glared at Kaiser, and he ducked back in hurriedly. Camden and Wolf stepped out of the van together, watching impassively. Sara wished Wolf wouldn't watch her beat up a woman at least fifteen years her senior. It wasn't a fair fight, even without Thacker and Horowitz standing behind her with guns at the ready.

But Sara didn't really care about a fair fight tonight.

Thacker used his best stare on Anna. It wasn't Paul Vaughn's Iceman look, but it wasn't bad. "I'd like to know how many we face inside the house, ma'am."

"Fuck you," Anna snarled.

Sara backhanded her hard, and Anna's head bounced off the metal side of the van. Out of the corner of her eye, Sara saw Horowitz twitch.

"Try again, bitch," Sara snapped. "Answer the fucking question and maybe we won't feed you to the goddamn rusalka."

"Pretty sure it only kills men," Wolf said calmly.

Sara pushed her face right up close to Anna's. "I think it'll make an exception for this piece of shit. I got a pretty good idea what you've been doing up in that house. How much money have you raked in on those girls?"

Anna spat in Sara's face. Sara's knee drove into Anna's stomach, doubling her over. Then Sara clasped her fists together and slammed them between Anna's shoulder blades, driving her to the ground.

Anna lay in the dirt, retching and groaning as she cradled her midsection.

Horowitz knelt beside her. "Ma'am, please just tells us what we're facing inside. We don't want to hurt anyone if we don't have to."

Sara harrumphed.

"Well, except for the major here," Horowitz amended. "But I can keep her on a leash if we can handle this quickly and professionally."

Sara raised an eyebrow at that. Thacker grinned, unseen by Anna, and made a quick jerking-off motion.

Kaiser leaned out of the van. "Infrared shows five live bodies inside."

"You can't do this!" Anna protested.

Sara stomped on Anna's hand, feeling the snap of fingers. Anna shrieked in pain and Horowitz clapped a hand over her mouth fast.

"I can do whatever I damn well please, bitch," Sara said.

"Major!" Thacker protested, only halfway pretending, she could tell. He made a big show of pulling her away from Anna.

Horowitz released Anna's mouth. "Please tell me, and I'll do what I can for them."

Anna struggled to a sitting position, clasping her twisted fingers against her soft belly. "I could give a shit what you do to Clayne or Victor," she croaked. "But don't you hurt Terry. He never woulda done nothing to Natalia if it wasn't for Victor. Victor is one fucked-up dude, you have to know, he tells Terry what to do and Terry does it, it's not his fault, it's—"

"Shut the fuck up," Sara snapped. "So that's three: Clayne and the Keegan brothers. What kind of arms do they have?"

"A couple of handguns, I swear, that's all," Anna said.

"Anyone else?" Sara glared at her.

Anna looked at the ground. "Just the two girls upstairs. We ain't replaced Natalia yet."

Sara stepped forward and slapped Anna hard in the face. "That one's for her." Horowitz handcuffed Anna and pushed her away from the van.

Wolf sidled over to Sara. "A little much, don't you think?"

"No." Sara checked the load on her Beretta. "You'll be waiting down by the riverfront?"

"With bells on, metaphorically," Wolf said. "I'll have the spell ready, but I need the man alive to make it work. So, you know, try to avoid damaging him too much, okay?"

"You got it," Sara said insincerely, and waved farewell to Wolf as he disappeared into the trees. He was an old hand at hiking, even better than Sara, and seemed to melt between the trees as if they parted for him. It was a neat trick that Sara had never quite mastered.

Sara checked her earpiece. "Red, you online?"

"At your service, milady," Kaiser said with something approaching his usual smartass.

Horowitz crept into the woods, beginning a slow circle around the back of the house as Thacker took his place with Sara, standing behind the brush that hid the house from the road.

Sara turned to Camden. "Your weapon."

Camden fumbled out the simple .22 pistol she'd given him. Sara checked its load. "You remember how to use this thing, I hope? Genius that you are?"

He nodded. "I know my job, Harvey. Watch the front, cover Red."

"Because if anything happens to Kaiser or the van, we're pretty much screwed without comms," Sara said. "Feel steady enough to handle that?"

"I wasn't drinking," Camden said softly. "I ordered. I didn't drink it."

"And that's the only reason you're not locked in a box somewhere," Sara retorted. "It doesn't really endear you to me. Right now, I think you're the most useless member of this team, so try not to get any of us killed and maybe I won't shoot you myself."

Camden took his .22 back with hands that didn't shake. "Do you ever feel anymore, Harvey?"

Sara looked at him, sensing her Iceman stare chilling through her eyes without really intending it. That was apparently the only answer Camden needed. He lowered his eyes and ducked back into the van.

Sara and Thacker approached the front of the house, hauling Anna with them. "Harvey to Horowitz," Sara murmured.

"Copy," Horowitz replied. "In position. Green."

"We are green," Sara said as Thacker nodded.

"Copy that. Wonder Twins activate," Kaiser said.

Sara shook her head. "I worry about him." She and Thacker crouched beside the concrete stoop and Sara handcuffed Anna to the front-porch railing. "Call to Terry."

Anna shook her head furiously.

Sara kicked her hard in the leg. "You want him out of that house alive? Call to him."

"P-promise me," Anna whispered.

Sara aimed the icy stare, this time on purpose. "I promise you the only way he gets out of this whole is if you call to him."

Anna must have seen the truth in Sara's eyes, because she croaked out, "Terry... Terry, c'mere!"

Thacker pressed himself against the side of the front porch.

"Louder," Sara insisted.

"Terry!" Anna shouted. "Terry, I need you! Terry!"

The door swung open and Terry's head popped out. "What the hell do you—"

Thacker pivoted around and kicked the door wide open. Terry vanished like a jackrabbit, stumbling and crashing beyond Sara's line of sight. "Green!" Thacker called into his earpiece, advancing into the house.

Sara followed him into a dim, ramshackle living room with castoff, mismatched furniture and crappy lamps draped with old scarves in a vain attempt to look exotic. The smell of mildew and worse things permeated the entire house.

"Shit, lost visual," Thacker said, just as a bullet struck the wood paneling beside his head. He dropped like a stone, so fast that for a moment Sara thought he'd been hit. She dropped as well, firing a couple of shots wild into the living room for cover.

"Taking fire inside the house!" Sara reported.

"Moving in!" Horowitz replied.

"Negative," Sara ordered, as two more shots hit the paneling over the foyer area where she and Thacker crouched. Terry was firing from the kitchen, she figured. "Cover the back door, do not enter."

"Copy," Horowitz said, sounding annoyed.

Another shot and Sara popped up. She fired two shots blind into the kitchen and heard a thud.

"Shit, I hope you didn't kill the asshole," Thacker muttered.

"My fucking apologies," Sara replied, duck-walking past the couch toward the kitchen doorway. She saw a pair of muddy boots and legs clad in dirt-smeared jeans lying on the floor of the dingy kitchen, the rest of him hidden behind the standalone stove. She scrambled fast to the side of the kitchen door, covering Thacker as he advanced through it.

"Not him," Thacker said. "This must be Clayne."

Clayne lay writhing on the floor, blood leaking from a hole in the shoulder of his denim jacket. Thacker had already removed the crappy revolver from the floor where Clayne had dropped it.

"Bind him," Sara ordered. Thacker already had the zip tie out. "You search the rest of this level, I'll take upstairs."

"Wait for me," Thacker said, but Sara ignored him, moving back into the living room. "Dammit, Major!"

"Stop calling me that," Sara said, pressing her back against the wall at the foot of the stairwell. "Advancing upstairs. Horowitz, anything out back?"

"Negative," Horowitz replied.

"Stay where you are." Sara slowly climbed the stairs, her Beretta aimed at the upstairs hallway, filled with shadows.

No sooner did her head come level with the floor than a booming gunshot rang out. She dropped down to the steps—smart fucker was barricaded in the doorway of one of the rooms upstairs. And from the sound of it, he had something a hell of a lot bigger than that .38 revolver Clayne had been packing.

"House is surrounded!" Sara shouted. "Surrender and you might make it through this!"

"Fuck you, bitch!" This was punctuated by another shot.

That had to be Victor's cool and logical side. But Sara still couldn't go spraying bullets around up here—there were the two girls to consider.

On the other hand, Victor was shooting something pretty large. Shotgun of some kind. There—she heard the action break, he was reloading.

Probably.

Sara jumped up onto the landing and fired twice. The bullets slammed into the wall, splintering wood. Victor dove back into the room, dropping the empty shotgun.

"Fucker," Sara muttered, advancing quickly and kicking the shotgun out of reach down the hall. "Come out, you cowardly shit!"

"Harvey, report!" Thacker didn't sound happy.

"Green! Find that fucker Terry!" Sara snapped.

Victor swung out into the hallway, but he wasn't alone. In front of him he held a bone-thin Latina girl of no more than twelve, one hand wrapped around her narrow waist and the other holding a large hunting knife to her throat.

"Back off, splitass," he growled.

Sara backed off a step, but kept her gun trained on him. "This really how you want it to go down, Victor?"

"You ain't no fuckin' cop," Victor snarled, taking a step forward. The girl's foot tangled with his and he nearly lost his balance. "Inez! Cut it out!"

Inez had a dead stare that chilled Sara's bones. On second glance she might be older than twelve, but that was only in her eyes. Her body was that of a young girl, covered in bruises and welts. Her clothes were ragged and torn, but overly sexual for a girl of her apparent age: a very short skirt with clearly nothing on under it. The too-tight shirt seemed to have been thrown on with haste.

"Busy, were you?" Sara snarled, her gut twisting in disgust. "Let the girl go."

Sara had a half-decent line of fire—Inez was not so tall that she could really protect Victor's head. But that assumed Sara could drill him right in the eye before he had time to twitch the knife into the girl's throat. Sara was not quite that sure of her aim.

"Drop the gun and I'm walkin' out of here," Victor ordered.

"Not happening."

"On my way, Harvey," Sara heard Thacker say.

"Negative," Sara replied. "Situation hot."

"No shit," Kaiser said from the van. "Harvey, you need help up there?"

"You're surrounded," Sara told Victor again.

Victor shook his head. "You ain't no cops," he repeated.

"Drop it!" Sara shouted.

"Fuck you!" he shouted back, and a second later there was a horrid *thud* as something struck his head. Victor's knife hand fell away from Inez's throat, and he stumbled backward, blood leaking from a wound on the side of his head.

"Run!" Sara shouted.

Inez scuttled past her toward the stairs. Where Inez had been stood another girl, almost as thin as Inez but older, a blonde girl who would be pretty if not for the bruises and outline of bones against her skin. She held the empty shotgun, which she had used to brain Victor.

But the stupid never die. Reeling, Victor reached for the shotgun. The girl aimed it at him, but pulling the trigger only gave an empty click.

"Out of the way!" Sara shouted.

"Sasha, you sloppy-ass skank!" Victor howled, grabbing the shotgun. Sasha tried to hold onto it, but he yanked it out of her hands and raised it up over his head as if to split her skull. Sasha stumbled to the side—finally.

Sara aimed low and fired. The bullet took Victor in the meat of his leg, spilling him to the floor.

Sasha did not wait to see what happened next. She scrambled past Sara to the stairwell, where Thacker was advancing up the stairs. Sasha and Inez wrapped their arms around each other and instinctively cowered away from him.

"He's safe!" Sara called. She had no idea if the girls could even understand English. "Thacker, get them out of here!"

Thacker managed to coax the girls down the stairs toward the living room, while Sara kicked the damn shotgun out of Victor's reach again.

"Get up," she ordered.

"Fuck you," Victor spat for the ninetieth time.

Sara grabbed Victor by the arm and forcibly hauled him to his feet. He bellowed in pain and she half-supported, half-threw him toward the stairs. Partway down his injured leg gave way, spilling him down to the landing.

As Sara approached him, Victor tried to punch at her, a wild fist that aimed somewhere like her crotch and missed completely.

Sara kicked him in the jaw, feeling bone crunch under her boot. Victor howled in a gurgling mess of blood.

"Stay there," she ordered.

Thacker moved over to Victor and zip-tied his hands, though Sara was pretty sure Victor was done with the fight.

More gunshots, this time outside. "Goddammit, who's shooting?" Sara shouted.

"Under fire! The fucker came out the back!" Horowitz yelled. Another volley of gunfire, but this one Sara heard over the earpiece as well as through the thin walls of the house. "Yellow!"

Sara bulldozed through the kitchen, tripping over empty boxes that once contained cheap wine, and into a back bedroom that smelled like old gym socks. In the corner of the darkened bedroom, she saw the rear door and slammed out through it, shouting into the headset.

Horowitz lay on the ground, trying to crawl out from the scraggly bushes where he'd been under cover.

"Shit!" Sara skidded down the three wooden steps to Horowitz's side. The shot was in the chest, but high, practically at the shoulder.

"Fucker got past me," Horowitz wheezed. "Got…my gun."

"Camden!" Sara shouted into her earpiece. "Behind the house now! Horowitz needs help!"

More gunshots rang out, a patter of them farther away now.

"Can't!" Camden replied.

Sara's fists clenched hard as she pressed against the bleeding hole in Horowitz's shoulder. "Goddamn you Camden you miserable piece of shit! Get the fuck out here now or I swear to Christ I'll put a bullet in you myself!"

A moment later, Thacker scrambled out the back door and came to Sara's side, covering her while looking over her shoulder at Horowitz's wound. "Shit," he breathed. "Hang in there, pal."

"I'm sorry," Horowitz whispered. "Sloppy… I'm sorry."

"Shut the fuck up," Sara ordered, pressing harder. "I think it missed the lung, but I'm not a goddamn medic."

"Camden, this is Thacker," he said into the mic. "Direct order. Get your ass behind the house now."

There was no reply, only more gunshots.

"Fuck!" Sara cried, all the frustration of the past week boiling up inside her chest in hot fury. Her eyes blurred a moment, and she honestly couldn't tell if it was Adam Horowitz lying under her hands, or Kay Riordan, or Paul Vaughn.

She looked up at Thacker. "Take over."

For once Thacker didn't argue. He dropped to his knees and pressed his hands against Horowitz's wound. Sara grabbed her Beretta.

"Don't kill our medic until after he saves Horowitz!" Thacker called as Sara advanced around the corner of the house.

Sara felt horribly exposed against the dingy white siding, the moonlight outlining her black tactical gear as clearly as a cockroach on a wedding cake. She consoled herself with the knowledge that two of the three assholes were bound up in the house with multiple holes in them, so they were unlikely to be creeping through the underbrush around the house.

She edged to the front yard, where Anna was still chained to the stair railing. "You bitch!" Anna shouted, tugging fruitlessly at the handcuffs.

Sara took one glance at Anna. "Ran off and left you. What a prince."

She moved past Anna toward the van, moving around the stand of trees that hid the house from view. There was no sign of Terry anywhere, but there were a thousand trees and bushes that could be hiding him past the unkempt yard. Sara crouched low and got to the front of the van fast, pressing herself against it as she moved around the side, where the door was still open.

"Camden!" she called, scanning the brush beyond the van for any hint of movement. "You better be pinned under something heavy or fucking dead, I swear to Christ!"

There was no answer, but rustlings and heavy breathing inside the van. Swearing under her breath, Sara pivoted around and aimed her weapon into the van.

Camden had both hands in Kaiser's chest.

A blink later, Sara realized Camden's hands weren't literally inside Kaiser's chest, but pressing down on his wounds. Blood covered Kaiser from neck to groin, with at least two bullet holes in his torso. Incredibly, the tech was still conscious, blood leaking from the corner of his mouth as he gasped on the floor of the van.

Camden looked up at her, and for once Sara didn't want to belt him. There was fear there, but no panic. He was locked into doctor mode, and his hands did not tremble. "I can't leave, Harvey. He'll die."

"Fuck," Sara muttered. "Did you get Terry?"

Camden shook his head. "He tried to steal the van. I could've sworn I hit him, and I heard him cursing, but he ran off."

"Should've given you something bigger than a .22," Sara said, her mind racing.

Camden looked at her. "How bad is Horowitz?"

Sara stared at Kaiser, her gut twisting inside her. Everything in her wanted to order Camden to abandon Kaiser and run behind the house, save Horowitz.

"Not this bad," Sara said. "Stay here."

She reached past Kaiser to the control board and quickly keyed in her code. "Harvey to Motherbird, need emergency medevac and cleanup crew."

Merrifield himself answered. "Harvey, can't you pick up a single civilian scumball without—"

Sara slammed her fist on the board. "Merrifield. Suck my dick. Get out here and help my people."

She grabbed an extra magazine and stepped back out of the van.

Beneath her, Kaiser managed a ghost of a smile. "Suck your...what?" he whispered.

"Shut up and stay alive," Sara said. "That's a goddamn order."

Camden tilted his head toward the trees. "Thataway."

Sara stalked away from the van, moving through the tall grass. It suddenly seemed very clear, very quiet. She could see every blade of grass, every branch in the cold moonlight, the thin spatters of blood standing out as if it were daylight. Camden must have hit Terry Keegan, with this kind of blood trail.

Sara stepped into the woods, listening to the quiet susurration of the river. The snap of a twig turned her to the right, and she saw a form slipping between the trees. She almost fired, but that cold clarity that had fallen over her stopped her—they needed the fucker alive for the spell. She couldn't risk killing him.

He stumbled over something—he must be in a panic, crashing into the dead wood and crunching through dry leaves without a care for what sound he might be making.

Sara drew closer, and now the black tactical gear worked to her advantage, helping her blend into the shadows. She moved between the trees, trying to emulate Wolf's trick of making nature move around her.

Terry stepped away from a tree, and she saw him clearly in the moonlight. Blood dripped from a gash in his left arm, and Sara made a mental note to put Camden on the firing range for some serious target practice.

Terry staggered further away and tripped over a dead log, landing squarely on his ass.

Sara took her chance and jumped over the log, landing directly on top of Terry. She aimed the gun at his head, but in a panic he surged upward, flinging her off into a low bush. She hit the ground hard, and the gun dropped from her hand.

Terry scrambled toward the gun, but Sara was faster. She swung her legs out and connected hard with his ribs, rolling him away from her gun.

"Stop fighting, you fuckhead!" Sara shouted, grabbing the gun. "I'm not gonna kill you!"

"That's not what she says!" Terry gibbered, scrambling backward in a weird crab-walk that had to hurt like a son of a bitch with his arm injured.

He got to his feet and Sara faced him. "I should fucking kill you for what you did to my team," Sara growled. "But I need you alive."

"No! I won't let you!" Terry shouted, and raised a pistol.

Sara dodged to the side as he fired, the .22 hitting her vest like a sledgehammer. It knocked her backward in a mass of pain, but it took her only a moment to realize she wasn't badly injured. A bruised rib, maybe. She got back to her feet and went after Terry, who was running in a blind panic toward the river.

She was only steps behind him when he burst onto the little inlet, spreading his arms wide before the silvery glow of the moon over the river.

"I'm here!" Terry shouted to no one in particular. "I'm here, you fucking bitch, so stop singing! For Christ's sake *stop singing!*"

Sara heard nothing. That didn't stop her from jumping at him from the trees, knocking the goddamn .22 out of his hand and into the water.

Terry brought a fist back around in a looping haymaker, and Sara dodged it easily. "You're dead, bitch! Dead!"

"I've heard that before." Sara hocked a knee into Terry's groin and jabbed her fist into the side of his jaw. Terry dropped to his knees.

"Wolf!" Sara shouted, stepping behind Terry. She pulled out a zip-tie and quickly bound his hands.

"She won't stop," Terry whispered. "Won't stop. Her voice, it never goes away, never ever…"

"Yeah, well, we'll take care of that," Sara muttered. "Wolf! Now would be a good time!"

"Sara…" Wolf's voice came from behind her, and Sara turned. At the curve of the inlet about twenty yards away, Wolf stood at the water's edge. His candle was sputtering on the ground beside a smoldering bundle of sage, a few other bottles and pouches scattered at his feet.

"Oh shit." Sara stared at him. "Wolf, what the fuck?"

Rivers of tears cascaded down the older man's face. Tears…or water? "Sara, I can't… She's singing…"

Sara stepped toward Wolf, turning away from Terry for a moment. "Can you fight her? Wolf, come on, man. I need you. I need this goddamn spell."

Wolf reached toward the sage, but his hands trembled and he pulled away as if it burned him. "I can't…"

"Please, I can't take it anymore," Terry begged, shouting up at the moon. "I can't! I'm sorry, I only did it because Victor made me, I'm sorry, I'm so sorry…" He turned to the water and shouted. "*Otpusti menya!* Please, Natalia! Let me go!"

Sara grabbed Terry by his injured arm, ignoring his howl, and dragged him toward Wolf.

But another look at Wolf told her he was beyond helping—he couldn't even speak. Wolf dropped to his knees, writhing. He leaned over and a rush of river water flowed out of his mouth.

"Oh shit," Sara whispered. "No, not him. Come on, you watery bitch, not him too! Goddammit!" For a moment, Sara thought of trying the Russian spell she'd used before, but the slip of paper Wolf had given her an eon ago was long vanished and she had no hope of remembering the words.

Sara turned to the river. "Natalia!"

Wolf's writhing slowed, and he coughed up more river water. Did that mean the rusalka was listening?

Behind her, the dark woods seemed to come alive, creaks and snaps as if unseen things moved between the trees. The river water flowed with a different energy than her cool, soothing ocean that swallowed hot pain and grief and made it dissolve beneath the waves. This water was power, it was life and death and life again, drawing its energy through the center of the land and flowing to this place, where the rusalka drew close. It was the water that had swallowed boats and souls without pause, and buried them in its constantly shifting, flowing energy.

It seemed as though Sara could see Natalia's face beneath the murky water. Perhaps it was a trick of the moonlight, but the water swirled in patterns like a young woman's hair over her shoulders.

Sara forced Terry to his knees again, winding her fingers in his greasy hair to hold his head still.

"Here he is," she told the rusalka.

Terry screamed, his whole body taut beneath Sara's hands. "God, she's so loud! I can't stand it! Make her stop, make her stop, I'm sorry I swear I'm sorry *make her stop!*"

Sara stared into the water, that cold clarity falling over her vision. She could see Natalia's face as clear as glass, lying beneath the surface of the river.

Sara pulled her combat knife and tilted Terry's head back by the hair. Unfortunately, that put Terry staring up at Sara's face.

"Will she ever stop?" he pleaded.

"Yes," Sara told him.

In one quick motion Sara drew the knife across Terry's throat. The blood spurted and flowed, obscenely hot over her hand and down the front of his shirt. He choked on his own blood, his whole body convulsing between her hands.

Sara let go of Terry's head and shoved him into the river. His bloody body fell directly into the image of the rusalka, dispelling it into the river in a splash of brownish water.

Sara knelt beside the water, rinsing Terry's blood off her hand and knife, splashing it up onto her sleeve.

She stared into the water for a long moment, but no face appeared. She could feel the change in the energy, the rusalka fading away from this place, melding with the river itself. At peace. Washed clean.

Then she looked up.

Wolf stared at her in horror, still coughing but alive. Kneeling beside him was Thacker, an identical expression of shock on his face. A tiny voice at the back of her mind asked who was with Horowitz if Thacker was here, but it seemed a minor question.

The water pushed at Terry's still body, turning him over. His face was frozen in that last moment of terror, above the ugly slashed wound across his throat. There was no more spurting blood; Terry was gone.

Then he blinked.

"*Ssssara...*" It whispered.

And grinned.

Sara stumbled backward, pulling her Beretta as Thacker scrambled to her side, his own gun aimed at the body.

Terry sat up, seemingly content with its new deadness. "*Sssara by the ssseassshore,*" it chanted, and began to laugh. And laugh.

Sara and Thacker fired together, striking Terry in the head and chest at least five times. Its body flew backward into the water.

The water rose up and enveloped him, drawing the body into itself. It was too big and fast for a normal wave, but Sara was willing to take anything on faith now.

Terry's legs and feet were the last of it to disappear beneath the opaque surface, sinking beyond sight. Swallowed whole by the river.

But Sara could still hear it laughing beneath the water.

Merrifield closed his file folder and handed it to Gina Wotosi. "I believe that concludes the review."

Thacker shook his head. "We haven't discussed the disposition of the team."

Merrifield drummed his fingers on the gleaming mahogany wood table and glanced at the silver-haired man sitting to the side of the conference table next to Gina Wotosi, watching silently. "I'm not sure we need to go over personnel changes at this time, Colonel."

"We absolutely do, Mr. Merrifield," Thacker replied, with a slight emphasis on *mister*. "The team needs direction, and they can't do their jobs with a sword dangling over their heads."

"'Team.'" Merrifield snorted. "You lost four operatives on their first major operation, caused a huge mess we spent a fortune to contain, and your alleged team leader killed a man in cold blood in front of a civilian witness. What kind of team do you call that?"

"A Blackfire team." Thacker directed his comments to the silver-haired man in the corner as though Merrifield didn't exist. "First: we lost three members of the team, not four."

Merrifield waved his hand dismissively. "Kaiser is too compromised. The last report I saw said he'll never walk again."

"Not true, he's making progress," Thacker said. "Even if he were permanently disabled, he has valuable skills not dependent on mobility and is an asset to the team."

"We already have a replacement for—" Gina began, but everyone ignored her.

"Second: containment costs are the costs of doing business," Thacker said. "You cannot send our teams in to fight uncontrollable elements on American soil with half-classified information and no backup and not expect a mess. In this case, our investigation busted up a human trafficking ring that was responsible for God knows how many rapes and murders, rescued two civilians—"

"Prostitutes," Merrifield said.

Thacker glared at him in white heat. "Age twelve and fourteen." Gina looked ill.

"And the 'civilian' Major Harvey neutralized had already shot at several of our people including Harvey herself, and was threatening the civilian witness," Thacker continued. "That's without considering that she appeased the rusalka and eliminated another supernatural threat from our agenda."

The silver-haired man spoke for the first time. "Is it your belief, then, that Blackfire teams should operate without oversight?"

"That isn't close to what I'm saying, Senator," Thacker snapped. "Oversight is essential so we don't have rogue elements wandering the countryside. But oversight means putting a military liaison with each team. Oversight means filing reports holding team members accountable for their judgment. Oversight should be conducted with neutral parties and…no agendas."

The last line was directed back at Merrifield, who busied himself with his leather-bound portfolio.

Thacker stood in front of them, all the better to flash his medals on his dress uniform. "Major Harvey has endured more than simple reports can show for this organization and for her country. In my opinion as military liaison and observer, she acted in the best interest of the team and of Blackfire, and by the way for the safety of the rest of the world. Her team was badly hit, but they deserve to be healed and return to the field. In fact, they're already on another case now, and we are better off with them standing between us and the critters out there."

Gina raised an eyebrow. "Critters?"

Thacker almost allowed himself a smile. "Team parlance, ma'am."

"Thank you, Colonel, we'll take it under advisement." Merrifield signed something and put it in a folder.

It was a clear dismissal, but Thacker turned once again to the white-haired man. "And Katrina Roberts deserves her father's pension."

Merrifield slapped his palm down on his precious folders. "Colonel, that is an internal matter not up for debate!"

"And it should stay that way." Thacker stood at attention. "Parish Roberts died doing the work of this organization, under the umbrella of the United States military. He died a hero, and he doesn't even have a grave for his family to visit. His daughter should receive the full pension he was promised."

"We all feel badly for Mr. Roberts' family," Gina said. "But surely you understand to grant her the pension would entail explaining his death, possibly creating another Dale Vaughn situation –"

Thacker leaned forward, placing his palms on the immaculate mahogany conference table and staring at Merrifield. "I don't care what idiotic cover story you have to come up with. Scholarship, bequest from a dead uncle, winning the lottery. That girl gets her father's pension." He stood at attention again. "It would be terrible indeed if the public were to learn of a man who gave his life in service only for his family to be screwed over by a military contractor no one ever heard of. It might invite the kind of scrutiny that we try so desperately to avoid in this line of work."

The senator spoke again. "Is that a threat, Colonel?"

He shook his head. "Of course not, sir. Just following through this line of reasoning to its obvious conclusion."

"Indeed." The senator looked at Merrifield, who was doing his best to avoid the senator's gaze and glare at Thacker at the same time.

"Thank you, Colonel." Merrifield couldn't make the dismissal more obvious in his voice.

This time Thacker took the hint. He turned and stalked out of the room, into the marble-lined corridor where Harvey was waiting for him. She lowered her sunglasses to look at his face, and when he gave her a slight smile, she fell into step behind him as they walked out of the building into the sunlight.

INTERLUDE: DEAD HEAT

DEAD HEAT

Sara groused as she climbed out of the van. "I hate the cemeteries."

St. Andrew's Cemetery was a strange one, even for historic cemeteries in midwestern river towns. Probably chosen because the land was too hilly to farm, the entrance faced a two-lane road few bothered to drive. The oldest graves lined the driveway up by the entrance, but the terrain dropped off at a steep decline down toward the dark woods. The further down the driveway one traveled, the newer the graves, and by the time the driveway circled around to go back up the hill toward the road, the graves disappeared completely. They hadn't quite finished filling all the land to the tree line, save for a few stray graves at the bottom of the hill. From the late-1700s settlers up by the gate to the grandmas of the twenty-first century at the bottom of the hill, traveling down the steep inclines of St. Andrew's was like walking through history.

Sara turned to the team climbing out of the van. "Come on, people. This is a simple haunting, let's get our shit together."

Camden checked his goofy sensory device that probably cost the taxpayers a few hundred thousand bucks and made for a good paperweight as far as Sara was concerned. "Is there really such a thing as a simple haunting, now?" Camden asked. "Life after death should be a little complex, shouldn't it?"

Sara didn't bother to respond, grabbing an extra canister of salt just to be safe.

"I thought you didn't believe in life after death, Dr. Camden." Father Spellane climbed out of the van and straightened his collar. Sara had told him he didn't need to wear it on mission, but Andrew Spellane was first and foremost a priest, and he would not be dissuaded. He was startlingly young, late twenties and fresh from the seminary, and sooner or later Sara meant to find out how he ended up tied to frigging Blackfire instead of baptizing babies in a parish somewhere.

"No disrespect to your trade," Camden said, but the snark in his voice told Sara he was just warming up for another verbal tussle with the priest.

"Can it, Camden," she ordered. "We've got work to do."

She walked past the crew to the passenger side of the van and opened the door. "Okay, kid," she said softly. "Tell me what you see."

Mark Kaiser didn't move. He didn't move much these days. He was thinner than he'd been when Sara met him, and his beard grew in scraggly. His left lung hadn't fully healed yet, so he tended to be short of breath. Thacker was planning to put him back into a rehab center so he could get up to 100 percent again, but Sara had held him off with a crucifix long enough to get Kaiser's help on this mission. Figuratively speaking.

"Kaiser," she said softly. "You with me?"

His head turned, and then he remembered to grin with a shade of the old smartass. "Yeah," he said. "I'm with you, chief."

She shook her head. "I guess that's better than 'major,'" she said. "What do you see?"

Kaiser closed his eyes for a moment, and when he opened them, he fixed his gaze on a grave about twenty yards off the road, away from the van. He got visibly paler, and pointed.

"There," he said. "There's the bride."

Sara could see nothing, of course. She saw rows of century-old graves, some leaning to one side like rotted teeth, and the dark shadows of ancient oak trees that loomed over them in the late afternoon sunlight.

"She's maybe twenty, but it's hard to tell because her face keeps blurring behind the veil," Kaiser said, and she saw that he had switched on his recorder just like he'd been trained. "Dark hair, slender, veil over her face. The dress is… I don't know clothes or anything, but we're definitely talking prewar, white lace and long, down to the ground and up to a high collar. She's walking between the third and fourth row and her hand is trailing along the gravestones."

Sara motioned to Camden and Spellane, and they flanked up and downhill from the row.

"Moving up toward you," Kaiser called out to Camden.

"Is this when we do the salt?" Horowitz's voice came from behind Sara, and she almost jumped.

"Don't sneak up on me like that or you're gonna end up with another bullet in you," she snapped. "Yes, salt time."

Sure enough, Camden and Spellmeyer were pouring salt in a circle around the graves.

"Uh, Sara…" Kaiser's voice trailed off.

She turned to him. "Yes? Don't keep it to yourself."

"She's…she's looking at me."

Sara turned by reflex, but again, she could see nothing. Not for the first time, she cursed the fact that she had an esper rating practically in negative numbers. Most Blackfire recruits had some level of sensitivity, but that was one skill that had simply skipped her.

"It is crazy cold!" Camden yelled. "Tell me that's some freak weather coming on!"

Sara glanced up at the late-June sunlight. "Try again, science boy. That's the bride." She looked back at Kaiser, and he was shivering. "Talk to me."

His eyes were fixed on the third row of graves. "She's staring at me, and she is pissed. It's like she's not even looking at the salt line, she's pissed at *me*. How can she register me at all? I thought you said the dead don't notice us."

The rules are changing. Sara wasn't hearing Paul in her head as much as she used to, and she almost missed it. Almost, because she felt like she might be regaining a tiny bit of sanity. But whether it was really Paul or just her inner voices pretending to be him, he wasn't wrong. Everything seemed a little off—or had been, ever since Memphis. Since the Island. Since Haiti. Since It. "Father. You're up."

Father Andrew walked forward toward the salt circle. He couldn't see much of anything either—the second-lowest esper rating after Sara—but he didn't let that stop him.

"We mean you no harm," Father Andrew said, lifting a small, simple cross he wore at mid-chest. "But your time in this place has come to an end. It is time for you to move on. You no longer belong here."

Kaiser moaned, and Sara was at his side in a moment. "You good, kid?"

"Her face," he whispered. "She is so angry… Oh god, she is so angry."

"She's got a right," Sara replied. "Go on, Father."

"You no longer belong here," Father Andrew repeated. "We offer the peace of our hearts to aid you. Follow the pull of your soul and be at peace."

The blast of cold air that came from between the graves hit Sara full-on like a wintry gale. Goosebumps lumped up on her arms, and she saw the same on Horowitz's skin.

Father Andrew switched prayers. "In the name of Jesus Christ, I bind every evil spirit and every evil plan made for this place. By the power of His cross and blood, I bind any spirits, powers and forces and command that you may not speak, manifest or move about this home."

Technically it was a cemetery and not a home, but Sara wasn't about to offer the priest literary criticism if it worked on the bride.

Kaiser shook his head. "Nothing. She's still there, and her face...her face is skeletal now, I can see it through the veil."

"You may do nothing," Father Andrew said, pulling his vial of holy water and sprinkling it in the shape of a cross as he moved closer to the salt line. "You may do nothing! You have no power here!"

That rolling wave of cold grew stronger, and even Sara could hear a faint cry. Kaiser clapped his hands over his ears—God only knew what he was hearing.

"You have no power here," Father Andrew said, more quietly now and with compassion. "I rebuke any—"

"Father!" Sara shouted. "Watch your feet!"

Father Andrew looked down and saw his shoe had smudged the salt line. He jumped back, but it was too late. Something unseen—at least, unseen by Sara—knocked him flat on his back, and the buttons on his shirt ripped off as the collar flew into the air.

"Shit!" Sara ran forward, opening her canister. Horowitz was a shade faster. He swung the iron bar through the air above Father Andrew, and a second later Sara doused the priest with salt.

"Quick, repair the line!" Sara ordered, and Camden got there first. More salt, and she could feel that icy coldness retreat a little.

Father Andrew sat up, spluttering a little as he wiped the salt off his face. "Apologies, Major Harvey," he said. "That was...quite sloppy of me."

"No worries," she replied, but her heart rate hadn't quite slowed yet. She'd protested attaching an actual priest to the team, as he was going to be a prime target for cranky critters with a hate-on for traditional religions, but she had to admit his expertise so far had been useful—at least in terms of research and prayers. Clearly he needed some refreshment on fieldwork and safety.

Kaiser called out from the van, and she saw he was trying to get to his feet. "Sara, she's back—"

"Stay in the van!" she ordered, and turned to face the ghost. It was like sticking her face into a chest freezer, waves of frigid cold blasting her cheeks despite the warm June sunlight. She pulled an iron spike from her satchel.

"Bad idea, bad idea…" muttered Horowitz, but she ignored him.

Sara stepped over the salt line into another time.

It was as though the entire cemetery suddenly faded to sepia, and her team vanished as though they had never been there. The graves vanished as well, save for the one newly dug a few feet ahead of her. The coffin rested on it, and the gathering beside the grave was respectably large and very much not from the twenty-first century. The women were in long skirts and high-button shirts, the men in hats and coats that clearly came from the early twentieth century. A pastor mouthed words at them, and so many were crying.

Holy carp, I can see after all.

One man stood separate from the others, and Sara moved closer to him. His young face blurred in and out as though a camera was having trouble focusing.

She felt rather than heard the bride beside her. There wasn't any point in looking. "Your husband?" she asked. "Thomas. He was the one that killed you, right? On your wedding night."

The cold rose up again in fury, and Sara saw.

As if a curtain drew over the cemetery, she saw another place, a bedchamber from a time very long ago, elegant and well-appointed with mirrors and a balcony and a four-poster bed with covers tastefully drawn back. She saw the bride sitting before a mirror, pulling another hairpin from her elaborately coiffed hair and smiling. She was still in her wedding gown, but the veil had been removed and carefully set aside on a chair.

Sara saw a dark figure stepping out of the closet, and the bride turning toward him, her smile changing to a scream.

A scream that didn't come, as the shadow pushed her to the ground. Her hands beat ineffectively against him as he drew a knife, trailing its tip slowly down her neck to the center of her chest. His other hand was clamped over her mouth, forcing her to swallow her screams. *No no no,*

Sara could hear inside her head, but she knew it never escaped the bride's mouth.

The knife plunged deep, staining the white lace of her wedding gown a dark red turned brown in the strange sepia tones surrounding her. Her body arched against the knife, shuddering to a stop beneath him.

Sara saw the man rise and slip out through the balcony door as the footsteps came, and Thomas opened the door to his honeymoon suite.

He froze in the doorway, his smile turning to a rictus of horror, then he raced to her side. He fell to his knees, his body wracked with silent sobs over the bride's body, flickering in and out as though in a silent film.

"Holy shit," Sara said. "They couldn't charge him, but the rest of his life they suspected Thomas. Even we thought he did it. For the money."

He got away with it.

Not Thomas, Sara knew—the dark figure with no face, the man-shaped shadow that slipped out the side door. "You knew the man who killed you?"

The bride's fury rose again in a wave of polar cold, and Sara remembered why she was here.

"Your time in this place has come to an end," she recited, and her body rocked back as the bride tore at Sara's clothes the way she had at Father Andrew. A long rip appeared in her sleeve, and Sara steeled herself against the buffeting waves that felt like wind. "I offer you the…the peace of my heart…"

Such as it is.

Sara dropped to her knees and drove the iron stake into what she fervently hoped was the bride's grave and not the wooden floor it appeared to be in the illusion surrounding her. A keening wail began underneath Sara's hands and rose into the sky in a cyclone of polar-cold air.

A moment later the sepia light washed away, and she was back in the June sunlight. Horowitz was by her side in a second. "Are you okay?"

Sara glanced down. Long clawlike rips showed in her shirt. "Well, my wardrobe took a beating, but yeah," she said.

Father Andrew joined them, having apparently found his collar in the grass. They looked at the grave of one Sarah Linden, nee Meyer, who bore her husband's name for approximately forty-five minutes before someone killed her.

"It wasn't the groom," she said as they walked back toward the van.

"There were no other suspects," Camden insisted.

Sara shrugged. "Just telling you what I saw, Peter. An intruder killed her, ducked out right before the groom found her, and he never got caught. Your basic crime of passion, maybe someone who wanted her and didn't get her. Extra icing on the cake if they had enough to hang Thomas."

Father Andrew was trying and failing to fasten his black shirt without any buttons. "I'm so sorry, Major—"

"Hey, you softened her up for me," Sara said. "If you hadn't started the ritual right, she'd have shredded a whole lot more than my cheap T-shirt." She clapped him on the shoulder. "You've got potential, Padre."

"That's nicer than she's ever been to me!" Camden called as he and Thacker climbed in the van.

"Me too," Kaiser added.

Horowitz opened his mouth, and Sara shut him up with a glare. "We're outta here, folks."

As Horowitz started the van and it rumbled back up the hill along the driveway really too narrow to be more than a path, Sara took another look at the graves lying still under the oak trees—and could swear she saw the shadows move.

The rules are changing.

Sara sat by herself in the interview room, but she was not alone.

They hadn't switched the lights yet, so she could see Thacker and Wolf on the other side of the two-way. Thacker gave her a thumbs-up sign that was probably meant to cheer her up, but it seemed ghoulish, given where they were.

Wolf didn't meet her eyes at all. He had trouble looking her in the eyes since the night at the river. He spoke to her as little as possible, and not at all since he turned down her offer to join the team. "I don't like who I'd be working for," he'd said. She didn't press him on it.

The door swung open, and they brought him in.

Sara's first thought was that he had aged. It hadn't been all that long, but the thin beard and lines around his eyes made James Bell look at least ten years older than the day she and Paul Vaughn had brought him here. He was no longer Jimmy the Kid, the naïve tech she had hijacked from Farson and taken on a whirlwind tour around the world.

Travel the world, meet exotic creatures, and kill them.

"Hello, Sara," Jimmy said, grinning as they dumped him in the chair opposite her. They quickly chained him to a rail on the other side, which Sara had protested, but it was apparently a dealbreaker.

"Hey there, Jimbo," Sara said. "Wanted to see how you were getting on."

Jimmy's grin grew wider. "Better drugs than college," he said. "Come to spring me?"

Sara shook her head. "Not today, kid."

"Too bad," Jimmy said, though his grin didn't falter. "I hear you got a new team. Thought maybe there'd be a spot on it for me."

Sara glanced down at her hands. "I don't know who's feeding you your info, Jimbo, but it isn't exactly—"

He leaned forward. "You know who tells me things."

Sara looked at him. "I didn't know, Jimmy. God's honest truth. I didn't know. I thought—"

"You thought I was crazy," Jimmy said, grinning even wider. "Crazy little Jimmy, the boy whose mind got blown apart by It. That's what you thought, you and Paul. Have a few bad dreams, start talking to someone you can't see, and suddenly you're in the rubber room."

"It was a lot more than that, Jimmy," Sara said quietly.

Jimmy whistled a little and tugged at his restraints.

Sara forced herself to keep eye contact. "Who talks to you, Jimmy? Who is it?"

"You know." For a moment, Jimmy's pleasant voice deepened, with a touch of the clipped near-French accent of Haiti.

The voice of It.

Sara glanced over Jimmy's shoulder at the mirror, but of course she could no longer see Wolf and Thacker. "We know It's alive, Jimmy. And It can do different things now. But we don't know why, and we don't know how to stop It."

Jimmy tittered a little, and a bit of drool escaped his mouth. Sara tried not to notice. "It talks to me all the time, Sara. Sara by the seashore. It told me about that, about watching you from the water, from the eyes of dead things. It can live in the dead now, and It says you did that. Gave It to the dead. Set It free."

Sara bolted to her feet. "That's not possible. I killed the fucker. Electrocuted It and then blew It the fuck up."

Jimmy cackled, rocking back and forth in his chair. "Killed It dead, sure, but not before It had control of other bodies. That set It free among the dead, Sara by the seashore. Now It can take over anything dead, anything that still has feet that travel, and with each one It gets… stronger."

Sara sat down in her chair, her head spinning. "We're fucked."

Jimmy shook his head slowly from side to side. "You killed It twice, Sara. You can do it once more. It knows that. That's why It wants you. Wants you dead or crazy, because It's still not strong enough that you can't kill It."

Sara leaned forward. "How do I kill It?"

Jimmy shrugged. "It isn't going to tell me that, Sara by the seashore. It only tells me enough to make me scream, keep me from sleeping, laughing at me in my head. Sometimes It sounds like Parish, or Gary, or the boss himself. Sometimes It sounds like other people I don't even know, but underneath it's always It, you know? They give me the drugs and It shuts up for a while, but then I wake up and It's chanting again."

He grinned, drooling more onto his shirt. "Sara Sara quite contrary, how does her garden grow? With broken skulls and bloody throats, with knives and guns and—"

"Stop it," Sara said, hating the sound of weakness in her own voice, and the knowledge that Wolf was listening behind the glass.

A bit of malevolence entered Jimmy's eyes. "Everything you touch turns to blood, Sara by the seashore. Everyone you love dies."

Not everyone. Sara clung to that, willing herself not to say it. If It could speak to Jimmy, It could read Jimmy's mind, and the last thing she needed was to give It ideas.

Sara rested her hands on the table. "You need anything, Jimbo?"

Jimmy shrugged. "A nail file and a really long rope would be nice."

"Maybe next time," Sara said, standing up.

He looked up at her, all the malicious humor gone from his eyes. For the first time since that awful night in Haiti, Jimmy's eyes were clear, young and frightened, just as they had been all that time ago. Before It got inside him. Before It drove him mad.

"Kill It, Sara," he whispered. "Please. Kill It before It's too strong. Set me free."

Sara's voice almost broke. "I don't know if I can, Jimmy."

Jimmy's eyes pleaded with her. "Then if you can't…kill me, Sara. Please."

Do not let me go that way, Sara. Paul stood in the Haitian moonlight, making that one request of her.

"I'll be back, Jimbo," Sara promised, and though they had warned her not to do it, she put a hand on his shoulder. He was skinny and horribly bony, as though only a skeleton rested beneath the thin cotton. He didn't move or try to hurt her. "I'll be back, I promise."

She moved away and signaled for the guard to let her out.

"Will you do it?" Jimmy asked, his head bowed over the table. "Will you set us free?"

"Soon," Sara said, gazing out the tiny window in the hallway, where Thacker waited for her. "Right now, I've got work to do."

ACKNOWLEDGMENTS

This book is at least partially Frank Fradella's fault. Frank was the founding publisher of New Babel Books and a member of the Sleepwalkers, a writing group that included Frank, Jeff Strand, Kit Tunstall, Jay Smith and me. Frank came up with the idea of a Sleepwalkers anthology of novellas and assigned us each a traditional monster to write in a nontraditional way. I was assigned zombies, and *The Cold Ones* was the result. The anthology never happened, but eventually the novella was picked up by Sam's Dot Press. We premiered it at the Archon convention in 2009, and it sold out the whole press run in forty-eight hours. It hasn't stopped rolling since.

No one writes a book without help, no matter how much we writers want to pretend we are lonely geniuses on a mountaintop. Certainly no one gets through a whole series without a boatload of help. The *Blackfire* series is no exception. I know I'm forgetting a lot of people, given that this series has been going for more than a decade now, so if I've left you off, please forgive me.

Thanks to so many people who helped with endless research, focus groups and first reads, including David Szucs, Becky Zoole, Angelia Sparrow, Marna Martin, Dr. Karen MacDonald, Dayton Ward, Stephen Reksten, Kori Tyler, Jamie Dent, Dana Franks, Kate Yates, Mitzi Trout, Mary Koppenhofer, Gary Bunker, Beth A. Wojiski and Meri Weiss. And probably so many more.

Thanks to my cohort in the MFA program at Southern Illinois University Edwardsville, and my mentors Valerie Vogrin and Geoff Schmidt, who guided me through my development as a writer in the program.

Thanks to my son Ian Smith, who helped me devise what the heck is going on with Juliet and Tommy, and has been carrying boxes of my books since he was old enough to pick them up.

Special thanks to Rachel Brune, editor extraordinaire and military expert who published *Yanaguana* in its initial release through Crone Girls Press and also speaks Russian because of course she does; to the editors of *River Bluff Review*, who selected "Dear Katrina" for their journal; to Tyree Campbell of the late great Sam's Dot Press, who gave the series life from the beginning; and of course to John Hartness, the publisher who gave *Blackfire* new life at Falstaff Books.

Thanks to my wonderful Patrons, whose ongoing support through Patreon makes it possible for me to continue infesting places with ghouls and beasties while supporting my family, and that's a gift without price.

Throughout the series, I owe gratitude and cups of coffee to the real people who let me steal their names for Blackfire characters beginning nearly fifteen years ago, including Parish Roberts, Jim Bell, Pam Spinks Smith, the late great Vic Milan, Katrina Roberts, Russ Matthews, Jeff Pagliei, Kathy Oh, Nicole Lanahan, Danny Chamberlin, Kim Hill, Mark Kaiser, Joy Keeling, Roy Michel, Shane Spellmeyer, and Woof "Bob the Skull" Stewart.

As always, my heartfelt gratitude to my henchman David Tyler, who answers my rambling messages at two in the morning; the good folks of the Eville Writers, who have lived and suffered through each of these stories; and to my husband Jim Gillentine, who always has my back.

For the record, the only supernatural critter I completely made up was the Raptor in Chicago, though I may have used a little creative license in their representations. Sadly, the human monsters involved in sex trafficking are all too real. But the redcap, aswang, rusalka, vrees, even the Incan demon are all based on the mythologies of various cultures. The redcap, for example, inhabits the ruined castles along the border between England and Scotland, and you really do fight it by quoting Scripture at it and trying to dry out the hat while it loses teeth. You think I could make that up?

The popobawa torments the people of Tanzania; the rusalka is a cross between mermaid and siren from Russia; the aswang is a ghoul popular in the central islands of the Philippines; and everyone knows about the djinn. Oh, and those Haitian zombies.

There is little in fiction that can match the creativity and rich dimensions of our own mythology, as our ancestors were the first to devise what might be hiding in the shadows beneath the bed.

Sleep tight.

ABOUT THE AUTHOR

Elizabeth Donald is a dark fiction writer fond of things that go chomp in the night. She is the author of the Blackfire urban fantasy series and Nocturne vampire mystery series, as well as other novels, novellas and stories in the horror, science fiction and urban fantasy genres.

She is a three-time winner of the Darrell Award for speculative fiction and finalist for the Prism and Imadjinn fiction awards. More recently, she received the Mimi Zanger Literary Award and was a finalist for the Imaginarium Screenplay Competition and the Knost Award.

She is the founder of the Literary Underworld small-press cooperative; an award-winning journalist and essayist with more than 25 years in journalism; a nature and art photographer; freelance editor and writing coach.

She holds a masters degree in media studies and an MFA in creative writing from Southern Illinois University Edwardsville, and is a professor of journalism and English composition at St. Louis-area colleges. She serves as president of the St. Louis Society of Professional Journalists and the Eville Writers, and is a member of the national SPJ Ethics Committee, Association of Writers and Writing Programs, Sigma Tau Delta, Authors Guild, Authors Against Book Bans, St. Louis Writers Guild and more writing and trade organizations than is healthy. She lives with her family in a haunted house in Edwardsville, Illinois.

In her spare time, she has no spare time.

FRIENDS OF FALSTAFF

Thank You to All our Falstaff Books Patrons, who get extra digital content each month! To be featured here and see what other great rewards we offer, go to www.patreon.com/falstaffbooks.

PATRONS

Dino Hicks
John Hooks
John Kilgallon
Larissa Lichty
Travis & Casey Schilling
Staci-Leigh Santore
Sheryl R. Hayes
Scott Norris
Samuel Montgomery-Blinn
Junkle
Vickie DeSantos
Quincy J. Allen
Allison Charlesworth

Thank You for Supporting Independent Publishing!

We believe that you should be able
to read your books, your way.
That's why this Falstaff Books
print edition includes a digital copy
at no additional cost!

Just scan the QR code with your device,
follow the directions on Prolific Works,
and enjoy!
You can also join our newsletter when prompted,
and never miss an awesome Falstaff Release!